PRAISE FOR THE NOVELS OF AVA GRAY

SKIN TIGHT

"Gray has crafted a tight, suspenseful tale that will have you up at night turning pages." —*Romantic Times*

"Ava Gray immediately sucked me in with this book. Her writing is compelling and addictive. The way she sets up the stories is brilliant . . . I honestly couldn't stop reading this book and finished it in twenty-four hours. *Awesome* doesn't even begin to describe it for me." —*Pearl's World of Romance*

"*Skin Tight* is heavy on the smoldering tension . . . Ava's writing really does grab you from beginning to end." —*Babbling About Books*

"A supertaut romantic suspense thriller." —*Genre Go Round Reviews*

SKIN GAME

"Ava Gray at her best. Smart, witty, and bursting with memorable characters so real you can practically touch them, *Skin Game* delivers a powerful punch of danger and nonstop adventure . . . Ava Gray is a must read!"
—Larissa Ione, *New York Times* bestselling author

"Sexy, clever, and tightly plotted . . . Ava Gray has some serious writing magic." —Lauren Dane, national bestselling author

"Adds a tiny touch of the psychic to a riveting romantic suspense novel. Strong, nuanced character development adds depth to the danger . . . [The] chemistry sizzles." —*Publishers Weekly*

continued . . .

"Ava Gray has written a very hot romance between two incredibly fascinating characters . . . The characters have a remarkably strong chemistry between them. Gray never skimps on the connection between the two, even as the story barrels along, full of action and excitement . . . *Skin Game* is a fast-paced, exciting story featuring fascinating characters, a terrific romance, and a thrilling conclusion."

—*Romance Novel TV*

"Brilliant . . . The perfect package . . . Fascinating characters, excellent pacing and story line, tons of nail-biting suspense . . . and off-the-charts hot sexual encounters . . . My favorite authors make the characters come alive. And Gray has accomplished this in a truly unique and unexpected fashion."

—*Penelope's Romance Reviews*

"Sexy . . . The delicious tension . . . adds spice to the story . . . The romance was particularly well done." —*Dear Author*

"Compelling, mind-blowing . . . Raw and candid writing that allowed complicated emotions to come through loud and clear. It's wonderfully written with a perfect pace, excellent character development, and an intriguing plot . . . *Skin Game* is a very good read for readers who appreciate romantic suspense with paranormal elements and a perfect must read for those of us craving unembellished writing, raw action, and strong characters . . . [Ava Gray] is an admirable storyteller and a most talented writer." —*Pearl's World of Romance*

Berkley Sensation titles by Ava Gray

SKIN GAME

SKIN TIGHT

SKIN HEAT

SKIN DIVE

Anthologies

PRIMAL

(with Lora Leigh, Michelle Rowen, and Jory Strong)

SKIN DIVE

AVA GRAY

BERKLEY SENSATION, NEW YORK

THE BERKLEY PUBLISHING GROUP
Published by the Penguin Group
Penguin Group (USA) Inc.
375 Hudson Street, New York, New York 10014, USA
Penguin Group (Canada), 90 Eglinton Avenue East, Suite 700, Toronto, Ontario M4P 2Y3, Canada
(a division of Pearson Penguin Canada Inc.)
Penguin Books Ltd., 80 Strand, London WC2R 0RL, England
Penguin Group Ireland, 25 St. Stephen's Green, Dublin 2, Ireland (a division of Penguin Books Ltd.)
Penguin Group (Australia), 250 Camberwell Road, Camberwell, Victoria 3124, Australia
(a division of Pearson Australia Group Pty. Ltd.)
Penguin Books India Pvt. Ltd., 11 Community Centre, Panchsheel Park, New Delhi—110 017, India
Penguin Group (NZ), 67 Apollo Drive, Rosedale, Auckland 0632, New Zealand
(a division of Pearson New Zealand Ltd.)
Penguin Books (South Africa) (Pty.) Ltd., 24 Sturdee Avenue, Rosebank, Johannesburg 2196, South Africa

Penguin Books Ltd., Registered Offices: 80 Strand, London WC2R 0RL, England

SKIN DIVE

A Berkley Sensation Book / published by arrangement with the author

PRINTING HISTORY
Berkley Sensation mass-market paperback edition / July 2011

Cover design by Lesley Worrell.
Cover illustration by Danny O'Leary.
Interior text design by Kristin del Rosario.

For information, address: The Berkley Publishing Group,
a division of Penguin Group (USA) Inc.,
375 Hudson Street, New York, New York 10014.

ISBN: 978-0-425-24214-8

BERKLEY® SENSATION
Berkley Sensation Books are published by The Berkley Publishing Group,
a division of Penguin Group (USA) Inc.,
375 Hudson Street, New York, New York 10014.
BERKLEY® SENSATION and the "B" design are trademarks of Penguin Group (USA) Inc.

PRINTED IN THE UNITED STATES OF AMERICA

10 9 8 7 6 5 4 3 2 1

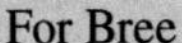
For Bree

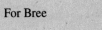

ACKNOWLEDGMENTS

Thanks to Laura Bradford, Cindy Hwang, Bree Bridges, Donna Herren, Lauren Dane, Jenn Bennett, and Carrie Lofty.

Thanks to my readers. Thanks to my family.

I appreciate you all more than words can say.

PROLOGUE

TEN MONTHS AGO
THE EXETER FACILITY, VIRGINIA

Gillie froze at the knock on her door. The only person who ever visited her was Dr. Rowan, but she would've sworn it was too early for him. The man lived like a vampire, working all night, sleeping all day. She wouldn't be surprised if he did slash people's jugulars to maintain his creepy immortality.

With great trepidation, she opened the door—if she didn't, they'd come in anyway. To her surprise, it was Silas, escorted by some man she'd never seen before.

"One hour," the orderly said, and then he was gone.

Gillie closed the door. Her heart beating too fast, she took in the stranger with absolute befuddlement. He stood just less than six feet tall, and he was pale, like her. Chestnut hair, green eyes. On closer scrutiny, she saw he bore bruises on his arms, and more on his back, most likely, if he'd been disciplined.

That made him a test subject, just like her. *God, please don't let it be some mating agenda. If they expect me to breed with him, I'll kill myself.*

"Do you speak?" he asked at length.

She shook herself out of the near panic. "Of course." Though it had been a long time since she'd met anyone new, she extended a hand, trying to be polite. "I'm Gillie. Nice to meet you."

Humor crinkled the corners of his eyes. He had a weathered face, as if he'd once spent a great deal of time outdoors. The sun-kissed hue that had led to the lines had long since faded, however. "You, too, Miss Manners."

"I don't mean to be rude," she said in a rush. "But . . . who are you? Why are you here?"

"That's a deep question for a new acquaintance."

She felt heat rising in her cheeks. "I didn't mean you should define the purpose of your existence. I meant—"

"I know what you meant. I'm here because they turned me into a crazy beast, and then they snapped me up on the streets a few years back. Now the doc's done something to my brain, something that left me going, *holy shit, I wish I were dead*, only I'm not, and I wanted to make the best of this fucked-up situation."

Gillie sat down. "I still don't understand. They never let me see anyone."

"There's nobody sane down here for you to talk to, besides the staff." He reassured her by taking the chair opposite. If he was meant to mate with her and he only had an hour to get the job done, surely he'd be more aggressive. "And that's debatable."

A reluctant smile curved her mouth. "Yes. That's certainly true. So you're here . . . for company?"

"Is that okay?" He hesitated. "I also demanded a visit to piss off Doc Rowan. He seems to think he holds your title."

"That's one way of putting it." She tried to control her revulsion, but he saw it.

Maybe because of the cameras, he didn't acknowledge the revelation. "Do you have anything to drink?"

Gillie could only think, *Holy crap, my first houseguest.*

"Of course. I should've offered. I can make tea or coffee, if you like. I also have some oatmeal cookies I made this morning."

"You bake in here?" His astonishment wounded her, as if she'd surrendered everything by wanting to make the best of things.

"Yes, I'm a collaborator," she said, feeling wretched. "Do you want the cookies or not?"

"Tea and cookies in hell." He shook his head in wonderment.

"That about sums it up." Relieved that she wouldn't have to

fight off a determined rapist—a worry each time Rowan came in—Gillie got up to make the refreshments. "You never told me your name."

Pure hatred flashed in his green eyes. "They call me T-89."

"Do you remember who you are? Do you have a family?" She put the kettle on, nearly weeping with the pleasure of human contact after so long.

"The T stands for Taye. I'm sure of that. The rest . . ." He shook his head, gazing at his clasped hands. "Only bits and pieces. I think I might have a family out there, but I'm not positive. I'm pretty sure they'd given up on me, long before I was taken."

"I'm sorry."

Was that true of her as well? Gillie knew a pang, wondering whether her parents had accepted the tale of her death. Did they have more children? *Do they miss me at all?* With the ease of long practice, she banished the darkness. Living in the present kept her sane.

He shrugged. "It's all scrambled now. Doesn't matter whether I was a crazy bum, begging for spare change and tinfoil for a hat. I doubt my family would want me back, if these flashes I get are true."

"Well, Taye, I'm glad to have you here. I didn't think I'd ever see a friendly face."

Shadows lurked in his jade eyes. "Nor did I. Mind if I use your bathroom?"

"No, help yourself."

By the time he'd finished, she'd laid the table with cookies and hot tea. He joined her. Gillie had always thought it funny they gave her two chairs, until the day Dr. Rowan sat down across from her. Since then, she'd lost some of the joy she took in doing small, everyday things for herself.

"This looks fantastic."

In truth, the cookies were a bit overdone, and she'd gone wrong somewhere else in making them. The raisins had soaked up all the moisture, so instead of being rich and chewy like her mom's, these turned out dry and crumbly. But perhaps with the tea, he wouldn't notice.

"You're being polite."

He broke a cookie in half and took a big bite. "Not at all. I haven't had any sweets in a long time. I used to . . ."

"What?"

"Like marzipan, I think. Or was it peanut brittle?" His eyes went distant, as if all the neurons weren't firing in sync.

Just how safe was she with him? Gillie eyed him warily. Sure, she knew about the cameras, but this guy could do some damage before help arrived.

"I'm not going to hurt you," he promised. "I just . . . can't remember certain things. If it makes you feel better, one condition of my visits is that I'm never to touch you."

Because she could envision Rowan laying down such terms, she considered that a mixed blessing. Still, she didn't want him to feel unwelcome. Anyone was better than the mad scientist.

"It does, thank you."

"I think I haven't seen my reflection in a while because when I looked in the mirror earlier, I didn't recognize my own face." His conversational tone belied the grief in his gaze. "Does that ever happen to you?"

Tell me I'm not alone, his eyes begged.

Gillie shook her head, wishing she were a better liar. She had no comfort to offer a man who found a stranger in the mirror; she could only change the subject. "Silas said we have an hour?"

Taye nodded. "Today, and every day hereafter. I made it a condition of my cooperation."

"If the question doesn't strike you as too forward—"

"What can I do?" Wisely, he guessed she wanted to know his ability.

"I'm curious."

"I'm drugged, so I can't show you, but . . . I manipulate energy. I absorb it, displace it, and discharge it. Energy is never created or destroyed, but I can transmute it. They're interested in finding out what, exactly, that entails and what my limits are."

"They would be. Sadly, they don't need me willing," she said softly. "It just makes life more bearable."

He cocked his head. "So they can use your gift, even if you don't want them to?"

While he ate, she explained. She'd never imagined she would have anyone to confide in. Even knowing they were listening to every word, it was still a relief. Sympathy shone in his gaze by the time she finished the story.

"Jesus, that's . . ." He curled his hand into a fist, as if that spoke for him better than words. “Well, I can only say—I don’t know how you’ve borne it.”

“I’ve thought of dying,” she whispered. “They think they’ve eliminated everything I could use to harm myself, but I have a few secrets. Sometimes I still think of it.”

Before he could reply, a knock sounded at the door. “Time.”

“I’ll see you tomorrow,” Taye said, eyes on hers. “Take a hot bath and try to relax.”

That seemed like such an odd and pointed instruction that as soon as they left, she went into the bathroom. With something like hope dawning in her heart, Gillie read the note he’d scrawled on a scrap of toilet paper:

We’re getting out of here. Be ready.

TWO WEEKS LATER

Gillie slumped, bowing her head over the sink. “You can’t keep sneaking around like this. They’ll kill you if they catch you.”

“If. Don’t worry about me.” He offered a cocky grin.

“I have to. You’re the only friend I have.”

“C’mon, sweetheart. You have to admit you like the adrenaline. You kept Tightass happy by feeding him my breakfast, and then sent him on his way thinking you can’t wait to run off with him. That’s genius.”

Her lips curved into a half smile, despite the fear-induced nausea. “It was kind of funny listening to him talk about you, knowing you could hear every word. Do they know you can leave magnetic impressions on digital recordings?”

Taye shook his head, sitting down at the table. “No, and they won’t until it’s too late either.”

“So they don’t realize you’re manipulating all the cameras down here.” She cracked some more eggs, scrambling them deftly in the skillet. “Or that you have a third power.”

“That’s me.” Bitterness tainted his voice. “The biggest freak in the sideshow.”

Gillie aimed her spatula at him. “At least you’re not the freak who laid the golden egg, nor does the chief torturer want to bang you silly.”

He widened his eyes in mock surprise. "Your language is appalling."

"There's something seriously wrong with Rowan."

"Ya think?"

"I mean it. He doesn't want a real woman. He wants one who doesn't argue, doesn't eat, doesn't have bodily functions . . . just lives to gratify him."

"Yeah, that's pretty pathological. If he wasn't down here torturing us lab rats, he'd be on the streets cutting people into bite-sized pieces."

"Thing is, this is familiar to me." Gillie gestured, and he came into the kitchen to serve himself. "There was a serial killer . . . I saw something when I was a kid. I'd only just arrived here. He killed because he was trying to create a lobotomized sex slave."

"Dahmer," Taye supplied. "You think Rowan is like him?"

"I think they share certain fantasies. I doubt he could perform with a woman he didn't perceive as completely submissive."

He arched a brow. "Should I be worried that you know this stuff?"

"You wouldn't believe what comes on late-night TV."

"And you watch it because you don't like sleeping at night."

A shudder rolled through her. "No. I don't want him coming at me while I'm unaware."

"No wonder he scares you," he said quietly. "If he figures out you're not who you pretend to be—"

"It won't be pretty. But I've done what I must to survive."

"If his obsession with you ever reaches the next level, he'll come to your bed."

Gillie propped her elbows on the table. "I know."

"And what will you do?" There was a peculiar tension in him now.

"I'll lie there with doe eyes and take it. I want to see the sun again, Taye. Maybe you'd rather I play the medieval maiden and say I'll die rather than let him sully my body, but he can't touch me where it matters. I can put up with anything, as long as it means my freedom in the long run. And once I have it, I'll never let anyone take it from me again."

"Relax, I'm not judging you. I think you're incredibly strong." He dug into his breakfast, probably starving from the time he'd spent hiding in her bathroom.

She dipped her chin. "Are you being funny?"

"Not at all. Not all strength comes from brute force. Ever heard of the power of passive resistance? Gandhi?"

"I hardly think that comparison is appropriate."

"Look, Gillie, I insisted on these visits because I wanted to stick it to Rowan. I knew it would get into his craw and chafe. But in the past few weeks, I've come to respect you. Not everyone could adapt and thrive as you have. You're a rare person." He cut a square of French toast and looked away. "You give me someone besides myself to think about, someone to fight for. I'm not sure what kind of person I was before Rowan worked on me that second time—and from certain fragments of memory, I don't think I want to know—but I'm not that guy anymore. I could be better, if I only had the chance."

His intensity moved her. Gillie reached out and covered his hand with her own. "We're both getting second chances, and we won't waste them."

Taye threaded his fingers through hers. They were both pale, but his hand was a good deal larger. Ordinarily it amused Gillie that he could tweak the cameras to show her sitting alone at the kitchen table, lulling all of Rowan's suspicions. Now she had the thought that he could do more than hold her hand.

Unlike with Rowan, the contact didn't give her the creeps. Taye felt warmer than a normal human, as if his gifts fevered him. But his eyes didn't reflect a febrile glitter. Instead they were the calm, cool green of tropical waters. She'd seen them many times on cruise line commercials.

"What?" he asked. "Do I have food on my face?"

With his free hand, he wiped his mouth with a napkin as Gillie shook her head. "I was just thinking how lucky I am to have you. Before, I only had inchoate dreams. *Now* we have plans."

Taye inclined his head and withdrew his hand, leaving her faintly disappointed. "Speaking of which, we need to use our time wisely."

"Yes, I'm sorry. Your ability isn't foolproof." Using electricity, he could manipulate the locks on the cell doors, and not long ago, he'd managed to get himself free. But he wasn't sure enough of himself to risk their one chance at escape . . . yet. So Taye came to her in these practice runs, bright with the pleasure of sticking it to their captor. Silas knew, of course, but he had his own reasons to hate Rowan. The doctor could compel his obedience, but not cooperation; the two differed vastly.

"Nor do I have it wholly under control." For the first time, his voice reflected a touch of strain, and she realized belatedly that the whole time they'd been talking, he had to concentrate on the cameras. It was a wonder he could communicate at all.

"God, I'm so stupid. Show me walking to the bathroom."

Taye grasped her intent at once and followed her. Gillie made a habit of checking the toilet for audio bugs, and there was no place to hide a camera. The room was small, but they squeezed in. She helped matters along by stepping into the shower stall. That gave him the space to flip down the toilet lid and take a seat.

"Thanks," he said. "Now I can focus on you fully."

Gillie put her back to the wall and slid into a seated position. The tingles his words created—however he'd meant them—signaled sexual attraction. It wasn't unexpected; he was the only viable potential mate in her social sphere. She had to ignore the feelings, regardless how intriguing and new they were.

"Good. Now, last time, we established the timeline. You've been laying the groundwork with the cameras. How long before we're ready to go?"

"Another week at least," he answered. "Possibly two. I'm still working on control. I won't hurt you when I blow the equipment, and right now I'm not good enough with overload to guarantee your safety."

"So you keep practicing. What's my role?"

His mouth twisted. "I need you to keep Rowan distracted. I hate asking you, but—"

"I don't mind. I've been playing to him for years. I can handle another week or two. I just hope I get to show him how wrong he was about me before the end." Gillie smiled with fierce anticipation.

"I can't believe I'm saying this, but if comes to a choice between making sure he's dead and getting out of here, we have to choose the latter."

"I understand. Freedom is more important than revenge. You can count on me."

"I'm aware. You have the heart of a lion, Gillie Flynn."

She didn't deny it. A lesser soul would've broken in the crucible of her life, but hardship had steeled her determination for things not to end here. The world awaited her, and she would do wondrous things.

"Thanks. But you, you give me something I sorely needed."

"What's that?" He should have looked absurd, reclining on her toilet. Instead he turned it into a throne. There was a faint, almost perceptible aura of power about him as if through the cruelty of a madman, he had transcended the human condition.

"Faith. For all my dreaming, I don't know that I could've gotten out of here alone."

At least, not without yielding to Rowan, becoming his creature completely in the hope of once more living in the light. Sickness coiled through her, and she put trembling fingers to her face. She didn't realize he'd moved until he brushed her hair back.

Gillie didn't recoil. He crouched before her on the bathroom floor, all concern. You'd never know he could turn an electrical device into chain lightning by looking at him. His tenderness threatened to undo her completely.

"What's the matter? I'm sorry. I don't remember how to deal with people. Did I do something wrong?"

"No," she whispered. "You do everything right. You're the *only* thing that's right."

And then she kissed him.

Gillie had been alone for two days.

That wouldn't have been a problem, except during the past few weeks, she'd grown accustomed to company. She didn't know if something had happened to Taye, or if she'd scared him with that clumsy kiss. God knew, he hadn't seemed swept away by it.

She tested the memory of his reaction like a sore spot on the inside of her cheek and found it still tender. For all of ten seconds, he'd kissed her back, his mouth fever-hot and hungry, and then he'd shoved her away, as if he were a frightened virgin.

"That's not a good idea," he'd said quietly.

She'd hunched her shoulders. "I'm sorry. I just thought—"

"No. We're getting out of here. Soon I won't be your only choice, and you'd be sorry if I hadn't stopped things." Taye cupped her chin in his hand, eyes searching hers. "You don't have to dispose of your virginity like this, as a defense from Rowan."

"It was just a kiss," she'd muttered. "It's not like I demanded sex."

With determination, she shoved away the faintly humiliating recollection. A kiss she'd instigated on the bathroom floor hardly qualified as magical. The awkwardness didn't prevent her from worrying about him, however.

Her heart skittered in her chest as she stepped out of her quarters. They had long since ceased locking the door. Rowan deemed her no flight risk; that much was sure. Of course, the crazy bastard also thought she wanted to run away with him, so there was no accounting for the way his mind worked.

The white, clinical corridors contrasted markedly with the mock normalcy of her décor. She liked to pretend she was an ordinary girl with a small apartment, a television, and a job she hated. That was one reason she never came out into the facility proper; it destroyed the illusion. There was no grass, no sky, no sun, just endless white and soulless metal, as far as the eye could see. Overhead, the fluorescent lights offered the same wattage day after day. She didn't know how Rowan could choose this life for himself when the whole world beckoned.

Every instinct told her to return to her apartment. It was safe in there. Instead, she picked her way carefully down the hall. Silas often brought her this way for treatments, and she knew the cells lay past the treatment rooms. She had been kept in one until Rowan grew confident she could be trusted.

And what will he say if he finds you wandering, hmm?

She got her lie ready. *I was looking for you. It's been several days since I saw you.* Yes, that would work. If the words fed his ego and his delusions, he'd believe them. Gillie could envision how his face would soften and he'd give that awful smile. This time he might kiss her. She steeled herself against the possibility. *At least it won't be my first.*

Gillie tiptoed past the treatment rooms. From within, she heard low moans of pain. That meant the techs were working, carrying out the doctor's instructions. She hardly dared to breathe as she went by.

She continued down the corridor. The horror of the cells struck her anew. They were eight by eight, and each contained only a commode and a cot. An industrial drain lay in the middle of the floor, necessary because the test subjects were hosed off once a week from a spigot in the ceiling.

Some of the walls were spattered with blood, or other, less readily recognizable substances. A few of the subjects sat and rocked; others lay in the fetal position on their cots. Two paced like animals. Another pressed her hands against the glass as Gillie went by. She stopped, unable to help herself, unable to deny the woman this moment of connection. Aching, she pressed her palms to the glass from her side. There was cognition in the other woman's eyes.

Kill me, she mouthed.

Gillie tugged on her pink scrubs, which were the only things Rowan ever ordered for her to wear. She found that faintly creepy, but at least she was out of the gray, institutional pajamas the other subjects had on. At last, the woman seemed to realize Gillie wasn't wearing a badge.

The woman pointed at her cell door, a plea in her eyes, and Gillie had to shake her head. "Sorry," she whispered. "I can't."

When the girl turned away, she walked on. Mercifully she could remember little of her time in these cells. They'd kept her sedated while they studied the limits and requirements of her gift. She didn't know how the others bore it, and as for the ones who couldn't, well, the madness was understandable.

She found Taye in the last cell. His swollen jaw and black eyes made him difficult to identify at first, but she knew the shape of his hands and the breadth of his shoulders as well. Not to mention the tousled dark hair. His gray pajamas were stained dark in splatter patterns. All too clearly she could see the crunch of cartilage and bone echoed in the discolored fabric. Gillie recognized Silas's handiwork; he executed the doctor's punishments, but she'd never received the impression he enjoyed it.

Goddamn you, Rowan, what have you done?

He lifted his head as if he sensed her. His eyes took too long to focus, and Gillie had watched enough medical TV to know that meant a concussion. *If only I had the key code.* As if Taye read her mind, he extended a hand. Blue sparked from his fingertips, echoing in the panel, and the door popped wide, but he wasn't steady enough to stand.

He tried and fell.

Which explained why she hadn't seen him. Mindless of the cameras, she hurried into his cell and knelt beside him. "I have to get you out of here. He's going to kill you."

"Won't." His voice came out slurry through puffy lips. "He's selling me to China."

"What? How do you know?"

"Overheard."

"So that's why he had you beaten?"

"Also suspects I see you more than an hour a day. Couldn't prove it." He gave her a hard look. "Now he can."

She helped him to a sitting position, an arm around his shoulders. It was hard to know where to touch him that wouldn't hurt. An ache sprung up inside her; he had been beaten because of her, because of a madman's obsession.

"I was worried about you."

"Go. Will try to wipe the cameras before anyone notices."

"The pain makes it hard to focus," she guessed.

"Yeah. Please go."

Impotence made her angry. She had spent her whole life obeying orders. She was tired of toeing the line for fear of consequences. Rowan held the unspoken threat of the cells over her to compel her cooperation, and now, the one time she'd dared disobey, Taye was trying to banish her back to the safe walls that held her prisoner.

"Not just yet. When you aren't injured, how's your control?"

"Good." His green eyes reflected anger and frustration. "Might be another reason why he had me beaten. Was nearly ready."

"Then you just need a few days to heal. Try not to piss him off." Gillie held up a hand, forestalling his instinctive protest. "I know you love to provoke him, but remember, I can't get out of here without you. I need you, Taye."

"I'll be good," he growled.

She couldn't do anything else for him, but she knew who could. Gillie hurried out of the cell, which locked behind her when the door clicked shut. At this hour, Silas would be eating in the small employee lounge. As she'd suspected, he was spooning up some soup while staring at the television. He wasn't homely per se, just . . . unnerving.

"Silas," she said softly.

He turned to regard her with dead, black eyes. "You're not supposed to be in here."

"Neither are you, I think. Do you like your job?"

The big man made a sound like an inner tube deflating and

studied his enormous hands as if he'd never seen them before. "No."

"You hurt Taye."

"I know. Rowan made me."

"How?"

In answer, Silas turned his head and showed her a faint blue pulsing light, inset behind his ear. Jesus, it had to be a control mechanism. Silas wasn't an employee; he was a former test subject.

"I'm going to die here," he said, and went back to his soup.

Suddenly bolder than she'd ever been in her life, she touched his arm. He tensed at the simple contact and looked at her hand as if it were an alien appendage complete with tentacles. "What if I said you could get out? Would you do something for me?"

Silas put the spoon down. "I might."

"Taye might be able to help you. He could short out that gizmo in your head. I don't know where that would leave you, maybe you'd revert to however you were before, but at least you wouldn't be under Rowan's control anymore. That has to be worth something."

He didn't think about it overlong. "What do you want me to do?"

ONE WEEK LATER

"It's time," Gillie whispered.

Taye pulled himself off the floor. His bruises looked a lot better, and he seemed to have the control he needed to make this work. If he didn't, they were going to die slowly, along with everyone else in this place.

It was a miracle they hadn't been discovered. When Rowan showed up unexpectedly the day before, it was all Gillie could do to keep from panicking. She'd been sure he knew she was hiding Taye, and that Silas was conspiring with them. Instead he'd behaved like a deranged Victorian suitor. After he finally left, she'd brushed her teeth for five minutes.

In accordance with their plan, Silas had stopped giving Taye his injections altogether. With nothing damping his abilities, he could light this place up like a summer storm. But he had to be careful, too. Fire was extremely dangerous underground. If the lift shut down, they were done for. So the situation called for a certain amount of finesse.

"I'm ready," he said in answer to her unspoken question. "I'll sound the alarms at the far end of the complex and fry all the diagnostic equipment. Maybe put a short in some of the lights."

"Can you open the cell doors?"

"I *can*," he said. "But do you really think it's a good idea?"

Gillie thought about the woman who had pressed her hand to the glass. "Yes. I want anyone who has the will and the desire to be able to leave when we do. What happens past that point is up to them."

"They might do an amazing amount of damage up top."

She regarded him steadily. "So could you."

"Good point."

Taye's brow furrowed, and a soft blue glow surrounded him. She'd never seen him completely unfettered before. His dark curls lifted as if in the wind, but she knew it was electrical current. Voltage crackled from his fingertips, and the lights in her apartment dimmed. Then a siren went off, just as he'd promised. Gillie heard the sound of running feet—techs and orderlies running to check out the problem.

"Now diagnostics?"

He grinned. "That *was* diagnostics."

"Wow. Impressive range."

With the air of a kid showing off, he set the lights to flickering. They should be able to move from her apartment now. If anyone interfered with them, Taye could handle nearly anything, and Silas would arrive soon to provide muscle.

She'd been horrified to learn that Rowan held Silas prisoner, too. Staff lived off-site, but since Silas had been part of the original experiments—a failure—the orderly wasn't permitted to leave. However, the moment Taye shorted the implant in his neck, the life had started returning to the big man's eyes. Gillie knew they could count on him.

Nausea rolled through her in a hard wave. Now that the moment had arrived, she was frightened of leaving, frightened of the wider world, of which she knew nothing but what she'd seen on TV. Taye misunderstood her expression.

"Is there anything you want to take with you?"

"No," she said quietly. "There's nothing."

"Then let's go."

Gillie followed him out of the apartment. In the distance, they heard cries of fear. The electrical problems were growing worse. In passing the first cell, he extended a hand. Blue sparks lit up the keypad and then blazed along hidden connections, giving the wall an eerie glow. The doors snapped open one by one as Taye went by.

Most of the prisoners were too far gone to respond. It broke Gillie's heart, but there was nothing she could do, short of sacrificing her own chance at freedom. Others stepped cautiously into the hall, gazing around like frightened animals. Gillie quickened her pace. Maybe it was wrong, but she was almost as frightened of Rowan's subjects as she was of the scientist. She knew all too well his gift for twisting humans into beings both wretched and monstrous.

Spotting Silas at the next intersection, she broke into a run. Taye followed, but she noticed him keeping an eye on the escapees trailing behind them. The orderly fell into step as they headed toward the lift. They had no way of knowing whether Taye could make it work as he did the locks on the cells, but it was their only hope. This was the one portion of their escape they hadn't been able to test.

"Are you all right?" she asked Silas.

The enormous orderly gave a quiet nod.

From the other side of the facility came a distant boom. Something had overloaded. Acrid smoke trickled through the vents, stinging her throat. Gillie tugged her pink scrub shirt up over her mouth and watched Taye at the lift controls.

"It's much the same as the cell door security," he said, after a few seconds. "This should work."

"Then do it. Fast."

She couldn't figure out why they hadn't seen Rowan by now. Someone would've called him, and from what she'd gleaned from his odious, egocentric soliloquies over the years, he lived nearby. Still, it was an unexpected boon.

"Here goes." Taye touched his fingers to the keypad, and a pale ripple of energy flooded outward, enveloping the ret-scanner.

CHAPTER 1

NINE MONTHS AGO
ABOVE THE EXETER FACILITY, VIRGINIA

Taye prayed his nerves didn't show. He had a whole elevator full of people counting on him to make the right decisions. Insane when you thought about it. He suspected he'd never been in charge of anything before. He bore all the signs of a man who had never amounted to much; nobody was looking for him.

Not so long ago, Gillie had asked him, *Do you remember who you are? Do you have a family?* He'd answered, *Only bits and pieces. I think I might have a family out there, but I'm not positive. I'm pretty sure they'd given up on me, long before I was taken.* Which made it even crazier that these people were all looking to him to guide them out of this mess.

But hell, I got us this far.

As the lift rose, the sound of distant explosions carried from the facility below, even through all the metal and concrete. Down there, the workers were dying. *Because of me.* That probably made him a monster by most people's reckoning, but to his view, those who could cash a paycheck without trying to stop what had been done to Gillie—well, they deserved the big boom. The floor heated beneath his feet, and he imagined the wall of flames shooting up the shaft toward the car. There were only two stops, top and bottom, and the metal box rocked as it climbed. *Come on, just a little higher. Systems, don't shut down just yet.*

At last, the doors swished open, swamping him in a wave of crushing relief. *Promise kept.* Gillie glanced his way, seeking direction. She had to be scared shitless, but damned if she would show it. There was a word for a girl like her—indomitable.

Now let's see, where the hell are we? Four walls of textured metal. No visible door. But since the place had been built from panels—

"Start looking for a latch or a hidden exit," the dark-haired lady said.

Took the words right out of my mouth. The woman who had given the instruction seemed different than everyone else, less tentative, less damaged. She couldn't have been there long, or she'd carry fear in her face. Instead, she only appeared determined, as if this sojourn had proven a minor inconvenience. *Rowan didn't have a chance to work on her.* Taye took visceral satisfaction in that.

Eager for freedom, the others spread out; Silas found the panel after a brief search. The big orderly flipped it open, and Taye pulled the juice from his own body—precious little left now—to pop the electronic lock. Sizzle and spark, just like underground. When the door swung open, the scent of musty grain wafted in. Tentatively, they moved as a group, peering into the next room.

It wasn't what he'd expected. No barbed wire, no high-tech perimeter. There were no guards he'd have to fry. It was almost . . . anticlimactic. This outer room was lined with straw and held the remnants of an old harvest. That was all.

"Looks like a farm," a man with a faint Southern drawl said.

He was a little taller than Taye, but he wasn't as pale, which meant he hadn't been incarcerated long. The blond woman, on the other hand—Rowan must've had her for a while because she was damn near wrecked. And that was everyone: Gillie, himself, Silas, the Southern man, the confident brunette, and the broken blonde.

"We need to get out of here. Right now. Rowan could be arriving any minute." Fear rendered Gillie's words sharp and staccato with urgency.

That triggered a stampede, though nobody pushed or shoved. Silas hit the door first, and it wasn't locked, swinging open to reveal daylight. Taye shaded his eyes, unable to speak for the pleasure of it. Though it hurt his eyes, the fresh wind on his face felt amazing. It was late spring, he guessed, by the color and size of the foliage, so the weather was on their side, at least. Given all their disadvantages, they needed the break. Or it might be early summer, if weather patterns had changed while he was underground.

Taye gazed out over the furrowed fields, breathing in the verdant air. It was sweet and clean, hints of manure and compost, but no chemicals. No pine-scented cleaner. That antiseptic smell haunted him. Flashes still hit him from the time before, when his brain was scrambled, and he remembered screaming as they dumped some solution on him from the ceiling; Rowan aspired to complete dehumanization of his subjects, and in most cases, he had succeeded.

Beside him, Gillie trembled from head to toe. This had to be fucking overwhelming for her. He remembered how she had said, *I want to see the sun again, Taye.* That was when he'd known he'd do anything to make that dream come true, anything at all.

And here they were.

He touched her on the shoulder. "It's okay. We made it."

"What now?" the man with the drawl asked.

"We should split up." The black-haired woman spoke decisively. "Looking like this, if we stick together, we'll be caught fast."

Mental hospital pajamas, no shoes, no money, crazy eyes? No question. They'll round us up and put us on the first short bus they find.

"She's right," Silas agreed.

Gillie managed a grin. "Before we split, should we all agree to meet at the top of the Empire State Building in five years?"

And that was so Gillie. Lightening the mood, refusing to show fear. She might be quaking inside, worried how the hell they'd manage, but nobody would ever know it. The girl would spit in death's eye, and if he understood her past, she had done so more than once.

While the others gaped in astonishment, Silas gave a slow nod. "I'd like that. Five years—to the day."

The thin, blond woman spoke for the first time. "If I'm alive, I'll come. But for now, it's time to get moving."

A murmur of good-byes followed. Taye didn't take long about it, and he didn't ask Gillie if she wanted his company either. He laced his fingers through hers and gave a tug.

With a final backward glance at the silo, she followed him across the field. He pushed north, avoiding the highway, because they would attract attention from passing cars. People in their right minds didn't go for a hike barefoot in thin cotton pajamas.

They'd been walking for a while—impossible to say how long—when he glimpsed a white house set well away from the road in the middle of sprawling fields. Farmhouse. He didn't see any cars in the gravel drive, but there was a detached garage, so it was impossible to be sure.

"Let's go check it out."

"Why?" she asked.

He read the anxiety in her expression. Though she tried to hide it, she was freaked. She hadn't been out in twelve years, and it would be dark soon. Compounding that, they had no money, no food, and no shelter, and she had to rely on him for safety; that would trouble anyone with a lick of sense. Shit, it worried *him.*

"We're not gonna knock on the door and ask for help, if that's what you're fretting about. But we can't travel like this either."

She merely nodded. He pretended confidence, striding toward the house. The gravel drive bit into the soles of his feet as he crossed to peer into a garage window. No cars. That ought to mean nobody was around. Setting Gillie on watch, he broke in through the back and stole food, drink, and clothing.

As he came back out carrying a plastic bag, she called, "I hear a car coming."

In tandem, they raced across the property toward the fields; once they put some distance behind them, they paused to change clothes. His were too loose and short; hers looked like they'd previously belonged to an old woman. It didn't matter. At least the shoes worked, more or less, and socks made up the difference.

By then it was getting on toward nightfall, but they pressed on. He could think only of getting out of Virginia. To the north lay safety and freedom. Or maybe he was conflating old history classes about the Underground Railroad with personal motivation. Strange he could remember those kinds of facts, but nothing about the man he had been. That was unsettling.

Gillie stumbled beside him and he turned to her, shoring her up. "We need to stop soon, huh? You're not used to this."

She didn't deny being tired, but she didn't complain. "I can go on."

"No need." He pointed. "There's a barn up ahead. Just a little farther and we'll rest."

The red outbuilding was well kept and had been shoveled recently, so the smell wasn't overwhelming. In the stalls, the landowner kept cows, who lowed at the intrusion. Taye ignored them and scrambled up the ramp to the hayloft. There was enough straw to mound for a bed, and if someone came to investigate the restless animals, they should be able to hide behind the bales. *Good enough.*

"It'll get better," he told Gillie. "You'll have your own place. We'll find work."

"But we don't have any identification."

"That just means we'll have to do the jobs nobody else wants for a while. Just until I figure out a better way."

She didn't argue. Instead she helped him arrange a makeshift bed. Though he wasn't crazy about the idea of sleeping together—even like this—he couldn't leave her unprotected. He'd just have to tamp down the unwelcome desire she roused in him. Thinking about Gillie that way made him feel dirty and wrong, as bad as that bastard Rowan.

They ate some of the bread and peanut butter he'd lifted from the house a ways back and washed it down with tap water. It wasn't gourmet fare, but he could tell she enjoyed it by the way she smiled at him; that look made him feel ten feet tall.

"My first meal as a free woman," she said.

"The first of many."

Then he lay down and tried to sleep, but as the temperature dropped and she lay shivering in her thin polyester pantsuit, he turned with a reluctant growl. "Come here."

Just sharing body heat, that's all. Don't think about that kiss. You can't have her. Not now. Not ever. He gazed up at the slats above his head and tried to resign himself to that. The straw prickled, and they lacked both covers and pillow. *Not an auspicious start, genius.*

"Thank you," she whispered.

"I should've grabbed a blanket, too. I wasn't thinking about sleeping rough."

"I'm glad we didn't take more than we had to from those people. They had nothing to do with what happened to us."

"You're too nice."

Gillie didn't reply right then. Instead, she nestled into his arms. God, why did she have to feel so good, feminine without being fragile. Her small frame possessed a tensile strength; he knew she'd worked out in captivity to stay strong. Some days when he came to visit her, he'd found her running on the treadmill, as if she could outpace Rowan and his cameras, artificial lights, and doors that didn't lock.

Eventually she asked, "Do you want to split up?"

He understood the reason behind the question. After all, they'd decided as a group that it made sense to go their separate ways. *That would be the smart thing.* He sensed her tension as she awaited his reply; she wasn't ready to be alone. Which guaranteed his response.

"No. I broke out of there for you, Gillie-girl. I'm not going anywhere without you."

Not now. Not until you're ready.

The world seemed so big. Gillie had all but forgotten the feel of the wind on her face; today it didn't matter if it smelled of exhaust, not as fresh as she remembered. There wasn't much sun either, a gray day threatening rain that hadn't materialized yet. But the hint of it hung in the air, a touch of damp that charmed her. She remembered rain and she'd seen it on TV, but the visceral feel of the droplets hitting her skin . . . not so much. Would it strike lightly or sting? She so looked forward to finding out.

Though her feet hurt and her thighs burned from the long walk, the fact that she was free made all the difference. She wanted to dance and spin, but people would stare, and that'd piss Taye off for sure. He had been muttering about staying under the radar all morning.

They passed through the shabby downtown area and kept moving. She hoped he knew where he was going. Apparently he did, because he stopped outside a bank.

Gillie watched as Taye strode up to an ATM machine. He

touched his fingers to the screen and sent a gentle jolt of power. To her astonishment, the machine spat out a number of bills. He palmed them smoothly and hurried away, tucking the money into his pocket.

She followed. They'd hiked all the way to Altoona, across the Pennsylvania state line. He'd turned down two offers of rides even on the back roads, and she was wary enough to appreciate his caution; she knew their value to the Foundation well enough. They couldn't risk trusting strangers right now.

He eyed all the storefronts as they passed, until she felt impelled to ask, "What are you looking for?"

"Thrift shop."

"I guess we do need some stuff."

Eventually they found a secondhand store in a shopping plaza that had clearly seen better days; they bought jackets, jeans, T-shirts, and sneakers, as well as battered backpacks to put the clean things in. Since the place also sold irregular socks and underwear, it set them up to keep moving, blending in on the lower edge of normal. They changed in a convenience store bathroom, discarded the stolen clothes, and then walked on.

Taye tucked the food he'd stolen at the house in Virginia into his pack; they hadn't eaten since the day before because she'd been worried about buying more. After that ATM trick, maybe she didn't need to fret quite as much. Still, she didn't feel right about it; the money had to come from somewhere. The bank would pass the loss on to its customers, and that wasn't fair. But Gillie would do whatever it took to keep from going back.

God, sometimes it seemed crazy—the idea she could function in the real world. She'd never stood on her own two feet. Things other people took for granted—milestones like dates, job interviews, and birthday parties—she'd never known, and she hungered for the normalcy she'd seen on TV.

"I watched a movie," she said to Taye's back. "About a man who was in prison so long he forgot how to be free. He couldn't survive without someone telling him what to do."

"That's not you," he said roughly.

She didn't argue. He wasn't in the mood to bolster her insecurity, so it was better to ask, "Where are we headed?"

"Right now? The bus station, if I can find it." He stopped at a graffiti-covered pay phone then. This wasn't a nice neighborhood and the directory had been chained to the pedestal to keep people from running off with it. Many of the pages had been torn out, probably by people without pens who needed to take an address with them.

Fortunately, Taye found what he was looking for in the yellow pages under transportation. He didn't pull the page, just read it aloud. "Twelve-thirty-one Eleventh Avenue."

"I don't think that's far."

He glanced at the addresses on the nearby buildings and nodded. "Just a little longer. You can rest on the bus."

Taye has a maddening tendency to think I'm made of spun glass. But if they spent enough time together, he'd get over that. He would see she wasn't an ornament.

"I'm fine," she said.

The rain began halfway into their walk. Delighted, she turned her face up; it was cool and soft, dropping lightly on her skin. Other people hurried all around her, heads down and jackets pulled up. Annoyance radiated from those caught without umbrellas. They couldn't know what a miracle this was.

When Taye glanced at her, his aspect warmed. "First time in a while, huh?"

"Yeah."

"Go on." At her questioning look, he added, "Spin. I know you're dying to."

In response, she twirled, arms out, and belted the chorus to "Singin' in the Rain." He laughed quietly, ignoring the looks they received from passersby. A little dizzy, she stumbled as they walked on, but the distance didn't seem as daunting anymore. When they approached the terminal, she was shivering, and they were both soaking wet. He paused to tug her hood up. That seemed counterintuitive because she was already damp from head to toe. Gillie arched a brow.

"There are cameras inside," he explained. "Since 9/11, they track people more."

From his grave expression, that ought to mean something to her. She hunched her shoulders, feeling ignorant and debating whether she should admit as much. "What's 9/11?"

Rain trickled down his pale face, tangling in his lashes. His stillness told her nothing at all, but she felt sure he thought she was an idiot. But then his mouth softened, and he cupped her cheek in his hand. That was actually worse because she glimpsed sympathy: *poor little thing. She's a little lost lamb in the big bad world.*

Gillie bit him.

He pulled his fingers away, as if *that* was why, like he thought she didn't want him touching her. Men could be such impossible boneheads.

"Don't feel sorry for me," she warned him. "I mean it. Next time, I do worse. I used to fantasize about biting Rowan's pecker off, if he should ever push my head in that direction."

Taye eyed her, his expression mingled incredulity, astonished appreciation, and masculine horror. "Dear God."

"I know, right? I only look harmless. If you hadn't gotten me out of there, I was biding my time. We both know he was escalating."

"Yeah." Then he addressed her initial question. "About 9/11 . . . the situation is tense in the Middle East. There have been wars off and on for years, or military engagements, whatever the current buzz word."

"So . . . we're at war?"

"Kind of. It's more complex than that, though. Terrorists who work for enemy factions will target civilian sites. War's not just for armies anymore."

She thought back. "I remember bombings in other countries, something about an American embassy. But I didn't watch the news much as a kid, and that never happened here."

America was safe for *normal* people. That had to be true. At least . . . it used to be. Chills washed over her, coupled with a dire sense of loss, as if a way of life had ended before she had a chance to appreciate it.

"It does now," he said.

"And 9/11?"

"The Twin towers in NYC aren't there anymore. Terrorists hijacked a plane on September 11, 2001 and crashed into them. The death toll was astonishing. Since then, life in this country has changed a lot."

"Like cameras in bus stations."

He nodded and pulled his own hood up. "Let's find out where we can both afford to go."

Gillie wondered in frozen silence what other events she'd missed, how else the world had changed. Children's TV networks had given her some idea about changing fashion and how people talked, though she never knew how realistic it was, but she'd never gotten news channels. Rowan had locked almost all stations he didn't consider educational, controlling her entertainment as fully as he did every other aspect of her life, but as cable networks evolved, Discovery Channel started showing the most interesting programs—and that was the only reason she knew anything about the world. All her DVDs passed through his controlling hands. As she got older, she requested the things she wanted to watch and he decided whether to grant her wish.

And he might be out there somewhere, looking for you. He'll never stop. As long as he's alive, he will never *stop.* She refused to let that hateful voice take root in her head. With grim determination, she dug it out and cast those thoughts away.

Once inside the station, they didn't look any different from the other folks waiting to catch a bus somewhere. Most had backpacks, like them. Wore jeans and sneakers. *He's right. This is the perfect way to travel. Provided we can keep out of sight of those cameras.*

They had to stop somewhere, of course. But not so close to the facility; Gillie was with him on that point. She wanted to put miles behind them as fast as they could.

Rowan's face loomed up in her mind's eye—the anodyne taste of his mouth on hers—and she caught her breath, trembling with the fear that she'd find him one step behind her. Taye didn't notice, thank God, because he already thought she was breakable. If he knew how frightened she was of this enormous world with its brand-new rules, he'd never look on her as more than a child.

He moved toward the counter. "How much for two tickets to Pittsburgh?"

Big city, random choice. Good call.

The cashier tapped on the computer, which didn't look anything like the ones she remembered. Its monitor was thin and sleek, and the printer was so small. Most likely, they all ran on different systems, not that she had spent much time using her dad's PC as a kid. *Something else I need to learn.* But she could, no question.

"Seventy dollars."

"We'll take them." He counted out the cash.

"All right. Passenger names?"

If she asks for ID, we're stuck.

"Steve Mills and Clare Smith." Taye spoke the lies so smoothly that even she was impressed.

Luckily for them, the attendant didn't care about the rules; her bored face said she was only half here. The woman typed and then printed tickets. "Your bus leaves in an hour and a half. Listen for us to announce the terminal."

Since the building was small, that was probably unnecessary, but Taye thanked her and scooped up the tickets. He swept the room and picked out two seats away from the cameras. With innate wariness, he set his backpack between his knees and looped the strap around his ankle. The gesture fascinated her because it wasn't something she would have thought to do; it was a remnant of a homeless man, who only owned what he could carry and defend.

"Hey," she said softly.

"Yeah?"

"How come you can remember stuff like 9/11, but—"

"Nothing about myself?" he supplied in a low growl.

She nodded.

His knuckles whitened as he curled his hands into fists, studying them with unnecessary care. "I have echoes. Empty space. Sometimes I think they burned certain things out of me. They ran a lot of voltage through me, and gave me insane amounts of experimental drugs."

"So you think it's permanent damage . . . those memories are just gone."

He lifted his shoulders in a shrug. "I don't think I lost anything worth keeping."

Oh, Taye.

In self-defense, Gillie went to the bathroom; they had been making do at gas stations, but she needed to sponge off. Fortunately, she found paper towels and hand soap, which allowed her to do a decent job. After she finished in the stall, she finger-combed her red curls, pulled her hood back up, and then went out to join him, once she was sure she could offer a neutral face. Just as she didn't want his pity, she knew he wouldn't allow that from her either, even if his truths threatened to tug the heart from her body.

Taye had a soda waiting for her and a couple of peanut butter sandwiches. By the look of him, he'd cleaned up a little, too, wiped away the grubbiness from his face, at least, and that left his eyes more brilliant in contrast with his dark hood. He had a roguish wanderer's charm, like she imagined gypsies used to be. He wasn't a stick-around-forever guy; he was a steal-your-heart-and-run-off-into-the-night man.

"Feel better . . . Clare?"

Gillie laughed. She did, actually. It would be even better once they got on the bus, wheels moving. She couldn't remember if she got motion sick.

Hope not.

She ate in silence, feeling the twinge in her arm where the shunt had been removed. *It's a good thing I talked Rowan out of the fistula.* Yet she would always bear a mark there, more visible than those from the constant injections during her early days with the Foundation. Even in her new life, the scars from the old would follow her.

But it was only superficial, not soul-deep damage. Over the years, she'd safeguarded everything about herself that mattered, locked away from Rowan, wherever he might be.

I win, you bastard. I. Win.

CHAPTER 2

Pittsburgh was surprisingly green. Taye couldn't remember if he'd ever been here before, but it was pretty, gently rolling hills and bridges spanning numerous waterways. Somewhere in his head, he had a memory—or an expectation—of lots of steel mills and men in hard hats, teamsters screaming at each other on construction sites. The reality was quite different.

After a nearly four-hour ride, Taye tapped another cash machine and then bought a prepaid cell phone. Since they weren't getting a landline, one of them should carry it. So, basically, he got it for Gillie. Though he loathed the idea of letting her out of his sight, even for a minute, he knew she wanted to be self-sufficient.

"Oh, cool! My first cell."

He wished she wouldn't say shit like that because it reminded him how young she was, how completely inexperienced. In so many ways, she was like a kid . . . and that meant he shouldn't remember how pretty she'd looked curled up in her shower stall, or how amazing it felt there in the bathroom, when she'd eased forward and touched her lips to his. It was the first good, clean thing he'd felt since he came back to himself with electrodes attached to his skull. Sweet lightning had shimmered through him, all the way down to his toes, and he'd been so starved for pleasure that it took all his self-control not to wrap her in his arms and drag her across his lap for the mouth ravishing of a lifetime.

But damn, she'd puckered like a virgin. Which she was, of course. *Sweet little miss, never been kissed. And hell, maybe I haven't either.* At least, he didn't remember the first time . . . or the last. But he knew that wasn't how you kissed someone you wanted to fuck—instinctive insight, that. Might even be hard-wired into him. Well. *She* made him hard, anyway.

"Can you . . ." He trailed off as she slid the cell phone up and mashed the buttons. "I guess you can."

She frowned at him. "I've seen it on TV."

"Right. Well—"

The phone rang.

Gille grinned, mouthed, *Wrong number*, and put it to her ear. "Yes?" Her expression froze; she listened for a few seconds in silence, then she held it out to him. "It's for you."

What the—

"Who is this?"

"My name is Mockingbird, and you have about five minutes to get out of the city."

"This a fucking joke?"

Gillie watched him anxiously.

"It's no joke."

"How did you get this number?"

"Information is my game, T-89. You bought a phone—" He named the store. "There's a traffic cam on the corner. I've known about you since before you destroyed the Exeter facility, and I'm very interested in your progress."

"What the hell do you want, man?"

"I'm going to sum it up for you because time is short, and you have bigger problems. Rowan is dead. My agent, Shrike, killed him before he resigned. I run a crew of those united in common purpose."

"And that would be?"

"Destroying the Foundation. I have an inside line on their strike team deployments, and based on their chatter, you just powered up. You're on their radar now . . . they have one of ours. And she can track you since you zapped that ATM. For an outsider, the only way to stay hidden from Kestrel is not to do your thing at all."

"There's a retrieval team headed our way? *Fuck*."

A little whimper escaped Gillie, and she bounced up onto her toes, as if to run. He steadied her with a hand on her shoulder. *Good thing I got more cash this time. It'll have to last us until we find work.* But it had also given them away to their enemies.

"I can get you out of there, if you're willing to come work for me."

"Fuck you, buddy. I don't take favors that come with strings attached." Taye cut the call.

He snatched her hand and broke into a run. "We gotta make tracks."

"They're coming." Her voice broke on a note of pure fear.

It was late afternoon, crawling toward evening, and people on the streets headed home from work. The cars on the street zoomed by at what seemed like incredible speed, compared to how fast they could move on foot. *Need a plan. Fuck. I wish I knew more about downtown Pittsburgh.* They drew glares and shouts as they wove through the crowd on the sidewalk.

"Don't think about it. We ditched them in Virginia, and we can do it again."

"What did he say exactly?"

"No time for that now." But there was something she had to know for the sake of her sanity, though she would be mortified to realize he'd noticed how she whimpered in her sleep. "Rowan's dead. You won't be seeing him again. Ever."

Her shocked but grateful expression almost stopped him in his tracks. *God, nobody should ever be that beautiful.* She was every lovely, wholesome thing he could never have. *So focus on the problem you've gotta solve. Five minutes. Think.*

While they pelted through the throng, he heard raised voices behind. Running drew attention because people fled when they'd done something wrong. Still, it couldn't be helped. He dragged Gillie around a corner, where the sidewalk opened to a pedestrian walkway. There were quaint shops, ice cream parlors, and little eateries set in remodeled pubs. None of these places would offer cover from a supernatural tracker.

The cell phone pinged. Taye dug it out—text message, unknown caller, with an address on Forbes. *Consider this a favor. Will shield your signal.* Attached to the text came a map, showing their position relative to where they needed to go, route traced in red.

He hesitated, not knowing if he wanted to accept a favor from someone who offered help with strings attached. Sometimes the price wound up being too high. But the Foundation goons were closing, and Gillie's breath rasped in terrified sobs. *No, we got away. They're not taking her.* Making the call, Taye made a sharp right and cut down an alley, where they came up against a chain link fence. Broad daylight, it shouldn't have been frightening, but only that expanse of metal stood between them and sanctuary.

He cupped his hands and boosted Gillie with all his strength. She flew like a cheerleader, and then slammed hard on her landing. It took her precious seconds to steady, then climb over, and the sound of booted feet grew closer; shouted commands drowned the normal city sounds.

"I'm fine," she called. "Get moving!"

But he waited until she swung over the top and climbed down before he took his running start and scrambled up himself. The thugs rounded the corner just as he hit the pavement.

"We have visual!"

"Take them alive. They're too valuable to damage."

Ain't that a fucking relief. Taye didn't kid himself; there would come a time when those orders changed. But for now, the Foundation still wanted to recoup their investment.

"Step lively, Gillie-girl."

Per the cell phone map, they were almost to Forbes. Tranq darts pinged the ground on the other side of the fence, but it was hard to shoot through chain link from a distance, and by the time the goons got to the fence, they were already on the way out of the alley on the other side. *Left turn.* The two of them ran like hell, breath coming in great gulps.

And here we are. The four-story building was a nondescript, cream-colored block with crumbling mortar. Hoping like hell he was doing the right thing, Taye dragged Gillie through the darkened doorway. Hands immediately pulled them into the first apartment on the right, studio-sized, but it wasn't a residential setup. The place lacked furniture, and the walls had been painted with something that left them streaky.

The short, middle-aged man who'd grabbed him slid back a number of locks and a crossbar, then he turned. "I'm Finch . . . and this is our Pittsburgh bolt-hole. Mockingbird gave me the heads-up."

"Won't they find us here?" Gillie asked.

It was a good question. Tension kept Taye rigid, listening for signs of pursuit. But it was quiet, oddly so. The apartment itself had a single armchair upholstered in rust fabric and a small iron table with two chairs.

"Tungsten powder on the walls. Don't ask me why, but it blocks Kestrel. Once you get inside the perimeter, she loses signal. From there, strike teams can only do a building-to-building search, and normal people tend to call the police if men in black attempt to enter their homes."

"I would imagine." Gillie sank down and folded her legs like a little kid. She rubbed the fibers back and forth on the speckled shag carpet; the pattern reminded him of bird eggs and was faintly hypnotic. At least, she watched her own fingers like she saw secrets hidden in the pile.

But even down-turned and half in shadow, her face showed pale, frightened. Shit, she deserved better than this. How the hell was he supposed to keep her safe? He'd only just gotten his mind back and he didn't know if he'd ever had a knack for long-term planning.

"Just sit tight for a while. They'll clear out, and then you can move on. But I guess Mockingbird said, to pass undetected if you don't have access to our hiding places, you have to stop powering up. They're looking for you two, hard. I figure you've gotta be worth big money."

Taye stiffened and instinctively stepped closer to Gillie. "Excuse me?"

"Don't get your panties in a wad . . . I wouldn't roll on you for a billion bucks. It's enough to know I'm keeping you out of Foundation hands."

"You're one of us," Gillie realized aloud.

Finch snorted. "You make it sound like a cult. But, yeah. Anyway, I've got places to be. Stay as long as you like, until you think it's safe. The door locks automatically."

"Nice to meet you," Gillie said politely.

Taye laughed as Finch headed out; he could always count on her to make him see the humor in any situation. She regarded him with a haughty tilt of her head. Still smiling, he dropped down on the floor beside her. Artificial light caught gold strands in her red curls, and she was so pretty when she smiled back at him that his breath stuck in his chest, leaving him with a tight and fearful ache. *She has a dimple in her left cheek.* He wanted to touch a fingertip to it; the gentle simplicity of that impulse surprised him. Her skin would be warm and satin-smooth, but if he started there, he wouldn't stop.

It took him a moment to remember what he had to say. "Sorry I almost got us caught."

"You didn't know they had somebody who can detect us."

"Yeah, well," he muttered. "Excuses don't matter. But I'll do better, I promise."

She went on, blue eyes implacable, "You absolutely can't power up anymore. If we need money, we'll find work, once we decide where to go."

Good idea, as far as it went. "We're limited to where buses can take us. And some terminals may ask for ID."

"I'm not keen to spend forty hours on a Greyhound anyway," she murmured.

Considering what the short trip from Altoona had been like, he had to agree. "He said we could hide here for a little while. Maybe you should get some sleep."

"What about you?"

"I'll watch over you."

To his pleasure, she didn't argue; instead she laid her head in his lap and closed her eyes. In the sweet silence, he listened to her breathe, realizing he had no happier moment socked away. For him, sitting in the dark on the floor with her offered the purest pleasure he'd ever known. When Taye felt sure she was out, he let himself touch the strands of hair cascading across his legs. She murmured softly, turning her cheek onto his thigh. His cock hardened from her warmth and proximity, but he didn't mind the ache. It reminded him he was alive and capable of wanting her that much.

Sweet as summer honey, she was. And he'd do whatever it took to keep her that way.

ONE WEEK LATER
DETROIT

Gillie stood outside McGinty's Tavern for a full five minutes, hands in the pockets of her hoodie, while she worked up the courage to go in. Normal people did stuff like this all the time.

It was a crumbling redbrick building with a green sign with tarnished brass letters. The windows were smoky, permitting no glimpse of what the inside would be like.

Taking a deep breath, she pushed through the door and snatched the "Help Wanted" sign from the window, then strode boldly toward the bar. *Begin as you mean to go on,* her mother always said. An ache sprang to life at the stray thought; she tried not to remember her parents or to wonder what became of them, lest the hurt become untenable. Gillie knew damn well she couldn't look for them or contact them. That would paint a giant bull's-eye on her parents' back, presuming Rowan had lied, and they were still alive. She wouldn't make them targets or let the Foundation use them to coerce her back into captivity.

But today, the memory of her mother's soft voice with its faint Cork accent gave her fortitude to do what she must. She took a quick look around: neon beer signs on the walls, turned off because it was daytime, dark wood, and various stains—not a lovely place, but one where people came to drink away their memories.

An elderly man turned at her approach and shook his head. "We're closed, miss."

"I know. I came about the job." She placed the sign on the counter as if that gesture held the power to get her hired.

Bushy white brows shot skyward. "Dishwashing? It's too dirty in there"—he pronounced it "thar," with a jerk of his head toward the kitchen—"for a pretty mite like you."

"Please. I really need the work . . . You don't have to pay me much. I don't even know what minimum wage is these days."

The old man eyed her for a moment, as if trying to decide if she was on the level. In the new world Taye had told her about—where there were cameras on every street corner—maybe government men routinely tried to trap small business owners into proving they'd hire illegal employees. But Gillie gauged the precise moment he recognized the desperation in her threadbare secondhand jeans and the slightly too-large sweatshirt.

"You looking for a cash arrangement?" he asked.

"That'd be best. I'll work hard, harder than anybody who ever walked through that door."

A gruff laugh escaped him, then he turned and yelled toward the kitchen, "Hear that, you sons of bitches?" Facing her, he added, "It wouldn't take much to beat this lot. I got one waitress, I tend bar, and Manny makes burgers and cheese fries for the drunks. You'd be on cleanup. You willing to bus tables, too?"

"I'll do whatever work needs doing."

"Bathrooms, dishes, floors?" He raised a brow like he expected her to argue.

The fact of the matter was, the money Taye had taken from the ATM in Pittsburgh wouldn't keep them much longer. He'd rented a studio apartment, using most of it, so if one of them didn't find a job, they'd starve. If he powered up again, the consequences would be worse.

She nodded. "I know how to mop, wipe tables, and push a broom."

"Come back tonight. You'll work from seven to three, five nights a week. Five dollars an hour, one meal included in your pay, if you can stand to eat Manny's cooking."

"I heard that!"

"Ignore him. Anyway, I'm Michael McGinty . . . you can call me Mick."

Gillie extended her hand politely. "I'm—"

"Are you gonna lie to me?"

"Yes," she admitted.

"Then I'll save you some time and call you Red. Unless you mind."

"No, that's fine. I'll be back at seven then. Thank you."

It didn't surprise her to find Taye waiting outside, even though she had asked him to let her do this by herself. He felt responsible for her, and she couldn't seem to cure him of that impulse, no matter how much she insisted she wanted to make her own way. But at the moment, she was too pleased to have that argument again.

"I got the job." She grinned up at him.

He opened his arms, offering a celebratory hug, and she wished his affection didn't come with such labels on it. But she didn't turn him down; instead she ran to him and let him swing her off her feet in a slow circle.

Once he set her back down and they fell in step heading back to the apartment, he said, "Me, too. I'm loading down at the docks."

"Under the table?" she guessed.

"That's the only work we'll be able to find until I get us some new IDs."

"Which will take money."

There was an easy fix, of course. Taye wanted to gamble by using his ability and then bail before Kestrel could get a team to them. But Gillie wasn't eager to risk capture again; they couldn't be guaranteed of finding a safe hidey-hole again. She preferred to work and lay low. Living on their combined salaries, surely they could save enough to get new paperwork in time. They just had to take care until then.

"I'm working the day shift, but I'll be able to pick you up at night."

Gillie stifled a smile. "Thank you."

"We need to talk about living arrangements—"

"Why?" She raised a brow. "It makes sense that we share the apartment. We need to save money, remember?"

He gave her a dark look, but didn't argue.

That set the tone for the next couple of weeks. The work at McGinty's was hard and unpleasant, as Mick had warned her, but she liked pulling her own weight, even when it involved mopping up someone's drunken bender or plunging a toilet. By the time she finished at night, she was exhausted, but she always went home feeling like she'd earned her pay.

And she always found Taye waiting when she got off work. Though she'd never admit it, without him, she would have been frightened walking the blocks between the apartment and the bar. Half the time, the streetlights didn't work, and sometimes men hung out on corners and on front stoops until all hours. With him beside her, they didn't bother her.

Once they got home, she hung up her jacket and gave him the takeout container. She had gotten in the habit of asking Manny to make a burger or a steak to go. And he never charged her for it; she suspected he thought she ate the food herself, the following day. Since they both got fed once a day on the tavern's dime, it cut down on the grocery bill.

"So . . ." Taye asked tiredly. "The outside world. Is it everything you dreamed?"

"Yes and no." She sank down on the plaid couch and watched him stow tomorrow's lunch in the small refrigerator. "I won't claim I dreamed of escaping from Exeter to clean up after people, but doing this of my own free will is better than being Rowan's prisoner."

"No joke."

Taye sat down beside her on the sofa. He stretched out, arm along the back, and she longed to curl into him. Gillie knew better, though. His boundaries didn't extend to cuddling; by his definition, they were roommates by default, and he had no desire to get further tangled up with her.

Most days she tried to pretend it didn't hurt. So she worked to bury the pain. Constantly.

After they moved in, she'd scrubbed the apartment thoroughly. Since it was furnished, it came with all the scents and stains of the previous tenants, who had not been careful housekeepers. Now the place was relatively clean, if threadbare and cramped. The Murphy bed helped with the lack of space; they didn't pull it down unless someone needed to sleep.

Like right now.

But she wasn't eager to end the rare moment where she had his complete attention. So she'd milk a few minutes more. "If you could do anything, what would that be?"

Go ahead. Dream big for me.

"I'd like to be rich," he said. "Decadently so. With a private jet and my own island. Beautiful women to fan me and feed me grapes."

Wow. That was pretty far from her dream, so maybe he was right not to let them get closer. If that was what he really wanted, he'd never be happy with her. Gillie's dreams were smaller and quieter—to find a job she enjoyed and eventually, start a family. Maybe it was because she had spent so much of her life alone, but she craved being surrounded by people who cared about her and needed her.

Or maybe he's saying that to avoid letting you get to know him better.

"I don't believe you," she said, testing the insight.

When he cut her a surprised look, quickly veiled, she knew she was right. They were just empty words, a lock on the door he was determined not to open. Taye eyed her warily, as if suspecting she might be able to read his mind.

"How did you know?"

"It's a generic dream, something anyone might say, but it doesn't tell me about you."

"There's nothing to learn," he muttered. "Haven't you figured that out yet? I'm like one of those chocolate bunnies, nothing but air inside."

She touched the blue ink on his forearm. "I know that's not true."

Taye studied her fingers on his skin, but he didn't move away. "Yeah? Then why don't I know how I got that tat? Or what it means."

"It means Rowan hurt you. Not that there's no substance to the man you are now."

He pushed to his feet. "Aren't you tired?"

That hint was subtle as a brick upside the head. *Yeah, I get it. Don't get too close.*

"Go ahead and make the bed," she said aloud. "I'm taking a quick shower."

When she came out in her pajamas, fifteen minutes later, he was already asleep. That didn't surprise her; he had to be up in three hours. By this point, they had the routine down. He made more than she did, though not a lot. Between them, they earned seventeen-hundred sixty dollars a month, and this place cost four seventy-five. She'd worked out the public transportation system, taking the bus to Aldi once a week to do some grocery shopping. Twenty bucks went a long way there. By pinching pennies, they'd already saved a little, but they were still looking for someone who could hook them up with IDs.

Once you have papers and can register for college, or whatever, Taye will be gone.

Part of her wanted desperately to seduce him, provided she could figure out how. Living in close quarters hadn't driven him mad with lust. They shared the bed because it was practical, but he'd never given any sign he wanted to take advantage.

Everything will change soon, Gillie promised herself.

CHAPTER 3

Taye ached, and for once, it had nothing to do with Gillie. His work on the docks was backbreaking and it left him little energy for other things. But he hadn't come straight home from his shift even though he knew she had supper waiting. One of his coworkers had tipped him to somebody who might be able to hook them up with new documents.

That was why after eight hours spent loading containers of God knew what, he hopped a bus to the address Rodrigo had given him. The closest stop was three blocks away, and he fought the urge to pull—draw energy from an electrical source—as he walked down Cass Ave. He passed a number of bars and liquor stores before he found the right place. Taye stared up at the block building, the cement a faded, dirty gray. In the derelict bottom floor, he saw the remnants of a grocery store; they advertised fresh produce, but all the doors and windows had iron grills across them. Half of a red and white prescription sign hinted at a defunct pharmacy.

Shit, maybe Rodrigo sent me here to get rolled.

On the second floor, where he was supposed to go, all the windowpanes were intact, a good sign, he supposed. As he'd been instructed, he circled around back and rang the bell. The intercom crackled, and then an unfriendly male voice said, "What?"

"I've come for a consultation. Rodrigo sent me."

"Fucking illegals," the guy muttered. "You probably can't afford me. But come up."

The heavily reinforced door buzzed, indicating it had been unlocked. Taye went in before the forger changed his mind. A dark stairwell led up and he took the stairs at a slow jog. There were three doors: one to the left, one to the right, and one at the end of the hall. He was sure it had to be the latter because like downstairs, it was new and made of metal. A camera whirred, checking him out. And then:

"Take off your coat and boots."

He did, showing he wasn't armed.

"Leave them in the hall and come in."

The second door unlocked and he stepped into the man's office. He had a lot of computer equipment, more than Taye had expected. Not that he knew shit about this business. The dude was younger than he would've guessed, too, no more than twenty-one, also pasty, chubby, and unkempt. His sanctum smelled of ham and cheese Hot Pockets, and he kept his hands in his lap; Taye suspected he had a hidden gun trained on his gut.

"Did you bring cash?"

A wave of embarrassment crashed over him. "Not today. Rodrigo sent me over to talk to you about that."

The other guy swore. "I knew it. I don't take trades, I don't take credit, and I don't work on the installment plan."

"I just need to know how much and what you need from us."

"Us?"

"Two of us need papers."

"Just passport? Or passport, driver's license, and birth certificates?"

Honestly he hadn't thought that far ahead. "Probably the whole package. How much will it run?"

"For two of you, six grand. When you can pay in full, I'll need photos, the names you want to use, desired age, date of birth, and birthplace."

"And how long will it take?"

"Seven to ten days." He must've shown surprise because the guy added, "I have to find suitable documents and clone the RFID chips, if you want to pass immigration software checks. I can get you a fake ID in twenty-four, but I figure you want more than to get into a bar."

"Yeah, we might need to travel."

Somewhere she can have a real life.

"Thought as much. Come back when you're ready to do business."

As Taye left, he realized he'd never learned the guy's name, but it didn't matter. Probably better that way. Working as they were, it would take several months to save that much. They were living on around nine hundred bucks, which meant they could sock away eight hundred a month, if nothing went wrong. At that rate, it would take seven and a half months to save enough for the full package. With a faint sigh, he put on his jacket and boots.

Nobody messed with him on the way home. Maybe they read in his expression that he'd like nothing more than to fuck someone up. He covered the distance from the bus stop to the apartment in a weary fog. As he entered, he thought, *At least there are no bums asleep in the lobby today.* Though he'd never admit it, eagerness lent him speed. It had been a long-ass day, and he wanted to spend an hour or two with Gillie before she went to work.

As he stepped in, he smelled beef and rice. Too bad he couldn't eat enough to do her cooking justice. She amazed him with what she could create out of the most basic ingredients. But his stomach hurt more than usual today; he'd been hiding the pain from Gillie from the first moment they met, determined to give her no reason to fear. He'd promised to see her safe and settled, and he would, no matter what.

"You're home late." She smiled, making it an observation instead of chastisement.

Gillie served a plate with plain rice covered with beef and vegetables. Some folks called the dish *picadillo*, others goulash. And he had no idea why he knew that.

He hung up his jacket and then filled her in.

"That's a lot of money," she said when he finished.

"We'll be here awhile. The only alternative—"

"No. I don't want you pulling."

Taye didn't tell her that his control was shaky, and they had been lucky thus far. If he ever fucked up, he'd do anything to minimize the harm to her. Even let them haul him back, if it came down to it. *Whatever it takes.*

He picked at his food until she went into the bathroom to get ready for work and then scraped most of the meal back into the pan. She enjoyed doing for him so much that he didn't have the heart to ask her not to bother. And it made him feel good, even if he couldn't enjoy it like a normal guy.

"Want me to walk you to work?" he asked.

"It's still daylight. Plus I have my pepper spray and that alarm horn you got me." The amusement in her voice said she thought he was overprotective.

But in this neighborhood, it was all he could do to let her go out alone. Ever. Each moment she was away from him, he suffered all the torments of the damned because life without Gillie Flynn wouldn't be worth living. He wanted to lock her away in a tower like a princess, but that never worked out well. In stories, they always ran off with the first guy to spring them.

"I might stop in later for a drink."

Shit, of course he would, after he got a little sleep; he'd gotten used to doing so in swing shifts. It was a good thing McGinty's had a ninety-cent draft, or it'd take even longer for them to save enough for the ID packages. But Mick seemed to know he was there to keep an eye on Gillie more than drink, and he didn't mind Taye nursing the same beer for hours.

"Then I'll look for you when I take my break."

Three hours after she scrubbed up the vomit from the men's room, Gillie went into the ladies to freshen up. There wasn't a lot she could do before seeing Taye, but she did wash her hands twice with soap, run a comb through her red curls, and put on some lipstick. She had gotten smart about the gross cleaning jobs; now she wore an apron and took it off when she was done, so her McGinty's shirt stayed relatively fresh.

She pushed the door open and scanned the room. The usual drunks occupied their usual stools. Mick smiled at her from behind the bar, acknowledging she was on break, and she nodded at him. Taye liked the cracked leather booth at the back, where he could sprawl and read while pretending he was going to finish his beer. In a busier pub, maybe people would've gotten on him about ordering more or moving on, but this tavern was never more than half full, even when the Tigers were playing. The game had been over for more than an hour, and afterward, people trickled out. It had to be close to midnight now.

When he glanced up from his book—an old Zane Grey somebody must've left behind—his welcoming smile made her weak in the knees. In a minute, Phyllis would bring out her usual burger and fries, but until then, she could sit and smile at him like neither of them had anyplace they'd rather be. Even if she knew better.

"Rough night?" he asked.

"No worse than usual."

"I hate seeing you here."

She knew that. "Things will get better. This is temporary."

As the waitress approached, Gillie fell quiet, smiling in thanks. The other woman didn't have to wait on her, but it was her way of saying thanks. Before she came on board, Phyllis had to do a lot of the cleaning herself.

"I keep telling myself that, too."

"It would be worse if we weren't together," she said.

He studied her for a long moment in silence, and she feared he would lecture her about unreasonable expectations. And then he surprised her. "If I wasn't with you, I wouldn't bother."

A frown creased her brow. "With what?"

"Anything." That brought to mind questions but he changed the subject. "How is it you can work so hard and come out looking so beautiful?"

Her heart gave a wayward thump. Maybe he offered the compliment as a distraction, but hell, it worked, mostly because she read the sincerity in his face. He usually tried to hide any hint of attraction, fearing she'd get the wrong idea about his intentions. Tonight he smiled at her with his heart in his eyes, and it thrilled her from head to toe.

"Just lucky I guess," she said, breathless.

"I'm the lucky one. You could've gone off with anyone else."

"I couldn't. I don't trust anyone else."

Something fierce and stark flashed in his sea-hued eyes, but his lashes came down to veil the look. Instead, he studied her palm, flattened on the table. Taye took her hand and pressed a kiss to her fingertips. They were rough from the work she did; he didn't appear to notice, but she noticed the contrast between her skin and the softness of his lips. She knew him well enough to take it as thanks for her faith in him—still, a pleasurable chill rolled through her. Daringly, she grazed his lower lip with her index finger. Phantom kiss.

Their eyes locked and held. Her breath accelerated. She felt the heat of his desire as if it were a hidden flame, burning him from the inside out. For the space of four heartbeats, he let her touch him. His lips moved in another kiss, and then he drew back. Not a sharp, sudden movement, but a retreat nonetheless.

"You won't regret believing in me," he said softly. "You should eat."

Well, he was right about that. Manny's food didn't improve once it cooled off. Gillie ate half the burger and some of the fries, with extra ketchup, while he amused her with a story about the guy who had been trying to pick up Phyllis earlier. She listened with half an ear, appreciating his company.

"Was it the guy with the red and black plaid cap?"

Taye cocked a brow. "How'd you know?"

"Eh, Steve's not picky. Phyllis, me . . . sometimes Mick if he's *really* drunk."

Instead of laughing, he took on a ferocious edge. "You promised to tell me if anyone bothered you in here."

"He's harmless."

"What did he do?" The lines of tension beside his mouth alerted Gillie to the fact that this wasn't just overprotectiveness kicking in.

"Tonight? Slapped me on the ass and told me I had the freshest buns in the bakery."

A muscle ticked beside his jaw. "This has happened before?"

"Not that exact thing. Steve can be creative." Egging him on might not be the best idea, but it was fun. "I'd better get back to work. My fifteen are almost up."

As she stood, he did. He stepped into her space and cupped her face in his hands. To her astonishment, he bent and kissed her. Not a sisterly kiss. Not a friendly one. The heat of his mouth kindled a sweet blaze in her belly, and she parted for him. She might've done it wrong the first time, but she knew better now. His tongue brushed hers, once, twice, teasing glides that curled her toes. His lips lingered on hers deliciously, endlessly, until he nipped her lower lip as he pulled back. Dizzy euphoria filled her head—God, how she wanted him.

The few patrons in the bar, including Steve, were watching with varying degrees of interest. Taye put his hand on her shoulder and said to the room, conversationally, "I'll kill the next guy who touches her."

Her elation died. There had been a purpose behind the show; it didn't mean he wanted her. It meant he didn't want anyone else to mess with her—a fine distinction, and a bit dog in the manger. With a sigh, she went back to work.

Seven months in this place, seven months of endless temptation. She shrugged. *Still better than the alternative.*

CHAPTER 4

It was a beautiful day, dawning pink and silver. Sand crunched beneath his feet, along with sand dollars and miscellaneous seashells. The water shone a cool and brilliant blue. In the distance, a few fishermen had already gone out to cast their nets, but they were too far away to help Nico Margolis. Caleb Dunn jabbed the barrel of the Glock between his shoulder blades; if the twat had any mental capacity at all, he'd know he was being marched down to the beach to die. People didn't come out here at gunpoint to chat about the weather.

Sadly, he didn't seem to have worked it out, which explained why his brother-in-law wanted Nico dead. Something about being married to his sister, so he'd given Nico a job running numbers and drugs; he was spectacularly bad at both. Now the brother-in-law needed a permanent solution that wouldn't blow back on him.

Cale forced the man to his knees. Since he had a contract on his head and very little sense in it, he was begging for his life in guttersnipe Italian. Which might have helped his cause if Cale spoke Italian. *Might* have, but unlikely. In general, he didn't negotiate under such circumstances. Men would promise anything, even if delivering it lay outside their scope. They always thought a change of venue would help, if they could just buy ten more minutes, everything would be different.

Not this time, Nico. End of the road for you.

Dunn didn't think of himself as a contract killer. He was more of a jack-of-all-trades, a true mercenary. In his nearly two-decade career, he had driven fugitives across international borders, stolen a couple of planes, fought in five private wars, and seen two dictators die. One of them, he had shot himself. So plugging a lowlife didn't rate very high on his list of things he should never, ever do, even if the man was crying like a widow.

With a faint sigh, he put two slugs in the back of the man's head, as agreed under the contract. As usual, he wiped the gun, dropped it, and left the mark by the water. Some beachcomber would find him, hopefully before the tide came in. Cale jogged up toward the road and got into his rented Fiat. Everything had proceeded right on schedule. Now he had a plane to catch.

Paris would be nice this time of year. He'd take a little time off, maybe look up Lisette, who had promised to kill him if he ever showed his face again. It would be fun if she tried; that always led to the best anger sex.

Halfway to the airport, his phone rang. It was his dedicated sat-phone, a number only given to former clients, which meant he had worked for this person before, or they were a referral. He answered with a curt, "Dunn."

"It has work for you."

Bizarre voice. He couldn't tell if the caller was male or female—a little deep for the latter and too light for the former, the most purely androgynous tone he'd ever heard. The verbiage wasn't quite right, either, but maybe this wasn't a native speaker. Some smooth, awful thread ran through it, something . . . not quite human, as if it came from a mouth with too many teeth. But surely he was tired—imagining things. A job was a job.

"Lay it out for me."

"It desires two fugitives remanded to its custody."

Cale hesitated. "I take it you don't work in law enforcement?"

"It does not. This contract would prove lucrative."

"Are they dangerous?"

"Yes."

A thrill of interest surged through him. It had been a long

time since he had a worthy hunt. Most of his targets were stupid and predictable. They ate, fucked, and slept in the same patterns, so it was child's play to snatch them. He could use a challenge.

"I'll need a full dossier on each of them, last known location, and half a million dollars." He always started high. Any employer would be prepared for that, and haggling was fun. But within five minutes, this creepy fuck should come to an agreement if he or she was serious.

Instead, the voice said, "Half now, half when the job is completed."

Holy—

All of his alarm bells went off. When the other party showed no interest in negotiation, it meant the task was so difficult as to be impossible—that, or they wanted it accomplished beyond any rational reason. It whispered of obsession, which was never good in his line of work. Business was business, and it was best not to chase it with a crazy cocktail.

"How did you get this number?"

"The hunter worked for Gerard Serrano, yes?"

"Once," he admitted.

The bastard was dead now, and good riddance. He'd tried to cheat Cale out of his bonus for completing the job within the ten-day deadline. Regardless, Serrano had all kinds of shady connections, so there was no telling who might be on the other end of the line. His silence must have communicated some misgiving.

"It represents a consortium called the Foundation, which funds scientific research. Serrano was one of the initial members."

That sounded particularly spooky; scientific research covered a lot of ground, but the money was too good to pass up, just the job he'd been looking for in order to top off his nest egg and get out of the game entirely.

Cale swallowed his qualms and said, "You have a deal. Send me the paperwork."

"Excellent. Tickets to New York wait at the airport. One of its people will be at LaGuardia with everything needed to complete the task."

Damn. They were fucking sure of me, weren't they? That made him uneasy, too. *Focus on the money, mate. It's keen and green, and soon you'll be done with this shit for good.*

* * *

Puerto Vallarta was gorgeous this time of year. Some people preferred Cancun, but Tanager didn't like the tourist influence. She thought it was more like an American colony than a true reflection of Mexico. PV still had the feel of a quaint beach town, where she could stroll along the *malecon* and pretend she had nowhere else to be. There were also gorgeous resorts here at reasonable prices, private beaches, plus fabulous service. Not that she ever paid for anything. All she had to do was walk in the door, ask to speak to the manager, and then say, *You want to comp your best suite, an all-inclusive package.* Her siren voice did the rest. Though it only worked on men, there were enough males in the world that she always got what she wanted.

Which was why she found Mockingbird's resistance intriguing. Maybe it was the electronic interference on the line, but she had never been able to get him to do anything he didn't want to. That didn't stop her from trying. Everyone needed a hobby.

"Come on," Tanager said. "You know what you want to tell me."

She was the only one who got away with teasing Mockingbird. Lying in the chaise lounge with her feet crossed at the ankles, she sipped at her foamy piña colada. The umbrella kept the sun off her fair skin, but the warmth was welcome, and this vacation was long overdue.

"I'm not telling you my name," he said, sighing. "Not yet. But I will tell you this much now . . . I used to have another handle. People knew me as Apex."

"Huh." It was more concession than she'd expected, though it still didn't tell her much. But she might be able to do some digging and turn up some information. Most likely, she would choose not to, however. If she found out, it could cost everyone else down the line. It sucked that they lived in a world that demanded such caution, but it was what the Foundation had made it.

"Does that make you feel better, like we've formed an indisputable bond?"

"Haven't we?" she asked, her tone serious for once.

Funny, but Mockingbird knew her better than anyone else. He had been the one to save her, when everything went so disastrously wrong, after—well. *After.* She had known him for years, longer than any other agent; Tanager had been with him since before he realized their organization had to grow inexpressibly more paranoid and complex if people like them weren't all going to wind up in Foundation prison cells. She called damn few people friend, but he fit the bill.

An awkward silence followed. Sometimes she wished she could fucking find him and see what he looked like, the guy who seemed like he never slept, never stopped fighting the good fight. Only through his diligence did all the balls stay in the air, and God only knew what would become of everyone else if anything ever happened to Mocks.

"Yeah," he said finally. "You've been with me almost as long as Shrike, and you still haven't quit on me."

Shrike was an interesting case. He had executed some of the bloodiest revenge that their organization had ever seen, but in the end, he just walked away. Last they heard, he was operating independently, solving problems that didn't fit easily into any jurisdiction.

"I won't either. Can you see me giving up all this?"

He laughed. "Not really. Anyway, the reason I pinged you is twofold. First, I have news about the Exeter facility. I have confirmation . . . five subjects made it out alive. I already rescued a couple of them, but they weren't interested in signing on right then."

"Give them time. Once they see how hard life is for people like us without a little help, they'll take the recruitment package."

"I think so, too. I don't care as much about the healer, but we could use another warrior."

"Careful. You'll make me feel unwanted."

"Not my intention."

"So what's the second part?"

"I've been thinking about this, ever since Kestrel was taken. We used her before we discovered the tungsten-blocking properties . . . and she found a lot of test subjects for us."

"Made recruitment a dream," she agreed.

"So how did *they* find her? They didn't have anyone who could pinpoint locations like that. I've thought all along it couldn't be coincidence, and now I'm sure. Someone sold her out."

Fuck.

"Have you looked at everyone's financials?" Tanager sighed and shook her head. "Never mind, I know. Most don't even have their own bank accounts, just cards you gave them."

"Yep. All the money flows through me. Doesn't mean somebody didn't take a briefcase full of cash, though, and I have no way of tracking that. The Foundation makes payments all the time. Needle in a haystack, even for me."

"So what's my part in this?"

He outlined it for her.

"Really? Shadow detail?" She sighed in frustration. "I'm the last person who should do this. I draw attention. I *thrive* on attention."

"Tan," he said quietly. "You're the only one I trust. Everyone else is too new. I can't tip my hand . . . I can't let them know I'm not the all-powerful Oz—that I am, in fact, just the little man behind the curtain."

What must it be like for him? He had nobody in whom he could confide. *Well, except me. And I'm not exactly the most reliable person in the world.*

"So you want me to plug our leak. Am I permitted to use force?"

"As a last resort, if you can't stop it any other way."

"Cool," she said, sliding off the deck chair. "I was about ready for some action anyway."

CHAPTER 5

PRESENT DAY
DETROIT

Shapes loomed up from the darkness. Fearlessly, Gillie stepped forward. The metal door slammed behind her as she stepped fully through the employee's entrance, trash in hand.

In the distant, half-light thrown by the streetlamp, the Dumpster became a young dragon crouched against the crumbling brick façade of the bar where she worked. She could almost discern the scales in the flecks of rust where the paint had peeled away. She approached the dragon armed with nothing but a thin black plastic sack full of rubbish. With a fierce scowl, she wound up and slung the mess down the beast's gullet and pacified it for another day.

"You're welcome," she said to the dark and oblivious city.

That imagination had seen her through unbelievable horror. Sometimes she still found it hard to sleep at night. Hard to believe she was finally safe, or at least, more so than she had been. For someone like her, safety came in degrees ranging from *out of harm's way for the moment* to *about to die.* And sometimes her mind played tricks on her, making her think something terrible was about to happen, because it always, always did.

But she wasn't imagining the light crunch of footsteps over broken glass.

"You shouldn't have to do this." The quiet voice didn't surprise her.

When Gillie turned, she found Taye propped up against the opposite wall, a steakhouse that had long since gone out of business. Now it had grates across the windows and people still managed to break the glass. God knew, the bar was headed that way, but over these months, Mick had been good to her. Weird as it might seem, she didn't mind her job.

"You're wrong," she said. "This is what real people do."

She wasn't interested in replaying the conversation wherein he offered to get her enough money to set her up for life, though his ability hurt him and it meant the difference between freedom and capture. It was possible he was just working too hard, but Taye looked more haggard all the time, as though the electricity had sapped the life right out of him. In recent months, his outlook had darkened, too, so bleak and grim that most days, it was a fucking miracle if she could make him smile. She'd taken to memorizing dirty jokes that she overheard in the kitchen in the hope she could take him by surprise and banish the sorrow for a little while.

Plus, she wasn't interested in letting him steal for her. She wanted to work; Taye didn't understand that. He thought she should be ready for a life of leisure after her long incarceration, ready to bask in the sun and sip margaritas. Unfortunately, the easy road wasn't the best way, and deep down, he knew that. He just hated seeing her with her hands raw from scrubbing, and the guilt of feeling like he should do better for her made him surly.

Frost lay lightly on the ground, adding a crystalline layer to the grit-covered pavement. Snow touched his hair and melted immediately, as if he generated heat in each unruly strand. It was too long in front, and it hung in his eyes, lending him a roguish air. But that buccaneer swagger was deceptive; he wasn't playful. Like the electricity he commanded, he could turn deadly in a flicker.

By now, she should have gotten over the lightning that careened in her veins just from looking at him. He wasn't shiny and new anymore. They'd had months to get used to one another, and more than once, she'd flung a dish and screamed at him. More than once, he'd slammed out of the apartment as if he couldn't stand her proximity for another minute.

But he always came back, and she always swept up the glass shards of what she broke. Their extra-special brand of dysfunction wouldn't work with anyone else.

At their first meeting, Taye had frightened her. She'd believed him a punishment from Rowan or a herald of worse things to come. But shortly, she'd realized he was a reward for everything she'd endured. Or maybe, she'd thought recently, she just *wanted* him to be. Taye had other ideas.

"We're not meant to be like them." He pushed away from the wall and sauntered toward her, all loose-limbed grace.

"I want to be. I've never done any of this. Maybe to anyone else, my life might seem awful or pathetic, but . . ." She couldn't finish the sentence.

He had seen the truth. Taye knew where she came from—and it was why he escorted her to and from work every night. He'd gotten it into his head that she needed protecting, that she was too fragile for the world. Like so many men, he saw only the fair, almost translucent skin, red curls, and big blue eyes. He assumed her appearance meant she couldn't take care of herself—that the apparent physical fragility ran bone deep. But one couldn't survive what she had and remain emotionally vulnerable. Inside, where it counted, she had a steel core.

"There's nothing pitiful about you," he said softly. "Come on. Let's get home."

For a while, after that possessive kiss at McGinty's, she'd tried to get him to take that final step past friendship and into intimacy, but he wouldn't budge. He maintained a hands-off policy where she was concerned. Which Gillie thought was ridiculous. She was nearly twenty-five years old, and no man inspired by normal desire or affection had ever touched her. Rowan's real doll obsession with her did not bear close scrutiny. From what she'd observed, Taye's need to protect her fought constantly with his desire to keep his distance.

Though she knew he hated casual contact, Gillie curled her hand around his arm anyway, as though they were a normal couple. Did boyfriends pick their girlfriends up after work? She suspected they did in this part of town, if they gave a shit.

He glanced down at her fingers, pale against the dark leather of his jacket. The duster suited his rangy build. With it, he always wore jeans, plain white T-shirts, and motorcycle boots. Gillie had wondered if that style was left over from the person he was before, the one he could only remember in bits and pieces.

That lack of memory tormented him. While she lay in their chaste bed, listening to him breathe, she'd also heard fragments of his nightmares. At base, Taye felt like an incomplete person, a man blessed with abilities instead of memories. He did not know who he was—or what he'd done—only what he could do.

After a long hesitation, he didn't pull away; he let the small incursion against his defenses stand. And then he set off toward the main street, matching his strides to hers. That instinctive courtesy made her think he couldn't have been as bad a man as he feared, before the Foundation broke him and remade him in their image. He was only certain he'd been homeless, crazy from the first vaccine. It hurt her to envision what he'd suffered, even before the evil of those subsequent secret experiments. But it also let her understand him. Pain had forged him into a protector, but it had left him emotionally wrecked. He feared he had nothing to give.

Because she couldn't give up on him—couldn't let him slide in silence—she said, "I made cookies today while you were at work."

It was an invitation for him to stay up with her for a while and talk about his day. It also served as a quiet reminder of what they shared, and a statement that nobody would ever understand like she did. By the wry quirk of his well-molded mouth, he knew her intention; you didn't get that kind of subtext with just anybody. Taye thought she only wanted him because he was the first person who had been kind since the Foundation took her from her parents. He thought she lacked any frame of reference to make an educated sexual decision.

Gillie found that insulting. There were guys at McGinty's, kitchen help and the occasional patron, who had offered to take her home. She didn't want any of them. Eight months later, she still wanted Taye, but he said the dregs of society didn't count. Some days, *he* was the reason she threw things. Him, and his fucking stubbornness.

Yet he didn't demure or mutter an excuse about how he

needed to go straight to bed. She'd learned early on that he had a sweet tooth, so she angled a hopeful look at him.

"What kind?"

Maybe she ought to mind that her company wasn't enough. But she'd take whatever she could get with him, as he wanted to cut and run. Only a confounded sense of obligation had kept him hanging around this long. And that, she did *not* want from him.

But time was running out. Soon, they would have enough for the ID package, and they'd go their separate ways. The idea filled her with despair.

"Gingersnaps."

He sighed. "You do this on purpose, tempting me in the middle of the night."

"Of course." There was no point denying it.

They turned the corner onto their street. The studio he'd found for such cheap rent was in a terrible brownstone that smelled of mildew and urine. Around here, there were mostly closed businesses and buildings that had been condemned and taken over by squatters. Graffiti streaked the brick and cement; steel grates covered windows and doors.

"We need to talk," he conceded. "And cookies will make the bad news go down easier. But Gillie, sweetheart, you have to resign yourself to the fact I won't be around forever. I can't play house like you want me to."

Her pleasure at the endearment twanged with a sour note, swelling into astonishing pain. "I have. I know you won't stay."

She let go of his arm then and hurried up the walk, stepping over broken green glass that glimmered like pirate emeralds. His footsteps came on, slower but steady and sure behind her. He would be watching the street, looking for the Foundation trackers. The two of them were too valuable for their tormentors to yield pursuit without another attempt at recovery.

When she pushed open the front door, she found a man asleep in the foyer. Likely homeless, but this wasn't the sort of place where anyone would run him out. Just as well; it was cold outside, cold enough to see her breath even inside the doors. Taye paused, and she knew what he was thinking: *Am I this guy? And did anyone give a fuck?*

In silence, he dug into his pocket and pulled out a couple of bills. The overhead light guttered, making it impossible for her to see their denomination. He crossed the cracked black-and-white vinyl floor to tuck the money into the man's breast pocket. Closer, the smell of cheap liquor wafted from him. It was impossible to tell the man's age, but Taye himself seemed older when he turned toward the stairs, following her up to the first landing.

Gillie jogged up the flights without speaking, and then unlocked the door. It was a humble studio, smaller than the place where Rowan had held her hostage. But it was theirs.

After this, she wanted to go to college. She wanted . . . everything. But she wasn't likely to get a happy ending, not the one with a picket fence and the man of her dreams. Taye said she hadn't met enough men to make up her mind anyway.

And these days, she would settle for freedom.

While Taye prowled the place, checking the few dark corners where an intruder might hide, she pulled her chipped, misshapen cookie jar from the top of the ancient refrigerator. Feline in shape, the thing also had one deformed ear, giving it a tomcat look. When she removed the ceramic lid, dual scents of sugar and spice wafted from the container. Switching focus with predatory grace, Taye wrapped up his search and came to sit warily on the couch.

Gillie poured milk into plastic tumblers and put some cookies on a plate. Taye eyed them with endearing hunger, as if they nourished some need in him much deeper than the ingredients would suggest.

"Here you go."

He took one for each hand, ignoring the milk, and ate them before leveling a contemplative gaze on her. His irises gleamed the vibrant blue green of tropical waters. Some might name them turquoise or aquamarine, but those words seemed flat compared to the beauty of Taye's eyes, fringed with dark lashes, bleached lighter at the tips. He was tan now from his work on the docks; his lean jaw bristled with stubble, and it held a ruddy hue, slightly redder than his chestnut hair.

"I guess you know there's a reason I'm not going to bed."

She nodded. Though her baking had improved, it still wasn't irresistible. In all these months, she'd never learned what it would take to breach his walls. Maybe she didn't have the key, and one day he'd decide she could stand on her own two feet. That day, he would leave her.

"They're hunting us. I heard from Mockingbird . . . He tapped their network again and saw the new retrieval orders."

Cold, spiked horror spilled through her. As she recalled, Mockingbird was a counteragent, working against the Foundation. He wanted to recruit Taye to join his mutant army. Gillie had never spoken to him, but the first time he called, Taye had told him to leave them both alone. It couldn't be good they were hearing from him now.

A hard knot formed in her chest. Dammit, she didn't want to spend her life running. It didn't seem like too much to ask that she could just do normal things like pay bills and go to work at a job nobody else wanted. Quiet dreams—and perhaps impossible ones, as well. She forced herself to consider the problem rationally, setting aside her visceral emotional response.

"How long do we have?"

He didn't seem panicked, which led her to believe the Foundation team must not be local. *If they have to factor travel time, given Mockingbird's early warning, we can be long gone before they get here.*

"He said we should have a couple of hours. They're mobilizing from New York."

She nodded, trying to keep it together. *Collect the pertinent facts.* "And how are they tracking us now, after all this time? We've been so careful."

"It's my fault," he said quietly. "I . . . lost control."

"Taye, what happened?"

"I don't know. When I went past the power station—the same one I pass every day—something happened. I pulled. I didn't mean to. It just happened."

"Oh, shit. Maybe it was just too much juice. Involuntary response?"

"I guess," he muttered.

There was darkness in his face, pure despair, and she wanted so badly to wipe it away. "Don't worry about it. We'll bug out of here, and you'll get it under control. This won't happen again, I'm sure. We just need to find some tungsten-powder and lose her signal. Did Mockingbird give you a safe house this time?"

"Yeah. As long as we get moving and don't power up again, we'll be fine."

"That's good news. I didn't want to heal ever again anyway." Relief surged through her.

Something like pain flashed across his face and then was gone. "I understand that. Now I need you to go stand by that wall and smile for me." Taye pulled out his cell.

"Why?"

"Please?"

Sighing, she did as he asked. Then he clicked a few buttons on the phone and nodded as though he'd checked something crucial off his to-do list. He stuck it back in his jacket pocket; the dark leather contrasted beautifully with the pale, worn denim.

"What was that for?"

"Mockingbird needs a picture of you. He's preparing an ID kit."

Well, that's unexpectedly good news. If he was handling the paperwork, then they could keep all the money they'd saved. But it did make her wonder what their benefactor expected to get out of the deal.

Gillie put that aside for the moment, focusing on another aspect of the situation. "But to reaffirm, as long as we lose Kestrel, and then go back to living like normal people, they shouldn't be able to locate us, right?"

"That's the next bullet point. I've got more news and it's all bad."

She braced. "I'm tough, I can take it."

"They've put us into the system as terrorists and set a merc on us. And he's good. I did a little digging on him before I came to get you. I don't know yet what kind of news coverage we're getting, if any. Just because they've added us to a wanted list doesn't mean anyone is paying attention. It might not be that big a deal."

Yeah, right. She could tell when he prevaricated.

"Aw, fuck."

In reaction, Gillie leapt to the worst-case scenario. Given the right connections and sufficient media interest, their pictures would be plastered all over the place, making it impossible to lay low. Since their escape, she'd watched the news, trying to catch up on current events, even though it was always relentlessly grim, and she knew how this stuff worked.

"You see why I'm worried."

"Yeah. I guess I should call Mick and quit my job."

"It's not the kind of place where you need to give notice. It's time for us to get out."

She curled her hands into fists, nails biting crescent moons into her palms. "I'm not going back. I'll die first."

"Shh." Taye stroked a hand across her hair. Funny, he'd touch her only if she needed comfort, as if she were a child, not a grown woman. He did much the same, soothing her, when she lashed out. "They won't take you again. I promise, Gillie-girl. That much, I can do for you."

If she hadn't been fighting fear, she might have asked him to explain what he meant by *that much. Like he thinks he's no good for anything more.* But she could think only about leaving this apartment. Even though it wasn't much, besides Taye, it was all she had.

She turned her cheek into his palm, seeking his overwhelming heat. For brief, precious moments, his fingers traced along her cheekbone, thumb lingering as if her skin were the sweetest thing he'd ever touched. His gaze lingered on her lips—and then she saw the moment he remembered who she was. Gillie the innocent, Gillie who must be protected from herself.

For the first time, she drew away before he did. "I'll pack. There's no point in wasting time. If you say it's serious, I know it is."

He flinched and averted his eyes. "Don't trust *me* like that. Not me."

Always lines like that. Trust me, but not completely. Touch me, but not like you want to. Stay with me, but not really. Not forever. Taye could break a woman's heart with his inconsistencies. She ignored his idiocy in favor of getting her backpack. His was already packed. While she stuffed clothes into the bag, Taye paced, head canted. Maybe his mood was rubbing off on her, but she sensed the unnatural stillness, too. There were no dogs barking, no rush of tires on damp, salted streets. Since it was after three in the morning, that could be why.

But she didn't think so.

"Are we sure about the time frame? How long ago did you talk to Mockingbird?"

Gillie shrugged back into her winter coat. She opted to go without gloves, which would make her clumsy. His mouth compressed into a grim line as he met her at the front door.

"Too long. Stay behind me."

"I will. I swear."

Taye led the way. She flinched at every creak of the stairs, every shadow that trailed along the wall. Her breathing sounded impossibly loud, whereas he turned to silent ice. She wanted to be fearless. It was easy to dream about adventure when you were the princess locked in the tower, but what happened when you got free and realized you had no ability to survive? Being helpless made her angry, and that fire in her belly dominated the fright.

On the ground floor, the stink of sickly sweet copper overlaid other smells. Gillie recognized it before she saw the wine-dark pool spreading around the homeless man. The money Taye had left lay scattered like the stained green leaves of some terrible tree.

"They're here," he said, as a bullet popped the bare bulb in the fixture overhead.

Dark swallowed the room, blinding her. They probably had night-vision goggles. For them, it would be like shooting—or stabbing—fish in a barrel. Instinctively, Gillie dropped, making herself a small target. But she slipped in the blood; it smeared her hands, and she bit back a cry. It took all her self-control not to scramble away from the corpse.

I will give you nothing, she vowed to the bastards hunting them. *No help. No errors. I am* not *yours for the taking. Be still. Be quiet.*

And then blue-white lightning kindled in Taye's palm, wreathing him in the wrathful beauty of a pagan god.

CHAPTER 6

Save her.

The words looped in his head in tandem with his heartbeat. Defending her had become his sole purpose and his reason for living; he did not know how to lay down his sword and shield. If this were some old-school medieval movie, he would die for her. In fact, that was the way he wanted it, only he was selfish enough to prefer his sacrifice meant something.

Taye's nerve endings had long since overloaded, sending shocks through his system. This wasn't painless. Nothing ever was. But it was necessary. These men wanted to take them both prisoner again—and that just wasn't happening. He'd promised.

He didn't have much, not even his fucking name. That bothered him most of all. He'd lied to her at the facility. He didn't remember. Mostly likely, his real name *did* start with T; Rowan had been consistent in his methods. But Taye was just the first name he'd thought of that started with that letter, and he'd said he was sure so she wouldn't think, *Poor bastard, he's worse off than I am.* In those early days, he saw pity in her face mingled with wariness. She'd feared that Rowan's experiments had turned him into a subhuman thing, a monster that would hurt her.

Sometimes real memories nibbled at the edges of his brain, but most often, just fragments of cold and isolation, darkness and silence, broken by violent flashes. Of one thing he was sure: she deserved so much more than him. The Foundation had taken everything from Gillie. He wanted it to give it all back.

Even if he had nothing else, he had his word.

Taye stilled, listening. *First movement overhead.* The strike team had killed the homeless man because he was a potential witness and then proceeded to the first floor. Therefore, they must have just missed the trackers at the landing, but the team was heading down now, straight into ambush. He hoped they hadn't neutralized the other tenants; he hoped they hadn't suffered for living in this building. But the Foundation had no limits. No harm they wouldn't inflict to further their agenda. It sickened him, knowing they'd made billions from Gillie's pain, and that they intended for her to spend her whole life in their labs, without love, laughter, or sunlight.

No. Fucking. Way.

His power blazed brighter as the soft treads on the steps quickened. He felt the drain and acknowledged it as necessary. The agony blazed in his stomach, always there, like a web of barbed wire. Taye didn't care how much he hurt himself, so long as she walked away. By this point, they had to see the glow kindling from the stairwell.

That's right, bitches. Walk into the light.

The width of the stairs bottlenecked their enemies effectively. When the first two popped into view, he slammed them with twin arcs of live power. The lightning danced and crackled, sizzling the fat beneath their skin. A disarming stench kicked up, the smell of their eyeballs cooking in their skulls.

Screams of dying men broke the silence, but their comrades readied weapons as they stepped into the breach.

"Stay down," he called to Gillie.

He understood how it worked. His body produced a limited amount of power in its cells, so he had to pull from nearby outlets, drawing from the grid. A halo formed around him, limning his body in light much like the aftershock of a flash grenade. Neighboring buildings browned out, lights flickering as he drained the juice and funneled it toward the Foundation goons. They too howled as they died, their flesh charring. Two more ran from him, dodging blasts as they sprinted for the lobby doors.

He didn't blame them. They couldn't have known how far he'd go for Gillie Flynn.

Letting the power die, he held out a hand to her, and she scrambled to her feet. In the dark, she came to him without a single hesitation, without a single misstep. Her blood-slick fingers tangled with his, and his heart gave the most awful kick in his chest.

Oh, Gillie. Gillie-girl.

"Time to fly," he said.

And she led the way toward the exit, though he felt the trembling of her hand. He ached; his skin felt as though it covered a blackened husk. One day, he'd die of this. There was no doubt in him. Each time he powered up, each time he pulled, he felt the darkness growing, eating away at his insides. Since the symptoms first plagued him, he had done some reading. Learned about the link between increased risks of cancer and tumors for those who worked where they were exposed to strong electromagnetic fields. And his body was worse than a microwave oven.

The Foundation had turned him into something that could only kill and kill some more, then die of it. No future in that. Perfect disposable weapon, in fact. The loose end would tie itself off. If they could make the gift a little more virulent, they could create an army of assassins who existed only to serve and be discarded. But he had to focus on escape.

Most likely, there would be more outside. The other two wouldn't flee the scene. They'd go for backup or to choose better ground for the fight. He had to stay sharp, even though his head swam with weariness and pain. If he breathed too deeply, it felt as though he had powdered glass in his lungs; that only added to the awful burn in his stomach. The cookies he'd consumed threatened to come back. He forced the weakness and nausea aside. No time. Not tonight.

Outside, the snow still fell. It stuck in irregular patches, dusting the ground white. Not nearly thick enough to draw out snowplows, though salt trucks had come around. Michigan was used to much worse. But winter gave the night a wondrous quality, the air crisp and cold. Soothing. Taye scanned the street both ways, searching for the remainders of the strike team.

"Anything?" she asked.

The ping of a tranq gun pierced the night, and he spun her

too late. Gillie flinched as the dart sank into her shoulder. Her blue eyes filled with terror, glimmering in the dark, and then she crumpled to the ground. Diving for cover, he couldn't afford to catch her, but they'd pay for this, every last one of them. Fucking bastards. Her backpack fell to the ground, dark against the snow; its contents spilled. She had taken such pride in picking out those shirts, those jeans, the first clothing she'd ever bought for herself.

When will you fuckers stop stealing from her? When?

The mailbox shielded him from two more shots. Then he leaned out far enough to draw Gillie in beside him. The apartment building behind him ought to prevent them from sneaking up on his six. Feverishly he scanned the area, seeking an escape route.

"It doesn't have to be like this," a smooth voice called. British accent. "Come quietly, and we'll make sure they don't hurt her. She'll enjoy all the comforts of home."

"Everything except free will," he growled back. "If it's all the same to you, motherfucker, I'd just as soon kill you all."

"You don't have the juice. Plus, you don't know precisely where my men are. And I only need to land one shot to take you both." Because it was true, it wasn't a boast.

It was also absolutely the wrong fucking thing to say. White-hot rage filled his head. He'd promised her. *Promised.* And he had nothing in the world except his word to Gillie.

"If you want me, come get me."

He spun in the crouch, eyeing the streetlight. From this distance, he might be able to tap the grid. Normally he wouldn't do it twice in one night. That would only accelerate his deterioration, and he could barely keep his cookies down on the best of days. But he had Gillie sprawled beside him, her face pale and still. She counted on him not to fail.

Fine. She's worth it.

Then his gaze lit on the parked cars lined up along the curb. *Could I . . . ? Fuck yes. It's the only way, in fact.* Instead of trying to find the men in the dark, he'd light this block up like the Fourth of July and use the subsequent fireworks to make his getaway.

Taye threw out a hand and opened his veins. At least that was what it felt like. Instead of blood, lightning arced from his fingertips, drawing like response from the bulb. It popped and white light sparked forward, spiraling toward him. He guided it with a twist of his arm and slammed it all into the gas tank of the nearest car. The explosion rocked the pavement, sending a gorgeous fireball skyward. *Another. And again.* Each time he did it, the pain built in his chest, crawling toward his belly. It sank cruel tendrils into his spine until he could feel the blood boiling behind his eyes. The fires burned brighter, more explosions rocking the street.

He grabbed Gillie up and sprinted forward, using the burning cars as cover. Darts still peppered the ground behind him, but the fire and swirling smoke made it tough for them to see him, especially when combined with the light snow and wind. With an elbow, he smashed the window of the one vehicle he hadn't sacrificed in Zeus's name. Once he unlocked the doors by reaching through the shards of glass, he slung Gillie in through the passenger side and then vaulted the hood. He didn't know why he knew how to steal a car, but it came naturally. More proof he hadn't been a good person before he lost his mind.

Taye slammed his foot on the gas and the car fishtailed away from the curb. He drove with his head low past the row of burning cars. Sirens wailed in the distance, which meant the Foundation goons would scramble like rats for their holes in the wall. Soon the authorities would be on scene, trying to figure out what the hell had happened.

Mockingbird had told him where to go. Safe house—or so the man claimed. He had no reason to doubt; they owed him their lives already. Taye didn't like the idea of being indebted to anyone, but he couldn't see any way around it. He couldn't manage this on his own.

That was what he hadn't shared with Gillie—the price of Mockingbird's intervention a second time. But if he had to indenture his remaining days to ensure her safety, so be it. Better to fight and die for her freedom. She had enough joy in her to live for both of them. Marriage. Kids. She should have every bright and shining thing, including a decent man who could tell her where he grew up and all the names of his childhood pets.

Not that it gave him any pleasure imagining her with anyone else. Most days, he fought the idea that the universe had given her to him. And she didn't make the battle any easier with her stupid hero worship and her rose-colored glasses. She refused to see him as he was.

While she slept, he drove to the airport and found a poorly secured long-term parking facility. Being cheap had its risks. He ditched the stolen car and found a new ride. This one likely wouldn't be reported missing for a while, as according to the paperwork stowed in the visor, the owner wouldn't be returning for a month.

With great care, he tucked Gillie into the passenger side and belted her in. Then he hurried around and started the car. Easier when you had the keys. It hadn't taken much effort to get into the flimsy metal prefab building that served as the lot office. Too bad. People should really take better care of their belongings.

He had been pushing west along I-94 for an hour or so by the time Gillie stirred. She moaned as she woke, her fear instinctive and bone deep. It took all his control not to put a hand on her thigh to soothe her. She consistently struck a nerve, one that made him want to claim and protect her. But it didn't matter what the fuck he wanted. His song was nearly done, and it would be unforgivable to let her love him for the time he had left.

"We made it," she said in wonderment.

"Told you I wouldn't let them take you back." He didn't look at her, knowing that expression of hero worship would have deepened. Sometimes it made him feel like Superman, and sometimes it made him want to set something on fire just to watch it burn. Because he could never be as good as she thought. He was only going to let her down.

"Where are we going?"

"West. We're meeting some allies."

"Mockingbird," she guessed. "Can we trust him?"

"I don't know. But we don't have anyone else."

She acknowledged that with a nod. "Are you going to work for him in exchange for my protection?"

How could she know that? But maybe it came from how well she knew him; it was hard to keep secrets from her. Though he'd kept one. One vital, miserable secret.

Taye shrugged. "It's not important."

"But just a few months ago, you didn't want to."

"Circumstances change." He hadn't been lying when he said he wouldn't be around forever, though he'd never leave her by choice. Arrangements had to be made.

"What aren't you telling me?"

She was so damn smart and she noticed too much. Gillie knew how to read his silences, the spaces between his words. Sometimes he caught her staring as if he were a puzzle she was determined to put together.

He laughed softly. "So many things, Gillie-girl. But don't worry. I've got this."

"I'm not helpless." Her tone frosted over. "I'm not incapable of looking after myself."

In this world, she was. He didn't say it aloud. But she knew. She was a healer, not a killer. Not like him. Most days, he wouldn't mind watching the whole world burn. And that silent knowledge made her give him her shoulder as she turned her face to the foggy glass. The highway zipped past outside. Taye wished—ah, fuck. It didn't matter. There was no magic in the wishing well, just the dead dreams of hopeful children.

Yet he didn't like it when she was mad at him. He'd grown too accustomed to her smiles. So he tried to pacify her. "I don't mind, really. We need his resources to start over. So I run a few missions for him and then we're free and clear."

It wasn't a matter of money anymore. He didn't dare trust her fresh start to a contact he'd found asking around at work on the docks. Mockingbird would do it right.

"Really?" she asked softly. "You don't imagine he'll want to keep you on, once he realizes how powerful you've become?"

I won't be around long enough for it to matter, Gillie-girl. That, he could never say aloud. It was his fondest dream to see her settled in a new life, her identity buried so deep that the Foundation could never find her again. Mockingbird could make that happen. Taye wanted her to go to college and get that dream job, whatever it might be. Most important, he wanted her to *live*. She would be his gift to the world. It was that simple.

"He'll be open to negotiation when the time comes. I'm not without leverage of my own."

"But you won't tell me what that might be. Is it too complex for my pretty head?"

That stung. After everything, she shouldn't compare him to the crazy bastard Rowan who . . . treated her like her thoughts didn't matter. Like she existed only to stroke his ego. He wasn't doing the same thing, not exactly, but it was close enough to give him a twinge. Wanting to protect her was no excuse for treating her like she didn't have a good brain.

"I'm sorry," he said.

But he couldn't tell her he was dying. Not now. He didn't want to see the pain in her eyes, mingled with pity and confusion. Better that she wear those fucking rose-colored shades a little longer. Taye could handle that better.

"I don't like that you're bartering your freedom like this."

"Me either. But the alternative is worse. At least by throwing in with them, I'm fighting for something I truly believe—the Foundation *must* be stopped."

"I'm with you there."

"And we'll get to meet other survivors, more people like us. That's not a bad thing."

She flashed him a wry smile. "Are you trying to convince me . . . or yourself?"

"Little of both. I'm wary of everything and everyone at this point."

"But not me."

"No. Not you."

Never you. He would trust her to reach into his chest with her bare hands. Christ, hadn't she done that to him already? The ache never left, not entirely. Not even when he was sick and sore and full of despair. He had been nobody at all when Rowan first cleared him to visit her—just a maddened thing spitting defiance and rage. But from the first moments in her faux-apartment, he'd felt like a white-hot sword, doused in the tempering waters that made it strong.

By midmorning, he couldn't drive farther. He pulled off the interstate at a cheap motel that looked like they'd take cash and not ask questions. In daylight, they both looked pretty fucking rough. She was blood-smeared and his white shirt carried red spatters. Simple enough to hide in his case. He buttoned his duster and ran a hand through his hair.

"Wait here. I'll get us a room."

Inside, it was much as he'd envisioned. A tired old Pakistani woman came out from behind a faded blue curtain. Her face creased in an insincere smile, but she took his money, asked no questions, and gave him a key, which was all he needed from her. Thankfully, there was no TV in the lobby, or she might have seen their faces on the news already. He had no way of knowing what angle the Foundation would choose, or what kind of terrorists he and Gillie were supposed to be. Taye hurried back out to the car and pulled it around back; he'd asked for a room on the far side of the motel, away from the freeway noise.

He didn't kid himself the British merc would give up the chase. But at least he couldn't track them using extraordinary means, and questioning people took time. Taye would use that time to rest and move on. In two days, they would make the safe house rendezvous with Mockingbird's agent.

Barring trouble.

Gillie slid out of the car as soon as they parked. She hadn't asked him to stop so she could use the bathroom, but from the way she hurried past him toward the facilities, she had to be in pain. Dammit, he would've found a restroom for her. But she hadn't asked. And that was Gillie. She had borne her lot in silence for so long that it had become second nature. Her anger came if it wasn't personal, if it was just a mood. But when she really needed something, she couldn't ask because that acknowledged her own impotence—and that she would *not* do.

Instead she closed the door quietly and turned the water on so he couldn't hear her pee. Or maybe, he thought, so he couldn't hear her cry.

But he heard . . . and it broke his heart.

CHAPTER 7

Gillie wiped her eyes.

She wondered if this would be it, if the sum total of her life would amount to running—narrow escapes and endless death. Maybe she shouldn't feel sorry for the men Taye had killed. They hunted their fellow human beings without caring if their prey deserved it; that made them reprehensible. But she couldn't help but question whether they had families.

She needed to stop giving a fuck. The lines had been drawn, and they were at war. If she didn't want to end up a casualty, she had to toughen up. Once she fought past the initial reaction, she washed her face and hands, watching the blood swirl down the rusty drain. That homeless man had been less than nothing to the men who came into their apartment building, just a potential complication. She had to remember *him* when she faltered.

By the time she finished in the bathroom, Taye was already in the bed with his back turned. It was a small room full of dings, dents, cheap furniture and interesting stains. He had pulled the curtains so the light only shone around the edges, creating a peculiar golden rectangle.

This morning, a cruel impulse possessed her. Since his intentions were so pure—he'd proven she didn't interest him over months of platonic cohabitation—she saw no reason to sleep in her bloodstained clothes. In economical motions, she slipped from the McGinty's Tavern T-shirt she wore and then unbuttoned her jeans.

He stirred then, risking a look over his shoulder and then turning his eyes forward in a rush. "What're you doing?"

"Getting ready for bed."

A long silence greeted the words. And then: "Are you sure that's a good idea?"

"I'm safe with you, right?"

"Yeah." But he sounded none too sure whether he could trust himself.

It was nice to know her bare skin discomfited him, even if he had no intention of doing anything about the quiet attraction. Denied the larger prize, she would take small victories. Gillie slipped into bed behind him and turned her back, facing away. She'd stay on her side, but while he tried to drift off, he could think about what she wasn't wearing. He wasn't immune; she knew that much. But he was determined not to "sully her innocence." Absurd. She hadn't been innocent since they took her from her parents. She was merely untouched.

"Then I see no reason why I should sleep in filthy clothes."

"I'm not a monk." The admission sounded as though it had been ground out of him.

"Are you concerned you'll forget yourself in your sleep?" she asked sweetly. "I mean, if you happen to bump up against a mostly naked woman?"

"I might."

"I promise I won't scream for help."

"I know," he muttered. "That's the problem."

That bit deep. He made her feel like she had thrown herself at him repeatedly, and that wasn't the case. Before she got the message, she'd dropped a few hints—that was all. But he'd made it clear he preferred to treat her as a younger sister, or perhaps a sexless great-aunt. They'd lived as roommates without a single misstep; that track record could get a woman down.

She pretended it didn't matter. "Sweet dreams, Taye."

Over the years, she'd gotten good at shutting her mind off and falling asleep on demand because her body needed rest. Gillie did so then. And when she woke, she found herself nestled in his arms. She didn't wonder who held her; there was simply nobody else it could be. He'd left his jeans on but had removed his shirt. His fever-hot skin blazed against her bare back.

More intriguing, he'd rolled onto her side of the bed, seeking her in his sleep. That had never happened before. Maybe she'd implanted a suggestion of sorts, teasing him just before they slept . . . or maybe it was the fact that she was naked. Whatever the reason he'd done it, if she were as wholesome as he believed, she wouldn't even consider encouraging him. As matters stood, she couldn't pass up this opportunity.

One of his arms draped over the curve of her waist. But not satisfied with that claim, he'd also thrown one leg over her, so that his entire body curled around hers. His chin rested on top of her head. Seductive warmth stole her breath, leaving her languid.

She shifted ever so slowly. Considering he "didn't" want her, his cock was doing an excellent impression of an iron spike. In response, he growled in his sleep, such a drowsy, sexy sound. A shiver rolled through her when he nuzzled his face into her hair and drew her tight against him. He pressed a palm low on her belly, positioning her so he could grind against her ass. It felt fantastic; he'd never forgotten himself this way before. Countless nights, she'd lain awake wishing he would. Then he went further, trailing upward until he claimed her breast.

He cupped and caressed, deliciously gentle. With great effort, she swallowed a moan. Dear God, that felt good. Her nipple tightened against his fingertips; Gillie hardly dared to breathe, afraid he'd wake and stop. For long, luscious moments, he played with her, gradually gaining confidence; his touch grew demanding. Her breath came in little gasps. The moans she strangled as he stroked his way south, lingering over the curve of her ribs and the concave dip of her belly. He rubbed himself against her in slow, firm thrusts, growing more aggressive. She wanted to reach back and pop the buttons on his jeans and invite him to take her from behind, but not like this. It couldn't happen like this, or he'd never forgive her.

Taye nuzzled the side of her neck, licking and biting. The shivers just didn't stop. His fingertips brushed the top of her panties, and he paused. Probably, in his dream, she was naked, wide-open, and ready to be fucked.

Touch me down there, she begged silently. Her body dampened, the ache intensifying. She tensed her thighs; that had helped in the past, but she needed friction for her clit. During her days in captivity, she'd perfected the art of masturbation so nobody could tell what she was doing. Quiet, furtive. Just "sleeping" on her stomach, muscles tensing and releasing, with a slow twitch of her pelvis. She could do it silently, the orgasm flooding her system until her muscles went limp. But not today.

Gillie sensed the moment he woke, the real world imprinting over fantasy. Tension filled him, and then he rolled away with a smothered curse. He pulled the pillow over the top of his head and muttered, "Take a shower. Please."

"You know," she said softly, as she rolled out of bed, "I think I'd be within my rights to call you a tease. It's not fair to start what you don't intend to finish."

"Your objection is noted." He didn't budge.

In reply, she eased off the bed and made no attempt to cover herself on the way to the bathroom. Once there, she sponged the worst of the blood off her clothes and took a quick shower using the rudimentary toiletries the motel provided. To forestall an argument, she also dressed in there. Fifteen minutes later, she emerged with her hair wet and falling in soft curls. He had left her backpack lying in the street, but since he'd saved her life, it didn't seem right to complain about wearing the same clothes for a second day. They'd sort it out.

"Your turn," she said.

Taye offered a scowl in answer, as if she had been secretly responsible for his nocturnal shenanigans. Once he closed the bathroom door, she muttered, "Not hardly."

If she had any input on what they did in bed together, it wouldn't end *that* way. But it wasn't the time for such thoughts. The longer they stayed in one place, the greater likelihood someone would find them before they made the rendezvous with Mockingbird's agent. Since she had nothing to pack, she donned her jacket and went out to the car, where she checked the lot.

Everything seemed quiet enough, but she still locked the doors behind her. Taye came at a dead run a few minutes later, his hair still streaming water. When he saw her sitting quietly on the passenger side, he closed his eyes for a long moment. Relief etched his features in pained lines, and it struck her then. He cared. Whether he wanted to or not, he did. She hadn't meant to frighten him.

But he didn't chide her as he climbed in. Merely started the motor in silence and pulled back onto the interstate. It might be better if he did because then she would feel like he'd staked some kind of claim. Right then she felt like an obligation he couldn't shift.

"How much farther?" she asked.

"About five hundred miles."

They covered the distance mostly in silence, punctuated by workaday exchanges about food and other biological urges. But it wasn't a companionable quiet. Instead Taye seethed, angry about something he wouldn't share. That irritated her in turn.

By the time they reached their destination, she was stiff, cranky, and spoiling for a fight. They pulled off the highway and followed a complicated series of turns to a house in the middle of nowhere. Somehow, she had expected a high-rise office building or something equally glamorous with an impressive security system and a bunch of armed guards. Buried in the boondocks, this looked like a secret base for rumrunners in 1924. The paint had long since peeled away, leaving this wind-washed structure. Simple architecture—the porch ran along the front of the house. It had a second story, but no attic, at least as far as she could tell.

"This is it. We arrived ahead of schedule." Taye opened the car door and swung out onto the gravel drive. He arched his back, pulling the leather taut.

Best she could tell, they were somewhere in Kansas. Snow lay cool and white in the surrounding fields. There were no trees for cover, but that was a good thing. Nobody could approach this house by land in any direction without being seen for miles distant. Given their current situation, she reckoned that a plus.

"That means we wait."

"Yep." He headed up the path to the front door and claimed the key hidden beneath the welcome mat.

"Definitely the right place." The isolation was spooky, she thought.

Since their escape, they'd stuck to cities, where they could blend in with the numbers. Never had she been able to gaze around and see nothing but open space. Never had the only answer to her voice come in cold wind and icy silence.

"Don't be scared," he said quietly. "They're going to help us."

Maybe she was more cynical and wary because Gillie saw this as an attractively baited trap. Once they lured him in, they wouldn't let him go. They'd use him to fight their war until it destroyed him, and she didn't want safety at the price of his soul. Not that Taye would listen.

He unlocked the door. A musty smell wafted out, not unpleasant, but long unused, as if the house heaved a sigh of relief to feel wind within its walls. She followed him inside and set about turning on the lights. Twilight lent the place a desolate air, and she didn't like the shadows. Sheets covered the furniture; the place was so old it didn't have carpeting. Instead, scarred hardwood floors showed the marks of many years. Children had run up and down this hall. Gillie could almost hear their voices, echoing down the decades. The house carried a particular energy, not happy or tragic in particular, just . . . *busy*, as if many things had happened within these walls. They too bore the marks of a Tungsten-spiked paint job.

"Wait here. I'll scope the place out." Taye loped up the stairs without looking back.

Wouldn't he be surprised not to find her waiting, someday? Because it struck her as pathetic, she didn't stand by the door, obedient to his will. Instead she went to see if the previous guests had left anything to eat. She hadn't imagined she'd ever miss anything about her captivity, but she'd enjoyed cooking for herself—and later, for Taye.

In the kitchen, she found a few staples she could use to make a passable macaroni and cheese from a box mix, powdered milk, and vegetable oil. It wouldn't taste exactly right, but it had to be better than what they'd been getting from the drive-up. Gillie heard him prowling through the house, ceiling creaking overhead. Doors opened and closed as he searched the place. Doubtless he expected her to wait by the front doors for the *all clear.* He found her from the rattling pots. By his expression, his temper couldn't take much more of her silent defiance.

"I didn't say anything before," he bit out, "but this can't go on. You scared me at the motel."

That shouldn't please her as much as it did. She shouldn't want to cause him pain. But since he wouldn't permit her to give him pleasure, Gillie craved the other side of the coin.

"I was careful . . . I checked before I went out." Pretending she didn't know why he was agitated, she put the pot of water on to boil.

"That's not the point. I'm trying to keep you safe, and you're not cooperating."

She gave him her sweetest smile. "You're about to learn how very truculent I can be."

Fabulous word, truculent. It pleased her. Sounded like a woman digging in her heels, impossible to shift as an eighteen-wheeler.

"Don't fight me, Gillie. I don't have the energy or the patience right now."

"Or what?" she mocked gently. "You'll zap me? I don't have to obey you, and it's about time I started making my own way. I'm going to offer my *own* services to Mockingbird."

His jaw went rigid. "No."

"You don't think he'll be interested? I bet he would be. Think of all the lives I could save. His agents would be so grateful."

"It *hurts* you."

"Yes," she admitted. "But what you do hurts you, too."

"That's different."

"Why? Because you're a man?"

He shrugged. No, with him, it wouldn't be that simple. Taye wasn't a chauvinist. His chivalry had layers and edges, vast dark chasms where she could lose herself and her budding autonomy if she wasn't careful. God, she almost wouldn't mind—and that was the most dangerous part about him. He didn't want to love her; he just wanted to *save* her, and she wasn't willing to take one without the other. Not anymore. She had to learn to live without him if he was determined to maintain this distance.

"It's complicated," he answered.

"It always is. Put some salt in the water, will you?"

He obeyed without hesitation. A woman could get used to that. In contemplative silence, she measured the powdered milk and mixed it with tap water.

"Don't do this," he said quietly. "I don't want you to."

Gillie turned then, her gaze snaring his. "And who are you to ask that of me?"

Those lovely eyes searched her face, and for just a flicker of a moment, revealed much more than he likely knew or wanted. Such hunger; he burned with it. And then the shutter came down, obscuring his emotions.

"We're friends."

"Ah. Of course. But friends don't arrange their lives to suit one another."

"You won't listen to reason because I refuse to fuck you?" He meant to humiliate with his hard, mocking tone. Oh, he had a cruel streak, but generally he didn't turn that razor tongue on her. He'd always pulled his punches because he figured she was fragile.

God, he knew her so little when it came right down to it. He saw what he wanted, not what existed, what life had made of her. She was like those unbreakable toys. Use them, abuse them, and they spring right back into shape. Sure, she had scars. But they would not end her.

She was supposed to gasp in shock. Her eyes ought to well with tears. But she merely crossed her arms and stared at him, brow lofted. "Honestly, Taye, you think so highly of yourself. You imagine I'm scheming to do you? Very well, say I am. How many men would I need to fuck before I'm dirty enough for you? Five? Ten? Should I do them all at once? Would you like to watch?"

His hands curled into fists, and *he* was the one who flinched from the mental picture. *Don't like imagining that, do you? And yet you keep pushing me away.*

"I can see there's no talking to you right now." He stalked from the room, shoulders tight.

She wished she could make it better, but he wouldn't *let* her. Beyond a certain point, he had to fight his own demons. Everyone did.

He'd left the cell phone on the table. Mockingbird's number would be in the recent calls, unless he'd remembered to delete it. Making a decision, she picked up the phone and dialed. Time to put her money where her mouth was.

CHAPTER 8

Out in the cold, Taye took several deep, calming breaths. The urge to set something on fire faded. *She wants to work for Mockingbird.* The very idea enraged him. He wanted to see her safe, not risking herself against the Foundation as part of some counterwar. Why the hell did their agents all have bird names anyway?

When he closed his eyes, he could still see how Gillie looked, clad in nothing but a pair of pink panties. Her skin was so fucking—

Stop, he told himself. *Don't remember.*

But he couldn't drive the image out of his head. He hadn't been with a woman in . . . well. Taye couldn't recall. Presumably there had been some. Maybe many. But right now, he could only find the memory of one he couldn't have.

A knot formed in his stomach. Sooner or later, she would meet someone else. Given how beautiful she was, it would be sooner, inevitably. She just needed a new life. If he stayed focused, he could open that door and carry the mental picture of her walking through it toward hope. Walking away from him.

No. Even if he felt like losing her would kill him, he couldn't fixate on that now. One step at a time. Six missions—that was the deal. And in exchange for his blood, they'd liberate Gillie from her tormentors. He could do this, no matter how it turned out for him. Guys like him never ended up well anyway. This, then, was the best he could do.

In keeping with his mood, the sky hung heavy overhead like a blood-filled bruise. Night fell fast in winter. As he paced, the shadows lengthened and snow drifted down, swirling in the icy wind. Reasonably he couldn't expect their contact to arrive before morning tomorrow, which meant he was alone in the middle of nowhere with Gillie. That didn't bode well, considering how much he wanted her, and how good she had gotten at goading him.

But surely he could make it through the next twelve hours without losing his mind or his self-control. They were safe here, at least. No neighbors to report on their movements. She preferred the city; after her long isolation, she loved being surrounded by people and noise. He had no doubt she found it comforting, which meant she wouldn't like this spot one bit. Her nerves would be on edge, and he couldn't leave her alone to listen to the silence.

Sighing, he squared his shoulders and went back inside. He found Gillie eating at the table by herself. The kitchen was a bright room compared to the rest of the house, faded yellow curtains and gold tiles. She had filled a bowl for him and brewed a cup of tea as well. Quietly thoughtful—she'd known he would linger in the cold to get his head straight, letting the weather take the edge off his temper. Taye wasn't displaying any particular grace in dealing with the prospect of his own demise. Maybe it would be easier if he shared the burden with her.

But he couldn't.

So he dropped onto the chair and refused to meet her eyes. "I know you aren't thrilled with this."

She shrugged. "It's the best of a bad lot. You should eat."

Refusing wouldn't accomplish anything except to make her more suspicious, but it hurt him to shovel it down these days. Still, he had to try. So he took a few bites. He needed to stay strong as long as possible and hide what was happening beneath the skin. And the food was good, considering what she'd had to work with.

"Thanks."

Outside, the snow fell fast and furious, deepening by the minute. Gillie followed his gaze. "Are we likely to be snowed in?"

"I don't know. Maybe."

Taye could think of worse fates than a delay on his first mission and having her all to himself, possibly for the last time. Unfortunately, it would also test his resolve, which wasn't made of steel. No matter how many times he told himself she wasn't meant for him, his body didn't believe it. In his darkest moments, he asked what it could hurt. But the answer was simple—it would hurt Gillie. She wasn't the kind of woman a man leased for a month or two.

"Can you tell me anything more about how they operate?"

No point in asking who she meant. "Mockingbird serves as the hub. He coordinates all the agents in the field and he sends them on missions. Generally, they work solo, though there are special exceptions. The type of mission varies according to the agent's skill set."

"Then they'd send *you* on black-ops type stuff," she guessed.

He'd forgotten how much she'd learned watching TV. Uncomfortable, he gave a curt nod, hoping to discourage further questions. He didn't want her seeing the blood on his hands.

"Does it bother you?" Her blue eyes looked like summer, hot, lazy days where the sky was so blue it hurt to gaze up into the cloudless expanse. Sometimes he thought he saw angels in her aspect, so fierce and pure that it might be enough to burn him clean.

Other men had memories of their childhood, of school vacations and camp and youthful mischief. They recalled their parents and their birthplace, the house where they'd lived. But no matter how deep he dug, his first memory sprang from a dark place. Two men: one weeping, the other striking repeatedly. The sound of fist meeting flesh made a distinctive sound. And there was red neon. It wasn't raining, but it had been. The pavement was wet, oil-slicked rainbows sparkling in the dark. The crimson flashed on and on, in tempo with the beating. He had no attachment to the memory. Taye didn't know if he'd been the man on the ground moaning in agony, or the one delivering the pain.

"Killing?" He couldn't lie to her, not even if it made her flinch from him in disgust. "No. In fact, each time, I like it a little more." Naked admission. He might possess a human exterior but inner darkness had turned him into something else.

To his surprise, she gave a jerky nod, her pretty face sharp with anger. "I struggle with it. Part of me *likes* watching them die. Likes seeing them pay for what they've done. When you call the lightning, I feel very Old Testament inside. Then a little voice reminds me they're still people. That their families love them. Yet the hate's part of me now . . . I can't help it. And I want them to pay."

"I didn't realize," he said, startled.

Her pretty face held a ferocity he didn't associate with her. Clearly, he should.

"You think you know everything about me, but you don't. You make assumptions, but you never talk to me long enough to find out whether they're true."

"I'm afraid of getting too close to you." Gillie drew the truth out of him, and that meant he had to be wary of her.

She smiled, but pain shadowed her eyes. "I know. Is it because you think I'm breakable?"

"What you went through would've destroyed most people." Taye shook his head. "You've been a fucking prisoner for years, and you're still not free. Do you even understand why it's so important that I do this for you?" His voice cracked.

How humiliating. He was supposed to be this badass who could protect her, but he couldn't check his own feelings. It was getting harder to stand apart, present but uninvolved. God knew, it would take a stronger man than him to remain indifferent to Gillie Flynn.

"I think it's because you feel like helping me will settle your account somehow."

Maybe so. Though he'd never thought of it in those terms, he decided she was right. In the back of his mind, he saw her salvation as the one selfless thing he could do. If he took anything from her, even physical affection, then his efforts lost all altruistic merit.

"You're not wrong."

She propped her chin on her palm. "I want to work with the homeless."

The seeming non sequitur surprised him. "What?"

"I've been thinking about what I'd like to do, if we ever get clear . . . and I want to open a shelter. Teach classes. Provide help and counseling for those struggling with addiction."

"For God's sake, why?" That wasn't what he envisioned for her at all . . . not that it was *his* decision. But he'd imagined a sweeter and more wholesome ending; he hated to think of Gillie spending her life surrounded by human garbage.

"Because of you. Because the lost need to be found."

An ache bloomed in his chest. Setting down his fork, he curled his hands into fists and rested them on his thighs to keep from reaching for her. With only her soft voice, she peeled him down to the raw places. *Just a little longer,* he told himself. *Tanager will arrive tomorrow and you'll leave Gillie in her care when you receive your first mission.* Yet he had seen to her safety for months now; relinquishing that charge brought him no joy.

Right then, he ought to say, *Don't build your life around me.* But the words wouldn't come. His desires were too diametrically opposed to his moral sense. So he merely gazed at her over the length of the table, unable to speak, unable to break free from the snare of her gaze.

She rose. If she touched him, he was lost. He had no more reserves, no more willpower. The reasons why not felt a million miles away. Instead, as if she sensed his weakness, she brushed past. Her steps retreated up the stairs and down toward the bathroom on the second floor. He felt as though he had been given a reprieve from an inevitable conflict. The water started, groaning in the elderly pipes.

This was a different kind of cruelty. Now he had to imagine water sluicing down her fair skin, beading on her breasts. In his mind's eye, he envisioned how she looked with her head tipped back, hair wine dark and tangling about her throat. God, she was gorgeous, the prettiest woman he'd ever seen, and sheer need maddened him.

His hands shook as he rose to clear the table. He stuck the macaroni in the refrigerator and tried to calm himself via mundane tasks. It didn't help. His cock strained against the zipper of his jeans as he stared out the kitchen window at the falling snow. Through his blurred reflection, the night glowed in a study in contrasts, moonless sky and field of white, like an old Ingmar Bergman movie. He didn't know how long he stood gazing out, but her voice startled him.

"Could you look at this?"

He turned reflexively, and swallowed a groan. Gillie stood dripping on the kitchen tile. Her bare feet were pink. His gaze traveled upward, devouring slim ankles, shapely calves, and deliciously inviting thighs. The towel hid nothing of her elegant curves. She looked almost as sexy after the shower as he'd imagined she would be beneath the curtain of water.

"At what?" Surely she didn't just mean to tease him.

"It's sore where they shot me." She indicated the back of her shoulder.

Ah. The tranq dart. Good to know she wasn't pointlessly cruel. "Come here."

She padded toward him and then spun, holding her damp hair aside, so he could assess the damage. The site was puffy with light contusions from the impact, but he didn't think the puncture showed signs of infection. She had delicate skin, which meant she bruised easier than most. When her gaze met his over the slope of her shoulder, his whole body surged in response.

"How bad is it?"

"You'll be fine. It'll take a day or two to heal."

Walk away now. Go put on some clothes. She wasn't stupid; far from it. So she had to sense his desperation. She must realize how hard it was to live with her, day after day, looking but not touching. For the past month, he'd woken in a hot fever, cock straining. Once he'd even tried to sate the urge with a girl from McGinty's, but he couldn't drum up the desire. Gillie would doubtless be delighted to learn she'd bewitched him and rendered him impotent. If he was a lock, she held his key.

"Thanks."

She turned then, just as he withdrew his hand from her shoulder. He didn't plan it; God knew he had no desire to torture himself. But Taye caught the towel and it pulled free, wafting to the floor. He had his first look at her fully bared body, and it hit him like a sledgehammer in the gut. Christ, he'd never seen anything as lovely as the sweet flare of her hips. And that ass—

No, don't turn around. But she did. His breath went in a rush and Taye stared at her in dumb fascination. He felt like a teenaged boy confronted with his first naked woman. There must have been others, but he could recall only her with that cream and rose-petal skin, the smooth indent of her waist, and the coppery curls at the lee of her legs. And her breasts . . . so pert and pretty, rising and falling with each breath. The berry nipples firmed as he drank her in.

He might have managed not to touch her if only he hadn't

looked at her face. But one glimpse of those wide eyes and parted lips, and Taye lost the battle. In her he saw echoed hunger, and the fear that he would not find her pleasing.

She had kissed him before, a clumsy caress that left him reeling with pleasure. He'd kissed her at McGinty's to get the bastards to leave her alone. This time it would be different. He snared her hand and spun her into his arms. Lowering his head, he claimed her lips with fierce longing; he parted them with a single movement and then touched his tongue to hers. She whimpered, a sound full of innocence and curiosity. It set him on fire.

Naked in his arms, she was utterly at his mercy. Conversely, he was determined not to take this too far. Nothing irrevocable. Delight consumed him, as he realized nobody had ever touched her like this, smoothed a hand down the graceful slope of her back or cupped her heart-shaped ass. In this, he could give without taking.

Gillie writhed against him, falling into the kiss with a passion that made the top of his head tingle. She followed his lead, press and taste, slide and thrust, until their bodies echoed their mouths, straining together. He fell back a step, and she cried out in protest.

"Not again. Not this time."

He soothed her with little caresses and kisses, edging her with his body back toward the sink. In a smooth motion, he lifted her and she splayed her knees unselfconsciously. In that moment, she was a creature of fire and silk, burning for him endlessly. Taye knelt, paying homage with featherlight kisses dusted on the inner curve of her thighs. That didn't shock her. Instead her eyes turned sultry, dropping to half-lidded expectation, and she tangled her fingers in his hair. He smiled as he inched upward, teasing her with teeth and tongue.

"You have to tell me what you want before you get it."

Though he half expected shyness, she answered with bold confidence. "Lick me, Taye. Suck on my clit. Put your finger in me and play with me until I come."

Maybe he didn't know her as well as he thought. Maybe she was right. She didn't use the dirtiest words, but this was all new to her. For someone who had never been touched before, it was an impressive showing. She *wasn't* a demure little virgin—and that turned him on fiercely.

"Your wish is my command," he growled.

But she wasn't prepared for the heat of his mouth; he could tell by the way she jerked, eyes widening, and then her hands tightened in his hair. Her hips shifted in restless, seeking surges. He licked her in slow strokes, denying her a fast release. He wanted her sobbing and screaming before he was done. *If I can't keep you, sweet girl, then I'll give you a memory that'll stay with you always.*

She tasted so fucking good, fresh and clean, with a hint of musky sweetness. Taye did precisely as she asked, kissing and nuzzling, using his fingers and his lips to drive her ever higher. Her encouraging words melted into incoherent sounds and then sobbing pleas. He eased a single finger inside her; she was astonishingly small. Imagining her pussy wrapped snugly around his cock almost made him come in his pants. She didn't react as if it hurt her. But nobody had ever touched her. That electrified him on a primitive level.

He worked her body with ruthless expertise, muscle memory filling in what his mind had lost. She arched and sobbed, contracting on his finger as he sipped at her clit. Gillie wrapped her thighs around his head and bucked. It took most of his strength to keep her balanced on the counter. Taye nuzzled her through another orgasm before her pleasure sounds drifted toward pain. Then he dialed it down, little kisses and soothing touches to calm her nerves. She fell limp into his arms, eyes glazed with satiation and perfect trust.

Words rose up inside him; he had spoken them to her before or some similar permutation. *Don't look at me like that. Not* me.

"Nothing for you?" she asked dreamily, curling into his arms.

He smiled and shook his head. Incredibly her delight dulled his own ache. It felt manageable, almost pleasurable, down at a low hum instead of that endless roar. She was the cool river that could slake his most dire thirst; he would like to lie down in her like a green valley and let his soul absorb her peace.

"Not tonight."

Not ever. But she didn't need to know that. It would only upset her, and he would like to spend this one night holding her. He could allow himself that much: scraps from the banquet. Perhaps it was selfish, but he'd earned this much of her.

As the snow became a blinding curtain outside, Taye carried her toward the stairs.

CHAPTER 9

The routine snatch and grab had turned into a complete goatfuck. Cale had lost his whole team, trying to bring those two in alive. Now he was inclined to peg them both in the head when he caught up to them, but that wouldn't get him the rest of his payday. The terms of the agreement were clear. He had to take them alive, if he wanted his other quarter mil. That was crazy money. Which was why he was starting to wish he'd passed.

Over the years, he'd become selective about the jobs he accepted, no more grunt work, no more body dumps. He should've known this was too good to be true. It would've been nice if his freakish employer had seen fit to tell him just how creative the male target could be. The row of burning cars and all the subsequent explosions inspired his admiration; if he hadn't seen it with his own eyes, he never would've believed it. He had been forced to scramble before the cops showed up—and it'd been a long time since anyone got the best of him. This game had gotten boring, but the potential for catastrophic failure and death? That rendered the chase interesting. It was also the only reason he didn't refund the Foundation's money and say, *To hell with this.*

He squatted in a condemned office building across the way,

waiting for the heat to die down. But when the fires were out, and all the city personnel and insurance adjusters disappeared, he eased out of the structure and down the stairs. It was early afternoon, and he got a good look at the destruction. Impressive, really. No less than seven cars. Bits of them had been left behind when the city towed them away. The heat was such that it had scorched the pavement. Dirty snow mingled with the metal shards and seared plastic.

Considering the mess it had been the night before, the street appeared quiet and clear. He had watched the scene long enough to be sure they hadn't left any surveillance behind. He jogged five blocks south to where he'd parked his car. In a stroke of good luck, it was untouched, and given the neighborhood, that was saying something. But he'd deliberately chosen a nondescript vehicle, nothing that would arouse interest or envy. If they'd known what kind of gear he kept stashed in his trunk, though . . . yeah, best not to tempt fate.

Cale drove back to the scene and risked parking nearby. It shouldn't take him long to roll the apartment and see if they'd left any clues as to their next stop. He already had a complete dossier on Gillie Flynn, at least until age twelve. Truth be told, he felt a bit sorry for the moppet, but this was business. Her protector offered nothing but question marks, which seemed odd. The Foundation ought to have records on him. But his case files—and the more recent documents on Ms. Flynn—had been blown up in some lab mishap and they weren't the sort of organization that left data backups all over the place. Most likely for good reason.

He swung out of the car and unlocked the trunk. The jacket concealed his weapons. *Should be no need for them.* Therefore, he only needed one thing from here. Cale snagged the aluminum case and headed for the brownstone. Part of the lobby had been cordoned off with crime scene tape. He skirted that and went up the stairs.

They'd occupied the first apartment on the left, top floor. It was a total armpit of a place, stained with the procession of tawdry lives that had passed through the door. Dirty brown carpet, peeling paint—one room with a kitchenette and bathroom. The furniture looked like it hadn't been replaced since 1976. There were dishes in the sink.

After donning gloves, it took all of five minutes to flip the place from top to bottom. Nothing. With a shrug, he shifted to plan B. Cale cracked open the case and assembled what he would need to dust the place for prints. Maybe he could learn something about Electro by putting him into the system.

The inner doorknob was the obvious place to start, and he got lucky. Two sets of clean prints, which he lifted with tape. Then he packed his kit and headed downstairs. There was nothing for him to find but clothes. Nothing written down or tossed in the trash. They were extraordinarily careful. After years of unqualified success, Cale didn't mind. He enjoyed pitting himself against an intelligent opponent.

In retrospect, he knew where they'd gone wrong. His men had secured the perimeter *too* well, neutralizing any potential interference. That resulted in a lack of normal ambient noise. He wouldn't make the same mistake again. No, these two he would capture himself, alive, as the Foundation wanted. After this last job, he'd retire. The paycheck would certainly permit a life of leisure, somewhere tropical. He'd earned it.

No point in delaying here any further. Cale bugged out, moving down the stairs with his customary watchfulness. He didn't think Electro had anyone watching his six, but one could never be too careful. Not in his line of work.

Once he left the brownstone, he drove for a good ten minutes to clear the neighborhood and then he found a motel, one of the low-end chains that offered wireless Internet as its greatest amenity. He needed a little privacy to do some digging.

The clerk looked tired, though it was only three in the afternoon; the guy had enough luggage beneath his eyes for a European vacation. His thinning hair stuck to his oily scalp, revealing patches of eczema. The heat inside the lobby steamed the front windows and created low visibility. If he worked in here, that wouldn't stand. He needed to see what was coming.

Cale handed over his credit card and ID, then tapped his fingers, giving the unspoken signal for *hurry the fuck up.* Despite his appearance, the attendant was efficient, and pretty soon he had a keycard for room 208—second floor, overlooking the parking lot. Perfect. He went back out into the cold and skimmed the cars. Near the street, a couple of guys stood wrapping up a drug deal; at least he surmised as much from their furtive looks and the exchange of cash for a brown bag. Eight cars, not too many guests. This was a decent place to do some research.

Grabbing his gear, he went up to his room and checked the place thoroughly. Paranoia perhaps, but it had kept him alive where other mercs ate a suitcase bomb. He made a habit of scouting any place he intended to spend more than a minute or two. But other than some slovenly housekeeping, this motel appeared to be clean. After pulling the drapes, he set up his equipment on the prefab desk. Once he had the prints ready to go, he dialed an associate at Interpol. Direct line, important business only.

"Hausen?"

"What?" He sounded none too pleased to hear from Cale, especially at this time of night.

"I need you to run some prints for me. Unlikely to be anything internationally, but you have access to US databases, yeah?"

"Don't you have any American friends you can bother?"

"None that owe me favors, like you do."

Heavy sigh. "Right. Send them to the usual address. I'll get the info as soon as I can. But I'm knocking another off the tab. Now you only have one marker left."

"You'll need me to save your arse again soon, I have no doubt."

Hausen cut the call with a derisive sound, but the truth was, he called whenever he had a mess that needed clearing up. In the past, Cale had specialized in that sort of thing. Sometimes interrogations took a turn for the worse, and he did whatever paid best at any given time, making him a true mercenary. In general, people didn't cross him because he knew where the bodies were buried.

He was somewhat concerned about dealing with the Foundation, however. Their enemies—and even their allies—had a history of disappearing, so he'd laid contingency plans, making sure they knew certain information would be sent to the press, should anything happen to him once he completed his end of the contract, leverage to keep the corporate kraken honest. Done for the moment, he put away his scanner and laptop, stowed both in their cases and slipped them beneath the bed. Better if he showed no sign he was different from any of the other faceless patrons.

Then he made a second call. "You didn't tell me everything I needed to know. Were you afraid I'd charge more if I knew precisely how dangerous the target was?"

A cool, inhuman voice replied; this Foundation drone gave

Cale the creeps because he could discern neither emotion, nor gender. "Irrelevant now. You agreed to its terms."

"You have information on some of their agents, yeah?"

"It has certain dossiers."

"Then you'll forward all that information to me. I need to know about anyone they may contact, anyone who might help them."

"The intel will arrive presently. Is there anything else?" Cold as ice, that reply—*Don't even think about backing out on me,* it said.

Cale suppressed a shiver, and it took a lot to unnerve him. He'd once stood in a drug baron's compound and watched him slice a traitor's eyelids off. "Do you have any other resources that might help me get the job done?"

A pause. They must have muted him because all the ambient noise went away as well. Frowning, he drummed his fingers on the desk. This whole outfit gave him the fucking creeps. But as long as they paid on time, he'd finish what he'd started. And then Fiji or maybe St. Croix.

Eventually the ungendered one came back on the line. "It has a girl. It uses her for tracking others. It is amenable to lending her for the duration of this task."

Bloody sweet. A feral grin curved his mouth. "Let's set up a meet."

Time to get some sleep, because when he woke, Hausen should have some data on the target, unless Electro had avoided the system entirely. Nobody managed that from birth in this day and age, unless they knew a world-class hacker willing to scrub for them. Therefore, his man would find a trail, however faint, and the girl would help him even more. The hunt could begin in earnest.

Cale would not make the same mistakes twice.

"A snowstorm," Tanager growled. "You gotta be shitting me."

She had been so happy to hear she was getting off shadow detail. For the last several months, Mockingbird had her stalking their own. So far she hadn't found anyone working for the Foundation, but his itchy feeling wasn't going away. That had to be back-burnered, however.

New instructions had come in while she made her way toward Kansas. Instead of providing Gillie Flynn with an ID packet and taking charge of T-89, she was bringing the little healer into the fold. Hawk would have the honor of working with T since he was the only agent accustomed to doing so, thanks to the time Tan had spent with Hawk in limited partnership.

Mockingbird was going to be pissed; he wanted T-89 locked, loaded, and ready for the good fight as of yesterday. Not that she could help the weather. While she could find a driver or a pilot and make him take her where she wanted to go, she'd be an idiot to risk her own skin. And she hadn't survived her life by being a dumbass. *Just because you* can *do something, it doesn't mean you should.*

Ordinarily she didn't swing toward caution, but it was really coming down out there: fat white sticky-wet flakes that would bring a twinkle to the eyes of little children everywhere.

Instead of being in Kansas, she was stranded on the Iowa border.

That'll teach you to screw around on those Midwestern gambling cruises. It had been a mistake to stop in northern Indiana, though it was a barrel of fun, plenty of motherfuckers she could ask for their gambling money. She figured they were just gonna lose it anyway. It could serve much better in her pocket. Then, instead of getting on with her mission, she'd spent a day shopping the Magnificent Mile on Michigan Avenue. Okay, so maybe she hadn't needed the hundred-dollar, tall red leather Doc Marten boots, but they were just so damn hot. And they went with her plaid leggings. She'd left Chicago too late that day, and the snowstorm hit with a vengeance, leaving her stranded. It should have been a simple matter to find a pilot willing to drop her off in bumfuck Kansas. Except for the weather.

She studied the brick building with the white trim, a duplex-style condo. Tanager had been casing the place for the last hour. A divorced man lived here; the wife had left recently. Poor bastard looked tired. Overworked. Fucking perfect.

Tan strode up the walk, her boots leaving impressions that the swirling snow quickly filled. After ringing the bell, she propped herself against the side of the portico, wearing a wide smile. Tom Sweeney, according to the mailbox, answered the door, his expression even more hangdog than it had been through the frosted windowpanes.

Because he was still a man, even if a pitiful one, his gaze swept her from head to toe. “Can I help you, miss?”

“No. But I can help you. Have you noticed how tired you are lately, Tom? You should sleep. Eighteen hours ought to do it. Don’t worry. I’ll come in and look after the house for you. Make sure nobody robs the place, and the pipes don’t freeze. Wouldn’t it be nice to let me drive for a while?”

His eyes glazed over. “Yes. Come in. I’m going to lie down.”

She popped her cinnamon gum as she stepped over the threshold. No hotels for her, no sirree. Nice place, too. Mahogany floors, marble tile, cut-crystal in the fixtures overhead. No wonder he was weary; he had most likely bought this condo to impress the woman who had left him. Sad sack Tom.

Within five minutes, the sound of snoring filled the bi-level condo. *Fuck. If only I’d told him not to make any noise. Ah well, too late now.*

Anyway, MB was a bit anal, so he liked to know when plans changed. She pinged him with a text and waited for him to call back. He also preferred to handle all calls between himself and agents; he always scrambled his own voice, which she thought was taking caution too far. Who the hell would ever try and get someone to ID him from how he sounded? Then again, maybe there was a special misfit out there who could do precisely that—find people based on their voices. It wasn’t so different from what Kestrel did, just a different form.

A few minutes later, her cell phone buzzed. The number came up blocked. They had one number to text, and MB always rang back on a different one. All so complicated, and it sucked they lived in a world where it was necessary, but the Foundation would latch on to any information they left behind and use it against them. They had done it to her sister, after all.

“Tan here,” she said brightly, forcing the memories down.

“Everything all right?” Even through the distortion, he sounded concerned.

Funny how he could do that. They had come together only virtually with him proving himself to her every step of the way. *Go to Chi-town, collect the gray backpack in the locker at Union Station. Use the money to open an account at Fifth Third. Identification will be provided for you.* In that way, he had earned her trust in baby steps when all the plans worked out just as he said they would. And only then had she been willing to use her ability to further his agenda. He'd never once failed to get her out of a tight spot, no matter how dangerous things were, where she was, or who was shooting at her. She'd do damn near anything for the sneaky son of a bitch, and he knew it. Most likely, the rest of his agents felt the same way.

"Small wrinkle. I'm stuck in Dubuque."

Stern crackle of anger, unmistakable. She liked when he got all *you're a very bad girl* on her. Made her think about disciplinary action. "What the hell are you doing there?"

"Waiting." The smirk showed in her voice, even to Tan's own ears.

"You had four days to get to the meet. What happened?"

"Snowstorm."

"That was on the five-day weather forecast. Didn't you plan for it?" She held her silence, knowing he'd remember who he was talking to. Sure enough, the sigh came a few seconds later. "Well, there's nothing to be done now. I've got Hawk heading that way, too."

She already knew that, thanks to their prior chat. Gillie calling to request they take her on, too—that move surprised her. Women didn't usually sign on for revenge, unlike Tanager, who lived for it. They had other dreams, other goals, and working with Mockingbird was just a stepping stone toward them. Not her. She couldn't ever imagine doing anything else.

"I miss the big guy. How's he doing?"

They had been partners for a while, but once he got closure on all the victims who had passed away down in the Foundation's Virginia facility, MB split them up. Tanager worked best alone anyway—she hated people telling her what to do and how to do it—but she'd gotten used to his face. And she'd found his devotion to his girlfriend oddly endearing. Juneau was a good sort, and she didn't lead him around by his prick, at least.

There was a long silence, as if MB found her interest inappropriate. Damn, it wasn't as if she fancied Hawk. She didn't like men to be more colorful than herself.

"He's fine. Helped wipe another facility, this one in Utah. Just imagine what he could do alongside T-89."

Yeah, she could picture it. Tan gave a little shiver. The carnage would be . . . delicious. "I'm sure. He's got quite the arsenal if it comes down to it."

"No shit," he said grimly. "I guess you didn't hear about the drama in south Detroit."

"I don't watch the news. It's always so fucking depressing."

That surprised a laugh out of him. "Yeah. Well, T blew up half a city block getting away from Foundation bloodhounds. Pretty spectacular."

"I like his style already."

"Just sit tight and make the rendezvous when it's safe. They're not moving in this weather. That'll give you some leeway."

"You warned him not to power up, right?"

"Of course."

"'Kay. Will Hawk get to the meet in time?"

"Shouldn't be a problem."

"I'll ping you when I get there." She disconnected.

No rush, right? Gotta wait for the weather to break. That was also why she wasn't worried about Kestrel. She wouldn't be looking for Tan, and in this weather, she wouldn't be able to deploy with any efficiency either.

After Tanager poked around the condo, made some food, and kicked back to watch cable TV, she fell asleep on Tom's ivory leather sofa.

So the strike team caught her flat-footed when they hit, spraying the front room with bullets. *Shit. They are* not *interested in taking me alive.* Tanager vaulted over the back of the sofa as she took one in the back of the thigh.

Smothering the pain, she called, "Put down your weapons. You don't want to hurt me."

Silence. No sound of guns being dropped. Either they were all deaf or they'd gone with earplugs. Which meant they knew about her ability. They were here hunting *her* specifically. *How the hell did this happen?* Shots slammed into the sofa; sooner or later, one would push through and splatter her brains.

She had to fight, no other option. But she had no weapon, and she was already injured. The odds didn't look good. Tanager ripped the flounce off her skirt and tied off the wound, reacting silently to the pain. While they went full auto on the furniture, she crawled toward the kitchen.

Each movement felt like a stab wound, and despite the

makeshift bandage, she left a blood trail, visible against the blond hardwood floors. She inched to the kitchen while they closed in behind her. Thankfully they were methodical, securing the perimeter as they went and taking extreme caution because Hawk had taught the Foundation that resistance agents were dangerous.

The lights were off in here, which helped. Dubuque wasn't Palestine; the neighbors would be calling the cops soon, which meant both she and the strike team needed to be quick. Tan pulled herself up on the counter and swallowed at the anguish burning her thigh. Dragging a dish towel behind her to mop up, she limped toward the walk-in pantry. The doors were wide enough for her to take a position to one side.

Need a weapon. With shaking hands, she hefted a big-ass can of peaches. Then she remained still and quiet, listening for the approach. Most likely they would split up once they realized she was hiding. *Wonder if they'll kill Tom. He's sound asleep so there's no need.* But with the Foundation, you could never tell.

Quiet footsteps. The tracker didn't click the light on. Tanager tightened her grip on her makeshift weapon; she would only have one shot at this. The next thirty seconds would determine if she lived or died. He flung open the doors and she struck, slamming the can against his temple with a two-handed grip. Full strength.

The guy wavered and went down, dazed but not wholly unconscious. Her breath coming in terrified rasps, she bent and pulled the plugs from his ears. While he stared up at her blearily, she gave his instructions. "You will tell the others the kitchen is clear. When you find the rest of your team, you will kill them. They're a threat to both of us. We can never be together as long as they're alive. As soon as you can stand, go. I'm counting on you now. Don't fail me."

It didn't matter that she'd powered up again. Kestrel—for it could be nobody else—had already tracked her here. She didn't have the ability to triangulate room by room.

Within a few seconds, he stumbled away and she scrambled back into the pantry, the pain in her thigh increasing exponentially. This was going to cause all kinds of trouble for Tom. If he didn't wind up dead, the police would never believe he hadn't seen or heard a thing. They'd demand drug tests and then wind up utterly mystified when the guy came back clean. Despite the dire situation, she had to grin at that. There was nothing more fun than fucking with people in positions of authority.

For a little while, there was only silence. And then the shooting started. Because she had given him the goal of getting back to her, her warrior would fight harder than the others. He would be more careful and cunning. He would snipe them in the dark. Endless moments, she listened to men dying, and it didn't trouble her at all. After all, they'd come to execute her for being different.

According to the glowing face of her phone, it took him ten minutes to complete her command. She limped out of the pantry to watch his progress. He shuffled toward to her, bleeding in five places. Only willpower and her compulsion kept him on his feet.

"You did well," she told him softly. "Rest now. Rest."

And he fell dead at her feet.

She stepped over his corpse in a pained motion and gimped to the front room to claim her bag. Sirens screamed in the distance; if not for the snow, the cops would have been here sooner. Time to get the fuck out. But this complicated her life considerably. Tan had used her power twice in a relatively short time, and the dark urges built in the back of her brain. If she didn't pay the piper, the sitch would get ugly—death by bloody aneurysm. And nobody wanted that.

Well, a few people did, actually. But they didn't count, and most of her enemies were dead. More to the point, how the hell would she find somebody willing to fuck her in the midst of a blizzard, while she was bleeding from the thigh? It would take a special kind of freaky to make that shit work.

Mockingbird was going to be *so pissed.*

CHAPTER 10

Taye was gone when she woke.

At first Gillie wondered if it had been a dream, but she smelled like him this morning, so it couldn't have been. When she rolled over, she saw the indent of his head on the other pillow. Like a sentimental idiot, she drew it to her and pressed her cheek to it. She didn't kid herself that this meant something permanent, but it had been so good to sleep in his arms that she couldn't bring herself to get out of bed just yet. Doing so would mean acknowledging the night was over.

But eventually, she had no choice. The only bathroom was down at the bottom of the stairs. This was a small house, which was convenient; it wouldn't require tons of gas to heat the place. After she used the facilities, she went back up to the bedroom. Walking around naked didn't seem like the way to spend the day. Maybe there was something in one of the dressers, clothes left behind.

To her astonishment, she found sweats in small, medium and large, still with the tags on. No underwear, but this was nice planning on someone's part. Maybe Mockingbird assumed anyone who wound up here had a sad story to tell, a halfway house for fugitive weirdoes. But then, this wasn't his first rodeo. He had gone down this road before with other recruits, and he had to understand how the Foundation operated. If he had never been captured, he was a powerful and worthy ally.

Though she'd been fucking with Taye when she first told him she'd work for the resistance herself, by calling Mockingbird, she had committed to the idea in earnest. If she did it of her own free will, maybe it wouldn't be so bad. If she chose to help instead of having someone else's filth and disease forced on her . . . well, it still gave her a cold chill. But maybe she could fight past that reaction.

Whatever, she had time to acclimate. It would take a day or two to get these back roads cleared, though the snowfall had tapered off. Going commando, Gillie dressed in the small tracksuit, but the fleece was soft enough not to itch. Then she went to find Taye.

He too had snagged a pair of clean pants, and that was all he wore. The sweats hung low, revealing the curve of his hipbone. Heat filled her, but from his expression, he didn't want a repeat of last night. His eyes were sad and distant, his jaw bristling with morning-after scruff.

"So here's the bad news. The roads won't be open for a couple of days, which means we're stuck here."

"But this is the right place?" It had to be.

He nodded. "Our contact is late. She was supposed to be here by now."

"Maybe she got caught in the storm."

His shoulders lifted in a shrug, drawing her attention to the movement of his muscles. "Could be. I don't like sitting and waiting, but I don't know what else to do."

"You think we're not safe here?"

"We are. At least, as much as we are anywhere. We can't move without risking arrest."

With that, he clicked on the TV and turned on the VCR. Outdated technology—even Gillie had a DVD player down in her dungeon cell. But he'd recorded a news broadcast from early that morning. She watched with growing trepidation.

The handsome, dark-haired anchor read from the teleprompter. "These two are armed and dangerous, responsible for a multiple car bombing in Detroit. As yet, no terrorist organizations have come forward to claim credit for the act, but they are believed to be working with the IRA. No information at this time as to why they have moved their activities to American soil. If you see them, please notify local authorities at once or call this national tip line . . ."

Her breath went in a rush. "So we're wanted criminals? It's not just the Foundation after us, now. Mockingbird can't scrub all these records. He can't wipe the memories of everyone who saw this broadcast. What are we going to do?"

"I'm working on that." He paced the length of the living room and back to the windows, where he gazed out at the white field stretching toward an endlessly gray sky. "They can probably find a doctor willing to change your face. You can color your hair and get some contacts. It's not impossible."

"Would that work for you, too?"

He hesitated a fraction too long before saying, "Sure."

Gillie fought with the urge to ask again for his secrets. By now she knew he wouldn't surrender them. The wall between them hadn't come down last night; he had just scaled it for a little while, and now he stood again on the other side, peering at her through cracks in the mortar.

"Don't lie," she snapped. "If you don't want to tell me the truth, fine, but don't insult me with bullshit. I'd like to think you respect me a little."

"More than a little." But there was nothing personal in the words; he wasn't the lover she'd known last night. Taye might have been observing the quality of a basketball player's jump shot. "But this doesn't change our plan materially. I still go to work for Mockingbird, and you get a new life. It'll just take a little more effort on your end."

"I don't want a new face." It was stupid to protest anything that would grant her freedom. Stupid. But she didn't have anything that was her own. Changing her looks, her hair, her eyes . . . who would she be then? She had always been Gillie Flynn. But she'd lose her name, too.

"I hate the idea, too," he said, as if he were personally responsible for the newscast. "You're just so goddamned beautiful, it's a crime to consider messing with how you look." From his stricken expression, he hadn't meant to add the last part.

A smile lightened the tightness of her chest. "You never said that before."

"What does it matter if I say it or not? It's always true."

Gillie laughed softly. "Idiot. It *only* matters if you say it."

"I'm not gonna survive you," he said, so soft and low that for a few seconds she wondered if she'd imagined the words.

"I don't understand."

"Never mind." He obviously regretted the momentary lapse, and that lit her up.

Anger provided a welcome boost; it was past time for her to protest—and not with yesterday's provocation. That, he could dismiss as an emotional response. So she kept her voice cool, belying the words she spoke. "I don't want a new life without you in it. We have to figure out some way to stay together."

He flinched. And when Taye hurt, he lashed out. "Don't say shit like that. I mean it. It only makes me think you're a brainless fucking romantic who can't be trusted."

But as she had told him countless times, she was tougher than she looked. "Aw. Is this where I cry and ask why you're being *so mean*? You saw how I lived, but I don't think you get it. Not really. Not even you."

"What are you talking about?"

"I remember, Taye. I remember my parents. And I remember the endless hospital visits and blood samples and feeling too weak to lift my head. I recall my miraculous recovery and bewildering the doctors. My folks were so happy that I'd finally get to be a kid. Play on the swings and fall in the mud and scrape my knees. But the Foundation took an interest. Instead of normal, we had to move and move again. They tried so hard to keep me safe.

"Then, of course, I remember being taken. After that comes a blur of drugs and torture. Then it gets crystal clear again—my years with Rowan, and all those days where I played the good girl to avoid something worse. It was like living in a minefield." She slammed a fist into her palm. "Do you get that? Twelve years. *Half* my life. And I had Rowan watching me. Lusting. Plotting. Nobody gave a shit what I wanted . . . I wasn't a person to them. I was a thing to be used and put away until some rich fucker needed me."

He put out his hand in a placating gesture. "Gillie—"

"Don't. When you came along, I thought I finally had someone who cared about me. But now here you are, treating me like I don't deserve a say in my own fate. Making *decisions* for me. You'll stop that—and right now. We're equals, or we're nothing at all."

She glared at him from a distance of five feet, fists balled up and ready to fight. This wasn't a game to her. He was the most important person in her life, but she would cut him off without a qualm if he didn't get past this notion that she was some china doll. Fuck, she probably would make mistakes and missteps, but they'd be her own, and she would learn from them. Though he might be a bit older, he sure as hell wasn't her dad, and she wasn't looking for paternal input. In another five seconds, she would go upside his head with something heavy.

Instead of escalating the argument, he stilled. And then, with his gaze locked on hers, Taye dropped to his knees. "I am so sorry. I told you before, I don't remember how to deal with people. But that's not an excuse . . . I need to listen when you speak. Can you forgive me?" He bowed his head, like a penitent in search of absolution.

Her hand hovered above his hair, and then she twined her fingers in the shaggy chestnut strands, tilting his face up. "I can. Just don't do it again. Don't dismiss me. This is *my* life. I appreciate your help but you don't make my choices. I do."

As if he couldn't help himself, he knee-walked to close the distance between them and rested his head against her abdomen. He wrapped his arms around her waist, and a tremor rolled through him, a man in tremendous pain. Taye, humbled and uncertain—in their months together, she had never seen him like this. Gillie stroked his hair with deliberate motions.

"Then why the hell would you choose me?" he whispered at last.

She recognized the power of the question instinctively. "I want you, partly because you're hot." At the way his chin tilted in indignation, she smirked. "Right, like I'm too pure to notice. You have a super-fine ass and shoulders that don't quit. But it's not just that. You get me, where nobody else could. I don't want to be with someone where I have to lie. Where I have to pretend constantly and invent memories to cover those lost years. I can be who I am with you. And some days when I am totally, unreasonably angry, and I break dishes . . . when I scream and throw stuff at you when you haven't done a damn thing, well, you understand that, too."

"I do," he admitted. "You have a right to be furious with the world."

He turned his cheek slowly against her stomach, the bristles prickling even through the fleece of her sweatshirt. It felt as though he were paying homage or worshiping her. The thought unsettled her; he couldn't possibly think he was so unworthy, no matter what secrets squatted in the midden of his past.

"Most of the time, it's not so bad. Up, now. I've forgiven you." She tugged him to his feet, but he didn't step away.

Instead his hands slid upward, resting lightly on her waist. "Is it wrong to admit I like it when you yell at me?"

She cocked a brow. "Why?"

"Means you trust me not to hurt you, no matter what."

A grin curled the corners of her mouth. "I bet you like it even more when I throw things at you. Crockery. Vases. Bowls."

"Aw, yeah. Now you're just *trying* to get me hot."

"How's that working out for you?" She leaned into him, and was astonished. "Never mind. Empirical evidence provides the answer." That revelation opened the most interesting doors in her head. "That's your button? You like when I'm mean and angry? What would you do if I ordered you to go up and get naked?"

His cock jumped against her belly.

Pure temptation. **It** would be the easiest thing in the world to let her take charge of him. Maybe too easy, because it was exactly what he wanted—his heart's desire while being absolved of all responsibility. *Yes, I'm aware she was a virgin, St. Peter, but she wouldn't take no for an answer.* Somehow Taye didn't think that defense would hold much weight in heaven. Not that he thought he was going there—and did he really need another sin on his soul? He could too clearly picture the devil roasting his entrails, while whispering, *She was too good for you, asshole.*

Gillie wasn't meant for him. He'd known that from the beginning, even before that first, enchantingly clumsy kiss. He couldn't repeat last night's weakness, or he'd never be able to walk away from her. But even knowing he stood on shaky ground, it took all his willpower not to obey her playful command.

"I'd say, 'not today.'"

"You have something better to do?" Her smile said she already knew the answer.

"I'm not ready." He could've kicked himself when he saw the light in her expression, because with those words, he implied he would be, someday. And who was the inexperienced one here, anyway? But in a sense, they both were, because he couldn't remember anyone else. Sex wasn't new to him, but for the life of him, he could find no past lovers in his head. Just Gillie. Only her. He might have been born with her face imprinted in his brain. The first thing he could remember—after Rowan began the second round of experiments—was being wheeled past her apartment as Silas brought her out, probably to heal someone.

"That's better than no," she said softly.

Not like she would believe it if he claimed he didn't want her. Just feeling her against him, savoring the clean soap and woman scent of her, drove him crazy. And she knew, dammit. She displayed new confidence, new seductive strength, in every gesture. Gillie had been dangerous enough to his equilibrium when she *wasn't* sure how he felt, or what he wanted.

Amusement got the better of him, and he fell into his role with a growing sense of appreciation. "Just give me a little time, okay? I don't want to rush into anything."

"I'll still respect you in the morning."

The next part, he meant, serious as a heart attack. "But *I* won't, if I do this now."

Gillie didn't know that, for him, the future was a mythical creature, like a griffin or a unicorn. If he could stall her long enough—without losing her affection—then maybe he could manage the situation. It would become a moot point.

"I don't claim to understand, but I won't press either."

"Thank you." He leaned down and touched his forehead to hers.

She wrapped her arms around his waist, and he hadn't realized until that moment how much he'd missed simple human contact. Though he had become a terrifying creature, portions of him still longed for comfort. She felt like the last tether holding him to this life; if she ever gave up on him, if she ever let go, then he'd morph fully into the monster he feared, the one that fed on fire and death. Simply put, Gillie held the silver cords to his soul.

He realized his mistake a few seconds later when she cupped his face in her hands and drew his head down. Taye had no ability to resist her at this distance, no secret well of strength. Instead he responded helplessly, hungrily. She had learned too much in a short time. Her lips toyed with his, playful and luscious.

"Gillie," he bit out, feeling ridiculous. "No means no."

"I'm not unfastening your pants, am I?" Her not-so-innocent blue eyes laughed up at him. "It was just a little kiss."

Bullshit. There was no such thing where she was concerned, no more than an arsonist could set a small fire, or a junkie could stop at one fix, just enough to take the edge off. And Taye felt every bit as compulsive where she was concerned. The long months of denial were driving him insane. He broke her hold on him gently and stepped away.

Taye winked, donning the cocky mask he wore when the pain bit deepest. *Thank God she hasn't figured that out yet. It'd be the end of me.* "I guess I gotta come clean. You're too much woman for me."

She liked the implied compliment; he saw it in the proud little lift of her head. "I might be, but I could teach you to handle the pressure."

"Maybe. Like I said, just give me a little time."

The one thing he didn't have. Such irony curled his mouth in a bitter smile, but he turned away before she could read his face. *Keep your secrets. Keep her safe.* It didn't seem like too much weight for a dying man.

"What now?"

"I'm gonna go shovel the drive." Exertion would help, although it wasn't the kind he wanted or needed. Excess sexual energy might give him an embolism before their contact arrived, and it would take all his mental acuity to keep Gillie from figuring out his game. "We want our contact to be able to get to the house once the weather clears for good."

"Need some help?"

He wouldn't try to shield her from hard work. Her message had penetrated in that regard, at least. Gillie had to be free to do what she wanted, what she *chose* to do. "If there are two shovels, sure. Otherwise there's no point in you standing in the cold."

And she appreciated the shift in his attitude. Gillie beamed a smile at him, and it made his heart twist in his chest. Another man would one day claim all those smiles, all her kisses. He'd have *everything*, and that inevitable outcome made Taye want to set the whole world on fire, nothing but scarlet flames, from

Atlantic to Pacific. But that was the monster talking. He strangled it to silence.

"I'll bundle up. Then we can check the shed."

It didn't take long to get ready for outdoor work. Just his luck, there were two shovels. His and hers. Which meant more time in her company. But she seemed to like the physical force. Though she'd had a treadmill in her little apartment, apart from washing dishes at McGinty's, she'd never done much in the real world. Never shoveled snow or felt chill wind on her face, kindling brightness to her eyes and the roses in her cheeks. To her, this probably felt like freedom.

Later, after they shifted the snow to clear a path, then warmed up with tea and leftover macaroni, Taye landed in the unenviable position of entertaining Gillie in a way that didn't end with both of them naked. The safe house, while plenty safe, didn't offer many amenities. When he suggested TV, she glared at him.

"No. *Nyet. Nunca*. I'd rather take a beating than watch another minute of TV."

Fuck. He'd forgotten it had comprised her chief entertainment and company for so many years. Yeah, that was right out. *Let's see, there has to be something else we can do . . .*

But while he searched the dusty bookshelves, she went into the kitchen and came back with a wine bottle. *Oh no.* She wasn't getting him drunk to take advantage of him. Pained self-disgust washed over him. When had he become a fucking Victorian spinster afraid to show his ankles? It should *not* be this hard to stave off her advances.

"I'm not sure that's the best idea."

"Bullshit. This looks old, which is supposed to be good for wine, right? So let's see if age made it delicious. And while we drink, we'll play Truth or Dare."

The words rang a faint bell in his memory, but he wasn't positive what she meant. Best to make sure. "What's that?"

"It's a game kids play. Usually, at least according to TV, they make each other do gross, embarrassing stuff. Or answer awkward questions."

"I'll have to take a lot of dares," he reminded her.

"Doesn't that depend on what I ask?"

Without awaiting his reply, she headed back to the kitchen, presumably for glasses. He heard her rummaging in the cupboards, then water ran. Rinsing them, maybe. When she appeared in the doorway, her cheeks were flushed pink, and she held a corkscrew in her teeth. *I can't deny her this,* he realized. As long as it didn't end in sex, Taye figured he could give her some of the fun she'd missed. Even if he was acutely conscious they were not children.

The glasses, she set on the pasteboard coffee table. He took charge of the bottle and the corkscrew. Though he didn't think he'd used the device often, he managed to open it and decant the wine without making a huge mess. The vintage smelled strong, a rich ruby red in the glasses.

Gillie took a sip and her nose wrinkled. "Is this supposed to be good?"

How the fuck would I know? Somehow he suspected he hadn't been a fine-wine guy in his past life. Still, he tried it and offered his best guess. "I think. Probably?"

"It's funny."

"What?"

"I feel like we're both discovering the world for the first time."

"So we are."

"And how do you feel about wine?"

"I don't mind it. But I like the lager I had at McGinty's better." But he took another drink because the spreading warmth appealed to him.

It uncoiled his muscles and made him worry less about what would come. Before he knew it, he'd downed the entire glass. Gillie watched him with a faint half smile, half of hers still remaining.

"More?"

"I better not."

"Then let's start the game. Truth or dare?"

"How does this work anyway? I just have to pick blind?"

"I think so."

"Truth, then." He figured it would probably progress to dare when he couldn't remember the answer.

"If you could do anything you wanted with me, what would that be?" No mistaking the sexual charge in her eyes or the provocative tilt of her head.

Aw, fuck. She'd come up with a new way to torment him. This was, absolutely and for certain, not a children's version of the game. But maybe he could have some fun with this. From her intent expression, she wanted to hear him talk about the dirty stuff. Yeah, he could work with this, strictly no touching. Just words.

Taye raked her from head to toe with his gaze. Anything he wanted? "I love looking at you, so I'd make you get naked. And then I'd make you sit on that chair"—he pointed to a ladder-back in the corner of the room—"and play with yourself while I watched you get off."

Her breath caught, her cheeks flushing a deeper pink. "Really? That's what you'd want, out of anything at all?"

"Right now? Yeah."

If she asked the follow-up question in the next round, if she asked *why*, he'd have to answer, *because I can* have *that.* She watched the chair with unnerving intensity, and then she downed the rest of her wine. *Dutch courage, maybe.* But maybe his desires diverged down a different path from hers, and she didn't need it.

"Your turn."

This game might wind up being fun after all. "Truth or dare, Gillie-girl?"

Her full, rosy mouth curved into a smile. "Dare."

Taye wondered if she thought he wouldn't go there. But she'd set the tone, after all. If she'd opened with a question about his favorite sandwich, they wouldn't be hovering on the cusp of a challenge so hot that he felt like his head might explode.

"I dare you to shuck your clothes, go sit in that chair, and execute my truth."

CHAPTER 11

He doesn't think *I will.*

But Gillie had enough wine in her to make it seem sexy. Some people got off on watching; maybe Taye did. The way her body responded to the idea, she might be one of the others, one who enjoyed being watched. After a lifetime of surveillance, she'd never have guessed it would be the case, but it wouldn't with just anyone. Only for Taye could she consider putting on such an intimate show—and possibly not if she were fully sober. She eased to her feet and walked to the center of the room.

Confidence. Certainty. She peeled out of her sweats slowly, top first. No bra, of course. Which meant in one more garment, she would be naked in front of him, but it wasn't the first time. He sat very still, hardly breathing, as she worked the pants down her hips. A lift of her thigh, and they pooled on the hardwood floor.

Starting to relish the display, she ran her fingers gently through her pubic hair, fluffing it. Gillie became aware how soft it was, fine down, barely there. She didn't have enough to hide what she was doing.

"Sit down," he said softly. "Legs open."

Amending his script, she brought the chair to the center of the room, just on the other side of the coffee table, so she could prop one leg. If he leaned forward, he would be close enough to touch. By his tormented expression, he realized that as well.

"I've never done it this way," she admitted, breathless. "I've only ever come on my stomach . . . or in your mouth."

A groan escaped him. "But you'll try for me."

"Of course. That was the dare."

Eyes locked on his, she spread as he'd requested and stretched her right leg out, her foot braced on the table's edge. He licked his lips, and that little motion sent heat straight to her cunny. She'd heard that word in a period drama, one with lots of sex and treachery, and that was the term she used in her own head, though it was a little silly and old-fashioned.

Without hesitation, she touched her labia. Dew misted them slightly, but when she parted them, the wetness grew more intense. Gillie slid her thumb up and down, gone breathless at the sensations. She'd never done this. Ever. And it felt so delicious, especially beneath his hot, hungry stare. At first she stroked up and down, getting to know her body. His breathing rasped in the silence, adding to the soft, slick sounds created by her explorations. She imagined these were his fingers, and the sensations spiked with new ferocity.

She slid down in the chair a little, giving herself a better angle and him a better view. He murmured his appreciation in low, guttural tones. Sweet words, encouraging ones. This time, she tapped her clit, gentle little strikes that sent sparks rolling through her pelvis. Would it be too dirty to use both hands? One to stroke up and down, the other to play right there? By his moan, she guessed not as she brought her other hand into the action.

Reaching down, she worked her index finger inside, marveling at the smooth heat. It hadn't hurt when Taye touched her the other night; it didn't now. Just then, Gillie could only be grateful that it felt so fucking good. The pleasure swirled higher, and she forgot about putting on a show, forgot he was watching. She whimpered a little as she discovered the rhythm she liked best, both within and without. Throwing her head back, she worked her hips, utterly without shame or inhibition.

"You're getting close, aren't you?" His voice was a low, sexy growl.

"Yeah." Breathless agreement.

"You're the sexiest thing I've ever seen. Come on now, Gillie. Come *on*."

With her eyes closed and Taye urging her on, she tightened her thighs on her hand, bearing down with the other, and that did it. Just the right pressure. She came endlessly, sobbing his name. By the time her body steadied, cool sweat covered her skin.

"Well?" she challenged. "Did I win?"

He laughed shakily. "I think I did."

She felt incredibly content. "Call it a draw and pour me some more wine."

His gaze devoured her as she dressed and went to wash her hands. When she returned, another glass of red awaited her. She sat beside him on the sofa, and without meaning to, she skimmed a look at his lap. *Oh, how lovely.* There was no hiding his arousal in gray sweats.

"It's your turn," he said, "unless you're done playing."

Gillie sipped her wine. "I'm just getting started."

"I was afraid of that." But he didn't sound scared. Instead, anticipation radiated from him in glowing waves. She wouldn't have been surprised to see lightning crackle from his fingers.

"So truth or dare, then?"

"After what you just did, truth would be a pussy move, wouldn't it? Dare."

Mmm. She had high hopes for this evening. "Only fair for you to show me yours, wouldn't you agree?"

He raised a brow. "Are you allowed to turn the same stunt back on me?"

"Do you *really* care about the rules? Don't you want to?"

From his visceral response and the tension of his body, he did. He considered for a few seconds, eyes distant, then he stood and circled the coffee table. She sat back as he had, obeying the unspoken rules. Look, but don't touch. Admire, but don't move.

He only wore those gray sweats, and they came off fast. His body carried numerous scars; a small pucker on his side looked like a scar from a gunshot wound. His skin told secrets his brain had long since forgotten; but maybe that was for the best. By the look of him, it wasn't a happy tale. And yet he was so beautiful it hurt. He had little body hair and a broad, gorgeous chest, tapering to lean hips and tautly muscled legs.

She had seen erect penises before, but only in pictures. His took her breath away. At this distance, there were more veins than she'd expected, and his balls hung heavy between his thighs. Taye sat as she had, but he slid down farther, a frown building. She gleaned from his impatience that the straight chair wasn't the best place for him.

"Would the couch be better?" she whispered. "I can move to the other end."

"Yeah." His voice held a raw, guttural note, as if each delay caused him pain.

Belatedly, she remembered he hadn't come the night before, so he must be desperate for relief. Gillie wanted to provide it, but she'd play the game by his rules. Hands off, for now.

He retraced his steps and sank down on the far edge, angling his body so she could see his erection. The tip glistened slightly, and he hadn't even touched it yet. Taye slid into a slouch, his head resting on the back of the sofa. He slitted his eyes, still focused on her, and wrapped his hand around his cock.

A pained sound escaped him. "How do you want it? Slow? Or should I just go for it?"

Torn, she hesitated. But from the restless movements of his hips, she thought he needed the latter. So she said, "I want to see how quick you can come."

"Thank you," he breathed.

He stroked hard, more pressure than she would've guessed could feel good, and so fast his hand became a blur, pumping up and down. She wanted to lick his thighs, to bite and nuzzle and cup his testicles in her hands. She feared even blinking, afraid she would miss something delicious. His abdominal muscles tensed as he worked, his face fierce with pleasure. Soon his breath came in loud rasps, punctuated by the sound of his fist on his cock.

"Watch me," he whispered. "Don't look away."

"I won't. You're beautiful."

"Tell me you like it, Gillie."

"I do. I'm imagining how lovely you'd feel inside me."

At that, he gave a pained groan and lifted his hips, hunching upward even more furiously. "I'm your first."

"You are. Only you." She saw how her words fueled his urgency and she gave him more. "You're going to fuck me so hard."

His eyes opened, wide with this wild longing. That look begged for the rest, a verbal picture of what she could only imagine. But for him, she'd try.

"Feels so good. Don't stop."

"It doesn't hurt?"

Faster now, harder still. Impossible to conceive that felt

good, the rough way he tugged and pulled. But she'd know not to be too gentle with him later.

"No, love. It's perfect. I need you."

As if those words constituted the key to his release, he roared and bucked, coming in long waves. He tensed and jerked, the fluid coating his fingers, belly, and chest. Without being asked, she got a damp cloth and handed it to him. God, he was magnificent in repose, the essence of masculine beauty. The air of leashed violence that always clung to him dissipated somewhat as well. He reminded her of a well-fed lion, indolent after a kill. Taye cleaned up with languid motions and then slipped back into his sweats. Then his eyes drifted shut and his head fell back against the couch once more.

Cuddling up would be the perfect end to the game, but she wasn't brave enough to see how he'd respond. It couldn't always be her, reaching for him. There had to be some reciprocation. So she merely sat down with every appearance of calm, although his reaction would determine their course, going forward, whether this was the start of something, or its end.

Taye watched her through his lashes. Though he knew later he'd probably regret what they'd done, right then, he felt pretty damn good. But she seemed nervous. Without realizing he'd made a decision, he leaned over and anchored her to his side. Her coppery curls spilled across his skin, soft as silk. He was pretty sure nothing in the world had ever been so good. He ran his hand through her hair, watching as the red strands feathered around his fingers. *So pretty.* She was made for sunshine and smiles.

"Here's the deal," he said lazily. "No dares, because that would require moving. But I'll give you more truth."

"It's your turn anyway."

So it is.

He thought about what he wanted to know most and shied away from the question. So he settled for the next best thing. Taye would take her in slivers and glimpses, like light glimpsed through a tangle of tree limbs at dusk. "What's your dearest memory?"

Gillie curled into him, resting her head on his chest, and he had the wild idea that for him it would be the memory they were making right now. No matter what came after, the gentle grace of her weight against his side, her heart beating in time with his, nothing could ever be sweeter. He'd take this moment to his grave.

"After I got out of the hospital for the last time. I was cured, not just in remission. My parents were so happy." She paused, face gentle with reminiscence. "On the way home, my dad stopped at a doughnut shop. I hadn't been able to eat much for so long, but before I got sick, he'd bring home a dozen on Sunday mornings before church. It was two in the afternoon, and we had doughnuts for lunch because we *could*."

"I get that."

"Yeah," she said softly. "My turn, I guess?"

He ran his fingers through her hair, luxuriating in the moment. For this stolen span, he would act like he had the right to hold and cherish her. "Shoot."

"How do you feel about me?"

Taye muffled a curse. He ought to have known she'd cut to the core of the matter. No bullshit for Gillie Flynn. *Has the heart of a lion does my girl.* The possessive thought slipped free before he could stop it, leaving cyclone-style devastation in its wake. He couldn't afford to indulge in fantasies; it would only make walking away harder down the line.

"You're the most important person in my life." In that he could be honest and hope she didn't press for more. Not that he could give it. That honor would go to some other guy.

I'd kinda like to kill him.

Her face lit as if fueled by sunrise, and he wished he didn't have that much power over her emotions. This could only end in tears. Yet he didn't resist when she curled closer.

"I think we'd better stop here," she murmured. "It's not going to get any better."

Prophetic words, Gillie-girl.

"Are you tired?"

"Unbelievably."

Together, they fixed some food in the kitchen. It was simple fare, plain boiled rice, because that was all that was left. This place hadn't been meant for long-term residents. Gillie ate far more than he did. The knives were back in his stomach, endless carving until he tasted copper in the back of his throat. It was only better when he touched her, like her proximity possessed some healing magic.

"Not hungry?" she asked.

He shrugged. Good thing this interlude was almost over. Taye didn't know how much longer he could hide his illness from her. She paid far too much attention.

In the bathroom, he studied his reflection in the mirror. Shadows below the eyes, scruffy face. What the hell did she see in him anyway? He pissed, washed his hands, and then did his best to clean his teeth with his finger and some old half-used toothpaste in the cabinet. She took her turn while he waited with imperfect patience.

Just one more night. That's all.

Once she finished, Gillie snagged his hand, leading him up the stairs. With tousled hair and bare, lightly freckled face, she should not have been the most beautiful woman he'd ever seen. But she was, and he suspected she always would be. The warmth of her smile tied him in knots.

Get me through this, he silently begged the joker who ran the universe. As usual, the bastard answered only with silence.

Together they went up to bed, but he fought sleep because it was his last night with her. Despite his best intentions, Taye fell.

The night was black and cold; he'd staked out a place over a heating grate. Others huddled nearby in their own boxes, their own nightmares. One of them was singing "We'll Meet Again" in a drunken-gravel bass, low and mournful like a foghorn heard over long miles. As the rain came down, the cardboard grew sodden from the weight of the rain, and so he curled deeper. He couldn't remember why it was so important they didn't find him. Only that it was.

They hunted him. He saw their faces everywhere. Fear and cold chilled his skin, so he took a drink from the bottle in his hand. Mad Dog induced numbness, but not enough to make him forget the danger. Never enough for that. If he let down his guard, even for a minute—

"They're not hurting anyone," somebody said.

"I don't care . . . I don't want them on my property. They're scaring away the customers. Shoo 'em out of here, before I shitcan your ass."

"You pay me to bus tables, not transients."

"Fine," the man growled. "I'll do it myself."

Footsteps came closer. He downed the last of the Mad Dog and braced for an attack. His fingers tightened on the bottle. If he broke it quick enough, he could turn it into a weapon. They wouldn't take him. They wouldn't. Not like they'd taken the others.

Everyone thought he was crazy. They called him . . . He couldn't remember the word. But it wasn't happening to him. He wasn't going to disappear in the dark.

"Look. You gotta move on. Don't make me call the cops."

Around him, other homeless men and women gathered their belongings. Headlights down the other end of the alley highlighted their drawn, hopeless faces, etched with weariness and despair. He looked just like that; he had no doubt. Best place to hide. They'd never look here.

But before he could decide what to do, the guy laid hands on him. *Don't touch, don't touch. Don't. Touch.* His leg lashed out, slamming into the man's crotch. He doubled over, moaning in pain, but it was just for show, trying to make him sorry and drop his guard. He was one of *them.* He followed with a blow to the face and the man went down. Another voice cried out in distress. The homeless who offered perfect camouflage melted away in the rain.

Cold, cold rain.

In the distance, he heard footsteps running. He stared at the man at his feet, seeing him for the first time. He was short and middle-aged, inadequately dressed for the weather. His dress shirt was plastered to his back, his slacks stained with the alley's filth. *He's not one of them. You're crazy.*

When he saw the red and blue lights flashing down at the other end of the alley, when the men in uniform came for him, he didn't resist. The bottle dropped from his hand, shattered into diamond-bright shards at his feet. He raised his arms slowly, as instructed, and put them behind his. *Let them take you. You'll be safer in prison.*

Taye awoke with a shudder; Gillie slept on, oblivious, beside him. In the faint starlight, he traced the blue tat on his arm. Prison ink? He guessed it must be, though he couldn't remember serving time. He didn't even remember what had happened in that dream. It felt like watching someone else's life, someone else's insanity.

Still trembling, he gathered her close and she rolled toward him with a sleepy murmur of pleasure. *No. You don't know who I am. You can't. Because I don't.* He held her like that until dawn lit the sky; he couldn't let her go just yet. Not when his greedy heart craved her closeness. The parting would come soon enough.

CHAPTER 12

The next morning, Gillie woke with a strange female perched on the side of the bed. Taye was nowhere to be found, so she could only presume this was their contact. She was small, slight, and had spiky platinum hair. Though it couldn't be very late according to the slant of the sun, she also wore heavy eye makeup and black lipstick. Her bouncing had woken Gillie.

"So you're the Miracle Girl." Low voice, touch of a Boston accent, but not so thick as some she'd heard.

"I guess."

"I hear you're joining us."

Grateful she hadn't gone to bed naked last night, she sat up, groggily rubbing her eyes. "I don't think I'll be much of an asset in the field. So what will I be doing?"

"Mockingbird gave me your assignment, and we'll get to that in time. How does T-89 feel about your recruitment?"

She shrugged. "He didn't ask my opinion of his master plan. I figure I have the same right as he does."

"So you're willing to work?"

A flash memory of being led down the hall to the treatment room. Of siphoning the sickness out of someone else's body and then the unearthly pain while it was drained out of her by a dialysis machine. Gillie puffed out a long breath; this was it, no backing out after this point.

She made herself speak the words aloud, just as she had on the phone. “I’m willing to do whatever you need. The Foundation has to pay.”

The woman drummed her painted-black nails on the mattress. “Can you heal injuries or just diseases?”

An excellent question. Thank God Rowan never asked it.

“Honestly, I’m not sure. There was no cause for me to treat wounds down there. Only the diseases and syndromes of people who could afford me.”

“We’ll need to test that, then.”

“Right now?”

Her eyes widened with dismay. It was morning; the sun was shining, shifting some of the snow, so that icicles formed as it melted off the roof, and then refroze because the temperature must still be below freezing. And she did not want to find out whether she could close a gash in someone else’s flesh. There wouldn’t be awful poisoned waste, she suspected, like with a disease, but she feared what the consequences might be.

“Forget it,” Taye said from the doorway. “Leave her alone.”

Tanager flashed him a scornful look. “Ah, men, always the last to know. I guess you didn’t tell him you called Mockingbird, huh? This should be fun.”

“I’m sorry,” she said to Taye.

Doubtless he’d thought she was kidding about signing on, using it as a way to poke at him. But he didn’t know her if he thought she would passively permit him to arrange her future. She couldn’t permit him to make all the decisions like Rowan had. If these people wanted her, she’d pay her own way.

“Is this for real?” he asked Tanager.

“Oh, it’s happening,” the other woman answered.

Gillie slid from the bed. “Did you want to run some kind of test now?”

“Not yet. I’ve given Crow—you’d be best served to forget any other name—his first mission. He’s supposed to be on his way already, in fact. Hawk’s downstairs waiting for him.”

A knot formed in her stomach. While they were working in Detroit, not a day had passed when she hadn’t seen Taye; living together had been the practical solution. And maybe that was a sign she'd grown *too* dependent. It was time for her to find her own path.

"Christ, Tanager. I was going to ease her into it."

"Yeah, 'cos peeling the bandage off slowly works so much better." She got up and sauntered toward the door. "I'll give you guys five minutes. Then I expect *you* to head out, and for her to come with me."

"No problem," Gillie said.

Was this why he didn't want to sleep with me? Well, have sex. They'd slept together plenty over the past months.

Tanager walked out, quiet treads carrying her down the stairs. That left Taye—or should she call him Crow, now?—watching her in silence. She recalled they weren't supposed to use given names. Generally, nobody in the resistance even knew them. But special circumstances and all.

"Hawk is Silas," he told her, like she cared about that. "I didn't expect to see him again . . . but he got here a couple of hours before Tanager. When she arrived, I guess I should've wondered why they sent two contacts for one recruit."

"I knew if I told you, we'd spend our last day together arguing or with you sulking at me. That's not how I wanted this to go."

"Better we should drink wine and play Truth or Dare." But there was no recrimination in his tone, only tender regret. "I don't want to say good-bye to you."

"It's not forever. Is it?" Surely he wouldn't agree to those terms.

"I don't make the rules. Mockingbird does." His voice sounded strange. "I go where he sends me. That's the deal."

It hurt more than she could have ever imagined. The world, however unfamiliar, never frightened her until this moment because she knew he was nearby. She wondered if a baby bird, poised at the edge of a great height, knew such an instant of disorienting terror, or if it was simply all instinct and the need to fly overwhelmed everything else.

"Me, too," she replied. "But I didn't escape to trade one prison for another. I don't want to be wrapped in cotton and protected like a glass figurine. I'm going to work for them. And *live*."

"That's all I ever wanted for you, Gillie-girl."

"Oh, God." She put out her hands, and he took them, drawing her in.

For a moment, she leaned her head against his chest. His hands sifted into her bed-tousled hair, seeking the nape of her neck. As always, his touch roused the most delicious shivers. And then she ached because she didn't know if she would ever see him again. The reality of it might break her heart.

"Can I kiss you?"

Sometimes the man could be such an idiot. There was nothing he needed to ask her for; it was all his for the taking, but she wasn't bold enough to say so aloud. If he hadn't gotten the message by now, then he was a fool. So she merely nodded and lifted her face.

When his mouth touched hers, it held layers of bittersweet—all gentle farewell and *I wish it could be different.* That was when she understood. He did not expect to see her again. His lips clung and clung, but did not claim. Tears started in her eyes, but she didn't permit them to fall.

"Someday." It was a promise, the only one she could offer.

Someday when I *have the power, when the bastards are all dead—*

He offered a twist of a half smile and then turned. Gillie closed her eyes so she wouldn't see him walk away. Long moments later, she heard Tanager return, smelled her distinctive perfume, notes of orange blossom, honey, and vanilla. It was a more delicate scent than she would have associated with the woman's visual presence.

"I'm not sure if you know, but we maintain a pretty strict policy of noncontact between agents. If you don't know where any of them are, you can't tell."

"So you don't know how to get in touch with anyone at all?" That sounded scary, but she would be damned if she'd let the unknown intimidate her. At this point almost everything was unknown. Except Taye.

Outside an engine started. Silas must be taking charge of Taye. But she wouldn't get to find out where they were going. The less she knew, the less she could betray.

"Just Mockingbird. He didn't used to be so rigid about it, but there were . . . casualties." Her eyes darkened, remembered pain twisting the painted curve of her mouth.

"I'm sorry."

"Yeah, well. Shit happens, people die, and the world turns."

Despite such nihilism, Gillie couldn't help going to the window, seeking one last glimpse of him. She spied an SUV pulling out of the drive they'd shoveled together. Dark. Plates obscured by snow. It shouldn't hurt this much; it felt like dying.

"He's gone," Tanager said. "Off to mission impossible."

"Will it be that bad?"

The other woman shrugged. "Not for you to worry about. Do you need to pack?"

"No. I didn't manage to bring anything with me." *Not that I had much to start with.* "Where are we going from here?"

"Wichita. It's big enough for you to blend in."

"You don't think people will recognize me from the news?"

"Are you kidding? The only picture of you the Foundation could scrounge up was years old, and grainy to boot. We'll dye your hair, get some contacts, and nobody will look twice."

She hadn't focused on the quality of the picture on the tape, only what the newscaster was saying. "I'm glad I don't have to change my face."

"Blonde or brunette, then?"

Much as she hated to dye her red curls, it was better than the alternative. "Brunette."

"I have disposable contacts in green or brown. Which?"

"Green."

"'Kay. We'll do the makeover here before we head out."

To Gillie's bemusement, Tanager took charge of her, leading her to the bathroom downstairs. "You have the hair stuff with you already?"

"I come prepared, Cardinal."

"Is that my new name?" She didn't hate it. In fact, when she paired them together mentally, she kind of liked Cardinal and Crow.

"Yep. Mockingbird assigns all the names. Don't ask me how or why. I'm just the minion." But from her cocky grin, Tanager didn't believe that. "Now cop a squat on the toilet and let me do my thing."

Gillie did. First, the other woman drew out scissors and went snip, snip, snip. Just as well she couldn't see how bad it was. Based on Tan's own do, it might be terrifying. Red curls dropped to the floor, and she squeezed her eyes shut. But when Tan aimed her at the mirror, she saw it was pretty nice. She'd taken it off at the shoulders and given her some flirty layers.

"I like it."

Tan smirked. "I'll notify the queen." She rummaged in her bag and found a box of color in chocolate brown. "I'm gonna wrap some of your strands, so they don't get covered. The rest will go brown, and the red will look like highlights that you've put in. Nobody would ever suspect a natural redhead of going plain brown."

"You're good at this. Do you have training?"

"Kinda." Her tone discouraged further questions. Then she added grudgingly, "I do everything to my own hair. But I know lots of styles. I'm a bona fide beauty school dropout."

"Like Frenchie from *Grease*?"

"Sadly no guardian angel ever came to sing me back to high school."

"Would you have gone?"

"Hell no. Bend forward."

Gillie leaned down, elbows on knees, while the other woman deftly twined up some locks of hair in foil. That process took more than a little while. She sat quietly because she didn't know how to talk to people who weren't holding her prisoner. Well, except for Taye.

The chemical smell of the color permeated the small bathroom. Honestly, it felt kind of nice to have someone messing with her hair. She'd missed most of the years where her mom would do braids or curl it or help her fix it up for dances. Not that she thought Tanager was in any way mom material. But still . . . nice. It almost took her mind off where they'd send Taye—no, Crow—and what he'd be doing.

"Thanks for helping me."

"This is my *job*," Tan said briskly. "All right. We've got forty-five minutes to kill."

"I take it you have something in mind."

"Of course. We're gonna test you."

That sounded like an unpleasant echo of her days in the lab, but this was a house, not an underground secret facility. Sure, there was snow on the ground, but there were no locks or guards. Gillie told herself all that to calm her thumping heart. But her eyes widened when Tan raised her skirt and lowered her leggings.

"Uhm—"

"Relax. I've been shot in the back of the thigh. Hurts like a motherfucker."

"And you want to see what I can do about it."

"Unless you have a better plan for what to do while we wait."

"No, I'll try." She studied the wound and tried to remember.

Back in the labs, even with a blood connection, the process didn't start until she touched the patient.

So maybe I have a true laying-on-of-hands thing. Gillie took a deep breath and sealed her hand over the wound. Nothing.

"Shit. Maybe you can only do disease? Bummer." By Tan's tone, a disease-magnet wasn't going to prove too helpful.

"I think it's something about my blood. Come on." She removed her hand and led the way to the kitchen, where she pulled a knife out of the utensil drawer and made a tiny cut on her fingertip, just enough to draw a few drops.

This time, it was different. She tingled from the roots of her hair to the tips of her toes, as if energy was building there at the wound. Gillie touched Tan's thigh again, and anguish spiked into the back of her own leg, like she'd been shot herself. *Aw, fuck.* Her eyes went blind for a moment, but she didn't pull her hand away. She let the wild sensation continue its one-way rush, biting down on her lip to keep from crying out. A faint blue glow pulsated from her fingertips.

And when it was done, she felt sick and shaky. She pulled her hand away and found smooth skin on Tan's thigh.

"That hurt you," the other woman said softly.

"As you said, like a motherfucker."

"Pull down your sweats. I promise I'm not being a freak."

Gillie eased them down and craned over her shoulder to look. *Yeah. New scar.* It looked like an old gunshot wound, similar to the one in Taye's shoulder. "Looks like there's a kind of transference in what I do. But it seems I can heal wounds."

"Are you willing to do that again to save the lives of agents who are working against the Foundation?"

"Yes," Gillie said. "Absolutely."

Her body might well be a patchwork quilt of damaged flesh by the time they finished this war. That was fine. It would be so worth it. The people who fought against the Foundation needed her, and it would be a different kind of healing, cleaner and more satisfying.

"Sweet. Let's finish your hair and then we gotta scram. Your new life awaits."

CHAPTER 13

"I wonder why they decided to call you Crow," Silas said.

Oh, Taye knew he wasn't supposed to admit to knowing the man's name. But this guy had been his prison warden for years, though he hadn't been anything like coherent for most of them. And in the end, Silas had played an instrumental role in their escape.

He looked different these days. Not bald for one thing. He'd added ink. But there was life in his black eyes now; they were no longer the abyss where all hope went to die.

They both had their cases full of credentials, papers, cash, and weapons . . . and more important, their first target. After six hours of driving, they stood outside the warehouse. From the outside, it looked like any other abandoned building on the docks with broken windows and rusted panels. According to Mockingbird's data, it hid a facility similar to the one in Virginia, although it had fewer subjects and staff.

The sky was black, moonless, no stars either. A fine mist of clouds dotted the darkness, threatening rain, and a seaweed and dead-fish stink assaulted his nostrils, mixing with the smell of diesel fuel. It was almost time.

Leaving Gillie had just about killed him, but that was the deal. What she did past this point was up to her. Taye did have faith they would look out for her, though. Probably better than he could. These people had stayed a jump ahead of the Foundation for a long time, and now they were striking back. That took intelligence and organization.

"No idea. Why did he decide to call you Hawk?"

"It's a bird of prey," he answered, as if that explained everything, and maybe it did.

"Then I guess he thinks I'm a death bird." Shit, MB was more right than he knew. Before they went in, though, they needed to clear the air. "Are we supposed to pretend we don't know each other? Clearly we have . . . colorful history. How does he know I won't lose my shit and fry you like a chicken?"

The other man shrugged. "You want an apology? You've got one. But you can't hate me more than I hated myself."

When Taye examined his levels of hidden rancor and resentment, he realized he bore none for this man. The chip in his head had left Silas helpless to fight back. If a person did terrible things with a gun to his head, it wasn't the same as choosing that course. *So, yeah, clean slate.* He made a conscious decision to let it go.

"You were a victim, too. I get that. And you're evening up the score . . . I intend to help."

Hawk nodded, his dark eyes showing gratitude that he'd made it simple. "Since this is your first mission, I'll run the op. Once you've acclimated, we can switch. Mockingbird wants to see how we'll do as a tag-team wrecking crew."

"You handle the personnel, I make things go boom?" he guessed.

"That seems best, though I'm all for you watching my back."

"And vice versa."

Hawk nodded. "I'm good with that. Shall we move?"

"Why don't we wait until midnight? In the Exeter facility, they pared down the staff for third shift."

The other man checked his watch and then nodded. "Another half hour."

"What kind of resistance can we expect inside? The info was a little sketchy."

"It always is. The last place I hit had some orderlies, no professional guards. Most of the subjects couldn't be saved."

"Too wounded or mentally wrecked?"

"Both."

That could so easily be him or Gillie. The pain in his stomach jacked to excruciating—one day soon, he needed to get some pain meds, as it would soon become more than he could manage through willpower and determination.

"How do you fucking do it?"

"I tell myself, every place like this we find and shut down, that's more resources they lose. It has to hit a tipping point soon . . . they can't continue like this. The government's already getting interested."

Taye wished that made him feel better. Sadly, he could imagine the government picking up where the Foundation left off. "I hope you're right."

"Let's circle around and start taking out the cameras. That way we'll be ready to move at the witching hour."

"Roger that."

They crept along rows of shipping containers, all marked and coded. Some looked like they hadn't been touched in years. At the back of the warehouse, Hawk gestured silently at the first video camera.

"You want that blown up or for me to make it loop?" He could do both, something he suspected the Foundation still didn't know.

"Damn." Hawk drew the word out as he considered. "Looping would be best if you can configure it so it doesn't stop before we strike inside."

"As long as they're not too observant, it should work. The time of night is on our side."

Taye built the image in his head and then transferred it to the camera. He didn't know exactly how that worked, but it felt like an electrical surge. The air crackled a little as he executed the maneuver and it left his fingertips smoking a bit. That dark mass inside him swelled a little more. Knives sharpened against his stomach lining; it had been damn near impossible not to show how much he hurt in front of Gillie. These days, he didn't even want to eat. But he could hold it together through six missions.

Hawk gave him a thumbs-up. "There are two more, but as long as we angle our approach, I don't think we need to mess with them. We can slip in on this side."

"Sounds good."

Any excuse not to power up more than he had to. Burning

the candle at both ends might yield a bright, bright light, but it was fucking hell on the wax.

They crept along the blind spot to the back of the warehouse. Here, oil had spilled not too long ago; it pooled on the pavement in oily rainbows. Rusty barrels stood watch on either side of the door, probably in hopes of camouflaging the fact that the door itself was brand new, shiny metal in a building that had seen better days.

"What kind of security are we looking at?" he whispered to Hawk.

"Complicated. I need you to fry it."

He didn't need any extra juice for this. Throwing out a hand, a blue ripple trailed from his fingertips to the keypad beside the door. It shorted and the door clicked open. "Alarms?"

"Silent. They'll be ready for us from here on in."

Even his time down in the Exeter facility hadn't prepared him for what he found within. Taye gaped at the rows of cots and monitors, so many human beings thrown away. *So many.* Counting, he realized there were fifty beds in here. He imagined field hospitals in war zones must look like this. Only a couple of attendants on duty in the main room; there might be other staff on premises. If he shorted out the electricity here, these people would die, no question.

But maybe the better question was, were any of them truly alive? He glanced at Hawk for a signal. The big man was busy, face pale, and at a gesture, he had the two workers on the ground. He clenched both fists, and they clawed at their throats until their eyes bulged. Then they went limp.

"Dead?" he asked.

"Yeah. I don't leave witnesses. Unless I see hardware in their heads, I know they made the choice to be here. Money for misery doesn't profit on my watch. Let's clear the place."

In the second ward, they found more cots and more orderlies. Hawk took them out even faster, but his face looked like white linen afterward. His hands shook and he popped some pills. That didn't bode well for his long-term health.

Taye arched a brow. "You good to go on?"

"Yeah. It's not as bad as it looks."

"If you say so." He followed Hawk around the edges of the room, and they went out the far door into a dark, institutional hallway.

This was a cellblock, more of what he remembered from Exeter. Here, there was wailing and the pounding of fists against walls and doors. A woman wept in soft, heartbroken breaths.

He exhaled, knowing they'd have to make a decision about all these people. He was here because they wanted him to blow the place.

"I didn't expect so many," the other man said quietly. "I think this place is still functional. It's not just . . . storage."

"Is that what you found before?"

"Pretty sure."

"Fuck." The idea offended him.

"They've come down in the world, huh? No more expensive underground facilities. But I guess even mad scientists suffer from budget cuts." Hawk shook his head. "Let's see if we can find the labs. Mockingbird wanted me to copy any data we found."

Taye didn't ask why. They snaked down another hallway, and the labs lay at the end. Light came from beneath the doors.

"It's you again," he said. "If I go to work in there, I'll wipe all the drives."

"Or fry them."

"Either way," he gestured at the door. "Be my guest."

Hawk kicked the door open and terrified the sole lab monkey working on premises this late. He fumbled a slide and damn near pissed himself. But he didn't have time to plead long. Hawk snapped the tech's neck quick as a dog with a chicken wing. The reverb shook him that time, but the pills must be helping. He didn't blanch or stagger back. Calmly, he pulled out a flash drive. Fortunately, the goon's computer hadn't gone to screensaver yet, so no password required. They downloaded everything; Mockingbird could determine its value.

"I'll be back once we sort those folks out."

Hawk nodded and led the way back into the prison area. As he'd done months before, he overloaded the locks one by one. The doors kicked open.

Taye called, "We don't work for the Foundation. We're here to set you free."

"If they attack, they go down," Hawk said softly. "I feel for them, but we can't set them on an unsuspecting populace if they're unable to tell friend from foe."

"Got it."

They stood back, waiting for the exodus to begin.

"So this is Wichita. Why am I here exactly?" Gillie asked.

"Here" was a pretty apartment complex, picturesque with the delicate cover of snow. The buildings were Colonial New England style, cool blue, bordered with spacious walks and well-maintained private roads. They passed through an electronic gate with no trouble, so she guessed Tanager had been here already.

Tan signaled, driving with greater care than she usually did. Gillie might not have a brand-new ulcer if the woman didn't have a lead foot and a predilection for playing chicken with oncoming cars. It might also be the light layer of ice on the road, or it might be their surroundings. Respectable, no question. Quiet.

"This is your new home."

Her eyes went wide. "Really?"

"We rented you a one bedroom with den. Or you can use it for arts and crafts or to keep exotic animals. We really don't care. The point is, this is your home base."

"So I won't be doing field work?"

Tanager laughed softly, maneuvering around a curve. "You're not a fighter, Cardinal."

Her breath caught as the other woman parked the car. It was a nondescript sedan, but sleek and modern. She still couldn't get used to the new lines of the cars, even though it had been months. They seemed fragile to her, at least more so than before she had been taken.

"Neither are you, technically."

"No, but I can make men fight and die *for* me."

Gillie had no response to that. "Do I have a cover?"

"Yep. You're Grace Evans, a transfer student from Ohio."

"Transfer student?" She hated parroting like an imbecile, but everything had happened so fast. One minute she was in Taye's arms, and the next, he was kissing her good-bye. Gillie shoved the ache down, trying to focus on the here and now. Surely he was doing the same.

Tan swung out of the car, snagged a manila envelope out of the backseat, and beckoned impatiently. Her gaze cut in a wide circle, making sure the charming landscape didn't hide any unwelcome surprises. Since they had driven straight here and the woman hadn't used her ability, Gillie didn't see how it could. They should be safe. For now.

"I'll show you the apartment and give you the synopsis. Then we'll run some errands."

Christ. Talk about overwhelming. Tanager hit like a train wreck, and Gillie felt like the body being dragged along the tracks. Nevertheless, she ran up the walk behind the other woman, who let them into the building and went up to the second floor. Inside, the building was still clean and welcoming, quite a step up from where she'd stayed in Detroit.

The other woman unlocked the door to her apartment with a flourish. *My God. It's huge.* And it was pristine without resorting to the clinical white she'd hated underground. The carpet was beige; the walls were eggshell. All the fixtures shone, and the ceiling fan showed not a single speck of dust. She walked through, forgetting she was supposed to be briefed.

The front door opened into a good-sized living room. Angled in the far right corner, the kitchen was visible from that space, adjacent to the small dining area. To the left, she had a balcony overlooking a copse of trees. Taking a deep, disbelieving breath, she went on down the hall. First room on the left was presumably the den Tanager had mentioned. Next, she found the bedroom; it was considerably larger and had an enormous walk-in closet. Bath and laundry sat at the end of the hall on the right.

Finally, she turned and raised a brow at Tan. "Am I living here alone?"

"Yeah, why?"

Thank you.

"It's fantastic. I guess you want to tell me what I'll be doing now?"

"That'd be nice. Unless you'd like to open all the kitchen cabinets first."

Gillie grinned at her. "'Kay. Be right back."

"Noob." But there was certain amusement in her tone.

Once she explored to her satisfaction, they sat down cross-legged, facing each other on the living room floor. Gillie petted her carpet. "I'm listening."

"Like I said before, you're Grace Evans, a transfer student from Ohio."

"What happened to her?"

"The kid died on vacation, and Mockingbird snagged the death notice before it could make its way through channels, and . . . now you're her."

"Does she have family?" It seemed inordinately cruel if she did.

"None that we could find. Only child, adopted by older parents who passed on during her first year of school."

"That's so damn sad."

"Focus. We figure it's unlikely anyone will see an IRA operative in the innocent face of Grace Evans from Ohio. Crow told us you want to go to college. Well, we can work with that."

"I wanted to go for real."

"And you will. You have sixty-three hours of transfer credit. She was studying business, but she hadn't gotten deep into her major. Those taken are mostly humanities and liberal arts requirement classes."

"Which I haven't passed."

"For fuck's sake. Read *The Odyssey* and smoke a bowl with a philosophy major."

"I'll look up the required reading."

"Seriously?" Tanager shook her head. "Whatever floats your boat, I guess. Anyway, you're smack in the center of the US, which is perfect. Among other things, we'll be using your apartment as a safe house for agents recovering from wounds. I've already proofed the place. Painted with the special tungsten blend, and then did a cover coat. You can power up safely within these walls, and we'll expect you to care for anyone we send your way. In return, we pay your living expenses and your tuition. You can study whatever the fuck you want."

Gillie considered. "So counseling is fine with you?"

"Ah, Jesus. You want to be a headshrinker? That's hilarious."

She bridled. "Why?"

"Cardinal, you gotta be beyond fucked up from your time underground. Maybe you just want to poke in other people's neuroses to avoid your own?"

Maybe.

Tanager went on, "We do expect you to act like a college student. You're supposed to be three years younger than you are, but you're small, so I don't think it'll be a prob."

"I'm . . . twenty-two?"

"Twenty-one. Don't be a smart-ass. I know you haven't hit the quarter-century marker yet."

Gillie nodded at the packet Tanager was twirling on the bare floor. "Is all of this in there? The facts I need to know about Grace?"

"Yep. You'll need to go get your student ID tomorrow. We have a driver's license in here for you, but I'm thinking you don't know how to drive."

She arched a brow. "When would I have learned?"

"You make a good point. You're less than five miles from campus, so you might take the bus or you can get a bike."

"Bike."

"So I take it you know how to ride?"

Gillie smiled. It was one of the best memories she had. After she recovered from the leukemia, her dad had taught her—a few years later than other kids, but yeah. She still remembered the pleasure of pumping her legs and flying down the sidewalk, wind in her hair. Her dad's laughter rang out: bright memory, a silver star of childhood.

"Yeah."

"Final business before we head out. Mockingbird wanted to furnish for you, order online. But since this is the first place you've ever had to decorate yourself, I figured you might want to pick your own stuff out."

Pure happiness. Gillie launched herself and hugged Tan. The other woman warded her off with an *oh what the hell* look. "Uhm. Yeah. You're welcome."

"No guy would have ever understood. But you're so right. I will be *so* much better equipped to deal with whatever comes my way here, as long as I can put my mark on this place."

"Right. Anyway, you have a Visa card in the packet. Nice limit. MB will take care of clearing it for you. Last thing—there's a cell phone in there. You need to have that on you *at all times.* It needs to be charged *at all times.* He has to be able to get a hold of you if we need you for an op."

"I thought I wasn't doing field work."

"You're not. But it's a just-in-case precaution, and part of the deal. Take it or leave."

"Sold."

"'Kay." Tan pushed to her feet. "Then let's get to Crazy Jay's. You have some furniture to pick out, and he has some nice shit. After that, you need clothes suitable for a co-ed."

Nuts. I don't have a wallet for my credit card, a purse for my cell phone, or any idea how to drive a car, and yet I have a license to do so. That gave her a clear idea how powerful her allies were. Taye had certainly made the right choice because she was feeling more hopeful than she ever had. Maybe if she cooperated and saved some lives, they would relax the "no contact between agents" rule. If she fought hard enough, she'd see him again.

"Toiletries, too."

"Yeah, yeah. I have orders to make sure this place looks like a normal person lives here by the time I leave town."

"Then let's get to it."

CHAPTER 14

Chicago bit in winter, but this was where the Foundation wanted to do the exchange. Since it wasn't too far from Detroit, and he had been eager to put the motor city behind him, Cale had agreed. Now he sat in Clarke's Diner in Lincoln Park, waiting for his contact. The waitress had already taken his order.

The place was close to DePaul University, so there was a mix of neighborhood folk and college students. He remained watchful as a man in a black knit cap walked in the door. It was angled so it didn't show much of the shape of his head, and the heavy beard covered the rest.

Cale lifted a hand, waving them over. He recognized the girl at least from an e-mail attachment. The man didn't linger long, just glanced at Cale's ID, then he muttered to the woman, "Siddown. The man's havin' dinner."

Rude little prick, aren't ya? He eyed the man as he left, and then studied the woman before him. She was tall, close to five-ten. His weird contact at the Foundation said her name was Kristin Shaw, but she only answered to Kestrel. She was also very thin—model thin—which would've been elegant if her skin wasn't so pasty. Her hazel eyes held a dull weight, and her shoulders slumped as she bore his scrutiny.

Yeah, there's something wrong with this one.

But she sat, as instructed. Misery covered her from head to toe.

"Care for a bite to eat?"

The waitress brought his meal as she shook her head. From the looks of her, she hadn't eaten anything much in a while. His foreboding about this assignment deepened. Cale needed the edge she could offer but he didn't look forward to spending long hours in her company. He ate fast and dropped a twenty for the server.

"You fine to travel?" he asked.

Somehow he didn't think the usual pleasantries would bear any fruit. She gave a mute nod and got up. It didn't seem right to accept charge of another human being without her saying a word, but these Foundation fuckers were a weird lot. There was no telling what they'd done to keep her cooperative and quiescent. At the very least, she was drugged. His unease returned; this wasn't the way he did business.

Cale led the way out to his car. She put her bag in the backseat and then climbed in front, obedient as a child. *Or a lobotomy patient.* This whole contract stunk to hell. *The last of your retirement fund,* he told himself. Smart mercs didn't stay in the biz after their reflexes slowed; as with professional athletics, thirty-five was old in his game, and he was three years past that. *So try not to think how pathetic she is. Focus on what she can do.*

"Is anybody powered up right now?"

They'd explained to him how she worked, but he couldn't imagine what it must be like. So he was trying to understand. To best make use of a tool, he had to grasp it from all angles. But now he found himself reluctant to use her at all, just from fifteen minutes in her company. That didn't entirely make sense, but he had a strong feeling he should give her back before it was too late. Too bad the man who'd brought her was long gone, making her Cale's responsibility.

"There are eight talents being used at this time."

"You can sense all of them?"

"It's like a tangled ball of yarn." Toneless. "I can see all the colors but I'm not sure where one stops and the other begins."

"How does that impact your tracking?"

"If more than twenty power up at once, I pass out." Still no reaction. She gave no sign the revelation bothered her. "I can't handle that much information."

"But you can track one particular person's ability."

"It's intermittent. I get a sense of where they are, and the closer we get in physical proximity, the more I home in. It works as long as they don't bombard me."

"Bombard?"

"A bunch of them powering up at once to incapacitate me. I think they do it on purpose."

"Fuckers. Are either of the ones we're looking for active at this time?" Cale started the motor and put the car in gear.

She cocked her head, probably sorting through the signals, but it gave her an oddly birdlike air. "No."

Then he didn't care who the other weirdoes were. He wasn't being paid to track them down. "I guess we'll have to do this the old-fashioned way for now."

She turned away in complete disinterest. Her eyes closed. He'd seen prisoners in war-torn countries behave the same way. Shut out the jailors, fly away from the torment. But he hadn't done a damn thing to her. It rankled. Generally when somebody treated him like this, he'd fucking well earned it. But there was no telling what the Foundation had done to her, and that bothered him. He'd expected a colleague, not a prisoner.

As he drove, the phone rang. "Dunn."

"I've got some news for you." Hausen's voice sounded crystal clear despite the distance, a wonder of modern technology.

"Go."

"Your boy's named Tyler Golden. Born in Miami. He's been picked up on multiple charges of vagrancy, loitering, drunk and disorderly, one count of public indecency. Did eighteen months for assault and battery. He dropped off the grid about five years ago."

Christ. "Did you find his next of kin for me?"

"Of course." Hausen gave the name and address, which Cale scrawled in the notebook he kept in the dashboard of his car. He glanced at his silent passenger. "Wanna go on a road trip?"

Didn't matter how she answered, of course. They had a job to do. And he might learn something about this Tyler Golden from talking to his family. Cale understood he had to learn his prey inside and out before he could run it to ground.

Not surprisingly, she didn't respond. He tapped the city name into the GPS and made a U-turn as soon as he could. Nothing dramatic. No squealing of tires or near collision. Yet she cried out. Pain etched her features, two blue veins throbbing at either side of her temples. Her lips were so pale they looked gray, and though she took great sucking breaths, she couldn't seem to get enough oxygen.

"What's wrong?"

Kestrel turned her head, regarding him with a blasted expression. He thought he'd witnessed every bad thing known to man, every horror, all possible types of damage. But in her hazel eyes, he saw hell.

"I feel them all."

"Who?" Despite himself, he knew pity for her, and something like kindness. It didn't seem right, what they were doing to her.

"The ones you want me to find. They're in my head. Along with so many more."

"Can't you turn the others off, focus on the two we need?"

"No." Tears welled from the corners of her eyes, but he felt sure it was wholly unconscious. She wasn't looking at him to see how he was taking her display. Instead her hands came up to cover her face, and she hunched over. "I'm up to nineteen now. I can't—"

Before she could complete the sentence, Kestrel slumped to the side, her face gone slack. *Christ.* Her agony made him glad he had human capabilities and limitations. Cale grabbed a jacket from the back, balled it up for her to use as a pillow, and tucked it beneath her head.

For her sake, he hoped she stayed out. Even if she could give him an edge in his search, he didn't like seeing women in pain, something of an Achilles' heel—one that had gotten him in trouble more than once. *Don't be stupid, mate. Not with this one. She's part of the job . . . and you can't save her.* With a sigh and a shake of his head, he stepped on the gas.

Tanager eyed Finch. He was the oldest of the agents, in his mid-forties at least. Short, dumpy, and balding, he was the closest thing to invisible without actually having it as a superpower. He always dressed in gray or brown, enhancing his low profile. She figured he had to hate meeting up with her because she was anathema to going unnoticed.

He gave her the once-over in turn. She grinned and struck a pose, hand on hip. Today she wore a plaid miniskirt, tall striped socks, combat boots, a white blouse, and a black tie. Her red tailored coat hung on the hook near the door. A rundown bar full of drunks and losers was the last place anybody would expect to find important business taking place; those same patrons would also never be able to give a credible description of either of them. That was why she'd chosen this place.

"I'm supposed to wipe the last forty-eight hours," he said.

"I know." Truthfully, she was a little sorry about that.

She'd enjoyed shopping with Cardinal. The kid clearly never had so much fun, which was pretty sad. But it was far safer if Tan couldn't remember where she was. Anyone who spent recovery time with her would get a visit from Finch. It was the only way to maintain privacy. The only way to make sure what happened to Ginnie didn't happen to anybody else. That had been before the code names, before the privacy, before all the rules. Shit, that had been before Mockingbird went into his bubble.

"It might get messy. It's hard to be precise about such a short time." He had a gravelly voice, that of a chain smoker. To her ears, he talked like Lou Reed sang. If she was a blind woman, she could get down with him.

"I'm ready."

Finch cupped her face in his hands and leaned in like he would give her a kiss. Instead he laid his head against hers. She didn't know if he needed contact to work his mental mojo, or if that was just his way of getting close to women he'd never otherwise touch. There was nobody like him on the planet. The Foundation had nobody who could implant suggestion and make a target forget. They'd come close to snatching him in Ecuador; Mockingbird took even greater precautions with him now.

The music throbbed low, John Lee Hooker crooning in the background, and the world wavered. A metal spike slammed into her brain.

Distortion. Reverb. Finch's face loomed.

Red lights. Wailing metal.

Ginnie was onstage, making love to the mic. To her baby sister, she was the coolest thing on two legs. Great voice, great bod. Everything she needed to be a rock star. Ginnie had an advantage, though, and it was gonna make her a million dollars. When she sang the words to "I'm Gonna Make You Love Me," a classic rebooted with raw power and a punk edge, the crowd fell for her. Every one of them wanted to take her home—male, female, or other—it didn't matter. Ginnie held them all in the palm of her hand.

Possibly because of their close blood ties, she didn't feel the same maddened pull. She did swell with pride, bouncing in the pit with her arms in the air. She'd dropped out of high school to follow her sister. With a fake ID, nobody cared she was fourteen, and Ginnie watched out for her. In fact, her sister kept a switchblade in her boot at all times. She was a total badass; it wasn't just show for the music. She had real ink and real attitude. It was the only way she'd kept the two of them safe over the years.

Their parents had died when she was twelve and Ginnie sixteen. She'd said the foster system was for suckers—they'd wind up separated, and there was no way in hell that they were letting that happen. Using her mother's license, they'd rented a shitty apartment and made do for a year with her babysitting money and what Ginnie could earn at minimum wage. But clearly they were meant for better things. Her sister sang like an angry angel, and she got in with a band. The next year was better—no more dead-end job. They'd traveled and partied and skirted the edge of bad, bad trouble.

Now raw talent—and that extra push—was paying off. The shithole clubs were scaling up. She'd heard of this place called the Rat, and groupies told her that acts got famous playing here. She fucking hoped so; she'd been all around putting up fliers for Dead Girls Dance.

One day, she and Ginnie would rule the world. With her brains and Ginnie's sexy-raw voice, they were going places. No doubt. No stopping them.

That night, she sang along in the audience, drinking in the energy—the sweat and the adulation. It carried an irresistible high. But to her surprise, Ginnie leaned down and hauled her up on stage. *Shit. She's never done that before.* She could sing and play a little bass, but Ginnie had never wanted her drawing the public eye. Protective shit.

But she leaned in, belting out the words to "Wrecking Ball," one of their originals. They covered a lot of the punk greats, but Ginnie wrote her own stuff, too:

You came, you saw, you conquered
Didn't you, motherfucker
Open my arms, open my thighs
You'd think I'd be goddamn wise
To a man like you/Swinging through
Like a . . .
Wrecking ball!/Wrecking ball!

The audience went wild at the rage in the lyrics, but she cut a look at her sister, who gave her an encouraging nod. She sang on.

The mood turned. A flip of the coin—love to hate. Maybe this wasn't the right song for the end of the set. Fear gripped her. Something was happening to her voice as she sang; it wasn't good. Not like Ginnie. It didn't inspire love. This was dark, dark—metal spike through the brain. It all went black. Past pain receded into the distance.

"Welcome back," Finch said.

"Christ. I *hate* that."

"Yeah. Sorry. I never was very good at Operation."

"I'd have more sympathy if you hadn't just made such a fucking mess in my skull."

"Bad one this time?"

"Yeah." She said no more. Too private. Too personal. That memory belonged to a different version of herself, one who had a real name, not just Tanager.

"I didn't erase anything I wasn't supposed to, did I?" Back in the early days, Finch would sometimes wipe too much, as if he were pruning roses with a machete.

"No." The ache was perfect and fresh. Maybe in a way, she owed him thanks for that. Time had a way of healing wounds over, leaving only the echo of phantom pain. Now she remembered why she was doing this, why the fight would never end as long as she drew breath.

"Can you tell me where you were yesterday?"

Blank wall. She shook her head and pushed off the bar stool. To the other patrons, they had shared an intimate moment—that was all. She snagged her coat and walked out the door, unable to speak for the tears tightening her throat. She still couldn't make people love her with her voice. Not like Ginnie. Tan was the evil twin; she had the darkness.

Sometimes Tanager considered asking him to blank her past completely. *Nothing to see here, folks, move along.* But even though they hurt like a bitch, she couldn't give up those memories. She had nothing else left.

CHAPTER 15

A skeletal, wild-haired witch came screaming out of her cell. She launched herself at Taye, paying no heed to his reassuring words. She didn't appear to have any words left; fire balled from her hand, and he dove wide. The flames slammed into the wall behind him. Without waiting for Hawk's call, he pulled, lightning crackling from his fingertips. The darkness inside him swelled, bringing the shadow-pain to life, but he ignored it as the electricity fried her.

The insane subject arched and screamed, giving pause to those shambling out of their cells. Most were pale, thin, and weak, but none of them attacked.

"What are we supposed to do now?" one asked.

Hawk answered, "If you can remember a number, I'll tell you who to call. If you're interested in fighting back, he can help you. Otherwise, you're on your own. Just be aware that there are hunters, and they can track use of your powers."

"I can remember," a woman said.

Taye gave Mockingbird's special ping-only line. As a group, their lips moved, memorizing it.

"I have a pen," Hawk added. "If anyone wants to write it down."

One of the men stepped forward, tall, thin, and freckled; he moved sluggishly, as if he was drugged. He motioned for the pen and wrote the number on his palm. Slowly, he printed more, and then flashed the message to Taye: *My brain's not what it used to be.* Somehow, the Foundation had stolen his voice.

"Mine either," Taye told him.

He had stood in their shoes. Right now he knew exactly how they must feel: terrified and helpless. Anger surged through him, so strong it nearly kindled the lightning without his will. The lights shimmered overhead, and Hawk cut him a sharp look. He could read the question: *You okay?* Taye nodded, locking the power down; the current steadied overhead.

For now anyway. There would come a time when the pain would be so great that he wouldn't be able to control it—or himself. The surges came more often these days, inexplicable and uncontainable. Hawk might have to put him down, if the power outpaced the disease killing him. But he wouldn't think about that today.

"Here." His partner was giving them each fifty bucks, more than they'd had when they broke out of the Exeter facility. "That will get you food, clothes, public transportation. The rest is up to you."

One of the women—short and plain with shadowed brown eyes and a shaven head—came up to Hawk and shook his big hand with both of hers. "My name is Holly," she said. "It would mean a lot to me if you said it. I've been H-156 for so long."

Hawk smiled down at her. "You're free, Holly. Good luck."

The others seemed to take that as a dismissal; they moved toward the exit. But an idea struck Taye.

"We should use them," he said, low.

The other man eyed him. "What do you mean?"

"Move the cots outside. I can't kill those people, man. I just can't do it. Some of them might wake up, if they're taken off the drugs and given proper medical care."

"So what, we move them out to the docks and—"

"Blow the place, as planned. Then we call 911."

"The authorities will have a field day trying to figure out what the hell happened, where all those sick people came from. And anything that makes trouble for the Foundation will be all right with MB."

"Wait," Taye called. "We need your help."

"I knew it," one of the men muttered.

"Too good to be true," another agreed.

Hawk shook his head. "It's not what you think. There are about a hundred test subjects like you in this facility. Only they're not ambulatory. We want you to help us get them out before we destroy this place. It'll take ten, fifteen minutes, tops."

"I'll help," Holly said. "I never thought I'd feel lucky but at least I can still walk."

The others muttered, and then a short, stocky subject said, "Okay. But can't we expect their guards to start arriving soon? There are usually more of them here and they can't be too far away, even though it's the middle of the night."

"If they come while we're working, then you fight," Taye told them. "Anything you can do. Power up. Leave nobody to tell the tale."

Short & Stocky nodded, his eyes fierce. "I can shake the place down to rubble."

"Leave that as a last resort," Hawk cautioned. "A quake might take out the people we're trying to save."

"Gotcha."

Taye asked, "So we're ready to rock and roll?"

"Aw, yeah." A dark-skinned man rubbed his hands together. "I am *so* down for this."

"Let's move." Hawk led the makeshift squad out into the second ward.

A gasp went through the subjects who had been kept locked up. Taye guessed they were like him: dangerous. But primarily to those who had run the experiments. None of them looked crazy like the woman he'd put down, and they all seemed horrified by what had been done to those lying on the cots.

"Take them out the back," Hawk called. "Out through the cell block and behind the warehouse. Crow, can you blow the lock?"

"On it."

He jogged back the way they'd come as the others each took a cot and a machine, wheeled for portability. Taye found the back door without trouble; it looked like a business entrance. There, he even found a time clock. Apparently, the guards worked regular hours; they punched in and out. What kind of bastards worked in a place like this and never experienced a crisis of conscience? It was insane. Doubtless Hawk wanted a clean getaway but he hoped the silent alarm brought the Foundation goons out in droves because he wanted to fry them all.

Taye popped the lock with a surge of current and swung the door open. The night was cold, so his breath whirled as he held it for Holly. She had the first patient, her face quiet and determined. Others followed her. He went to help with the rescue and relocation, but it was impossible to run as he wanted because of the tubes. Nobody knew what a loss in connection might do or what experiments these people had undergone. If a bunch of them woke up, crazed as the fireball lady, while they fought the Foundation, it wouldn't be pretty.

They had cleared the first ward when the sound of multiple engines came roaring across the docks. Taye sprinted to a window and peered out.

"SUVs full of Foundation goons," he called. "They won't be looking to take us alive."

Not like Gillie or him. But they didn't know he was here. So they'd hit hard with bullets, not tranqs. They undoubtedly had instructions to torch this place and leave no evidence behind. That was how they operated.

"Incoming," Hawk bellowed to those taking victims out the back. "Flank them. If you're combat ready, now's the time for you to shine. If you aren't, keep ferrying the others out. The Foundation needs to take this facility out now. It's become a liability."

"Understood."

Taye raced back and slipped out alongside the man who had been spoiling for a fight. Together, they hugged the side of the warehouse, sticking to the shadows. The goons were unloading, assembling weapons and gear. Outfitted in black, they moved like they knew how to bring the hurt, more prepared for action than the orderlies had been down in Exeter. Surface facilities offered greater security challenges than those underground, but they had to be cheaper.

One solitary voice barked orders outside. "Clean it. If it moves, put a hole in it. Jackson, I want you laying charges. Whatever the cost, our goal is containment. Nothing leaves, you got me? Nothing leaves."

Taye slid a look at the man beside him. The guy answered with a curt nod; he was ready to rock and roll. Without asking what the other man could do, he let the lightning come. It sizzled through him so he swore he could feel his nerve-endings going from medium rare to extra crispy. The current raised his hair, floating it around his face, and the guy gave him a thumbs-up.

"If we're fighting together, I guess you should know my name's Oliver."

"Nice to meet you, Oliver. I look forward to kicking some ass with you tonight." He didn't have the heart to tell the guy that Mockingbird didn't like them exchanging names. It was the best way to keep everyone safe. Taye understood from experience that he wanted to feel human again. Taking his name back was the first step.

"You know they called me O-298? I felt like a fucking prisoner in a concentration camp. I done time where I didn't feel so . . ." Words failed him.

Taye knew just what he meant. "I was T-89."

"That mean you were taken before me?"

"I guess. You ready?"

Oliver nodded, moving forward. A blue white glow kindled at Taye's fingertips and rippled along his right arm; he threw lightning arcs most often with it. He waited to see if his temporary partner needed to power up, but he shook his head and waved him forward. Whatever he did, it was instantaneous, like Hawk. This should be entertaining.

They hit the SUVs first.

You heard the man. Nothing leaves. Including you assholes.

Taye slammed the gas tanks, and the vehicles went up in an orange fireball, rocking the pavement. To dodge scraps of burning metal, he took cover behind some barrels. Automatic gunfire sprayed the cylinders, which sucked because they started spewing chemicals. God only knew what in a place like this. Could be anything from crude oil to toxic waste.

He scrambled away just as another round came in. Whatever was inside the containers, the shit was flammable. The liquid caught; fire blazed a path wherever it ran, and a chill wind blew it back toward the Foundation goons.

"Cover me," Oliver said.

In reply, Taye fired dual bursts from each hand, suppression rather than intent to fry. He didn't have the juice; these sparklers were just for show, and to ignite the liquid trickling toward the goons. The SUVs burned merrily, black smoke swirling up toward the dark sky; they also gave the only light for several hundred yards. Which meant their enemies couldn't see them too well. Taye would present a better target with the energy crackling around him, but he couldn't help that. He'd just have to keep moving. As he tucked and rolled, a spray of bullets hit the pavement behind him. Broken bits of cement stung him, even as something bit into his arm. Flesh wound.

He levered up with his good arm and saw Oliver going at a run. Shadow wrapped him like a living force; it was hard to get a good look at him for the roiling mass around him. He was like a walking cold spot, so wrong it hurt to look at him. His shadow drank those men in.

Their bodies wavered and went amorphous, lines pulled as if they were photos a kid spun through some weird Photoshop filter. They fought and screamed, but they fell into him as if he had irresistible gravitational pull. The shadow swelled, pulsing with an eerie black purple light. Then it dropped away, and Oliver stood alone, hands on his knees. Black sand at his feet blew away with the wind, skittering across the pavement toward the open ocean.

"Fuck," he breathed. "Mockingbird's damn sure gonna want to recruit you."

"I don't know if I'm down for that," Oliver said. "That shit . . . it don't feel right. I got parts of them inside me now. Like I can hear them screaming, I can feel every bad thing they ever done. I don't need more of that . . . I got my own burdens."

Damn. At least the lightning's just killing *me.*

"Well, hear him out at least. It'll be hard for you to stay free on your own . . . and I ought to know."

"You signed on 'cause they were hunting you so hard?"

"Yeah. They want to sell me to China, and I'm guessing what you can do would be worth a lot, too."

Screams came from the other side of the warehouse, reminding him that while they had won one fight, it wasn't over. Not by a long shot. And unlike the Foundation thugs, Taye cared about safeguarding those he could. These folks had suffered enough. Maybe it had been wrong to use them to try and evac the ones hooked up to those machines. Maybe he should have told them to run, blown the place, and let the unconscious ones die.

But he didn't have it in him to play God. Not after what had been done to Gillie and himself. He was a foot soldier, not a decision maker. This was Mockingbird's war.

"This way," Oliver muttered.

The other man took off. Taye knew a ripple of pride, watching him. *This is true bravery. The man's barefoot in the snow in his fucking prison pajamas, fire burning all around, and he cares. He* cares. Though the Foundation hadn't meant to—and despite Rowan's megalomania—they had, in fact, created a new breed of human, where pain lifted him above life's circumstances and made him willing to fight. That personal anguish refined the goodness in them and burned away the damage. Like him, some of these folks had probably been completely worthless before the Foundation forged them into something new, something strong and wild and utterly empowered. Sadly, the process wasn't working out the way the company had hoped; they weren't loyal drones. They were heroes.

It gave him chills.

Or maybe that's just the wind. Get a move on, dumb shit.

He followed Oliver around; they paused at the corner to check out the situation. Foundation goons had Holly and a couple of other women pinned down. They weren't fighters; but even these women, who—like Gillie—could not set someone on fire or break their bones, tried to protect the comatose patients.

The pop of automatic weapons cascaded. Four gunmen. Sparks brightened the night with each spray. One girl—she couldn't have been more than eighteen—took five bullets in the chest, standing in front of the gurney, blocking the shots with her fragile body. He didn't know who was laying on it. Taye doubted she did either. That wasn't the point.

True courage. He'd never seen it before this night. Blood spread across her thin, gray pajama top, and she slumped forward. Red stained the dirty snow, innocence lost.

That could be Gillie.

Madness took him then. The lights were still on, a bare bulb outside the back door. Knowing he'd die faster, Taye threw a hand out, drawing the electricity to him. It rolled through his body like a flashflood, kindling a weird amber glow beneath his skin. He took too much power this time; his skin pulsed with it. In addition to the lightning, his magnetism rose. He didn't use that much because he didn't have good control over it. Like the electricity, it hurt him.

His whole body blazed in white-hot anguish. The medical equipment beeped, drawn to him uncontrollably. *Shit, no. I don't want to kill everybody back here. Gotta keep from going*

Chernobyl here. I just want to take out these assholes. But the feeling just got bigger and bigger, swelling past what he could manage or contain.

The muzzles of their machine guns bent, yearning toward him. A couple of them lost their grips and the weapons flew, slamming into Taye. He didn't need guns. He was the fucking weapon, a bomb about to blow.

"Get them out of here," he said to Oliver in a guttural voice. "I don't know how long I can hold this back."

The other man didn't hesitate. While Taye gave chase, he went to work hustling the women out of the combat zone. It was an equal-opportunity decision; if any of them had been able to kill, they'd have done so already. Therefore, they needed to be out of harm's way.

His right arm burned from the combination of raging power and the gunshot wound; the feeling swelled like a rain-flooded river. In the dark, enemy radios crackled, but before they could call for help, he exploded them. Showers of sparks rose up, orange embers drifting on the night wind. They turned to run then. No weapons, no way to call for help, and the rest of the mercs on the other side of the warehouse.

Even Mother Nature worked against them. Their boots slipped on the frozen ground, and Taye flung himself after them. He *used* the ice, skidding onto his knees, arms upraised. Gillie was safe. There was nothing to hold him back anymore. Ball lightning exploded from his whole body and it caught the mercs before they got out of the blast radius. Equipment caught fire behind him, and he heard the groan of warping metal. The back door flew off its hinges and came banging toward him. He damped the magnetism and dove low, so that it struck the burning men like a giant battering ram.

That eased some of the pain, but Taye felt the damage settle deeper inside him. Now it felt like dark tendrils, gnawing their way through him. He stumbled to his feet, fingertips smoking, and holding on to the building, he staggered around the other side. Hawk fought alongside a couple more subjects. His eyes wouldn't focus, so he couldn't track the exchange too well. He leaned against the wall, trying to gather a little strength, and then, confident Hawk had it under control, he went to supervise the extraction of the remaining victims.

CHAPTER 16

Gillie rode a bike for the first time in over ten years on snowy sidewalks, and that sense of freedom felt exactly the same. Sure, there was some risk, some wobbling, and some sheer exhilarating terror. But it was all hers. She wore her winter coat, along with hat and gloves; people stared at her strangely from the steamy windows of their cars, but the apartment wasn't that far from campus. And those few miles flew by, despite the cold.

I'm not Gillie now. I'm Grace. Or Cardinal, depending on who's asking.

It wasn't normal to have so many names, but she wasn't looking for that anyway. She just wanted to live. This qualified.

She found the Rhatigan Student Center without too much trouble, and they directed her to the room on the first floor where she could get a photo ID. Her hands shook a little while she waited in line behind other students. Normal people. She kept expecting someone to call her out as an impostor, but the pointing finger of shame never materialized.

Eventually, her turn came and she presented her registration paperwork and her fake driver's license. She stifled a grin while Mrs. Mott typed away on the computer; her lack of personal attention meant she saw nothing wrong—just another student to process. Gillie could hardly contain her giddiness. Everyone else looked so bored . . . and why wouldn't they be? Standing in lines sucked if you were anyone else. But she'd never stood in one in her life, apart from shopping. It was all so gloriously new. Most likely, the crowds would be worse in the fall. These were midyear transfers or people starting late.

The girl who took her picture looked like she might be a student herself. She was friendlier than the woman at the window. "I need you to take off the hat. Do you want a minute to brush your hair?"

"Yeah, I guess I better." But she was new at this, so she didn't have one. Gillie tousled her shorter hair as best she could and smiled for the camera.

To her surprise, it didn't take long at all to make her Shocker ID card, and she nodded while receiving the spiel about everything on campus it could be used for, including the library and loading money for food or copy machines. Just like that, and she was officially Grace Evans, transfer student from Ohio. She would do her best to fit in, like Tanager wanted, while keeping her eyes and ears open. For what, she didn't know exactly. Maybe she would learn more if she found something out of the ordinary here, though part of her wondered, *In Kansas? Really?* But doubtless people thought Virginia was totally wholesome, too, and look what had happened there.

"Now don't lose it," the girl said, grinning as she handed the card over.

"Thanks."

And just like that, she became a student.

Gillie tried to acclimate herself to becoming Grace from Ohio. She read a bunch of classics in the evenings, attended classes, bought textbooks, rode her bike eight miles a day, and spent long hours in the library. In the back of her mind, Taye burned like a quiet candle, flickering warmth. But she couldn't have him right now. First she had to prove to herself—and to everyone else—that she could handle the real world on her own. She looked on this separation as a test, and once she passed—

"I see you here just about every afternoon." A kid—with his tousled emo hair and his rock T-shirt, she couldn't think of him any other way—stood beside her table, a backpack slung over one shoulder.

She nodded. "I switched majors. I feel like I have some catching up to do."

Was that normal? Casual tone, no big deal. But it was, actually. This was the first conversation she'd had with anybody on campus apart from *pass these back.*

"Oh?" Uninvited, he took the chair across from her.

She chanced a look around the library; this wasn't the only vacant table. From all the endless television she'd watched, he had either placed a bet with his frat buddies that he could bang her or he was interested in getting to know her better. Gillie stifled a grin, wondering how many people based their insights into human nature on teen dramas that aired on The WB.

"I was taking business in Ohio, but it's boring. When I transferred, I decided to try counseling. See if I can help people."

"That's cool. I'm majoring in music."

From the hair and the personal style, she'd surmised as much. "And you play guitar."

"How'd you know?"

"Lucky guess."

"I like your streaks," he said.

My . . . oh. Right. I'm a brunette now. If only she could get used to the contacts.

"Thanks."

When Gillie checked the clock on the far wall, she saw it was almost time for her next class. "Gotta bounce." Did people actually say that or was it a TV thing? She felt like such a loser faking this stuff.

"Hey, you didn't tell me your name."

Gillie.

"Grace."

"I'm Brandon."

"Maybe I'll see you around." That sounded suitably disinterested.

Gillie lifted a hand as she shouldered her bag and headed out. Over the next day, she noticed she was more earnest and dedicated than everyone else. The other undergrads milled around campus, met in coffee shops, and made plans to attend parties.

And that was the aspect of college she couldn't figure out. The classes were pure pleasure—and far easier to fall into the work than worry about socialization. But if she didn't find a way to break that last barrier, she might as well still be a prisoner with Rowan bringing her books. Sitting in classrooms with other people didn't make her free.

But she wasn't going to worry about that today. Not when the sun was out, reflected on the melting snow. She rode her bike home, backpack bulging with books. Tonight she had papers to write and assigned reading. Maybe it was weird, but she liked being graded—tangible reward for work.

But all the normal vanished in the blink of an eye. In her apartment, she found a strange man waiting. He was tall and thin, more than Taye, not as much as Silas. He had copper-cast hair and odd, achromatic eyes—a true gray, no color at all. His skin was heavily freckled, no scars or distinguishing marks. She took all that information in a glance, adding that he appeared to carry no weapons. He wasn't wearing a jacket either.

The silence grew weighty. She tried not to panic. If he was from the Foundation, he wouldn't be extending a hand for her to shake. But Gillie realized she was wrong belatedly; this wasn't a handshake. His grip became implacable, but he still didn't say a word.

Then the world flashed away in a blinding rush. At a carnival, before she was taken, she had once been on a ride that spun you so fast that it operated on the principals of centrifugal force. This motion felt the same, along with the same rising nausea. Just when she felt she couldn't bear it, the movement stopped, colors clarified, and they were entirely somewhere else.

The room was clearly rigged as an infirmary, and four people lay on cots. Blood and burned flesh scented the air. Her heart froze. Though part of her was still reeling over the way he'd brought her here, she knew he had to work for Mockingbird. She didn't think she could bear it if Taye was one of the people she had to heal. Gillie studied each of their faces, a cool trickle of relief spilling through her as she catalogued the injuries.

Once she'd finished, a large man with a wild spill of dark hair and colorful tattoos running up his arms stepped into the doorway. After a moment, she recognized him as Silas. He gave a tiny shake of his head. *No names. You don't know me anymore.* Gillie acknowledged that and waited for her instructions.

"I'm Hawk. These folks are casualties of a raid on the

Foundation . . . and we can't take them to a hospital without risking recapture, but they won't survive without treatment."

"Tanager calls me Cardinal. I take it he's one of yours?" She indicated the thin man.

"That's Heron. Sorry if he scared you. He doesn't speak."

For an instant, she wondered why not, whether it was something that had plagued him since birth or whether he could blame the Foundation. It wasn't the kind of thing she felt free to ask. Not on first acquaintance.

"So I noticed. Are they all—"

"Test subjects? Yeah. We lost a few. But we saved a whole lot more."

"I'll get started." She examined all four of the injured and then did something she never had before. Triage. Gillie touched them lightly in turn and listened to their wounds; it became immediately clear who needed treatment first. "This guy's not going to last much longer."

"Do you need anything?"

"Yeah. Sterilize a knife." She'd never tried to heal someone who had lost so much blood before. Remembering the scar she'd taken from Tanager's gunshot wound, she had the feeling this wouldn't be pretty.

God. I don't want to do this.

But if she didn't, he'd die. *Nobody's making you.* This wasn't for money. It was just to save the life of a man from whom the Foundation had already stolen everything else. Gillie squared her shoulders and waited for the blade. Hawk handed it to her presently and she sliced the tips of her index fingers and then laid her hands on the bare wound.

Blood to blood. A chemical hiss sprang from her fingers; he screamed and tried to pull away. God only knew what he thought she was doing to him. Gillie hung on, knowing when her healing kicked in. The rush made the top of her head numb, as if she were losing her own blood and health in the process. She didn't think she could do four in a row, but she didn't let herself consider failure.

With Hawk watching over her shoulder, she stood firm until the wound sealed. It aged before her eyes until it was little more than an old scar, and then that vanished as well, her blood drawing the damage as it did disease. Gillie raised her shirt and found a thin line bisecting her abdomen. *Shit. I guess I won't be wearing a bikini.* As she straightened, a wave of dizziness swept her.

"I could use some orange juice," she said. "Or cookies or crackers if you have them."

"Heron?"

The thin man nodded and headed out the door, which he closed behind him. Gillie had the idea they didn't want her to know the location or anything about how to find this place. Hawk helped her to a crate, where she sank down and put her head between her knees. Her vision showed sparkles of color, first signs of an impending lapse in consciousness.

She regulated her breathing and kept it together until Heron got back. Hawk tried to distract her from the welling nausea, but she lost the thread of his words, trapped in the cotton around her head. With trembling hands, she drank the juice and forced down the sugar cookies. These looked like the ones her mother used to buy in colorful Christmas tins.

"Better?" Hawk asked.

"Yeah. But there's no way I can do more today. It would kill me." Not drama. She felt weak and lethargic, almost as shitty as she'd felt as a kid. Those memories haunted her, along with the faces of thin-faced children who never made it home from the cancer wards. That, and the endless visits from magicians and clowns, like balloon animals could fix everything.

"That leaves us with a problem." He glanced at the other three patients and then at Heron.

The thin man got out a notepad and scrawled, *It would be better if I go back for her tomorrow.* Near as she could figure, people would call what he did teleportation, although it didn't feel instantaneous.

"Can you keep them alive until then?" she asked.

Not that it mattered. She had nothing more to give.

Hawk lifted a big shoulder in a half shrug. "I'll do my best."

"Is . . . Crow doing okay?" She'd almost slipped up. Almost called him by his name.

"Just tired. He's around here somewhere."

Oh, God. She ached for a glimpse of him. Just from a distance, just a smile, or a wave. It was pathetic, she knew. It hadn't been that long.

"Could you send him in?" Gillie held her breath, wondering if he understood the significance of the request.

"Sure. I'll go roust him." He proved he did know when he signaled Heron to follow, so she'd have a few moments of privacy with Taye.

While she waited, she paced—or she tried to. On her second circuit of the small room, it tipped sideways and she had to resume her seat on the crate, waiting for the world to steady. He came in then, clad as usual in jeans and a white T-shirt. No leather jacket; they were indoors, and it was warm enough.

"Thanks for coming to help. The situation was messier than we expected."

With such casual friendliness, he smiled like it hadn't broken her heart to say good-bye to him, as if he'd never made love to her with his mouth, and she didn't know what his face looked like when he came. Taye gave no sign he'd argued passionately against her working for Mockingbird, maybe because she had some chance of crossing his path, making a clean break more difficult. He didn't speak her name.

In her head, Gillie heard slamming doors, breaking glass.

"This is the first time he's used me. Wounds are easier than diseases."

Easier but no less painful, no lessening of consequence.

She drank him in. Taye propped himself against the wall, not stepping far enough into the room to approach her, his manner distant. But she saw through his façade—his eyes burned with green fire, lambent with banked longing; his skin held a nacreous gleam, textured by the red gold bristles of his jaw, and he didn't look quite human, more polished and finely drawn, as if his inner fire had burned away that part of him. As usual, he hadn't shaved in several days, and his face fell somewhere between the stages of *I can't be bothered* and *I'm growing a beard, really.* Shadows cradled his eyes as if he hadn't been sleeping well. But then they both had nightmares. Probably always would.

"Settling into your new life all right?" he asked.

No. It's empty, and I don't know how to do this without you. I don't want to. But that was a weak, quiet part of her, and one whose words she would never give voice. She was stronger than that, stronger than fear, stronger than captivity and confinement. Through the long looks and mutual assessment, Taye didn't reach for her. Other than his eyes, he gave no sign this was hard for him. Gillie took that as her cue.

"Yeah. I'm a good student."

"Knew you would be." Awkward pause. Long silence. And so many words she wanted to hear from him. They all died in that void. "Well, I'm glad you're doing fine, but I have to—"

"Me, too," she said softly.

Hurt, so much of it. It drowned her. *I can't do this again. Say good-bye,* she told herself, *and mean it this time.* It was possible she would never change his mind; he meant for the separation to be permanent. The next time Heron brought her to tend the wounded, she wouldn't ask about him. She would *not.* If they ever saw each other again, he could do all the running. And maybe some begging.

"Take care of yourself," he said.

Impersonal wish. Gillie lifted her chin and gave Taye the same careless wave she'd offered Brandon in the library. This time, she did watch him walk away. She wanted it emblazoned on her memory, so she'd remember the pain.

Hawk gave her five minutes to collect herself before sending Heron back. When the porter held out his slim, freckled hand, she was ready. The twist and pull didn't take her by surprise, though the spin didn't do her stomach any good. When they returned to her apartment, she dropped to hands and knees, breathing deep through her nose. He seemed unaffected, probably used to the movement.

In his notebook, he wrote, *You gonna be okay?*

Somehow Gillie didn't think he meant the trip. She nodded and held back the anger until after he ported away. *Stupid, stubborn bastard. He'll be so lucky if it's not too late by the time he realizes what he's lost.* She didn't weep; that was weakness. In her kitchen, she had a whole cupboard full of dishes to break, and it gave her tremendous satisfaction to smash that first plate, while imagining Taye's face.

Later, once her rage subsided, she decided she would never be helpless again, never looking to a man for guidance and protection; it was time to take back some power. Steely with determination, she dialed a local shooting range.

"You have classes for women? When does the next one start?"

CHAPTER 17

Initial intel from Hausen indicated T-89, born Tyler Golden, had grown up in Miami; that wasn't strictly true. They were deep in the mangrove swamp. Heavy trees overhung the road, and Cale imagined the whir of insects beneath the roar of the engine. He had been raised on a council estate in Seven Sisters, so while he was used to fighting and scratching, he wasn't used to nature. Even the army had sent him to cities and deserts in need of pacification. No swamps.

He wasn't clear on whether this was part of the Everglades, but it was hot, murky green, and sticky as hell. Beside him, Kestrel was quiet, but tears slipped down her cheeks now and then. He didn't know what to do in the face of so much pain and sorrow. Usually, there was something you could say or a solution to be had, but he didn't know how to fix it when the problem was in her brain.

And he shouldn't care whether she hurt constantly, but over the course of their journey, he'd offered caffeine, which sometimes helped with pain by dilating blood vessels. Coffee, chocolate, he offered them to her, feeling helpless and tentative. She drank the former and declined the latter. And at night, in their separate beds, he listened to her tossing and turning; he didn't want to sympathize with her. That would make it difficult to do his job.

"Don't you have something you can take?" he asked.

"Before I was betrayed, Mockingbird was working on finding medicine to help me. And in between tasks, he let me take sleeping pills, so I could rest. The Foundation doesn't care. They'll use me until I can't take it anymore and I find a way to kill myself. Or until my brain fries from the constant stimulus." She turned her head and eyed him with quiet resignation. "Just as you will, so don't pretend you're different. You only care about the money."

That hit pretty close to home, so he went back to driving. In silence, he navigated the last of the turns and parked. There was no proper drive; he had to park on the shoulder of the road and walk up the track that led deeper into the swamp. According to the GPS, this was as far as the roads went. Kestrel followed him, stumbling with pain and weariness, because the constant movement in her head wouldn't let her sleep. Wordlessly, he put a hand beneath her arm and guided her over the gnarled roots into what passed for the Goldens' front yard. When she didn't pull away, it warmed him; constant hatred and suspicion got old.

Before he could think better of it, he said, "I'll get you something when we leave here, so you can sleep at night."

She flashed him an incredulous look. "Why would you do that for me?"

"You'll be no use to me if you burn out," he muttered.

But that wasn't the truth, and by some feminine intuition, she knew as much. Her smile said so. Cale ignored her, walking on.

The house was worse than he expected, even given their surroundings—an ancient tar-paper shack with debris littering the area outside, old tires, a rusted cookstove, piles of scrap tin. This place could easily double as a rubbish heap. An old man sat in a lawn chair wearing a ball cap, a pair of overalls, and little else; his long beard grew into his tufts of white chest hair. He raised a can of beer as Cale came closer, but he didn't speak, nor did he get up. The old hound laying next to him raised his head and gave a halfhearted growl of warning, but it was too warm for even the dog to take it seriously.

"Are you Amos Golden?" he asked.

"Might be, unless you're from the government. But with an accent like that, I don't guess you are."

"No, sir. I've come seeking information about your grandson."

"Tyler? We ain't see that bastard in ten years and good riddance, I say." He spat into the weeds that grew around his ankles.

"Anything you can tell me about him would be helpful—his friends, his habits, his usual haunts. What do you recall?"

A greedy look dawned on Golden's face, but before he could capitalize, the door to the shack opened up, and a woman with her brown hair caught up in a ponytail came out. She didn't look old enough to have a grown son, except around the eyes.

"You're here about Ty?"

"Yes, ma'am. Could we come in for a moment?"

Her eyes went to Kestrel, who couldn't—under any circumstances—be considered a threat. It had been a stroke of genius to bring her along.

"Of course." She extended a small hand, which he shook. "I'm Dani Golden. I've got a pitcher of tea made. We'll have a glass and talk."

Inside, it was just as hot as it had been outdoors, and the small rooms didn't help. He didn't know how anyone could survive this place. Maybe Golden was a lucky bastard after all; he'd gotten out, at least, whatever had happened since then. Everything was worn and threadbare, cheap furniture years past its prime. On the walls, someone had hung dime-store art and yard-sale pictures of Jesus. He sank onto the sagging pink couch. That would slow his reaction time, should it come to a fight. Mentally, he reckoned how to compensate and waited for their hostess.

The woman brought three glasses of iced tea and then sat down in a rickety rocking chair. "Did you find him?"

Interesting.

"I'm afraid not. But that's what I'm trying to do, so any information you can provide would be helpful."

"Who's your quiet friend?"

"This is Kestrel." Best not to elaborate, or try to explain her silence. Let Dani make of her what she would.

"Is he in some kind of trouble?"

He'd worked out the cover story ahead of time, and she was the kind of person who would buy it—hook, line, and sinker. "No. But he participated in some drug trials a while back. There's since been a class action against the pharmaceutical company, and I've been hired to track down the participants, so they have an opportunity to opt in and possibly receive benefits from the lawsuit."

Someone who knew more about such things would ask who the hell would hire him to do that, but she merely nodded, trying to look worldly. "Is he gonna get sick?"

"He might be already, which is why it's imperative I locate him."

"Well, like Daddy said, we ain't seen him in years. I had him young," she confided, as if he hadn't discerned that from her face. "I was fifteen, a kid myself. I tried to do right by him."

It was clear she wanted to talk so Cale let her. Maybe he could learn something about his target from his mother's memories.

"But I guess he was about nine or ten when he started showing signs he wasn't right. I always thought maybe it was my fault . . . 'cause I drank and smoked before I knew I was pregnant with him. I did stop, soon as I figured it out, but—" Guilt shone from her like a beacon, creating sad lines beside her mouth.

"It's not your fault," Kestrel said softly, unexpectedly. "Tyler's problems didn't come from one cigarette or a couple of beers. There are indications now that schizophrenia is linked to genetic markers, zinc finger protein 804A and the chromosome six HLA. If there's no history of mental illness in your family, it might have come from his father's side."

Cale glanced at Kestrel in shock, both at her knowledge and her kindness. Dani Golden smiled in a grateful haze, her hands trembling so the ice in her plastic tumbler of tea rattled. To cover his reaction, he took a sip of the tea: over-sweetened but cold. The atmosphere in here felt cloying, as if nothing ever moved. No fresh wind, no progress, just slow stagnation, echoed in the mossy-mold smell from the swamp. From the old man came the sound of another beer can cracking open.

"I guess you're a scientist," Dani said. "Somebody who worked for the drug company, but then you realized the product was bad, so you turned whistleblower?"

That was a surprising analysis from a woman he had taken

to be completely credulous. He revised his list of queries accordingly. If he made her suspicious, she would throw them out before he learned anything.

Kestrel's answer came soft and slow, an astonishing word. "Yes."

Really? Or is she just playing along? Now he wondered if she had, in fact, worked for the Foundation at some point. But surely they would have told him. Cale had assumed she was a former test subject, like T-89, and Gillie Flynn, but hunter's intuition told him now that perhaps she had layers and secrets. If he could peel them back and learn her truths, he might be better able to make use of her.

"Well, you've sure set my mind at ease. I always blamed myself."

"You shouldn't," Kestrel said.

"He had his moods, that boy did. Sometimes he would seem normal as a blue sky, and sometimes, he was downright twitchy. But in either frame, he couldn't wait to light out of here for city sights and loud music. When he wasn't having one of his spells, he did like to party. Nobody could light up a room like Ty." The woman smiled, soft with nostalgia, as if remembering the sweet moments her son had given her.

He couldn't have asked for a better priming of his subject. Relaxed with relief, Dani Golden was ready to yield everything about her son. Smiling, Cale began his questions.

It was a cold, snowy day, not unusual for this time of year or this altitude. Tanager watched the man through the window of the café; her target was inside, all warm and cozy, drinking a cup of coffee. He gave no sign of a guilty conscience over what he'd done. She hadn't wanted to believe it at first, but gradually, the clues she uncovered spoke for themselves, and once she had clearance to go after him, the leak would be plugged once and for all.

This part of Denver was excessively trendy, SoDo or LoHo, or whatever the hell they called it, lots of upscale places and a pedestrian mall. But she liked winter because it let her wear her most kick-ass boots and jackets, so unless she was on vacation, she gravitated toward the cold. Fortunately, her work permitted certain flexibility.

She took care not to let the mark see her. To that end, she went into a shop across the way and dialed Mockingbird. *Come on, ring me back. Green-light this.*

The minutes ticked away. She pretended to shop, looking at overpriced knickknacks. From behind the counter, the clerk eyed her with a mixture of scorn and trepidation. Tan obviously didn't look like she could afford the prices in here.

"Can I help you?" the man asked at last, obviously hoping she'd move along.

Well, she would be damned if she'd wait in the cold, but she had to stay close. From here, she had a perfect view of the coffee shop across the way. It was tempting to use her voice to shut him up, but she couldn't afford to do that. Not after what happened in Dubuque.

But she wanted to; darkness stirred. Something in her liked breaking men to her will, leaving them helpless to resist any terrible thing she asked. This man was middle-aged, presumably innocuous. Yet he exuded a superior air, as if the fact that he sold expensive gewgaws for a living made him better than the rest of humanity. It would be sheer pleasure to humble him a little. Tan resisted the urge.

"I'm just looking," she said, forcing a smile.

"For anything particular?"

"My mom's birthday is coming up. She likes fancy stuff."

"Ah." He decided perhaps she belonged after all—even hoodlums loved their mothers—and stopped pestering her.

Tanager paced, though she concealed the movement by meandering through the store, ostensibly seeking the perfect gift. Near a selection of expensive cut-crystal perfume bottles, she pinged Mockingbird for the second time and received no reply. If this were a life-and-death matter, she'd already be dead. That couldn't be good; it had never happened before. Ever. It took half an hour for him to reply, and it was with a text, not a call.

Get your laptop. Somewhere private.

And that was all.

Oh, shit. Something is spectacularly wrong.

To keep from sticking in the clerk's memory more than she already would, in case someone came asking questions, she bought a pretty carved jade fan. "I think she'll like this."

Or she might, if she wasn't more than ten years dead.

Smiling, the man rang her up and became even friendlier when she paid cash. “A lovely choice. Come back anytime.”

As she stepped out into the cold, she took one last look at the man in the café and shook her head. She couldn’t take him out without talking to Mockingbird first, and it sounded like he had his own problems. His welfare took priority over her suspicions, no question. Tanager made tracks back to the bolt hole; the resistance had a number of them around the country. Ordinarily, she’d use her voice to find someplace nicer to stay, but they were on high alert at the moment and couldn’t afford to have her playing cowgirl, just for the satisfaction of making some bastard let her stay in his penthouse. This was a pretty humble place by comparison, a studio apartment with basic furnishings, but it got the job done.

Tanager sat down on the couch and opened her bag. Though she preferred traveling light, netbooks were small enough to tuck into a purse, which changed her policy of refusing to carry a laptop. She fought down unreasonable panic as she powered it on. While the thing ran through its system checks, her heart pounded like a freight train, roaring in her ears.

Calm the fuck down. It’s probably nothing, or at least, not as bad as you think.

Five minutes later, her phone pinged again, giving her the IP address where she could connect to him. This stuff was above her pay grade; she didn’t understand half the shit MB did for them, but she could follow his lead. When giving instructions to a tech dummy like her, he followed the KISS system.

Within seconds, his avatar appeared on her keyboard. *Hell of a chat room.* This wasn’t something other people could do. Though they had never talked about it, she was sure of that.

“I’ve got problems,” he said without preamble.

Tanager put aside her personal fear and sat forward. “What can I do to help?”

He laughed, though the sound held a darker current. She didn’t think that was feedback. “I wish you could, Tan . . . and I love that you asked with *no* regard for what trouble I might be in. I don’t have many people who would.”

“You’re freaking my shit out.” She tried for a light tone and failed as foreboding settled into her bones.

“Goes with the territory with us, doesn’t it? I appreciate

you, love, but there's nothing you can do. I have to handle this myself."

"Handle *what*?"

"It's . . . a transition, of sorts. I'll figure it out, but things may be a bit shaky for a while. I'm routing all my pings to your cell phone. Hopefully this won't take long."

"I don't like where this is going."

Dammit.

Never had she hated the distance between them so much. Mostly, it was easier to see him as words on a screen or pixels in the net, but lately he had become more real, a friend rather than someone she used or who used her in turn. There had been damn few of those in her life.

"I'm putting you in charge in my absence." He paused, a thread of weariness or pain woven through his words.

No. She didn't want this. *Bad, bad idea.*

His instructions went on, inexorable, horrible. "I'm sending logins and passwords to databases that will help keep things running. When people call, you can answer many queries by running a search. In these files, you'll also find the accounts from which I make payments to our agents. You'll have complete control of all finances while I'm gone. Finally, I'm sending a voice scrambler to the place in Denver. Using it, you can pretend to be me, live, if necessary."

"I can't hold this shit together without you. I don't have your mojo, Mocks. I can't scan the net and find escape routes or dig out the dirty stuff for leverage. Please don't put this on me. I'm gonna fail them. People will *die*."

"I know," he said. "I'm sorry."

And then he disappeared in a flicker of light.

CHAPTER 18

Taye wasn't surprised to learn Oliver had signed on. Of course, his name was Gull now, and he hadn't seen him since they cleared the warehouse a few weeks back. Mockingbird had sent the total headcount, and in the end, they saved eighty-seven of those coma patients. They'd lost a few in the crossfire, of course, and some of the other subjects had died protecting them.

He'd watched the news special on the incident with great amusement. The government called it the biggest case of unsanctioned medical testing in the country's history. Investigations were ongoing, of course, which meant important people would be bribed, and the story would be buried after the initial furor.

In ten minutes, he had to meet Hawk. Since he was the junior agent, he never sat in on the assignment calls with MB; his partner brought the targets and they struck without mercy. The property damage alone had been astronomical. *If I can do nothing else well,* he thought with dark humor, *I can blow their shit up.*

Since he was constantly on the move, it made no sense for him to have a home base. Consequently, he spent his downtime alone in seedy motels—and he missed the sense of home he'd had with Gillie like the phantom pain of a missing limb. He had fought so hard to keep her at a distance so his remaining days wouldn't seem like such a barren wasteland, all for nothing, it seemed. Because she had him; she haunted him. He couldn't close his eyes without dreaming about her, which would've been painful, except that she supplanted the nightmares.

Taye forced her out of his head, and dressed; he had gear now, all black from head to toe, and a flak vest. After catching his hair back in a short ponytail, he pulled on the black knit cap. Now he was ready to go meet Hawk. Bulbs flickered as he went by, responding to the lightning in his veins. *Fuck. I gotta quit that.* But his control wasn't getting better, which meant Mockingbird had to get his money's worth fast.

Hawk waited for him at the midpoint of the bridge, as arranged. He didn't know where the other man lived—or maybe he was like Taye, and just crashed wherever, a different place each time to make him harder to track down. Anonymous cell phones and e-mail accounts enabled them to set up such meetings.

"You don't look great, man."

"That's good since I feel like shit."

"Sure you're up to this?"

"Fuck yes, I am. Let's do it."

Via his inside link to the Foundation's network, Mockingbird had gotten intel on experiments being performed in an old factory, so they were heading over to check it out. As always, it was late, and nobody was abroad but them. It saved answering awkward questions on why they were dressed for a Special Forces black op.

Hawk just nodded and led the way. "I scouted the place yesterday, found the entrances. There don't appear to be any cameras or security measures in place."

"That doesn't strike you as wrongity-wrong?"

"It's possible they built downward. As we learned at Exeter, sometimes the best disguise is not to have the place surrounded with high-tech shit announcing something's there. But I'm prepared for the possibility that there's something skewed in this picture, too."

"Good to know," he muttered. "When I get my ass shot off, at least we saw it coming."

"You're manstrual tonight."

Taye laughed despite himself. "Sorry. I'll get my head in the game."

"Thanks. My girlfriend would appreciate it if you don't let me die."

Whoa. He'd never thought of Hawk as that guy, a family man, so to speak. He was huge and sort of ugly, even with the hair grown back. But he *had* noticed the difference in him, as if happiness had set him free, and when he fought against the Foundation, it was a job, but not one that owned his soul. He went home at the end of the day.

"How'd you meet her?"

"Dug her out of a rock pile."

"Dick. Fine, don't tell me."

Hawk cut him a grin. "Not kidding, actually. We survived the earthquake in Ecuador together . . . and then I went to work for Mockingbird after I got back stateside."

He remembered hearing about that on the news; they were still trying to rebuild. "So you haven't been together long."

"Comparatively, no. Feels like I've known her forever, though."

"And she's cool with the freelance violence?"

"She was with me when some Foundation mercs tried to end me . . . and her as collateral damage. I guess that helps her see my point of view."

Taye couldn't imagine bonding with a normal person; it was beyond his scope. But he also couldn't bone up for anyone but Gillie Flynn. So he probably wasn't the best gauge of what relationships could work, long term. If the woman could see past Hawk's terrifying exterior, then she probably *was* a keeper.

"I'd like to meet her sometime," he said, before he remembered that wasn't allowed.

No fraternization; those were the rules. Hawk knew that as well as he did, but he didn't point out the dumbassery of the comment, for which Taye felt grateful.

As they talked, they covered the ground between the bridge and the factory. Now they stood a hundred yards away; the structure sprawled over several acres with smokestacks rising against the dark. The gray concrete gave it an ominous air, and the rows of windows added to Taye's feeling that anything could be waiting inside. He hadn't been this unsettled at the warehouse, so he thought maybe thinking about Gillie had gotten to him.

"The fencing is down on this side." Hawk strode off, leaving him to follow. "There's an inner yard full of industrial junk with some utility buildings. They seem to be newer construction . . . and it's brick, not cement."

"Interesting." He just didn't know if that was a sign of Foundation presence; the original owners might have added on before the factory shut down.

"Let's go check it out."

Not until they crossed the parking lot did he realize what was bothering him, more than the general decay. "There's no light anywhere."

Hawk swore.

Most public streets had lights powered by the city, but there were none in a block in any direction. Everything around the factory sat dark, as if someone had shut the juice off on purpose. And they would only do that for one reason.

"It's a trap!" But his words came too late.

Hawk reacted like a defensive end, putting Taye on his back by hitting him with all his weight. The barrage of shots killed the broken pavement instead. More followed—Taye took one in the back, and even through the vest, it hurt so bad, he saw stars. If they didn't find their enemies, things would get ugly, fast.

"We're too exposed here. On my mark, we run for the inner yard. Keep your head down and you won't end up with a bullet in it. Is that clear?"

Damn, but this guy could bark orders. He wasn't sure he could stand, let alone run. Talk about your inflated expectations. "Were you in the army or something before they took you?"

"Fuck, no. I taught physics. Now *move*!"

The demand in the other man's voice had him up and running, low, toward the narrow slice between the factory wings. One side had probably been for production, and the other for packaging. For a moment, an almost-memory flirted with him; maybe his dad, or granddad, had worked someplace like this, he thought, but he couldn't summon a face or a name.

More shots sprayed the ground as they ran, and from Hawk's muffled curse, they'd gotten him, too. No time to stop and see if the vest caught it.

"How did they know we'd be here?" he asked, vaulting a pile of concrete cinder blocks.

"Dunno. We either have a leak or they know Mockingbird's compromised their network, so they're planting false leads to see if we take the bait."

"We sure as hell did."

The night fell quiet, no sign of their enemies. Which meant they were good, better than the usual Foundation goons, and considering the best tactics. *They could be flanking us right now. Might be that bastard from Detroit.* He'd certainly know to cut Taye off from the grid; if he couldn't pull, it severely limited how many volts he could throw.

Thank God for Hawk.

"They've got us pinned down, snipers in position." The other man was clearly thinking out loud. "I know you don't mag much because you can't control it too well, but can you do something with all the scrap metal?"

"If I had an idea, I could."

"Then you don't need juice for that."

"Nope."

"That's the plan, then. Feel free to be dramatic."

Despite the incredibly bleak odds, Taye smiled. "Bring it on."

While he watched the perimeter, Hawk pinged Mockingbird to let him know that the Foundation was onto him. Once MB called back, he summarized the situation and then asked, "Can you send reinforcements?"

"Not soon enough. I've got another fire to put out. Sorry, but you're on your own." Which was harsh, but not surprising.

"As I see it," Hawk went on, "we don't need to kill them all. We just need to escape."

"Which is why you told me to be dramatic." Taye scanned the inner yard, considering the scrap metal—and he *almost* had a plan. No juice. Just magnetism. "I form a fire shield. One piece of metal by itself wouldn't be enough to block high caliber ammo, but if I layer them—"

"We end up with makeshift armor plating. Can you make it mobile?"

It'd hurt like hell, but he could. Probably. "Yeah, no problem."

His control wasn't what it ought to be in using this ability, which meant they might get knocked around some. Better than staying pinned down here until the snipers found the right angle. He didn't know who his enemy was this time, but he couldn't assume they intended to take him alive. They might not even be hunting him specifically; they might have cut the power as a precaution, in case he was here. But they couldn't be sure.

Energy hummed in him, different than the lightning. It felt

like a vibration low in his aching stomach and the scrap metal groaned in response. Lighter pieces flew toward them and he halted their progress before they could pierce the skin. *Shit. I could make a shrapnel bomb like this. Good to know.* The pain scaled up as he added more pieces, guiding their flight toward Hawk and himself. When it looked like solid protection, he gave the go-ahead. Hawk moved out, and the shield stayed with them, but it required his constant focus to keep it in place. Sweat beaded on his forehead as they moved toward the parking lot. If they could get to the bridge, they had transport out. *Just keep running.* From a long way off, he heard shouts, and bullets slammed the shield with terrible force. He was all that stood between having their brains splattered.

God, it hurts. Felt like his whole head was on fire. Taye couldn't see anymore; it all went bloodred and he felt blindly for Hawk in front of him. Hand on his partner's shoulder, he kept running, focused on holding the shield in place. The outer metal exploded. One layer gone. *All it takes is one lucky shot.* The Foundation had gotten smart. Keep out of sight and the resistance couldn't fight back.

"We're almost to the bridge," Hawk said. "Can you keep it up?"

Yeah, he tried to say, but he couldn't form words anymore. His jaw locked from grinding his teeth against the agony.

More shots. The second layer gave, and something in his mind did as well. He felt a warm trickle from his ears. That couldn't be good.

"We're across. Stop now. Let it go."

But it took precious moments for him to remember how. Magnetism could fry his mind if he let it. But eventually the metal clanged to the ground, and Hawk caught him before he fell. Taye knew vaguely a sense of being dragged to the car, and that was all.

ONE MONTH LATER
WICHITA

"Ms. Evans, could I see you for a moment after class?" Her aberrant psych professor looked as she'd always imagined, down to the well-trimmed beard, glasses, and tweed jacket with patches on the elbows.

"Of course." But inwardly, Gillie cycled through levels of

panic. Whenever people paid attention to her, she assumed it was because they could see through her façade.

Other than Brandon. He'd taken a liking to her, and he was so nice—and young—that she didn't have the heart to shoo him away. She'd made it clear she wasn't looking for a serious relationship, and he said, *Duh, college,* as if that were a given. He made her laugh, at least.

With her nerves prickling, she waited until everyone had filed out of the room and then she glanced at the professor with veiled trepidation. She expected a question like, *What are you doing here?* or *Why is a psychology student taking classes down at the Bullseye?*

Her lives didn't align these days, but handling a gun made her feel safe, as if she could contribute to her own protection. Gillie had completed the women's handgun course, and she was now taking the required class to apply for a carry concealed permit; there didn't seem to be much point in owning a Glock if she had to leave it in her sock drawer.

"I was extremely impressed with your sample profile of a man suffering from narcissistic personality disorder, truly realistic and detailed, including the episodes of grandiosity."

"Thank you, sir."

He smiled at her. "I'm only stating a fact about the paper. As it happens, I have an opening for a TA. Ordinarily, I make undergrads vie for the position, but your work has been so exceptional that I'm offering it to you. I took a look at your records . . . and I'm glad you changed your mind about business. You have a real insight into human nature, something that can't be taught, and I would hate for the discipline to lose you."

No, she thought, remembering Rowan. *It can only be learned at a master's hand. Give me your crazy, your neurotic, your mentally ill, yearning to be made well.*

Realizing he needed a response, she said, "You're offering me a job?"

She wasn't clear on what a TA did, but it was pretty damn exciting to have the opportunity at work that didn't involve a mop and bucket. Money wasn't a factor, of course. But if she wanted a real career, even under a fake name, she had to start somewhere.

"I am. Are you interested?"

Gillie couldn't ask him for the information she needed on

the position; it was stuff a normal college student would already know. But she'd figured out the Internet with Brandon's unwitting help, and she was sure she could learn fast. The real world sometimes seemed like an endless game of catch-up.

"Yes, absolutely."

"Then you'll start next week. You'll need to go through the student employment center to make it official. I haven't even posted the job opening yet."

"I'll take care of it. Thanks for thinking of me."

Shouldering her backpack, she strolled out of the classroom feeling like she'd won the lottery. Her smile didn't dim when she saw Brandon waiting for her. He'd memorized her class schedule and she often found him outside with coffee in hand. Unfortunately, she didn't have enough social experience to be sure whether this was normal, friendly behavior. He didn't give off a Rowan-style vibe, though, so she figured she was safe. Over the years, she had seen a number of doctors while in Foundation custody, and he was the only one who made her feel like she might lose her soul if she looked in his eyes too long.

So yeah. I'm pretty good at spotting the nutjobs.

"What'd you do?" he teased.

"I wrote a kick-ass paper on narcissistic personality disorder. Prompted him to ask me to be his TA."

"You gotta watch out for Professor Reynolds. He likes to pick the pretty ones and then chase them around his office. Last time, it ended badly."

For a horrified moment, she thought he was serious, but then she saw the laughter dancing in his eyes. "You almost had me."

He chuckled. "Congrats, I'm sure you'll learn a lot."

"Thanks."

"You want to grab lunch?"

For once, she had no assignments due and she didn't feel like being alone. Gillie was sure Taye wasn't. He probably had a bimbo on his lap right this minute, and there was nothing stopping him from feeling her up. Anger made her smile extra bright.

"Sure. Wanna get a sub? My bike's parked outside."

"You ride that thing everywhere."

"No car," she said. "It's cheaper and I'm being green."

"Doesn't it make grocery shopping a pain in the ass?"

Wow, she thought. It was funny how much distance—and

entitlement—separated her from her "peers." He couldn't imagine what a pleasure she found it to walk out her front door and get on a bus, which would take her to a store, where she could spend as much time as she wanted considering her purchases. Such things were not chores for her; each time she bought a jug of milk, it was a minor miracle and a major victory against those who had never intended for her to be a person at all.

"I don't mind," she said. "There's a bus stop close to me, and I meet interesting people."

He laughed. "Yeah, and they're all too broke to afford cars."

Okay, right now she didn't like him very much.

"Sometimes it's not a matter of money, but a matter of choice," she said frostily.

"Hey, sorry." He wasn't an idiot, so he registered the change in climate and held up a hand in a placating gesture. "I think it's cool you care about the environment and stuff, seriously. But you don't run around throwing red paint on people and screaming *Meat is murder*, do you? Because I draw the line there."

There's no harm in him. He's a good kid. That was a laughable thought, considering he wasn't so much younger than her, but age was more than a number; it was also comprised of life experiences, and some days she felt about a hundred years old.

"No." Mentally, she sought the buzzwords that made biking and riding the bus admirable instead of the result of a weird and sheltered life. "I'm just reducing my carbon footprint."

"I get that. The baby boomers really left us a fucking mess to clean up."

As they walked outside, he rambled about the environment, clearly trying to impress her with his knowledge, and how big oil companies had suppressed green technologies. Gillie feigned interest because she thought Grace would care whether the electric car would catch on within ten years. That was who Brandon liked, after all—Grace Evans from Ohio with the pretty brown hair with the funky red streaks and fake green eyes. She wouldn't have thought it would be this hard, living a lie, when she'd never lived at all.

Four weeks into her new job, Gillie went with Dr. Reynolds to observe the pro bono work he did at the state mental hospital. He didn't have a private practice anymore, but he liked to give back by offering free group sessions once a month. What seemed like so long ago now, she had told Taye she wanted to offer counseling to the homeless—and this was a firsthand opportunity to see how it was done. All the classes in the world couldn't teach her how to connect with people. Maybe she did have insight, like her professor said, but understanding how things worked didn't always translate to an ability to fix them.

On Saturday morning, she presented herself early and locked her bike up inside. Her office was a small room attached to Dr. Reynolds's, and she shared it with another TA, but Roger wouldn't need the space on the weekend. Gillie had finished upstairs and just come back down to wait when her professor pulled up. He drove a silver BMW, but it wasn't new, probably paid for by prior years of private practice.

"Good morning," he greeted as she slid into the car. "It's an hour and a half drive. I chose the distance so I wouldn't have to worry about seeing any of my patients around town, if they should happen to get better and be discharged."

"Yeah, I can see why." That was an aspect of counseling she hadn't considered, how it would feel running into a patient on the street, when she knew about his bedwetting and his problems with his mother. "There won't be a problem with my sitting in on the session?"

"If anyone objects, then you'll have to wait outside. But you can ask permission to interview other patients while you're there. There are a number of interesting cases, and most welcome visitors."

"Good idea." So it wouldn't be a wasted trip.

Rather than make small talk, Dr. Reynolds played a classical CD. That was fine with her. Nerves ate at her for no reason she could name, until she realized it was because she felt like this hit a little too close to home. She was going to see people who couldn't leave; they were locked away, maybe for their own protection, but it still set off a chain reaction in her belly.

As they neared the hospital, he turned the volume down on Handel. "You seem tense."

"I'm nervous," she said.

There was no point in lying to him; he was trained to notice this kind of thing, and she had to make her anxiety seem normal. *I can pass,* she thought. *I can fake it well enough to fool even you, Doc.*

"Why do you think that is?"

"It's the first step in what I hope will be a long career, exciting but nerve-racking. I don't know whether my expectations are realistic, or if I'll actually be able to help anyone."

"Probably not today," he said. "But those are reasonable fears."

That's not what I fear. I fear seeing myself in those people. Only their minds are their prisons, and I can't imagine anything worse, because nobody can set you free from that.

She nodded. "Thanks for taking me with you."

"I don't mentor people. Or I haven't in a long time. It's exhausting." For the first time, she noticed the lines etched beside his eyes, as if he didn't sleep well.

"Why is that?" A therapist move, asking questions instead of offering opinions.

By the quirk of his mouth, the professor registered that as well. "Are you analyzing me so soon, Ms. Evans?"

"You should call me G-Grace."

Christ, I almost fucked up. Let's hope he thinks that was a nervous, girlish stutter.

"Only if you call me Will." He was smiling, like there was a joke implicit in those words, some pop culture reference she ought to get.

Got it. TV show. About a gay man and his best friend, as she recalled; she didn't know how much a parallel she was intended to draw. *Did he just come out?*

She laughed. "Is that really your name?"

"William, but I prefer Will to Billy."

"I would, too."

She appreciated him trying to set her at ease. His gentle manner must have made him a totally kick-ass psychiatrist, and she wondered what made him want to teach instead of practice. But that wasn't her business.

By the time they pulled into the drive, her fears had quieted. The hospital was one of the oldest still open today, built in 1888 and full of historical weight. It looked like an old manor house from a distance, eerily set in a white field, though she imagined in spring and summer, it was pretty. On closer inspection, she decided it was more like an old prison.

"Come, let's get you a visitor's pass." He clipped a volunteer badge to his jacket. "You did bring your ID, yes?"

"Of course."

Just not mine. Officially, Gillie Flynn was an IRA terrorist. There would be cameras in here; these days, they were everywhere. After Taye pointed it out, she noticed them more—silent devices tracking every movement. Remembering that, she adjusted her red and yellow hat and tugged up the collar of her coat, then followed him up the snow-framed walk.

Inside, Dr. Reynolds—Will—spoke in friendly tones to the woman at the desk, and then gestured Gillie forward. "I'd like my student to observe, but only if everyone agrees."

"I need your driver's license, hon."

She handed it over and received a temp badge in turn, which she draped around her neck. Will nodded in approval, and said, "I need to check with the group . . . it's really a formality. They let Roger"—his other TA—"sit in last year. Wait here for a moment?"

"Of course."

The woman at the desk, whose nameplate read "Laverne," went back to typing. Clearly, this wasn't as big a deal as it felt to Gillie. Likely nobody else could see the momentous weight, but this felt like a pivotal event. As Reynolds had promised, it didn't take long to get permission.

Her professor returned, still wearing his calm, reassuring smile. "It's fine. Let's go get started before we lose their attention. A few have ADD, along with various, sundry problems."

Gillie nodded, trailing him through the gray corridors. He entered the fourth door on the left, where eight men and woman sat in a circle. They all murmured greetings, and Dr. Reynolds introduced her. "This is my student, Grace Evans. I trust you'll show her the same respect you did Roger."

A mumbled chorus came in response to the words, more general welcome than anything else. She smiled and said, "I'll try not to inhibit the process too much, but thank you for permitting me to sit in."

The next hour illuminated her decision; before, she'd had only an inchoate desire, but after watching Will work—seeing him take mental pain and confusion and help these patients sort through their myriad fears—she knew beyond a shadow of a doubt this was what she wanted to do with her life. She could see that they trusted him, and by the time they walked out the door, she had a new respect for William Reynolds.

"Did you learn anything?" he asked.

"Yes, you're very good."

He laughed. "I wasn't fishing, but thank you."

Before she could reply to that, an alarm went off and a male voice came over the PA, making an announcement that she figured was in some kind of code. "What's going on?"

"Someone's broken out of the secure ward, where they keep the dangerous patients and the criminally insane."

"Does that mean—"

"Yes, we should find the lounge and wait. They won't let anyone in or out until they resolve the situation." He shook his head wryly. "I'm sorry, Grace. I didn't imagine this trip would take up your whole Saturday."

"Not your fault."

While staff hurried down the hall, presumably to widen the net, they went in search of the break room. The situation reminded her unpleasantly of the Exeter facility, but she forced the memories down, reminding herself nothing illegal took place here. The majority had come seeking treatment, trying to get better. While the same wasn't true of those who had been confined by the courts, they didn't need to be out in the world, wreaking havoc.

"I think it's just ahead." He quickened his step, and those three feet proved the factor that changed everything.

It all happened in a split second; the distance between them, a door opening behind her, and suddenly, she had an arm around her throat, and a makeshift shiv pricking the skin of her throat. *No,* she thought. *I don't die here.* Her captor was male and he smelled of terror sweat, the demons in his brain driving him on.

She made some sound of distress and Will turned. His whole body stilled, and for an instant, she saw abject fear in his face.

He didn't move, reaching out with only his voice. "Don't hurt Grace."

Step one—use my name. Make me a person to him.

Only silence came in reply, but the blade at her throat trembled, and dread seeped into her bones. The sting meant he'd cut her; warm blood welled up. While the professor might be an excellent hostage negotiator—she had no idea—you couldn't reason with crazy. There were no words that would convince this man not to kill her if he thought she was a threat.

"What's your name, sir?"

Step two—establish rapport and use a respectful manner of address.

Longer silence. "I'm not telling you. You're one of them." He turned to someone Gillie couldn't see and snarled, "You shut the fuck up, I'm in charge here."

Acute paranoid schizophrenia, chased with hallucinations. But diagnosing him wouldn't save her.

Will changed tactics. "You're doing well here. I can see you have the situation completely in control. What is it that you want, sir?"

"To get the fuck out of here."

"That can be arranged. Just let Grace go."

"I'm not stupid," he said to the invisible heckler. "I *know* he's trying to trick me."

The voices in his head were winning. She felt his forearm tense, which meant he was about to slit her throat. Gillie sank her teeth savagely into his knife hand, not about to die without a fight. Grace Evans might be too frightened to act, but *she* was not. The bite drew blood and forced him to drop the shiv. But her anger kindled a dark echo; they were both smeared with blood, his and hers, and her awful ability sparked to life, this time fueled by fury, and it sank its fangs into him like a snake. He went down, screaming and clutching his head.

Hands shaking, she swiped a palm across her lips. Will came over and put a hand on her shoulder; doubtless he thought she needed to be steadied and reassured. *You have no idea,* she thought. *I used to face worse than this before breakfast.*

"Are you all right?" he asked.

She nodded as hospital staff swarmed them, asking questions, which the professor fielded. From his perspective, it must have looked very odd. *A bite leads the crazy man to fall down screaming.* But Gillie knew the truth: somehow she had forced her disease on him. The cancer that should have killed her as a child had become a weapon in her hands.

CHAPTER 19

Taye knew he didn't have much longer. Stomach pain stabbed constantly now. He chased pain meds with whiskey and it barely dulled the agony, even on a good day. On bad days, he chewed the pills without liquor and focused on the bitter grit in his teeth, waiting for the moment when the lightning in his belly would drop to a slow throb. Pulling had become an exercise in special torment, engineered by a particularly sick mind. Rowan would laugh, if he knew; he'd enjoy Taye's suffering.

He had promised them six missions, and he'd run five. Freed a lot of people. Kicked a lot of ass. More important, he had cost the Foundation a hell of a lot of money. Over that time, he had become closer to Hawk—and Juneau—than he might've expected. His partner had broken the rules, taken him home after he nearly fried himself getting them out of the factory trap. His girlfriend inexplicably took a liking to Taye, and now, they were like family to him.

But nobody could replace the woman who had stepped into his heart when she first offered him tea and cookies in hell. At night, he still saw her face, as she had looked when he wished her well. *She deserves to kick me in the nuts if that's how she feels. It's time for closure.* Time to go home for a little while. He had wrestled with this and tried to fight his desire, listing all the reasons it was wrong, and why she was better off without him. But he wanted her so badly, and he could no longer resist her magnetic pull. Taye got out his phone and dialed.

"This number is for emergencies only," Mockingbird said.

He sounded . . . different, somehow. Different cadence, different in a way Taye couldn't put his finger on. But nothing in his tone said he had just woken up, though he had no idea what time zone the other man was in.

"Yeah."

"So if you don't have some Foundation bastards about to end you, I'm curious why you called." He didn't sound curious. He sounded tired and impatient.

Taye could understand. With the burden this man carried, it was a wonder he ever slept at all. Everyone counted on him to keep the operations running smoothly and to extricate them if they ran into trouble. And the demands never ceased. That knowledge wouldn't stop him, however. He was down to the point where he had precious little to lose.

"I'm asking a favor."

"Really."

"I've completed most of my missions now. They all went better than expected. No loss of life on our side, major hurt to the bad guys."

"True enough. So what do you need?" A little curter than usual, maybe—he seemed eager to get off the line.

"A vacation."

"Reasonable request. What's the catch?"

"I want you to tell me where Cardinal is."

Silence. The line hummed with the static he'd come to associate with Mockingbird, probably the voice scrambling gear he used. "That's strictly against policy. It's for her safety as well as your own."

Desperation trickled into his tone. "Look, I know you've sent people there for recovery, and then had Finch go to work on them. I'm willing to submit to the same treatment afterward."

"You want to spend time with her . . . that you won't remember? You got it bad."

Yeah, I kinda already know that. Despair made him willing to promise anything, say anything; he missed her so much it hurt. It had all but killed him to let her walk away—to act like the time they'd spent together hadn't meant everything to him.

By now, she might have moved on. She would've had time to meet other guys and see he wasn't special at all. And if that was the case, then she'd enjoy telling him to fuck off in person.

"Consider it a dying man's last wish."

"I wondered when you were gonna bring that up. Hawk said you were puking blood on the last run. Not a good sign, my friend."

"I know. And after this break, I'll make the final run for you. My word on it."

If that meant anything. He might've been a compulsive liar in his last life. *Yeah,* he told himself. *It does mean something. You're a new man now.*

There was a long silence while MB thought it over. Taye was prepared to beg if it came to that. The indecision surprised him, though. He'd expected a quick *fuck off* or *we can do this, but don't tell anyone* type reply. Quietly he wondered if the pressure was getting to MB.

Eventually, he prompted, "So . . . can you help me?"

"It's against my better judgment, but I'm not unsympathetic to your position." He hesitated. "I know what it's like to want somebody you can't have."

Interesting. He never would've guessed MB had any softer feelings at all. He always seemed borderline robotic, wholly focused on the mission. Despite his curiosity, he knew better than to press for more. He might just piss the guy off and change his mind.

"Where's Cardinal then?"

"I'll get you the address." There was a pause, and then he spoke it quickly, as if he wasn't sure of the choice he'd just made. *More unusual behavior.* Mockingbird never seemed less than certain about anything. That was part of the reason why people followed him without question. He was the answer man, magical, mystical, and never wrong.

But Taye was too relieved to push. "What's the best way to get to Wichita from here?"

"I'll hook you up."

"Heron?"

"None other."

Taye went immediately to his standard-issue agent laptop and did some Googling. "Could you have him drop me off downtown? I have something to do first."

"Not a prob. We don't offer much in the way of severance packages, but our fringe benefits are top notch."

"Thanks. I won't forget this."

Mockingbird laughed. "You will actually. And don't mention it. You've got three weeks. Make the most of them."

"I will," he answered, and cut the call.

Mockingbird sent Heron right away because he popped into the safe house before Taye had time to do anything other than grab his backpack. Heron scrawled, *Do you get motion sick?*

Though it was hard to tell how the whiskey and the OxyContin would affect his travel tolerance, he answered, "I don't think so."

Taking that as gospel, Heron seized his arm and jerked him out of the world into a wind tunnel full of melting spiders made of wax. At least that was how his brain processed it, and then they ported back into the known universe. Here, it was still and warm, a pretty day in late spring.

"Wichita?" he asked.

Heron nodded and disappeared. Nobody knew exactly what his deal was. He had a tongue, but his throat didn't work right; he simply couldn't speak. Some smart-ass he'd ported for recovery had started an urban legend that Heron screamed his voice away, when the Foundation first locked him up. Whatever the truth, Heron wasn't talking. *Heh. No pun intended.*

Because it was nice out and he had plenty of time, Taye walked the mile and a half to the health center. Maybe it was fucking presumptuous, but he would show up at Gillie's door with a clean bill of health, papers in hand. It wasn't like he could tell her about his partners; he didn't remember them. So before he laid a finger on her—assuming she'd let him—he would make sure he was safe. Emotionally, he wasn't safe for her at all, but he couldn't resist the need to be with her, at least for these very short weeks. He missed her too much to keep fighting the endless need. It was funny; her memory had conquered him with distance and absence.

Hoist with your own petard, dumbass. You thought once you got her away from you, it would get easier. It hadn't. Every day he'd been apart from her, the wound bled endlessly. *Well, if this last glimpse of her is all I get of happily ever after, so be it.*

Still he braced for the worst. *She might have moved on.* And if that was the case, he'd wish her well, and go for good.

There was simply no time to make himself worthy of her. Yet he would have felt like he was doing her a terrible disservice if he hadn't let her explore other options before swooping in to claim her, much as it hurt him, even more than the daggers grinding in his stomach. So maybe it was too late; maybe he'd only had a shot at her as long as she didn't see there were better men in the world.

Regardless, Taye walked into the redbrick building, went up to the fourth floor, and filled out the forms. In his leather duster and motorcycle boots, he didn't fit in with the other patients, who were all dressed in silk and cashmere. The receptionist—a silver haired matron—eyed him when she saw he didn't have insurance . . . because this was a pricy private clinic; he'd checked them out before he hung up with Mockingbird.

"Do you have an appointment?"

"I'm just here for some tests," he said. "I understand you can help me . . . draw blood and expedite the process. I'm paying cash."

Her demeanor grew a little friendlier. "Ah. What kind of tests?"

"Full STD panel and HIV finger stick."

"If we send the sample to the lab today, we can have results in three days. The HIV test we can do on premises. Results in about half an hour. The nurse can take care of you. No need to see the doctor."

"Excellent."

It didn't take long, as she'd promised. The HIV test came back clean, a relief for Gillie's sake. Hell only knew what he might've done in his past life. Taye left then, heading back to his hotel. They'd call when his lab work came back.

For three days, he sat and waited, watching bad TV and trying to ignore the pain in his gut. He wasn't sure he could hide his illness this time around; she would certainly notice the pills. Maybe he could convince her they were vitamins.

At last, the phone rang, and he swung by the clinic to hear the news. The relief when he studied the results surprised him. If he'd picked up anything, he couldn't have gone to her. He had almost been expecting it, given the scraps of memory that came to him in his dreams. But apparently his vices had been drink and violence, not unprotected sex.

Nerves crowded his head, but it was time. Taye called a cab.

Though there was an electronic entry, the gate opened without anyone asking who he was visiting. Maybe the guard thought he lived there. That was pretty fucking stupid; just because he had cab fare, it didn't mean he belonged here.

Then he got into her building itself without trouble when a neighbor was coming out. God, any bastard with killing in mind would have no trouble at all getting to her. It chilled his blood. He ran up the stairs, ignoring the knife in his side.

Before he got to the apartment, however, he heard laughter—Gillie . . . and someone else, a male someone; their voices hinted at intimacy and familiarity. Fear froze his steps, his hand upraised to knock. Before he could make up his mind, the door opened.

She was still a brunette with a flip cut. Contacts tinted her eyes green, but the gentle curve of the mouth was the same. She had freckles now, a sweet smattering across the bridge of her nose. If possible, she was even more beautiful than he'd remembered . . . because she looked happy. No more running, no more working terrible jobs for a pittance. What the hell was he doing here? Lines from a Trent Reznor song flickered in his brain. Yeah, he'd only hurt her. But he couldn't walk away either; he didn't have the innate altruism to deny himself again.

"Hey," he said.

Gillie recovered her poise swiftly, her smile locking into a shape he hadn't seen before. It had a false quality, like plastic fruit. "It's been a while. Steve, this is my friend, Brandon."

Steve. That was the name he'd chosen in the bus station, so long ago now. That last time, he'd walked away from her, made her think he didn't care, and now he'd reap the bitter harvest. *This is what heartbreak feels like.*

The kid stuck out his hand politely, and Taye felt a thousand years old as he shook. Sick roaring in his head almost drowned out the words, "Nice to meet you."

Normal. Be normal. But pain called more pain, and he felt the lightning rise. *Not here. Not now. Be. Normal.*

Gillie saw the danger signs in Taye's face. For all he'd pretended there was nothing between them, for all the lonely he had put her through—those long months without contact—there was an unbreakable bond between them. And the idea she'd chosen a baby like Brandon was driving him crazy. If she didn't take the situation in hand, someone would wind up fried.

"We have a lot of catching up to do," she said to Brandon. "I hope you understand."

"Sure." He grabbed his backpack and headed out.

Fortunately, he had been on his way already. He came over twice a week, ostensibly to study, though she knew he had ulterior motives. Brandon wanted to hook up with her—well, not her. Grace Evans from Ohio. With him, she had to be nice. Polite. No breaking dishes. No screaming. He wouldn't understand the anger, and so it would never, ever be anything but pretend. She couldn't be real with anyone but Taye. From the beginning, she'd known that, but men could be slow.

It hadn't been easy since the incident at the mental hospital. She had bad dreams, and she regretted what she'd done, so much. But she'd faced it alone, proving she was strong enough to handle anything. She'd passed a test. Therefore, it was fitting Taye would sense that and show up now. She was ready for him.

As Brandon went down the stairs, she took Taye's hand. "Dial it down. If you pull here in the hall, I'll have to run again, and that'll piss me off. I'm acing aberrant psych."

"You're not with him?"

Typical man. Took you ages to claim me, but the minute you catch someone else sniffing around, you're about to blow a fuse.

"We're friends," she answered. "Not with benefits. Relax and come inside."

"You're not mad at me?" His expression seemed faintly dazed.

She closed the door behind him, trying to decide how to answer. "I was at first. Went through all the stages, including *he'll be sorry* and *this is it forever*, but it always cycled back around to *it's him or nobody*, once the anger faded."

A little shudder rolled through him, visible to the naked eye. God, he looked like shit, so thin and hollow-eyed, his cheekbones sharp as knives. "You're serious. Have you dated at all?"

"Sure. Casual stuff."

"And there's nobody special."

"There's you," she said. "It's always been you. It'll *always* be you."

"I shouldn't love hearing that so much, but . . . Gillie, you're everything."

"I am?" God, she'd almost given up hope.

He reacted as if he had a world of words dammed up inside him. "Sweet, sweet girl, I want to dive under your skin."

The sweetest ache blossomed in her chest. It wasn't quite an *I love you* but it was closer than she ever thought she'd hear from Taye. Maybe he didn't know how deep he'd taken root already—that he'd woven himself through her soul in an infinite pattern. She'd resigned herself to a future without him, but she'd never wanted that, ever.

"You're there," she told him. "My heart beats for you."

His throat worked. "I want to be part of you so you can't ever cut me out."

"I didn't even try," she said quietly. "I can get by without you. I *have*. I can manage reasonable contentment, but I can't be me without you. I can only be Grace Evans."

"She seems nice. Brandon likes her."

Gillie laughed. "My point. I guess I only have one question—what took you so long?"

"I suffer from a unique genetic condition. It's called Dumbass Syndrome and, unfortunately, there's no cure."

"I'm a healer, you know. I can help."

"You're the only one who can. I have something to show you." Taye dug into his pack and produced a sheaf of papers.

Gillie took them, reading with a dawning sense of wonder. "You got tested?"

"I knew if I came to you, I had to do it with a clean bill of health. Unlike most guys, I can't tell you who my partners have been. I can't say how many women—or men—there may have been. I don't remember shit about my past, and I don't think I ever will."

"I don't care," she said softly. "We'll make new memories. I may as well have been born the day I met you, too, because it was the first day in longer than I could remember that I actually had hope. You have no idea what you did with that message you left in the bathroom."

"And you *believed* me. I have no idea why. At the time I wasn't even sure I could control myself enough to make it happen. Sometimes surges still get away from me."

"That's part of the magic, isn't it? In a place like that, we found each other."

"I taunted Rowan about you," he admitted.

She grinned. "I know. Silas told me."

"What the—"

" 'Word on the ward is: she's smoking hot. A tight little redhead with a killer ass.' " Gillie pitched her voice low, doing her best Taye impression. " 'I figure she'll be so grateful to see a new face that she'll be riding my pole in under a month. What do you think, Doc? Will she put out?' " She winked, continuing in her normal tone, "I totally would have, you know."

"Dear God."

"Relax, I thought it was hilarious. Only *you* could make him crazy like that . . . You knew just how to push his buttons. Silas showed me the footage after you freed him. I loved when you told Rowan he was the crazy butcher keeping me in his dungeon, so I was never gonna show him my titties and beg him for the cock. True, by the way. And awesome."

A red flush lingered high on his cheeks, but he was smiling, too. "It was kind of inspired, I must admit."

"And this is why it's you. There's nobody else with whom I can acknowledge those days, who would understand what's been done to me. I'm not normal. I never will be. I can pretend, and I can pass, but I have no hope of a real relationship with anyone else." It hurt her to admit this, like he was a consolation prize, and that so wasn't the case. "They took too much away from me, too many years. But you understand that because they stole your memories, too. We're the same, you and I. We fit."

"You don't need to convince me." He drew a deep, shaky breath, as if releasing some long-held tension. "I've wanted you so long I hurt with it."

"What changed your mind about us?" Gillie knew he'd intended to make the break permanent. That last time, he hadn't even left her hope, but sometimes you ran on faith instead.

"I felt like I should give you the chance to meet other people . . . and not just roll you under me without letting you do some comparative shopping first."

That wasn't all of it. From the shadows in his eyes, she saw a secret, maybe even the one that had him looking so thin and tired. But she wouldn't push for his confession. In time, he might trust her enough to confide on his own.

"Well, now I have. Other men tried to get in my pants, some with more determination than others, but I didn't feel anything for them. I always wanted you."

His voice went rough, and the gravelly tone sent a thrill through her. "At night, in bed, I get off remembering how you taste, the softness of your lips, and the way you sound when you come. Those are the only sexual memories I have. All you. Always, you."

A slow burn started deep inside, as Gillie imagined him tugging on his cock as he had that day at the safe house . . . for her pleasure. Every orgasm he'd ever had, she had caused in one way or another. How fucking hot was that? *Irresistible*. She figured this was how some men felt about virgins . . . because in a way, Taye was one, too. He couldn't recall anyone else, and that made him all hers. *Delicious*.

But before she moved forward, she had to be sure. "Tell me we're done pretending this isn't what we both want."

"No more waiting. I gave you a chance to find someone else."

"If I had, you'd have killed poor Brandon . . . and maybe everyone in the building as collateral damage."

"Not on purpose," he muttered. "But I'm not big on restraint. You're mine now."

Mmmm. The need spiked higher, making her want to grind against him, and he hadn't even touched her yet. Not once. They were going to blow the roof off, though not literally, she hoped. With Taye, it was always a possibility. The danger added a little spice, not that they needed additional chemistry. Almost from their first moment, she'd known it could be like this, if he would only let it happen. She would have fucked him on her bathroom floor down in Rowan's dungeon.

"Then let me show you my room. Did I mention it has a bed?"

"Fascinating."

Taye laced his fingers through hers, but she noticed he didn't lead. No sweeping her off her feet. Gillie registered the subtext at once—this was a decision they'd made together—no coercion, no seduction, just willingness and desire. That meant everything to her because he remembered what she'd said about needing to be equals. He didn't see her as a child to be protected anymore.

"We know you're clean," she said softly. "I obviously am. And I have a bonus prize. I got a Depo shot two months ago."

It had seemed like a smart, modern thing to do, taking control of her sexuality. Obviously, she would make love at some point. Best to get the contraception started and see if she had any adverse affects like hormonal swings or weight gain. After all his rebuffs, she hadn't dared hope her first partner would be Taye.

Brow furrowing, he paused beside her bed, and it was so good to see him there. "That's birth control, right?"

"Yep."

"That means—"

"You can go bareback." Thinking he'd laugh, she put her arms behind her head and executed a slow grind, nothing more than club dancing. It wasn't erotic; it was funny, her trying to be all sexy.

But a groan escaped him. "If you don't stop saying shit like that—and working your hips—I'm going to come in my pants."

She thought he was kidding, until she saw his pained expression. He had an enormous bulge in his jeans, and he rubbed it absently as if to ease the ache. Gillie longed to respond in kind, moving in slow circles as she recalled how it felt to have him thrust against her. A deep breath restored some equilibrium.

She turned down the covers on her bed. "Dirty talk does it for you, huh? And I remember you like watching. Pretty soon, I'm gonna own you."

"You already do," he said huskily.

If she had planned for this encounter, she would be wearing better underwear. They had a satin bow in front, but they weren't sexy enough. At least she thought that until she shimmed out of her yoga pants, and caught his avid expression. When she pulled her baby T-shirt over her head, his eyes went incandescent. *Ohhh. It was worth the wait for him to look at me like that.*

"Working for you?" She posed in her panties, hand on hip.

"No bra? I bet Brandon couldn't keep his eyes off your tits."

Honestly, she hadn't even thought of it. Her breasts weren't huge, so she often went without, particularly at home. But in retrospect, the kid might have noticed, and she didn't mind; it was a turn-on to be found desirable, and Taye's jealousy was . . . delightful.

"I didn't pay attention," she admitted.

"Do something for me."

If he wanted another private show, she'd scream in frustration. She was good at playing with herself; she had been doing it for years. But it was time to add to her carnal repertoire.

"What?"

"Take out your contacts. I need to see your eyes."

Oh. Something in her melted a little. Gillie hurried to the bathroom so he wouldn't realize just how completely he owned her heart. It was too soon; he had only just accepted the inevitability of a sexual relationship between them. At least according to TV, guys didn't always leap to the conclusion that physical rapport equated to happily ever after. She would have to ease him into the master plan. *After I fuck his brains out.*

As she came back, blue-eyed once more, Taye scrambled out of his clothes so fast she thought he might break a window with his boots—and she didn't care. Once he got naked, she saw he had lost weight, but this wasn't the time to ask if he'd been eating right. Now he had a gaunt and irrefutable beauty, strength refined to its essence. His muscles flexed as he lifted her into his arms, his heat shocking and delicious.

"Mine," he whispered. "Finally. Oh, God, Gillie."

CHAPTER 20

Taye trembled with need. Her angel blue eyes contrasted beautifully with her dark hair, though he missed her red curls. Gillie was every bit as lovely as he recalled, slim and shapely with small, pert breasts and gently flaring hips. Her thighs were thicker, but it was pure muscle, probably from the bike he'd seen in the foyer.

Get hold of yourself. You can't just ravish her. It's her first time. You have to make it special. Inwardly, he whimpered at the idea of controlling his lust, but at least the raw feeling tempered the constant agony in his gut.

"No," she said softly.

"What—"

"I don't need rose petals and moonlight. It's three in the afternoon on a Thursday, and I will die if you don't kiss me."

Freedom. Her words took all the pressure away, leaving only the longing. He closed the distance between them in two strides and drew Gillie into his arms, nothing between them but her tiny panties. She stretched up, and he leaned down; she made him feel irresistible, even though he was just an average-looking guy, and less than the romantic ideal of six feet tall. But since she was only five-two, he figured she didn't miss that last inch.

Her mouth brushed his as she wound her arms around his neck, a butterfly kiss. Taye refused to let her tease him, so he deepened it, parting her lips with his own. He nipped her lower lip and touched his tongue to hers. She murmured in pleasure, seeking more. He lost control when she sucked, and the kiss turned into ravishment, long drugging moments where he thrust his tongue between her lips in a delicious precursor to sex, symbolic and irresistible.

Every man in the world should understand how thoroughly she belonged to him—and she would until he bit it. Maybe that wasn't fair but he cared fuck-all for that now; he believed her. She was the strong one, damn near unbreakable, for all he'd worried about protecting her from harm. Losing him wouldn't end her. As it turned out, she was stronger than him because three months without her had wrecked him, stolen his will to do the right thing.

Got to have you. Can't die without being part of you. He gazed down into her eyes, and thought, *Gillie, Gillie-my-love. Stay with me.*

Taye ran his mouth along her jaw to her throat and took special pleasure in biting down; he sucked to create the bruise that would mark her. The next time she saw Brandon, he'd know. A little growl rose up.

She whimpered, arched her neck—such a graceful curve—and dug her hands into his back. Her whole body had a dusting of freckles now, the most delicious cinnamon and cream. He imagined her lying in the sun, drowsily soaking it in for the first time in years. In his mind's eye, he put himself in the picture beside her, lazily rubbing sunscreen on her. *Mmm, yeah. Time to pay attention to those pretty breasts.*

He lifted her and tossed her on the bed. She landed with a startled laugh and a bounce, but there was no trepidation in her look, only avid hunger. It shone from her blue eyes, clear as the heaven she offered him. *You don't deserve her,* he thought. But that lack didn't stop him from following her down. Taye swept his hands lightly over her body, barely grazing her nipples with his blunt nails. Her breath caught; he watched her face as he touched her. Surely there was nothing so beautiful in the whole damn world. He skimmed his thumbs back and forth, bringing each nipple to a tight point.

Silently, she drew his head down, and he teased her with

delicate kisses and flicks of his tongue. Gillie gave his hair a tug, so he relented, sucking one sweet peak into his mouth. She arched and moaned, hips lifting. Soothing her with gentle strokes to her belly, Taye worked his fingers downward until they found the fabric of her panties.

"Touch me," she whispered. "See how wet I am."

Invitation or order, he couldn't resist. Inside, he found her smooth and divinely slick. His touch faltered, and then he had to see to believe. With her help, he worked her panties off and slid downward, parting her thighs in a motion that was pure masculine demand. But from her happy little wriggle, it seemed to work for her. Taye's eyes confirmed what his fingers had discovered; she was completely bare. She'd been right, all those months ago. Gillie was no shy, backward virgin, and she knew what she wanted.

"I had it waxed off." Her smile offered pure temptation. "I was curious how it would look. Sometimes I like to get off in front of the mirror, and I can see better this way."

Too powerful, that mental image—he knew just how she did it. Raw lust careened through him, and it shook him from head to toe. Goddamn, for all his fears about her socialization, he might be the maladjusted one. He didn't know if he was allowed to study the way her body was made. If he'd ever done so, he couldn't remember, and it was fitting that her pretty pink sex would be emblazoned on his memory going forward. She was the only woman he'd ever want; his need for her had reached obsession levels, and he didn't even care.

"Can I look at you?" The question came out as a growl.

"Please. But no touching. If you play with me . . . or lick me . . . I'll come. And that's not on the agenda unless you're inside me. I've flown solo enough."

Aw, Christ. She might as well have a playbook telling her what buttons to push. The idea that he could get close and look but not touch? The heat ratcheted up to dangerous levels; for a moment, he was afraid he'd start drawing metal objects and pulling juice from the light sockets. Taye shook silently for a moment while fighting to separate sex from power. Gillie didn't make it easier when she parted her lips, showing him. Like the rest of her, she was small and compact down there, shiny with lust, her clit already tight.

"So you're saying I can either play with you elsewhere . . . or fuck you." He licked the inner curve of her thigh, adhering to the rules she'd set forth.

Her breath caught. "Is there a problem?"

"No, just clarifying my options."

"Have a clear picture n—*ohhh*—" Her teasing words turned into a moan when he caught tender skin with his teeth.

"Yeah, I think I've worked it out."

"I hope this story has a happy ending."

Oh, Gillie. The ache spread all over his body, and he couldn't tease either of them a minute longer, not when those moments were numbered and so precious. Taye slid upward, widening the space between her thighs.

"Tell me if I hurt you. Or if you get scared."

She gave a husky laugh. "Yes, the naked version of you is terrifying."

"Don't you know you're never supposed to laugh at a man in bed?" But he should have known it would be like that with her. Even imprisoned, she had been all light and sunshine, the one bright spot in the darkness. And that was why he'd known he had to set her free.

"Oh? Is that a rule? I don't read *Cosmo.* Too busy with my psych textbooks."

He grinned down at her, propped on his elbows. "You'll probably learn more about me in there anyway."

"So you're a deviant, then?"

Talking helped his self-control, permitting him to focus on her, not the pressure building in his balls. He angled his body, slid his hands beneath her ass, and tilted her to meet his thrust. *Dear God.* Taye had no experiences to compare it to, but this was the best thing he'd ever felt. She was sweet and small, hot and slick.

"Yeah," he whispered. "I love to fuck innocent girls."

"Damn. And here I thought you wanted *me*."

More than anything. More than life.

He didn't say so aloud, but she saw. God, she always did; she always knew. The only thing he'd managed to keep hidden from her was the cost of his gift, and if they hadn't spent the last three months apart, Taye had no doubt she'd know that by now, too.

"Good to go deeper?"

At her nod, he pushed, a slow and torturous penetration that threatened to melt his bones. The need to come boiled higher. Soon he wouldn't care at all if he felt good inside her, only that she was his. Merely thinking the word nearly undid him; Taye thrust three times, four, before reining himself in, shaking from head to toe.

"It doesn't hurt," she whispered. "I have toys. I used them and thought of you."

He remembered her saying, *Sometimes I like to get off in front of the mirror, and I can see better this way.* Too much stimulation, combined with the luscious heat on his cock. He lost his mind. Taye pounded into her with long, demanding strokes, angling her to meet them. In answer, she wrapped her legs about his hips and drew him deeper still. He had no yardstick to measure her expertise, but she felt perfect, each movement orchestrated to jack him higher.

As he got closer, everything faded but the heat of her body, the softness of her skin, the apple scent of her hair, and the unearthly blue of her eyes. He fell into them, drowning, and then breathing for what felt like the first time in his life. Beneath him, she shuddered and came, his name a broken song on her lips. Only then did he let go. The orgasm cracked him wide open. Too much pleasure, too much, and he was keeping such a secret from her. He almost wept, except it would be such a fucking pussy thing to do, and it would ruin the moment. Somehow he fought it all down as he got his breath back.

She went lax beneath him, her skin glowing with sweat and satisfaction. He rolled off, but carried her with him. They had too little time for him to take a single second for granted. After all, he had to live a whole lifetime with her in eighteen days.

Hours later, Gillie stretched like a contented cat. She hadn't meant to fall asleep, but after having mind-blowing sex with the man of your dreams, it came naturally. He was awake when she opened her eyes; the light had gone, painting the room in shadows. From what she could tell, he hadn't moved at all, except for his hands stroking her back.

"I thought it was the guy who was supposed to conk out and start snoring."

She laughed softly. "Sorry. But that was way better than when I do it myself. More relaxing, too, apparently."

"Good to know. Since I was winging it."

"You haven't practiced with anyone else?" It might seem like a casual question, but it so wasn't. Gillie had the same jealous, possessive feelings where he was concerned; she just didn't light up like a broken power line when they hit. He was hers—and she felt strongly on that point.

"No. I've spent all my time on missions, pretty much. Mockingbird has me working with Silas, er, Hawk. Not supposed to use his real name. He has a girlfriend now."

Intrigued, she levered up on an elbow. "Really? What's she like?"

"Kind of a hippie-chick. But nice."

"I'm glad. He hated himself so much for what Rowan made him do down there."

"We've freed a lot of people. It helps."

"Do they all go to work for Mockingbird?"

"About half. Some just want to find a place to lick their wounds."

Talking about his work brought up an important question. "How long can you stay?"

"A little over two weeks."

"Really?" Longer than she'd dared hope, at least for this first visit. A long-distance relationship where one partner regularly risked his life wasn't ideal, but military wives did it. Women who married spies did it. She'd do whatever it took to be with him.

"Yep. Can you put up with me that long? I warn you, I'm going to demand sex in payment for household chores."

"A blow job for a load of laundry?"

He laughed. God, she loved the sound. It banished his secrets and his darkness, at least for a while. "That sounds fair. But you gotta swallow if you want me to use fabric softener."

"Deal. But *you* stay away from curry."

"You're a sick, sick woman, Gillie Flynn."

"I know. It's part of my charm." She kissed him lightly on the mouth, marveling even now that they were naked, and there were no more reasons they couldn't be together. "How did you talk Mockingbird into this, by the way? He's all about the security risks and layers of protection for our true identities."

Not that she was living as her true self. But the question stood.

He hesitated, and those secrets swam to the surface again. So she gave him a sharp nudge with the elbow to indicate she wasn't having that. Not now. Not anymore.

"Finch is going to wipe out my memory of where you live."

Cold stole over her, the first whisper of dread. "Can he do that? I thought he could only take specific time periods."

"It'll be fine. Trust me."

Well, when he put it like that, she chose to believe in him. In *this*. In happy endings, and people getting what they wanted out of life, even though experience had taught her otherwise, again and again.

"So what will we do next time? Meet somewhere? MB might not like it, but we can e-mail each other. As long as we set up anonymous accounts and don't use names, I don't see why that would flag the Foundation."

"You're right," he agreed. "It wouldn't."

"Will you write me dirty letters?"

He heaved a mock sigh. "You've got the *real* me naked in bed with you and you're thinking about cyber?"

"I have to plan for the future. If you do, I'll use my toys when I read them."

"Dear God." From his tone and the erection he was sporting, he acted like she might be the death of him. "I can't go again without fluids."

"Are you hungry? I have some leftover soup."

"Not so much."

That drew a frown. "You don't look healthy. Have you been skipping meals?"

Guilt flashed across his face. "I guess. I don't have anyone baking for me these days."

"I'll make cookies while you're here. I've perfected the gingersnap recipe. Finally. Only took me twenty batches. I gave away a lot of them at homeless shelters."

"Thank you," he said gravely. "It means everything that you care."

Care? That was such a lukewarm word. People cared for their friends and for their pets. They cared about whether it would rain. Maybe it was time to tell him.

"You know I love you." Quiet statement, devoid of drama—it was fact, not a romantic declaration. No fireworks, no serenades. Gillie didn't cherish some idealized vision of him. She loved his moods, his temper, his bad attitude, his hidden laughter, his sometimes surly nature, and the fact that he would burn the world down to protect her.

She was prepared for refutation and for him to recite all the reasons this wasn't real, why it couldn't work. That had been the deal for so long. Gillie braced for more of the same.

Instead, he said softly, "I know. And I love *you* . . . with all the heart that's in me. That's not much, maybe, but I'll give you everything."

"All your Taye are belong to me?"

Not surprisingly, he offered a blank look. That was fine. She could catch him up on dorky Internet memes; they had a lifetime, after all. The realization sent a shiver through her. No more fear. No more uncertainty. He was hers; the next two weeks were only the beginning.

"What time are your classes tomorrow?"

"Early," she said. "I'll be back by two."

"So . . . we have plenty of time, then." He kissed the spot behind her ear that drove her nuts.

"I dunno. I have a quiz to study for."

"Want me to drill you?"

She flashed a wicked grin. "Thought you'd never ask."

CHAPTER 21

Tray in his hands, Taye stood for a moment and watched Gillie sleep. Without mascara, her lashes showed red gold against her skin. He could take pleasure in counting every freckle on her face, but that struck him as slightly obsessive. Instead he set the tray on the nightstand and leaned down to kiss her awake. Her lids flickered open; her smile sent a spear of pleasure straight through him. She tangled her fingers in his hair, giving a gentle tug. He loved seeing her like this, all pleasure and satisfaction.

She stretched lazily. "Breakfast in bed? What time is it?"

"I got up early." He never slept well these days. "It's not quite seven. You have plenty of time before your eight o'clock."

"I could get used to this."

You can't, love. But I so *wish you could.*

"We have scrambled eggs, toast and jelly, coffee, and orange juice. Am I allowed to eat in your bed?"

"Taye," she said with devastating sweetness, "as long as I've been waiting, you can do whatever you damn well please in my bed."

"It's cruel of you to say that when you're leaving."

"I prefer to think of it as delayed gratification. And I'm coming back. What will you do while I'm gone?"

An excellent question. "Read. What do you recommend?"

He couldn't remember if he had a favorite book, or whether he had ever read for pleasure. But he was willing to do as she'd suggested—fill his head with new memories and new information to compensate for what he'd lost.

"What're you in the mood for?" Gillie shoveled in some eggs without the refinement that had marked her manners in the facility. Now, she could do as she liked without someone watching and judging. Then she seemed to realize and grinned at him. "Book-wise, I mean."

"Right. Well, I was gonna suggest you ditch today so I can spend those six hours licking you all over."

"The leading cause of dry mouth," she quipped. "Anyway, I have some awesome books about demon brothers. Lots of action and sex."

"Sold."

"I'd totally skip, but I'm a TA for one of my professors, so I have to set a good example. Plus, I have work to do. Don't worry, I won't be gone long." But her radiant expression said she liked the suggestion.

Gillie took a bite of toast, smearing the red raspberry jam beside her mouth. Then she licked it away and he had the overwhelming urge to kiss her . . . taste that sweetness on her lips. So he did. No reason to refrain anymore. *Mmm.*

Afterward, he reclined against the headboard, watching her; it pleased him to feed her. Taye felt pretty sure anything more complicated than scrambled eggs was beyond him, though. Not that it mattered. She knew how to cook. Rowan had encouraged her to live a "normal" life.

"Aren't you eating?"

"I had something earlier."

These days, he was taking vitamins and pills in lieu of food. Proper meals just hurt too fucking bad. When the need for nutrition got to be too much, he would down a nutritional supplement and then curl onto his side for a couple of hours. Taye knew it couldn't go on like this much longer. Sometimes he thought about asking Gillie to heal him; she could take the disease from him, but it meant pulling all this pain into her body, and for him, it wasn't hyperbole to say he'd rather die than hurt her. He had selfish reasons for wanting to be the one person who never asked her for anything, who gave without taking.

On his darkest days, he still thought about requesting a cure, but since there was no banishing his carcinogenic power—and he couldn't always control it—this wouldn't be a one-shot deal. As he pulled, the disease would return; therefore, he would be committing her to a lifetime using a power that had nearly destroyed her. After seeing what the Foundation had done to her, he just couldn't. Death, however terrifying and unwelcome, proved a more viable alternative to hanging around her neck like an albatross. He couldn't take the risk that she'd get tired of him, and then she'd be bound to him out of pity. *Because I'd literally die without her.* And how pathetic would that be?

"So you were just joking about eating in my bed? I see how you are." She finished her breakfast and slid off the mattress.

With delightful exhibitionism, she stretched, showing him . . . everything. His cock hardened and the ache built in his balls. You'd think sex would relax him, but right then, gazing at her naked body, he felt frantic, as if she were leaving him for more than a few hours.

"How do you feel about a joint shower?"

"With or without extracurricular activities?"

He grinned. "Either?"

"I think I'm curious how it feels to be fucked standing up. Can you handle it?"

"If I can't, are you going to request a replacement?"

She leaned down and nipped his lower lip. "Is there a union where I can complain?"

"Not so much."

"Just as well," she said, serious then. "You're the only one I've ever wanted."

"Those casual dates you mentioned . . . did anyone ever touch you? Or kiss you?"

She hesitated. "Do we really want to do this?"

Bootless rage thrummed in him, nearly kindling an involuntary pull. Just in time, he locked it down, but she saw the near miss and put a hand on his arm, soothing him.

"Okay, sorry. I've been touched, but not intimately. I've been kissed, but not well. Does that help any?"

"Not really," he growled. "I kind of want to set them all on fire."

"Hey, you're the one who wanted me to window shop."

"True." It might be primitive, but now he wanted to fuck her even more.

He had to give her enough pleasure to last a lifetime. Taye wanted her to remember him, no matter who she ended up with, and he was vain enough to wish she'd never find anyone who could make her feel this good. Someday she'd find Mr. Picket Fence and have some kids, but part of her would always miss *him*.

"Still interested in that shower? I have to leave in half an hour."

With a wolfish smile, he took her hand and put it on his lap. "I'm thinking yeah."

She fluttered her lashes, falling into the role of the ingénue with delightful alacrity. "Oh. Does that hurt you?"

Evilly, she rubbed her hand up and down the fly of his jeans, adding just enough pressure to madden him. Taye snagged her fingers and rolled to his feet. The resultant burn in his belly would be almost enough to kill a normal man's boner, but he'd gotten to the point where pain and pleasure mingled together; he couldn't have one without the other. So it just made him harder. Making love to Gillie was an affirmation, the ultimate defiance of death.

"I don't think I can wait for the shower."

"You'll have to be fast then."

"I don't think I can be anything else right now."

Her breath came quicker now, his arousal driving hers. Her hands went to the buttons on his jeans, and she freed his cock with genuine expertise. *Gotta admire a woman who knows what she wants.*

Gillie gave him a little push and he fell back sideways on the mattress. "Mind if I drive?"

"You kidding? I get to admire how beautiful you are while you do the work."

Since he'd only put on jeans after getting up, it didn't take her long to strip him naked. Despite his words, Taye sensed he hadn't often done this; it felt unfamiliar to lay back and wait. *Guess I prefer to be in charge.* But if it meant he got to gaze up into her pretty face and see the joy as she opened her thighs and positioned him for her pleasure—well, he could lay quiet and let her go cowgirl on him.

Oh fuck yes.

She was already so wet, and she slid down on him slowly. This speed could be considered torture, in fact. He needed a fucking and she gently, slowly circled her hips, getting used to the feel of the position and seeking the perfect angle for penetration. When she found it, she cried out, her blue eyes wide with astonished pleasure. He responded with an upward thrust, giving her more, and that sparked her into motion.

Gillie braced her hands on his chest and began to ride in earnest, dropping down hard each time, her pussy tightening as her excitement built. He framed her hips in his hands and marveled at the beauty of her. She had new scars, but he didn't ask; he knew she'd earned them saving lives, and they only increased her loveliness.

Helpless to resist, he stroked the rosy skin of her bare labia; he felt so dirty for enjoying the sight of her riding his cock—and that turned him on more. From this angle, he watched as well as savored each movement. She closed her eyes, her breath coming in sobbing moans, but he had to see every shift, every flicker. He had never seen anything so fine as Gillie rising over him, her mouth parted. When his thumbs brushed her clit, she came, slamming down on him and jerking with each pulse. He wasn't quite there yet, as he'd gotten caught up in the satisfaction of watching her.

She smiled down at him dreamily. "Oh, look. You finally got me riding your pole."

God only knew why that did it, but the fact that she could joke with him after coming so hard? It unraveled him. She had always, always been love and light and laughter. Always. With a groan, he rolled her beneath him, caught her thighs in his hands, and went for it with hard, fast thrusts. She was sweet and soft beneath him, limp with satiation, but by the time he started getting close, she perked, as if she might go a second time.

"Think I can get you there again?" He leaned down and nuzzled her skin, every bit he could reach. "God, you feel good."

"Maybe," she answered, breathless. "Keep at it."

That sounded like a challenge, so he reined himself back and ignored the pressure building in his balls. No orgasm yet. Thankfully, the pain in his stomach helped to manage that. He watched her face and adjusted his pace according to her gasps and moans. She liked a slight angle and fast, long pushes. Taye gave her what she needed and Gillie rewarded him by screaming and clawing his back. It was like he hit the sweet spot, nudging her up a notch. Her intensity sparked his own and he came so hard his vision went spotty. Pleasure blasted him until he fell, lax and brainless, his cock throbbing inside her even as he softened. God, he wanted to do the dirtiest things to her, even now.

"I have five minutes," she breathed. "Gonna be the fastest shower ever. Wash my back?"

He did—and it was tender and lovely. The urge to cry rose in him again, but he refused, and impending loss froze behind his eyes. Quite apart from pain management, he hadn't wanted to miss a moment of holding her the night before, so he hadn't drifted off. Now exhaustion would make him careless if he didn't take steps.

I don't want her to know. Let these be our perfect, idyllic days.

And once she left, he took the pills that let him sleep.

Taye was . . . lovely. The past week had been everything she could have dreamed. He was different in some indefinable way, as if he had resolved some inner conflict. Before, he always had so much rage and turmoil that she worried about him, but it seemed working with Mockingbird had helped him achieve inner peace.

It was helping her, too. No longer did she fear and loathe her healing. If she *chose* to use it, the process didn't offer the same soul-killing agony. Sure, there was physical pain, but never the sense of emotional violation that accompanied the sessions in Rowan's lab. Since Gillie wanted to help people, she could only consider that a good thing. Now, she dared to think ahead to that homeless shelter, where she could treat the walls with tungsten powder and quietly save lives in addition to helping to heal minds—quite a big fucking dream for someone who had once only wanted to see the sun again before she died.

But these days, she had hope. Though she'd suffered, it seemed like she had finally come out on the bright end of the tunnel. She loved Taye so much it felt like a star inside her, glowing constantly with heat and need. And he loved her back, no doubting that.

At first, it was a little strange having him around all the time, but she liked the everyday details. Somehow, doing dishes with him made everything seem more real. People might fantasize about great sex, cuddling, or talking, but she was sure they didn't dream about scraping plates and sharing a sink. Therefore, he was here. He was hers.

Even with him present, dreams still haunted her. Sometimes she dreamt of Rowan and the lab; more often, these days, she dreamed the death of the man at the hospital. Nobody had ever pointed a finger her way, but there was no doubt she'd caused it with a single, terror-charged touch. Adrenaline had to be the chief difference, or this would've happened down below, too. But there, she had never been frightened in quite so visceral a fashion.

Mostly, she thought she had a handle on it, but on their eighth night together, he woke her from sleep with worry shining from his face. Her own cheeks were wet with tears.

"Shh," he said. "You're safe."

Guess you can't be cool about killing someone. She clutched him and tucked her face against his chest. *Christ, he's thin.* He stroked her back for a few moments, soothing her, until her breathing slowed.

"You want to tell me about it?"

Not really. But she didn't keep secrets from him either. So she eased back onto her side; it would be easier in the dark, at least. Gillie took a deep breath and relayed the events in a monotone. Some part of her wondered if this would change how he saw her.

"I'm guessing this is a new thing," he said, once she'd finished.

"Yeah."

"Gillie, you were scared for your life. I'd guess a defense mechanism kicked in. It's not your fault . . . he had a *knife* to your throat. In fact, I kinda want to kill him all over again for that."

"But he was nuts. He couldn't help himself."

"That doesn't mean he gets to threaten you."

"He didn't deserve to die for it."

"You shouldn't blame yourself. You didn't ask for this. If anything, it can be attributed to the Foundation, who first gave you that experimental injection."

"Yeah. My parents never had much money. They were good people, but dreamers, you know? Their master plan for future security was to win the lottery."

"At least you know that much about them."

She exhaled unsteadily and tucked her head against his shoulder. "I guess it's bothering me, too, because there were no consequences. Normal people can't see how I had anything to do with his collapse."

"You're punishing yourself," he said softly. "Isn't that worse?"

"Not worse than prison, from what I understand."

"I can see you're torn up, but for me, it's a relief that you can defend yourself when I'm not around."

That surprised a shaky laugh from her. "Yeah, anyone who grabs me, intending harm, is in for an awful surprise."

He smiled at her. "Before, I thought you were too good, too sweet, too . . . everything. But now you seem a little more like me."

"So you *like* my dark side?"

"I adore every side of you, love."

When he drew her back into his arms, she expected that line served as a precursor to sex, but instead he tucked her against him tenderly and rested his head on her hair. She thought she was too upset to sleep, but somehow, the heat and security of his presence made it possible for her to let go, and this time, the dreams didn't come.

On their fourteenth day together—and she tried not to panic over the way they speeded away—Gillie dragged Taye to her favorite bar. While he might prefer quiet evenings, she had spent enough of those to enjoy crowds, noise, and excitement. She liked to dance; she enjoyed the music, and on Thursday, she even sang. By a stroke of good luck, she could combine her passions: Taye, public spectacle, and karaoke.

In four days, he was leaving.

"Tell me you packed something nice," she said, grinning down at him.

Taye set down the paperback and stretched like a sleepy tiger. He really was reading the demon books she'd recommended, though they tended to spike his sex drive—not that it needed any boosting. She was worried about him, all told; he didn't eat much, and he seemed to grow thinner by the day. Soon he would pass from lean muscle to dangerous emaciation.

"Define nice."

"Something besides motorcycle boots and white T-shirts."

"Then, nope. I can buy something, though, if you tell me the occasion."

"We're going dancing."

To her surprise, he didn't protest. Maybe his loss of memory also wiped any aversion he might've felt.

"What's the venue? Upscale, downtown, hip-hop?"

"It's a place in Old Town, casual, but fun. You don't need to dress up much. Jeans with a nice shirt and a decent pair of shoes should do it . . . I don't think you can move in those boots."

He grinned. "I bet you're right. Wonder if I *have* any vertical moves."

"We're gonna find out." God, she appreciated his willingness to try.

While she got ready, he went shopping. Her lack of a car didn't bother him, though she had dated enough, even casually, to realize he was going above and beyond. A few college guys complained because she didn't have a car and couldn't do her share of the driving.

She put on a dark blue mini-dress, Chinese-inspired with silver embroidery and mandarin collar. It was sleeveless and deceptively simple, but with long blue silk opera gloves, a pair of matching heels and heavier eye makeup, she felt transformed from her everyday self. She knew a moment of regret that she couldn't go sleeveless without gloves, but she had to cover the needle marks. Generally, she didn't dress up much—college didn't require it—but Taye had never seen her best. It meant a lot that he wanted her, no matter what, but sometimes a woman needed to wow the man in her life. By the time he got back, it was dark, and she was ready; he stopped in the middle of her living room, his sea green gaze sweeping from head to toe and back again.

"Damn," he said.

Gillie had the notion she had stolen his bigger words, so she took that as a compliment. She spun slowly, so he got the full effect, and his face went dreamy with desire. Lovely, how he didn't attempt to hide it anymore.

"I suppose you need to go change." She tilted her head at the bag in his hand.

"Oh, right."

When he returned, he wore his jeans, new leather shoes, along with a blue and gray striped shirt, untucked but with his model-thin build, it said casual instead of sloppy. The narrow cut made him look lean and dangerous; his longish, tousled hair and the scruff he almost never shaved added to the impression. Gillie found him beautiful in the way of crystals encountered unexpectedly in a dark cave, a shock to quicken the heart.

"It's almost like you knew what I was wearing."

"My imagination's not that good, love."

They took the bus downtown and walked the rest of the way to the club. She liked the vibe and the DJs. There was a rooftop view, and people milled around outside since it was a pretty night. But it wasn't the sort of place where you had to impress a bouncer to get in, just a fun spot to cut loose, drink, and dance . . . things she had never been allowed to do before. Sometimes she felt like a confusing twist of nesting instincts and strangled youth.

"I'm pretty sure I can dance," Taye said, as they went into the club.

"Yeah?"

"I seem to remember that. Nothing specific, but I think maybe I used to be a party boy."

She liked imagining a time where he was happy, even if he couldn't recollect it. "Let's find out."

"Sounds good."

The floor had plenty of room, so as "Tik Tok" came on—a dance favorite among the college crowd—she led him out. She noticed the other guys danced in more or less the same shuffling style, nothing flamboyant, nothing unexpected. She could tell by their expressions they were out to please their girlfriends or in hope of getting laid, with possibly some intertwining of the two. With Taye, it was different; the music caught him, and he *did* have some vertical moves—smooth, fluid spins, graceful footwork straight out of a music video. Delighted, Gillie found herself hard pressed to keep up with him. He had no shame or inhibitions; he danced up against her, practically sexing her up in front of the whole bar. But he wasn't out for attention. Instead, he focused wholly on her. She caught other women checking him out, probably wondering where she'd found a man like him.

You wouldn't believe me if I told you, ladies.

When the song ended, she stood breathless and smiling. "You sure you weren't in a boy band during your lost years?"

He grinned back. "Hm. Should we check the *Where Are They Now* files in case someone's missing me?"

"No," she said. "I'd rather keep you all to myself."

It was a magical night, and the only downside came when she ran into Brandon. Beer in hand, he registered the intimacy between "Steve" and herself in one glance; though he wasn't studying to be a cryptologist, he could decode body language just fine. Fortunately, he didn't linger, instead heading to the bar with his buddies.

"He's jealous," Taye whispered into her ear. "All that time he spent playing the good 'friend' and *I'm* the one in your bed. Life's not fair."

She smiled up at him. The music had slowed, so he had both arms around her waist, hers about his neck, and they were shamelessly dirty dancing, old-school style. "But sometimes it works out exactly as it should."

Sorrow flickered in his face, a shadow she'd seen before but couldn't identify. "Sometimes. Sometimes it does."

"Is there something you want to tell me?"

Please. I deserve your secrets. You can trust me . . . I ought to have proven that by now.

"Just that you're the prettiest one here." By his avid expression, he believed it. Not empty words, and she took that desire in lieu of full confession.

Ah well. I'll find out in time.

Before they left, she had to get onstage. She studied the music selection and gauged the mood of her drunken audience carefully before she made her choice. Taye winced and laughed all the way through her over-the-top rendition of Peter Cetera's "You're the Inspiration." At one point, he covered his eyes so he wouldn't have to see her emotive crooning. *Hey, if you can't sing, at least you can have fun.*

When she finished, she pointed at him and said, "Your turn."

He shook his head as he lifted her down from the small stage. "I worship you, Gillie-love. I do. I'd do anything for you. But not that. Never. Ever."

He startled a laugh from her. "So karaoke is where you draw the line?"

"Absolutely. Be happy I can dance."

"Oh, I *am*."

"Can we go home, so I can show you how much I enjoy that up-and-down shimmy thing? Particularly when you do it right up against me."

"I can't think of anything I want more."

CHAPTER 22

Taye silently blessed the pills that let him get through the night. Without them, there was no way he could've danced as he had—and that would've been a crying shame, considering how happy it made Gillie. But it put questions in his head about where he'd learned those moves. *Maybe I was a club kid, before crazy got the best of me.* He liked the relative innocence of it.

They walked to the bus stop—so ridiculous to travel that way—but its simplicity suited her, and who was he to complain? Starry night, spring—Taye tried to memorize everything: the way the wind smelled, the sound of distant laughter, and the click of her heels on the sidewalk. She leaned back against him as they waited, and on the ride home, she rested her head on his chest.

He held her hand as they went through the apartment complex gates and followed the sidewalk to her apartment. Mockingbird had given him three weeks, and he had spent three of those days waiting for the all-clear. That left him eighteen, and two weeks had already flown by.

On Monday, he had to go. *Only four days left.* A devil lived in his head, counting down the time as if it were a doomsday clock—and maybe that was an apt analogy. Because his world would end when he left her.

Not thinking of that tonight. Go away, death. Go bother someone else.

The dress fit her like a second skin, both exquisite and erotic. He'd be lying if he said he didn't like the way other men looked at her. Hell, most of them wished they were him tonight. She led the way up the stairs, her hips swaying like a sexy metronome. In front of the apartment, she fumbled with the keys; she'd drunk more than he had.

Gillie smelled of apples when he leaned down to kiss the nape of her neck. As always, she reminded him of springtime, where everything was bright and green, burgeoning with potential, and she left him raw with her emotional honesty. He followed her in the door, admiring what she'd built here, wishing he could be a permanent part of it.

This apartment was the first home she had ever known, and it showed. He could tell how much care had gone into selecting the walnut brown furniture and the contrasting blond oak tables. Each abstract picture, every patterned throw pillow said something about her personality. As a whole, it was bright but comfortable, inviting but beautiful, completely Gillie. Remembering how they'd squatted in squalor, he felt a rush of shame that he'd denied her this.

If I'd said yes to MB sooner, she could've had this sooner. Of course you'd be dead by now. Always a trade-off.

"Did you have fun tonight?" she asked, as if it could be doubted.

He didn't remember ever having *fun*; it wasn't part of his lexicon. Sometimes fighting beside Hawk was satisfying, but it wasn't fun, at least not in the way she meant. Not light and happy and carefree. Fuck, *nothing* was; it couldn't be.

"Yeah. It was amazing."

You *were amazing.* He loved that she didn't care if she could sing . . . she couldn't. Still, she gave everything to that stupid song and had a blast doing it. Life with Gillie Flynn would be fun as hell, and he ached that he wouldn't see her old and gray, rocking a walker and maybe an artificial hip.

"I guess we have to go to bed and have sex now." She tried for a mournful tone, but the sparkle in her eyes gave away the teasing.

Christ, she's fantastic.

"I'm afraid so. I did the dishes today, and as I recall, we made a deal."

"It's fine. I can fake it again."

At that, he grabbed her with a growl and wound his arms about her waist, lifting her for a long, delicious kiss. "You're a wicked woman."

"I'm glad you finally noticed."

"Bed?" It wasn't really a question, but he felt obligated to check as he carried her toward the bedroom.

"Please."

That night, he took his time with her; hours kissing and nuzzling, teasing her breasts and making her writhe. She came three times before he fucked her, and she wept as she went for the fourth, her pussy pulsing sweetly on his cock. The drugs started to wear off then, making it hard for him to thrust without pain, and she saw it.

Rousing sleepily, she put a hand to his cheek and asked, "Are you all right?"

No. Oh, God, love, no. This is the beginning of the end.

He almost told her then. Almost. Because the love in her eyes was too much, and he didn't think he could get through the next few days while encouraging her to believe everything would turn out just fine.

You're not being fair to her, you bastard. She has a right to know.

But then she distracted him by gently nudging him onto his back and kissing her way down. Her mouth was hot and featherlight, teasing with every kiss. When she wrapped her lips around his cock, all thoughts of confession went away. She let him lay still and drink in the pleasure—and then she begged with silent looks for him to show her how he wanted it. God, that was the hottest thing ever. In response to his touches and gestures, her pace increased; the pressure grew. He blazed for her, such fierce need, it overpowered the pain, and then he came. She didn't try to pull away, instead drinking him down.

Afterward, he drew her up and kissed her in sweet, lingering desire, not gone, merely banked. She tasted of him, of salt and sweet, irresistible. As soon as she slept, he'd take something, but for now, the endorphins made it bearable.

"I love you," he said, because *not* saying it was unthinkable.

If he could, he'd say it a thousand times, so if nothing else, she believed.

"Mmm. I feel like I should say something clever in response but my brain is sleepy."

"G'night, Gillie."

But she was already out. He waited a few more minutes before slipping from the bed and going in search of the meds in his coat pocket. *Up to three pills at a time, now. Not good.* But he couldn't be sorry, if they let him function for this time with her. When he came back to bed, she stirred, turning into his arms with an instinctive movement that all but destroyed him. He drew her close and rested his chin against the top of her head, wishing he could preserve this moment in amber. Unfortunately, the drugs kicked in, and when he woke, she was gone—and he'd lost another eight hours with her.

By the time she came back from class, he had his mask in place. *Nothing to see here, no heartbreak.* Taye greeted her with a kiss and a question. "So what're we doing this weekend?"

"The same thing we do every weekend."

"Try to take over the world?"

She grinned. "Close."

"Don't keep me in suspense."

"I thought we'd take a trip."

"That's not what we do every weekend." At least, they hadn't the past two. For obvious reasons, plane travel was right out. Too many cameras, too many chances someone would see and recognize him. Though they had old pictures, aged via software, he couldn't risk her safety.

"Come on, play along. Where would you like to go?"

"That we can get to in one day? From *Wichita*?"

"Quit caviling. We don't like your kind here."

"Cavilers?"

"Yep. Your funny feathered hats and rapiers won't win you any points here, mister."

God, she always could make him smile, even now. "Fine. Let's go to Denver . . . it's about eight hours away. We could be there by late evening, and then come back Sunday night. In time for your classes on Monday morning."

"You get on my laptop and make some reservations. I'll pack for us. We can be ready to roll in half an hour." In a whirl of energy, she headed for the bedroom.

He always felt clumsy messing with computers, but they were simple enough to operate. He pulled up her browser and it opened automatically to her e-mail account. She had two unread . . . one from Brandon, whom he knew, and another from Will Reynolds. Though he knew it was a douche-y thing to do, he opened the first.

What the fuck, Grace. We spent all these months with you telling me you don't want anything serious, because we're in college. But you looked pretty damn serious at the club. So I guess it's just that you didn't want to be with me. *Don't bother replying. I get it.*

Taye actually felt sorry for the poor bastard. Marking that one unread, he opened the next one. It wasn't jealousy or even sheer nosiness, but more of an insatiable need to know her. He had to soak in as much of her as he could in this limited time.

Grace: First, I must reiterate this: what happened at the hospital wasn't your fault. The autopsy revealed a sizable brain tumor, gone undiagnosed, and it likely caused the patient's mental condition. I understand why you're upset . . . it was a traumatic experience. If you need counseling, I'd be happy to help, or to recommend someone if you're not comfortable with me in that capacity. On to other matters. I'd like to talk about an internship. When you come in on Monday, we'll discuss some summer opportunities. Have a great weekend. Will.

Ah, this must be the guy she worked for. *Seems decent enough.* Too bad he would never understand her sense of guilt. She'd killed the bastard; Taye didn't share her remorse because crazy or not, he had been threatening Gillie, which meant death was too good for him.

Quickly, he marked the e-mails unread and searched for a hotel. By the time she returned, bag in hand, he could say, "Got us a great room at the Oxford Hotel. They have a book lovers' package . . . apparently you get valet parking, your room, and a certificate for the Tattered Cover, which I guess is some big-deal bookstore nearby." He glanced around the living room, seeing the numerous shelves she'd already filled. Some were textbooks, but most she had bought for pleasure, books not screened and forced on her by Rowan. "I figured you'd like that."

Her face lit. "You, sir, are a genius."

"We can wander around downtown tomorrow. It's supposed to be nice."

"Let's go rent a car."

"Gillie," he said as they went out the door. "I read your e-mails."

"I figured you would."

That gave him pause. "Really?"

"Of course. You had to know if I lied, if I've been conducting a passionate affair behind your back." She smirked at him.

"No, it wasn't that."

"I know that, too."

That hit him so hard. The prospect of losing her felt like more than the end of the world, but he donned his cocky mask and shared a smile. He could get through one last weekend.

While she might not understand him as well as she claimed, Gillie knew Taye hadn't violated her privacy out of insecurity. With Taye, it was always something deeper. And she didn't mind; it wasn't like she had anything to hide. She wished he felt the same.

But she was too excited about the trip to linger on such thoughts. It was the first real vacation she had ever taken. Running from Foundation goons didn't qualify . . . and right then, those days seemed so far away.

Renting the car didn't take long, thanks to Mockingbird's quality ID and credit card. The attendant seemed a little squirrelly; he kept glancing at Taye as he processed the transaction. Gillie told herself she was worried over nothing, and they went out to their rented Honda.

Taye drove, of course, because she didn't know how. Interesting how he remembered motor skills, like dancing and driving, but actual memories eluded him. Privately she wondered how he could recall his name, if he couldn't anything else, but she'd never question him about it. He had the right to any damn name he wanted, after what they'd done to him.

On the way, they talked and listened to music. She held his hand. It was such lovely simplicity, such pure pleasure, that she should've known it couldn't last. They had been driving about four hours when red and blue lights appeared in the rearview mirror.

"Fuck." He slammed a hand against the dashboard. "That rat bastard called the tip line."

"Looks that way." Fear shifted its coils in her chest like a serpent waking from a long sleep. "As I see it, we have two choices. We can stop or we can run."

Either way, it wasn't likely to turn out well. If they stopped, if they went into police custody, the Foundation would pull strings high up the ladder and get them "extradited" for international trial. Her conscience wouldn't let him hurt innocent policemen, but she couldn't go back either. *If we'd stayed away from each other, if we'd followed all the rules in place for our protection, we wouldn't be in this situation. He did this for me . . . because of me.*

"I'm sorry, love. I wanted so bad to give you something to remember. One special day."

Tears pricked at her eyes, but she wasn't a weeper. Never had been. "You already did. It's not your fault . . . I forgot, too. And really, it's just bad luck he'd decide to report you on the off chance you turned out to be the guy."

"Tell me now . . . this is your call. What do we do?"

Behind them, the siren wailed; the cops were now signaling them to pull over to the shoulder. *I don't want this. I don't want to decide.* But she squared her shoulders and took the burden because he asked her to, and that meant he saw her as an equal.

"Stop. If we run, they might get hurt. This isn't their fault."

With a tense nod, he eased off the road and put the car in park. Her hands trembled and she clenched them in her lap. The next few minutes could change everything.

The cop came up and tapped on the window, which Taye powered down. He shone a flashlight into the car as if looking for weapons or hostages. That didn't bode well.

"License and registration, please." The stone-faced officer gave no indication what the problem was, and that didn't do anything to calm her nerves.

Gillie had studied enough psych to know what she shouldn't do, so she tried not to fidget as Taye handed over the paperwork on the rental car. The state policeman walked back to the patrol car and gave the documents to his partner, presumably to run them. She didn't know if they always rode together, or if they had taken the clerk's report seriously enough to proceed with caution. The first cop came back and studied them for a few seconds in silence.

"Are you the folks who rented the vehicle originally?"

"Yes." Taye looked too wary, and the guy had to be picking up on it.

Not good. Dial it down. We can walk away from this without trouble yet. But to say he had issues with authority—well, that'd be an understatement.

The officer asked a few more questions, clearly killing time until the other one got out of the car with the results. Gillie watched in the side mirror as the second cop came up on her side of the car. *Taking no chances,* she thought. *Guess they were warned to show caution with us.*

"Can you please step out of the car?" the first asked.

She closed her eyes for a second, knowing this wasn't going to end well. Flashing Taye a pleading, *don't kill them* look, she complied, keeping her movements slow so as not to alarm the policemen. He lifted his shoulders in a quiet shrug, promising nothing.

"What's this about?" she asked.

"The FBI wants to ask you some questions. We've been asked to bring you in until they can send agents to talk to you."

Gillie saw the tension coiling through Taye. When they got within ten feet of the car, he threw out a hand and pulled. Lightning blazed from the car's hood as he drained the battery, and then he slammed the gas tank with a blue-white arc. His face shone stark and white against the dark, electricity limning him in ragged light. The subsequent explosion flung her down, and it knocked the cops off their feet, too.

"Run," he said, extending a hand to pull her up.

This was an admission of guilt but she knew there was no way he could've gone with them and trusted it would work out fine. He had no such faith in the system. Most likely, that was wise, as a conspiracy like this one could only function with certain officials on the Foundation payroll. Otherwise there would be more press, more stories leaked. The fact that few people heard of anything unusual at all proved that point. She took his hand and sprinted for the Honda. As they drove off, one of the cops fired a few shots, but they didn't hit anything crucial.

Taye drove hell for leather, likely knowing those cops would be calling for backup. Soon this whole highway would be crawling with troopers looking for them. His face was still pasty, and he looked agonized, more so than she ever remembered after he did his thing.

"Call Mockingbird," he said hoarsely. "We need an immediate exit."

Fearful, she did as he asked. MB answered the ping fast, which was a good thing.

"They found us. Can you send Heron?"

He didn't ask for explanations. Thankfully, he also didn't offer recriminations or *I told you so.* That might come later. "I'll send him. Where are you?"

Gillie gave him the highway, mile marker, and the name of the truck stop where they were stopping.

"Good enough. What're you driving?"

"Red Honda Accord."

"I'll tell him it's a 911. Sit tight."

Terror made her juggle the phone in cutting the call. As Taye drove down the ramp to the station lot, mostly full of semis at this time of night, she noticed that his pain didn't scale back. Once he parked, he stumbled out of the car and puked. Terrified now, she ran around the car, only to have him fend her off with an angry gesture. In the yellow light shining down from the post, the fluid looked dark against the gray cement, horribly, awfully so.

"Tell me you've been drinking raspberry syrup."

"I can't lie anymore."

But whatever he might have said, she didn't get to hear it because Heron appeared and ported him away.

CHAPTER 23

Cale now had a good idea where he'd find Ty Golden, known to him as Electro. The research trip had been a good idea, and the Foundation had provided new intel. All helpful. He felt like he knew his target now. That meant it was almost over. But it was getting so fucking hard to pretend he didn't care how much Kestrel hurt.

They'd just stopped for the night when she said brokenly, "I know where he is."

"Show me." He got out the map, and after some resistance, she pointed, unable to defy the hardware in her head. Reluctant remorse coiled through him. Shit, he hated using her, rued the day he'd agreed to accept her on loan from that creepy bastard.

"On the road to Denver? You're sure?"

"Positive."

He had been certain the guy would gravitate to the cold, given how much he hated Florida. His mother had been clear on that point; Tyler had only ever wanted to get the hell away from the heat, the swamp, the bugs, and the gators. Damage reports from the Foundation confirmed someone was targeting facilities in the north and northwest. The MO and the repeated success of the strikes indicated the participation of T-89. That was why

Cale had laid a trap, asking the Foundation to plant false data, though the motherfucker had gotten away *again*.

Now he planned to play the odds. There was only one more facility in this part of the country. One place for the bastard to strike; he just had to get there first, and do a better job of laying the snares. He hadn't known about the magnetism; he'd bet the Foundation didn't either. Now he'd compensate. Gas him. No more tranqs. If he wound up subduing the whole facility as well, so be it.

"Wait." Her face crumpled. "He's gone."

"*Goddammit*. How the fuck's he doing that?"

"I don't know. They must've found some way to block me." She squeezed her eyes shut and dug her knuckles into her eyes. "I wish I could reverse engineer it."

She had become increasingly less useful as time wore on; he had been led to expect she could take him right to his targets. Now, she was more of a companion than a beneficial tool, so at this point, he should call the Foundation to pick her up, but something held him back. Maybe it was her obvious torment. Shit, he was such a sucker, and it had gotten him in trouble before.

Cursing silently, Cale stood and crossed to where she sat at the cheap motel desk. He'd wanted to do this for days now. He set his hands on her shoulders and kneaded, feeling the knots of pain and tension in her frail body. Christ, she felt like a little bird in his hands; this overture didn't come from a sexual impulse, but an instinct purer and more profound. Once, he'd been a good soldier, fighting so women like her could draw water from their wells.

"Are you going to send me back?" she asked, her voice low and hopeless. "I'm not helping you at all . . . they counter too fast, and I can't find them anymore. I'm just dead weight."

An affirmative answer trembled on the tip of his tongue. What the hell did he care what they did to her? This was a job, right? But then she bent forward, giving him access to the nape of her neck. He could see all the delicate bones, the little knob at the base. He could so easily break her in his bare hands; it seemed wrong that anyone should be so reduced. Anyone. Let alone Kristin Shaw, who knew about science and could show kindness to a distressed stranger, even after all she'd been through.

"Is that what you want, Kes?"

"No." She turned in the chair, her hands open on her knees, an oddly prayerful pose. "You're kind. You got something so I can sleep."

Such a fucking thing. What the hell had they done that she'd call a man like *him* kind? He shook his head without realizing he'd made a decision. "No. I'm not sending you back."

"Ever? Or right now?"

Cale knew he couldn't keep her. He didn't have the resources to take on the Foundation, and that gizmo in her head probably told them where she was. Sooner or later, they'd both wind up dead. But honesty hurt him.

"Right now."

"Would you kill me?" she asked. "I can't do it myself, because of the chip."

"*No.*"

Her eyes went feral and she clutched his hand, bringing it to her small breast. "I'll sleep with you. You can do anything you want to me, as long as you end it afterward."

He yanked away and stumbled back, unsure what horrified him most—that she'd been tortured so much that she'd ask such a thing, or that she thought he'd consider the offer. Shaken, he sank down on the bed and rested his head in his hands. Undeterred, she came up beside him and burrowed close, desperate with determination.

"What's the matter? Don't you want me? The guards did. The orderlies did."

Slam. Slam. Slam. Each word pounded like a nail into his brain. That was the outfit for which he worked. They took women like Kes, stripped away their will, and then forced them to any damn thing they wished. He'd always prided himself that no matter the pay, he'd never worked for human traffickers, but in its way, this was worse.

Great time for a crisis of conscience, mate. What the hell're you gonna do?

Under other circumstances, yeah. Perhaps. Sometimes he fought back glimmers of attraction because she wasn't whole. They'd broken her. But maybe . . . maybe someday. He just had to figure a way out of this mess first. That was, if he intended to give up a quarter million dollars for her. That was the big question, wasn't it?

"You're lovely," he said, trying to be as kind as she named him. "But I prefer women who come with a little less coercion."

At that, she broke and wept, falling into him as if he were her last hope for salvation. Unable to resist such despair, he brought her into his lap and rocked her, whispering endearments like his old mum had done when he was young. She cried herself to sleep like a child, and left him with a dilemma unlike any he'd ever known, at least not in years, not since he'd left the army, disillusioned with the orders he'd been given. From that point on, he'd sworn not to blind himself to the truth. There were no heroes, only men who did terrible things for pay.

Can you finish this, knowing what they did to her? he asked himself, gazing down at the top of her head. *Can you?*

Pretending to be Mockingbird all this time had totally sucked. As Tanager had known she would, she had lost some agents. It came to a head the night she chose to send Heron to save Crow and Cardinal. Others had been sacrificed because she couldn't find the information they needed fast enough. So far, two had been lost. Tan was at her breaking point, gazing around the small room with a sense of infinite doom.

Then her phone vibrated with a simple message. *It's done.* There was a map attached, showing an address and a route, so she knew he wanted her to come. It would be a bit of a journey from here, but not a problem.

"Holy shit," she said aloud. "Does this mean I finally get to meet him?"

Her heart lifted with anticipation. If it was true, then everything she'd gone through would be worthwhile. She packed up her stuff and bugged out, heading for the small regional airport outside town. There, she would find somebody willing to take her to Las Vegas. She wouldn't worry about Kestrel; Mockingbird's lair had to be proofed against detection or the Foundation would've shut him down long ago.

Six hours later, after having paid the piper for using her siren voice, she showered and did her hair. Maybe it was stupid, but there was no way she was going to him smelling of some other guy. Most likely, he had no interest in her, but y'know . . . just in case. Tan redid her makeup, put on her cutest skirt, her best boots, and her newest leggings before going the last mile and a half to where he waited.

The address turned out to be a rundown building built of stucco and cement on the outskirts of town. Beyond here, there was only the road into the desert and a tangled crisscross of electrical wires. All the doors were locked, so she broke a window and boosted in through the back. She passed through empty rooms on the first floor, dusty and empty, and she wondered if she had the right place. But when she jogged up to the second floor, she found a heavy steel door.

Tan tried the handle, and it was unlocked. Her heart pounding as she shoved it open, she called, "MB? I'm here."

No reply.

When she stepped past the threshold, a scent hit her in the face. Death. *No. It can't be him. He must've killed somebody who came looking for him. Any minute now he's going to come in from behind me and tell me everything's okay.* She took a shuffling step into the room and saw the body. Young, so fucking young—dark hair, with red and blue streaks—he had multiple piercings, and he was pale as moonlight, so thin she could practically see through him. There were no signs of violence, no injuries. Not so much as a bruise. He was just . . . gone.

Tears prickled the corners of her eyes, threatening to smear her makeup. She hadn't cried since the Foundation took Ginnie. She wouldn't start now.

"Christ, what the fuck," she swore.

At her voice, a computer powered up. The whole room was full of them; it looked like mission control for the space shuttle or something: so many fucking wires and plugs, hard drives and monitors, a wonderland of them. Lights twinkled and then his avatar appeared, shining from the screen. The cruelty of that made her wish she could punch the Mockingbird-shaped glow; the fucker must have recorded it before he died.

"Tan, I'm so sorry to ask this of you, but you're the only one who can know I'm gone. At least that part of me is. I need you to call La Paloma for me. Here's the number. They'll collect the body and do an immediate cremation. I don't want any services, just take my remains and scatter them in the desert, wherever you want."

Shit. Did he expect her to continue playing Mockingbird, now that the worst had happened? God, she was so done.

"You fucking bastard," she said, her voice strangled. "I hate you for doing this to me."

"I'm sorry, love. I wouldn't have, if I had a choice."

She froze. *That sounded like an* answer, *not a recording. How is that possible?* Turning to glance at his body, she saw it hadn't moved, still slumped in the chair, still dead.

"Are you . . . here?"

More lights on the computers flashed. "I'm here. Not there."

"I don't understand," she said shakily. "Not even a little."

"I'm the deus ex machina, now. Look, just get rid of that. Me. Whatever. We can talk more once it's gone."

"I need your real name."

"Shawn Devlin."

In a daze, she called the number he flashed on the screen and told them her friend had died, yes, natural causes, no signs of foul play. The cremation service agreed to send a retrieval team for the body. She waited, numbly, unable to process what was happening. He was gone . . . but not entirely. Instead of going to heaven, hell, or nowhere—whatever normal people did—he'd gone into his machines. Given his mojo, she supposed that almost made sense.

"Hey," he said. "It's not all bad. The meat was slowing me down."

"And you needed me to cover for you while you . . . died."

"Dying hurts. I couldn't concentrate well enough to handle the workload."

A short bark of laughter escaped her. "Yeah, I guess not. Do you have next of kin? Somebody I ought to call."

"No. There's only you, Tan."

She still wanted to punch him. He probably hadn't even tried to get help. No medical treatment. Had he stopped eating? *What the hell, MB.* This killed the tiniest dream she hadn't even known she'd borne—that she'd one day meet him in person and they'd click—that maybe they'd be together like normal people, and because he knew everything about her, he'd *understand*, and her weirdness wouldn't matter. He'd love her.

God, you're such a dumbass. You were never anything to him but words on a screen.

Eventually, the guys came from La Paloma. They asked questions. She mumbled her answers. They took Mockingbird—Shawn—and promised to call her once they had authorization from the county medical examiner.

She left the high-tech bolt hole as soon as they did. Tanager wished she could run, but she was committed to finishing this process and scattering the ashes. Too shaken to think properly, she actually used her credit card to rent a room and waited for news. During that time, she didn't hear from him, and she started to wonder if she'd imagined their conversation the day she found his body.

On the fourth day, they called to tell her she could pick up her loved one's remains. Tanager stole a car—a cherry red convertible—for this trip into the desert; it seemed fitting that he go out in outlaw style. She stopped at a cluster of red rocks, opened the white plastic container they'd given her, and let the wind take him; he went in a swirl of dust.

Tanager dropped the container and sank down on the sandy shoulder of the road to cry. She'd promised herself she wouldn't but she was the only one who knew, the only one who'd mourn him. And so she did—with the dramatic sobs she'd denied her sister. Her eyes stung from the eyeliner and mascara, streaming black tears down her cheeks. Her head pounded like a drum by the time she finished, and her eyes were so swollen she could hardly see.

Half an hour later, she washed her face, cleaned up the evidence of her despair, and ditched the stolen car at a truck stop. Tan caught a ride with a semi driver. Maybe she'd fuck him in the back of his big rig. God knew she had to pay for using her voice, and she didn't much care who anymore. One man was much like another.

Her phone vibrated and she pulled it out of her pocket. *Power up your netbook. We need to talk.*

Fuck you, she thought. *You died. You left me.* With a bright, false smile, she ran her hand along the arm of the guy beside her and listened to the wheels spinning against the road.

CHAPTER 24

Taye regretted that he hadn't said good-bye to Gillie. That roadside mess hadn't qualified as an ideal ending, and one of the cops had nailed him with a lucky shot as they fled the scene. It was the second time he'd been hit since he went to work for Mockingbird, which pretty much encapsulated his life expectancy. He hissed as Hawk's girlfriend worked on him.

"Don't be a baby," Juneau said.

She stitched Taye's leg with a lack of care that said she didn't come into nursing as her first vocation. Not that he was complaining. He couldn't easily reach the place where he'd been shot, and he sure didn't want his partner fucking around with his big hands. He felt lucky they'd taken him in; when Heron dropped him off, he had been in no shape to look after himself. It *sucked* being so weak.

"Sorry," he muttered.

"Relax, I was teasing you."

"What do you do for Mockingbird anyway?"

He knew she wasn't like them. Not a test subject. Not out for revenge. She was a normal woman who loved Hawk. And by the way the guy looked at her, he'd happily walk through fire for her, too. Though he'd spent plenty of time with her before, he'd never asked about her role in the organization. Mostly, she preferred joking around, making everyone laugh. She pretended she had no serious thoughts whatsoever, and she lived to see Hawk smile.

"Whatever needs doing. I do a lot of gopher work when it's too dangerous for him to poke his head out because bloodhounds are nearby." She spoke so matter-of-factly. "Kestrel can send a team pretty fast, though it's dependent on them being in the relative vicinity."

"We have a real advantage since we found Heron."

He had been among those they saved in the warehouse, along with Holly—who died shortly after she enlisted—and Oliver, now Gull; Taye hadn't seen him since they fought together. Heron's ability meant quick extractions when necessary and faster medical treatment when they had wounded. So they lost people less these days, between the porter and the new healing capacity.

Unfortunately that meant Gillie. He still didn't like it—even less now that he'd been her lover—but he couldn't argue. Not when he knew how important it was to her to make her own way. And after how he'd concealed the truth from her, she wouldn't give a shit about him. It was probably just as well. Now maybe a nice guy like Brandon would have a shot.

"What's the deal with Kestrel anyway?"

"She used to be one of ours. Foundation hounds grabbed her and implanted her with the same tech they used on . . . Hawk."

She almost slipped up. Almost called him Silas.

Juneau went on, "At first Mockingbird thought they'd used a mind-fucker, but they don't have one who can compel complete obedience. So they went with a hardware solution instead."

He remembered the chip, the one he'd shorted out, so Silas could help them execute the escape plan. He hadn't realized that about Kestrel. She was as much a prisoner as they had been, and now they were using her to hunt and hurt her former associates. Taye considered the problem as she wiped the stitches clean.

"How does it look?" he asked, craning his neck.

"Dashing." At his raised brow, she amended that to, "It'll look like your other one."

He thought aloud. "So if we find her, I could potentially free her and bring her back on board. She could go back to helping Mockingbird locate other weirdoes."

She frowned at him. "You know I don't like—"

"Yeah, yeah. But the question stands."

Juneau nodded. "Sounds doable to me."

"But you have to figure she won't be unguarded. Getting to her will mean a fight." Hawk sauntered out of the shadows, looking pensive.

The big man bent to claim a kiss, and Juneau wound her arms around his neck. "Mmm. He's all patched up, as promised."

They lived in a warehouse. She had decorated the upstairs and made it homey; Hawk liked all the space downstairs because it permitted him to rig the perimeter with traps and wires. God help the scurrying rats in this place.

Hawk turned to him. "Ready for your last mission? Mockingbird wants to—"

"That's what we were just talking about," Taye said. "Maybe you could call him with my idea. See if there's a way he can track her. He has access to all kinds of internal Foundation systems. Or I can call, if you don't want to."

"He's been prioritizing according to the greatest number of lives at stake. I don't know how he does it." Hawk shook his head. "That kind of pressure could make your head explode."

Juneau added, "He hasn't sounded right the last few times you've spoken to him."

Taye cut a sharp look at her. He'd noticed it, too. "In what way?"

She lifted her shoulders in a shrug. "Maybe it's nothing. I have a vivid imagination."

Hawk paced, a grim figure all in black. "MB hasn't moved on Kestrel because he didn't think we had the ability to fix what they did to her. Finch can remove memories, alter them or implant gentle suggestions, but he doesn't have anything that makes people obey. Not like that."

"Which should have been a clue," Juneau pointed out. "Tanager can do that, but it's her voice, not mind mojo. It's her siren call."

Hawk nodded. "And it only works on men."

Taye considered the implications. "If they used tech on Kestrel, that means they don't have a mind-fucker. Not even like Finch."

"Ask him to find Kestrel, if he can." Taye pulled his shirt on and grabbed his jacket. "I can free her, like I did you. I'm sure she doesn't want to work for them."

"We've been hurting her for months," the other man said quietly.

Yeah, the intentional bombardment—the way they'd powered up simultaneously to shut her down. It might have been kinder if Mockingbird had just sent someone to kill her.

"We could use her help," Juneau said softly. "And even if you can't save her, I think you should try."

That was all it took. Hawk made the call.

A few minutes later, Mockingbird appeared in the laptop. Taye didn't think anyone had instituted a conference call. It wasn't a video-chat. But an avatar appeared on screen—not human. It had no face, just the smooth shape of a head, oddly childlike, and a hole that moved in convex patterns for a mouth.

"You have your last mission," Mockingbird said. "What do you need?"

Hawk answered, "I thought we might want to go after Kestrel instead. Can you find out where she is?"

Silence. The unsettling, inhuman image disappeared. Then streams of data poured down the screen; words, numbers, symbols, and pictures flashed so fast Taye couldn't tell them apart, as if Mockingbird were using the whole Internet as his search engine. He'd never seen anything like it outside of a movie. Computers didn't work like that, particularly not stripped-down little netbooks like Juneau carried around. They didn't have the power.

It took only a few seconds, but MB said, "Sorry for the delay. They've updated their security . . . but it'll never be good enough to keep me out. They gave her to the merc. Caleb Dunn. I already forwarded a dossier on him."

Taye had skimmed the file when Mockingbird first got in touch with him and told him they needed to run. A British former soldier, Dunn had worked in most of the hellhole countries: Bosnia, Afghanistan, Cambodia, East Timor, Kosovo, and Sierra Leone, pretty much anywhere a man could make money fighting in private armies. His resume was impressive; he had a reputation for being tough and thorough.

Hawk said thoughtfully, "So if we find Dunn, we find Kestrel."

"Indeed. I can give you a little help there . . . he has a car registered to him. Forwarding DMV records. You have clearance to pursue this. I'd forgotten Crow developed a successful workaround for the Foundation chip."

Successful workaround? I just fried it, more like. Hopefully his control would be sufficient to do the same for Kestrel without melting her brain. The further his sickness progressed, the less likely that seemed. Time mattered. Then incredible foreboding hit him as he registered the latter part of what Mockingbird had said.

Forgot? Juneau glanced between Hawk and Taye, eyes wide. The big guy reflected the same incredulity. Fear percolated in Taye's veins. Mockingbird did not forget things; no detail slipped through the cracks. *What the hell's going on?*

"You okay?" Hawk asked.

"Fine." But Mockingbird didn't sound fine. There was interference in the line now. Feedback and data echoes, as if two radio stations were fighting for the same frequency. "Whatever happens with Kestrel, afterward please resume the mission I laid out for you."

That sounded oddly final, but before any of them could question his words, the laptop went dark. Juneau fiddled with the cords, but it was still plugged in. Nothing. The battery had just been completely drained.

Juneau shook her head. "Weird."

"Has that ever happened before?" he asked.

Hawk shook his head. "MB has what we call an unstable gift. Maybe because it's tech-related, it's constantly updating itself, whether you want it to or not."

Taye grinned despite himself. "Superpowers by Microsoft."

"Pretty much," the big guy answered. "Think we should call Tanager? She's known him longest. She might be able to tell us what the fuck's up."

Juneau bit her lip. "You know she cares about him more than she'd admit. I don't think it's a good idea until we know more. No point in worrying her before we're sure."

The big guy sighed. "I'm sure *something's* wrong, Junie."

"Don't call me that." She folded her arms and glared.

Taye shook his head, casting the tie-breaker vote. "I'm with her—not yet. Not now. Let's rescue Kestrel first."

Worry hollowed her out. Gillie tried pinging Mockingbird, but he didn't answer. That couldn't be good. She had no other numbers to call. They didn't send anyone else to her for healing, which made her think something big must be going down.

And so Gillie slid back into her life. Her ID hadn't been compromised. There was no surveillance footage of her at the car rental place, and any film the cops might have gotten on their patrol car had been blown all to hell. Therefore, she was safe as Grace Evans. The same protection inherent in playing a college student still existed.

So she went to class and took her finals. At night, she went to the firing range. By day, she graded papers for Will, and fielded desperate questions from students who had just realized their grades sucked. On the last day of school, Brandon found her in the library, as he'd done so often in the past. The e-mail he'd sent made her think this wouldn't be a fun conversation.

"So where's your boyfriend?" he asked.

"He travels a lot for work."

So much better than the truth . . . that he's sick and he didn't see fit to tell me. In retrospect, she should have paid more attention to the signs, but she'd wanted everything to be all right so badly that she'd glossed over them, accepted his lame explanations. *I don't know if I'll ever see him again.*

"Ah. So he's older. Probably got a great job and a cool car."

She stifled a laugh. Brandon thought she liked Taye for that? *Sure, let's go with that.*

"I'm sorry," she said. "But I made it clear I wasn't looking for a relationship."

"You didn't tell me you were seeing anyone either."

"Look, he and I have a complicated relationship. We're not always . . . seeing each other, but nobody else's ever going to measure up in my head either."

Brandon shook his head. "So even when you're not with him, you're still his. Christ. Does he have a gold-plated dick?"

"I'm sorry if I didn't make my situation clear to you."

He sighed. "No, you did. I guess I just hoped if I hung around enough, I'd change your mind. I don't take rejection well, and I'm sorry about that e-mail. I was a total douche."

Well, yeah, but it was the least of her worries right now. "Thanks."

"So we're cool."

"Absolutely."

"'Kay. I probably won't be around much this summer. I got into a band and we're the opening act, so I'll be touring."

"Wow, sweet. Congrats!"

"It's because of you," he said quietly. "I wrote all these tormented emo songs and the guys loved them when I auditioned."

"I'm glad I could help."

But Gillie didn't feel much like studying after Brandon left. She packed all her stuff and left the library, heading over to her small office in the psych building instead. Though she expected it to be quiet, instead, there was an argument going on. Roger, the other TA, was yelling at Professor Reynolds. Though she didn't intend to eavesdrop, it was impossible not to.

"I can't believe you're recommending her, instead of me. She's only been in this department for one semester . . . I've been busting my ass for you since I was a *sophomore*."

"It wouldn't be a good fit. There will be other internships."

"Everyone thinks you're fucking her," the TA said. "Did you know that? *Just* like the other girl. You just don't learn, do you?"

Well, shit.

She pushed the door to Reynolds's office open and planted her hands on her hips. "Do you want to ask me something, Roger?"

"Grace." Will looked sick with shame, but whatever he'd done in the past, he hadn't done a damn thing wrong with her, and she wasn't letting the other TA get away with this.

"Yeah. How often do you let him put it to you?"

"Never," she answered coldly. "Which is as often as *you* get laid, considering you're a spoiled, entitled little prick. It's time for you to leave, before you really piss me off."

Something in her face must've genuinely frightened him, because Roger's bravado failed him. Instead of continuing his diatribe, he grabbed his things and hurried out, leaving an awkward silence. Will sat down at his desk, shakily running his hands through his hair.

"You must be wondering what that was about."

"I gather you're recommending me for a position he wanted."

He sighed. "Not that part of it."

Gillie shrugged. "To be honest, it's not my business."

"Well, I feel I owe you the story."

At that, she took the chair opposite his desk and crossed her legs, waiting.

"Five years ago, I was married, and I had a promising young assistant . . . she was very driven and pretty. She was also quite unstable. She became . . . obsessed with me."

She nodded to show she was listening. It wasn't a surprising tale. Take a young girl with daddy issues and put her in proximity with a nice, decent older guy and shit like this happened. It was too bad for Will; she believed he hadn't encouraged the behavior. God knew, he had never been anything but polite, friendly, and professionally encouraging with her. But some people couldn't differentiate social nuances.

"I never slept with her, but Margaret told everyone I had. Her stalking escalated. Eventually, she went to my wife and exposed our 'affair.' Consequently, my wife, Judith, left me . . . our marriage had been troubled, so she was looking for an excuse."

"I'm sorry."

He shrugged. "If she'd loved me, she would've stayed. I don't think I loved her anymore either. We were going through the motions. I hated failing, more than anything else."

"I get that."

He went on, "Eventually, Margaret killed herself. I almost lost my job in the resultant scandal, but the university believed my side of the story, as it came out that Margaret had prior incidents. Restraining orders, tendencies toward obsession. Her biology teacher in high school received some of the same treatment."

"But you lost everything anyway, including your reputation." Which explained Brandon's joke, early on.

Will lifted his shoulders in a shrug. "Some prefer the lurid version, wherein I'm such a lover that I drove a young woman to her death at the loss of me. But since then, I've taken only male TAs or none at all."

"Until me. I'm sorry I caused trouble for you." This also explained why he'd been so frightened at the clinic. If she'd died on his watch, his career would've been done.

"People are assholes," he said, unexpectedly. "Roger more than most."

"Amen to that."

"I suppose you'd like to know if you got the internship?"

"No, thanks. I have something else to do this summer." She hadn't known she meant to turn him down until this second; this wasn't her life. She could pretend for fifty more years, but she wasn't Grace Evans from Ohio, and she'd fight to be Gillie Flynn.

"Are you sure? It's a once-in-a-lifetime opportunity."

"I believe you. Otherwise Roger would've been a little less irrational about losing out."

Gillie stood, glancing around his office. The textbooks had all become familiar to her, as had Will with his faint scent of tobacco smoke. Impulsively, she crossed his desk to hug him, though she made sure it was an appropriate embrace—not one that would make him worry she was crazy like Margaret. He responded with surprise and then a gentle pat on her back.

He stood back to gaze into her face with a speculative look. "I hope it's important. You're giving up a lot."

She shook her head. "Nope. I'm taking everything back."

CHAPTER 25

"We can assume it's another trap," Taye said.

Hawk nodded his agreement. "If we're lucky, that bounty-hunting bastard will be there . . . and so will Kestrel."

It was after midnight; everything was quiet. Mockingbird's new "intel"—the shit the Foundation was trying to feed him—suggested a farm as their next target, and it was a little too much like the Exeter facility for Taye's liking. The difference was, this time they knew they were walking into a minefield. There would be no test subjects here, just Foundation hunters looking to tag and bag them.

God, he felt like shit. He was up to four pills per dose now, and his time was limited. More than anything, he wanted to wrap this up. *Let me see the ending. That's all I ask.* He had no sense of whether that would happen, though, or if he'd drop dead on this mission. Since he'd eschewed all medical care, it was impossible to know how many weeks he had left, or whether, in fact, the span numbered in days instead.

"You fit to fight?" Hawk asked.

"Yeah, I'm solid." A lie, but one his partner didn't dispute.

Taye could always pull, no matter how much he hurt . . . and the pain pills they'd found for him didn't damp his ability, unlike the sedatives Rowan had pumped through his veins.

"Gull's going in on the other side. He's leading his own team."

Others they'd saved—it was amazing to know they'd made a difference. People's lives had been changed, thanks to them. In the end, maybe he couldn't ask for more.

"Let's do this."

Geared up and ready to rock, they moved as one. The weight of the flak vest was comforting; the night-vision goggles helped even more. This way, the world had a peculiar green cast. Taye scanned the perimeter and spotted the first Foundation goons. He gestured, alerting Hawk, who gave the orders with two hand signals. No weapons on their end—they didn't need them. *We are the fucking weapons.*

Hawk took the first two in a silent kill; their necks popped and they went limp. It didn't matter what kind of armor you wore if somebody could break your bones from the inside out. His partner crept over to make sure of the body count, and then beckoned.

"You still good?"

Hawk nodded. "I took my meds before the run, no worries. Don't be jealous. You'll get your shot before too long."

He grinned and crept along in the big man's wake. When Taye went to town, there would be no hiding their position, so they needed to crawl farther inside the line and locate Caleb Dunn, along with Kestrel. The bounty hunter wouldn't let her out of his sight; she was his ticket to finding his quarry in the dark. Now that Hawk had powered up, she might even be leading Dunn in their direction. In fact, they were counting on it. The pain pills left him feeling faintly euphoric, though not stoned as he'd be if he had a normal metabolism.

Bullets bit into the ground as they moved forward. They tore holes in the barn and Taye flattened himself against the side of it.

Hawk swore, diving for cover. "Shit, they've got men on the ridge. Too far away for us to touch them."

If not for the armor plating he'd jury-rigged last time, they would have killed Hawk and him the first time they tried this. But this location was better for the enemy, with very little he could use in that regard. Their chances didn't look good this time; the Foundation had factored all the angles, except possibly that so many of their subjects were willing to die to shut them down.

"Snipers." It was a smart move, but maybe Oliver—Gull—could counter. He was running support on this op, and it would help immeasurably if he could take out the sharpshooters.

"Let's get inside. We want Kestrel, that's all. If we hunker down, she'll come to us."

As they pushed for the barn interior, where they could hide behind machinery and in the stalls, Taye stayed low, avoiding the headshot, but a round still caught him in the back as he rounded the corner toward the open front doors. The impact forced a curse from him and it took him a minute to catch his breath. Hawk put a hand on his shoulder, steadying him as he drew him out of the line of fire.

"Did it go through your vest?"

He shook his head. "Might've fractured a rib. But I'm fine. I can finish this."

"We've got movement."

Taye wheeled on his haunches, and through the goggles, he could clearly see the bounty hunter edging his way across the yard toward them. He was tall, carrying solid muscle, balding but saying *fuck you* to the problem by shaving his head, so what little hair he had was short and prickly. A scar bisected the right side of his jaw. *Yep, that's Dunn.* A tall, slender woman clung to his hand quite unexpectedly; it didn't look as though Kestrel was frightened . . . at least not of the man beside her.

Her whisper carried in the night air. "Cale, be careful. We're right on top of them."

Taye exchanged a *what the hell* look with Hawk. The big guy shrugged.

"Then they ought to be able to hear me." Yeah, definitely Dunn—the accent was unmistakable. "I got no beef with you, mate. I'm trying to hand her off, here. Though the Foundation doesn't know it yet, I'm no longer on their payroll. They've done things to this girl that you wouldn't believe."

Yeah, I would. He cut a look at Hawk, who made the call.

"Come inside. If you're sincere about helping her, we'll let you go. If this is a trick, I'll snap your spine."

"Don't hurt him," Kestrel said as she stepped into the barn. "He's been helping me cope with the shit *you* guys throw at me."

Fuck. Yeah. Mockingbird's bombardment.

"I'm sorry about that," Hawk said. "It wasn't my call. But were we supposed to let you hunt us for our enemies?"

She gave a bitter laugh. "No. I thought, for the longest time, that someone would come to *save* me. Mockingbird can find anything in the Internet, right? Why didn't he find me?"

An excellent question.

Hawk explained, "They never put you in the system. We tried, believe me . . . and that was *after* I signed on. Mockingbird lost a lot of people trying to rescue you."

Outside, the sound of combat reached them. Foundation goons must be going up against Gull's team. Gunfire cut the night air, screams of pain and muted explosions.

"You don't have long," she said then. "Get this out of my head. They can see what I see, you know. They know I've found you. They're fighting this way."

Shit, that was his cue. "This won't hurt you."

At least he didn't think so. He hadn't fried Hawk's brain anyway. Taye turned her head gently, found the hardware, and pulled a fraction of his power. The resultant jolt sent her reeling, and the bounty hunter caught her, his eyes fearful. Yeah, the poor bastard cared.

"Y'all right, Kes?" Dunn peered down into her face.

She clung to him a moment, her breath coming in deep gulps. "Yeah. He shorted it out. I don't have Big Brother in my head anymore."

Dunn let go of her then. "That was the deal then. I get you to safety and walk away. This smells like a goatfuck, and I never liked goats."

"Thank you." She didn't have to stretch far to kiss his cheek. "I'll never forget this."

Hawk eased to the front of the barn. "It's getting hot out there. We need to clear out while Gull's wreaking havoc."

"No argument," Taye said, removing his goggles.

He pulled, lightning wreathing his hands. There was no reason to hide his light under a bushel anymore. Time to make some shit go boom.

They came out of the barn together into a nightmare of automatic weapons and live shadows devouring their prey. Taye threw out his hands, twin arcs of raw power striking Foundation goons, who were taking aim at Hawk. They screamed at the voltage, alarming their teammates, but nobody broke and ran. *Not yet.*

"Get her out of here," he told Hawk. "I've got this."

But before the big guy could move on the suggestion, a shot came down from the ridge. A red jewel blossomed on Kestrel's forehead, and then she fell forward into Dunn's arms. The bounty hunter dropped to his knees, holding her, while weapons sparked around him; it was like he saw or heard nothing else. He didn't head for cover. He didn't draw his own rifle, slung across his back.

Taye did his best to keep the man alive, slamming goons with electricity right and left. Fucking ironic, when you thought about it. Hawk fell in at his other side, and with his power, they turned the tide. In the distance, Gull's team mopped up those who fled, until, at last, the yard was quiet, and not a single one of the Foundation hunters still stood.

"They killed her rather than let her get away from them," Dunn said, straightening at last.

Hawk nodded. "They assigned someone for that eventuality."

"Why?" The question sounded torn from the bounty hunter.

"Because she strengthens us. She would have found more like us and bolstered our numbers. If she's not in their hands, they couldn't let her live."

Dunn swung Kestrel's body in his arms, his eyes grim in the moonlight. "She deserved better. I know I said I'm out, but not now. Not like this. They'll pay for what they did to her."

Gillie received two injured soldiers from Heron that night. Healing wounds always took a lot out of her, and left a fresh scar, but it was better than disease. Nothing hurt as much as that; the boiling blackness in her veins reminded her of Rowan.

The first patient had a bullet in his gut. Without her, he'd surely die. *What a fucking mess.* He'd gone in wearing a vest, she had no doubt, but this was a high-powered round, and it chewed through the Kevlar and into his belly. Thankfully, he was unconscious and didn't suffer unduly from her inexpert surgery.

Goddammit. I'm not a doctor. I shouldn't be doing this. That didn't stop her from washing up and donning gloves. By the time she finished, blood stained her hands, nearly to her elbows. But her fear wouldn't let her give up on him. Once she finished with that part of the process, she stripped off her gloves and got the scalpel. Gillie sliced both her palms—a little blood wouldn't do for him—and sealed them both over the wound.

The power built at the back of her head and then roared down her spine, flaring into her arms and out through her palms. Heat rose, sparking so she could almost see it. She felt his pain and surprise as the shot tore through his gear and into his gullet. The agony left her seeing black spots, but eventually it dulled, scaling back. By the time she had only twinges, she knew it was safe to pull away. With bloodied hands, she checked her stomach. New scar. It sat neatly next to the vertical slice. *Anymore of this and I'll look like a merc.*

The next patient wasn't nearly so bad off. She had time to clean up and knock back some bourbon before she tackled his flesh wound; that one hardly marred her skin at all. Heron popped in and out, ferrying the men back from whence they'd come. When he came back the second time, she stopped him.

"What's going on? Those were both gunshot wounds."

Heron got out his trusty pad. *They tried to save Kestrel.*

"Did it work?"

No, he wrote. *The Foundation killed her.*

"What's going on now?"

They're planning one final strike. With Dunn's help, Mockingbird can track the location of the central facility.

"Who's Dunn?"

The bounty hunter who was chasing you and Crow.

Shit. That would be a story and a half, if he was working for their side now. It sounded like there was more going on than she could readily squeeze out of poor Heron.

"Take me with you. I want in."

No more sitting around. No more waiting for word. She could fight if she had to, if she was threatened. She wasn't just a healer; she'd killed, too. As if she'd known it might come to war, she had been training on weapons—handgun, rifle, shotgun . . . she could use all with equal proficiency—since she arrived in Wichita. And she wanted to fight. It was time to put her inner steel to good use.

Heron merely nodded. And he returned for her once he'd delivered the patient he'd come for in the first place. The world swirled and melted; her stomach turned inside out. And then they arrived at the warehouse where everyone else was gathered. It was a huge, rusty place with broken windows and heavy metal rafters forming a catwalk overhead.

People sat around on oil drums, talking or playing cards. *Shit.* Gillie had never seen such a gathering of weirdoes in one place. Most, she didn't recognize. A few she did. This was incredibly dangerous, but if Heron had been telling the truth—and they really meant to end this, once and for all—then this was a necessary risk. Plus, if Kestrel was dead, then the Foundation couldn't locate them anyway.

"Everyone's here," Hawk said, loud enough to quiet other conversations.

But Gillie didn't see Tanager. Hard to imagine she'd let something like this go down without being involved. Still, she sat down and waited for instructions. So far, Taye—who was talking to a woman with long, light brown hair—hadn't noticed her arrival.

"Here's the plan. Dunn's going to ping his Foundation contact. When he calls back, MB traces the signal."

"Are we sure he'll call back? Doesn't he know Dunn turned?" That was the man Gillie healed an hour ago. He looked pretty damn good for someone who had been gut shot.

"He knows," someone—presumably Dunn—said. "But I'll offer irresistible bait. See, he's going to call and keep me on the line, long enough to triangulate my location. So he can send someone to kill me."

The crowd murmured in appreciation; it was delightfully devious. Now they'd pit Foundation hackers against Mockingbird's speed. Well, Gillie would put money on MB any day. His avatar stood ready in a glimmer of yellow light.

Hawk went on, "Heron will ferry us to the site, once Mockingbird gives us the location. We have to strike fast, before he has a chance to shut down and relocate."

So when their strike team arrives, nobody's home. Gillie knew a twinge of fear for Heron. From what she'd seen, most weirdoes paid a price for their powers, and it sounded like they might be asking too much of him. There had to be twenty people here. Twenty trips, in addition to what he'd already done? But she didn't object. Surely Heron would say something if it was too great a burden. Well. *Write* something.

"I'm ready if you are," Dunn said.

While everyone watched, he sent a text message. Within two minutes, as he'd predicted, he had a call back. "Dunn."

He listened for a moment, while Mockingbird arched in a river of light and then . . . dove into Dunn's phone. Not what she'd expected, but surely the most direct way to trace a call. She wondered what happened to his body, though, when he was so fully immersed in the net.

"I just wanted you to know you shot the wrong woman."

More listening. She could tell by Dunn's expression that the ranting on the Foundation end must be amusing. But his eyes carried a haunted shadow, belying the curl of his lips. No more than fifty seconds had passed when Mockingbird's avatar returned to its place on the keyboard of Hawk's netbook.

"You got me," the bounty hunter said eventually. "I lied. I should've known there's no fooling the Foundation." Silence, and then he nodded. "Yeah, that's where I am. You're too clever for me. See ya soon, mate."

In his inhuman voice, Mockingbird gave the location of the final battle.

Hawk cued the porter to begin and said, "Let's finish this."

CHAPTER 26

Taye spotted Gillie as soon as she ported. *What the hell—*

They stood in a white, high-tech room, surrounded by machines and people fed by tubes and wires like something out of a SF movie. Only they weren't people. Not exactly. Most had something wrong with them, something extra: arms or fins or spines or fangs. These were full-on monsters, experiments gone far beyond anything Rowan could've imagined.

Dear God.

And it was so quiet, it sent chills down his spine.

Hawk was dividing people into strike teams as they arrived, coordinating strategy with Mockingbird on his headset. For all he knew, MB lived in the damn thing. Nothing made sense anymore, and his pain meds were wearing off. Part of him knew this was it, his last hurrah. He wouldn't make it past this fight. Taye had been living for revenge and for Gillie, but sheer will could only carry you so far.

He strode over to her, anger blazing. "What are you doing here?"

"I'm here to fight, same as you."

"But you can't—" Only she *could*. Too late, he remembered

what she'd done to the mental patient who attacked her. "I wish you hadn't come."

"I wish lots of things," she said quietly. "But I'm not going to get them, am I?"

She didn't attempt to hide her pain, and it stabbed him deeper than anything ever had before, worse than the cancer. "I was going to tell you."

"When? Via posthumous DVD recording?"

So yeah, she knew. But this wasn't the time. "I tried to keep my distance. That's why. But you were too much for me to resist, no matter how hard I tried. I'm so sorry, love."

Her face said she had something bitter and angry to say, words that would eviscerate him and leave him bleeding at her feet. But Hawk interrupted with their assignments; in a gesture of delicious cruelty, he teamed Taye with Gillie.

"You two will be a good match. Watch each other's backs."

As long as I can, he thought.

To Taye, Hawk added, "Take the bounty hunter. If he tries anything, put him down."

Gillie stood beside him, not looking in his direction. He would like to kiss her good-bye, but it wasn't the time for that. Together, they watched the final few arrivals as Hawk went over the strategy Mockingbird had devised.

But the plan had to be modified when Heron made the last trip. Blood trickled from his nose and eyes; he stumbled and then fell forward, crimson splattering on the white tile. Gillie ran forward, but he could tell by her expression, the man was beyond help. A rumble went through the assembled teams, fury ratcheting up a notch.

"He chose this," Hawk said quietly. "He knew how important it is that we strike fast and cut off the head, once and for all. Don't let his sacrifice be in vain." He paused long enough to let it sink in. "That also means each team is responsible for getting out once the job is done and reaching the rendezvous point on their own. There's no backup, no emergency escape this time. Now let's do this, people."

Hawk strode over to where Taye stood with Gillie and Dunn. "I have a special assignment for you three."

"Yeah?" Taye asked, expectant.

"Take this flash drive. I need you to get to their servers. They'll be on that side"—he produced a schematic and pointed—"of the facility. Everything hinges on you making it there. Plug it in, let the program run, and then retrieve it. It's crucial you don't leave it behind."

If they were burning the place anyway, Taye didn't understand why it mattered. But it wasn't for him to question his orders. So far, they had been golden. Mockingbird ought to be just as brilliant for this final strike.

"Got it," Gillie said.

Hawk added, "Don't let me down."

"What's on that?" Dunn asked.

The big man shrugged. "Honestly, I don't know. Tanager gave it to me. She said it would wipe their system beyond recovery."

"I didn't see her," Gillie said.

Hawk nodded. "She came in late. She was working on the flash drive, I think."

"Something she got from Mockingbird?" Gillie suggested.

"Doesn't matter." Taye didn't get the point in debating what it might be.

As he saw it, the job was simple. *Fight to the servers. Kill anything that moves. Blow things up wherever possible. Then plug in the flash drive and wait for fireworks. Yeah, simple. Except for all the guys who want us dead in between here and there.*

The teams broke up, two- and three-person groups, heading out from here. The boss was no longer here in the room, though he could see the phone he'd used. They had to find the head honcho and finish this. Not caring if Gillie or Dunn saw, he chewed four more tablets and ignored the censure in Gillie's eyes. *Yeah, I should've told you. I'm a bastard.*

Dunn checked his weapon and said, "Let me scout. I can't imagine either of you has any experience in it, and you'll want to keep an eye on me anyway."

"Sounds good." Gillie fell in behind him without another look at Taye.

God, he didn't want her here. He'd tried too hard to shield her from ugliness and maybe, in the end, that was where he'd gone wrong. It wasn't like this shit surprised her. She had spent her life in darkness, after all.

Since their squad hadn't been assigned to deal with the freak show in here, they went down the west hallway; everything on this side of the facility belonged to them. They hit resistance fast, goons in black, but not battle-ready, no guns, no flak vests. *Caught you flat-footed, you bastards.* Dunn whipped twin guns up; equipped with silencers, he pegged both men square in the chest before they had time to turn and round. Here, the halls were gray, and the blood splatters added an interesting pattern to the tile.

"I don't think they were on watch," Dunn said. "So they won't be missed. Help me move the bodies."

Feeling lucky he hadn't come up against the bounty hunter in a fair face-off, Taye jogged down the hall. The knives in his belly had softened, stinging eels instead of sawtooth blades. He'd get through this. *One more job. I promised.* But though he wouldn't say it aloud, he was starting to feel disconnected; he didn't know if it was the drugs or slow death come for him at last. A quote came to him, though he couldn't remember the author: *well, we were born to die.* But he had no peace for it, no acceptance. All these months schooling himself to let her go and he still wanted to rage.

He hefted the shoulders while Dunn took the feet. Gillie opened a door and found an unused conference room, where they probably talked about what horrors to perpetuate next and then voted on it. She beckoned them forward, pulling out the chairs so they could hide the corpses. The second man went beside the first, and then she pushed the chairs back. There was blood in the hall, but short of finding a janitor's closet, nothing to be done about it. Then alarms went off in some distant part of the facility—other teams at work—and it became a moot point.

"Keep moving," he said, waving Dunn forward.

"We're in the corporate offices," the bounty hunter said as he cleared the next room.

It contained an executive desk, made of real mahogany. The computer equipment was top of the line. He took a moment to rummage through some memos in the inbox, and one line leapt out at him: *Circulate to all staff at headquarters.*

Elation surged through him. No matter what happened, it ended tonight. Everyone who walked away from this fight could do so without fear, no more looking over the shoulder, no more hunters. But for now, booted feet coming from behind demanded his attention.

Taye spun and pulled. Overhead, the lights flickered, giving the corridor a peculiar stop-motion appearance. Dunn laid down fire as the thugs rounded the corner. Most of them were disheveled or partly dressed; private soldiers didn't expect to be hit on their home ground. Two of them fell with bullets in them; the rest opened fire.

He flung his arms out, lightning exploding out of both palms to send the enemy flying back. Four men smoked and slammed the far wall hard enough to break spines. Behind him, Dunn worked cleanup in an economical fashion, plugging any of them who still moved or moaned. To his surprise, Gillie ran over to one of the bodies and snagged a gun.

"What're you doing?" he asked.

"Arming myself. My thing only works with a touch . . . and if I'm bleeding. I need a way to drop them at a distance."

"Do you know how to shoot?" Dunn looked ready to take the weapon away from her.

"I do. Just stay out of my way and you won't catch one in the back."

Good God, she handled the weapon like a pro, checking the magazine and the safety. Astonished pride curled through him. She had hidden depths, did Gillie Flynn. While she might look like a Botticelli angel, she was a warrior through and through.

"Feisty," the merc muttered. "Come on, then."

The smell of smoke permeated the facility, but the alarms cut off midwail, hopefully soon enough to keep the authorities from responding. He had no idea where they were, but police involvement wouldn't improve matters. According to the plans Hawk had shown them, they had three more turns before the server room, that many hallways to clear.

Taye paused. "If one of us falls, the others have to push on with the drive."

The other man cut him a look, as if he understood. "Agreed."

Excess electricity sizzled in Taye's veins, licking along his skin in blue white sparks. He ignored the blaze of his nerve endings, ignored everything but the sight of Dunn crouched and scoping out the next room. The bounty hunter signaled clear, and they passed another empty office, but another security team was heading their way. Gunfire popped; one of the guards had lost his nerve and gone full auto, spraying at shadows. The sound of his weapon was unmistakable. Stupid bastard. Since they were moving quietly, the goons didn't know they were right on top of them until it was too late.

Gillie and Dunn flanked him, laying down cover fire as he lashed out. New thing, lightning storm. The electricity danced around the thugs in blue waves, surging through them endlessly. They jerked and screamed, weapons discharging into the air. But fuck, that took a lot out of him. He swayed, black spots before his eyes, and he had to lean against the wall to keep from falling down.

"Show off," Gillie muttered. "Don't do that again. We don't need them to go out in such a spectacular fashion."

Dunn nodded. "True. They just need to die."

***He's not going** to make it,* Gillie thought. If she hadn't been so angry, she would be heartbroken. But Taye's face told the truth; he was all cheekbones and eyes, skin pale as parchment. Even his lips had lost all color and the sclera carried bloody veins, expanding each time he powered up. By the time he finished, they would be crimson. Of course, by the time this was done, he would be dead. Understanding why he'd been so determined to push her away didn't make it better.

He did dial down the juice as they pushed forward, clearing the corridors one by one. More men died. She shot some of them herself. The first time she nailed a guard, she expected to feel . . . something. Pleasure, guilt, remorse, but there was nothing. There was no room for anything but grim determination. Taye had the flash drive, but if—when—he fell, she or Dunn would take it from his cold, dead fingers and carry on.

No. The idea of a world without him in it threatened to end her. With iron control, she edged the pain aside. *I'm still here. Just because he made the choice for me doesn't mean it has to stand. If we get through this, I can save him.* The bastard had to have known she'd heal him; therefore, it rendered his refusal to confide inexplicable.

Live through this, Taye. Live. Afterward, we'll fight and I'll fix you. It'll be fine.

As he swung around a corner, Dunn executed some pencil-pusher who was working late. But Gillie didn't feel sorry for him. This was Foundation headquarters—a mythical place for her kind—and he had to know what went on here. No way to avoid the horror; it was everywhere.

She paused long enough to slice her palm. *Never know when*

the plague-touch will come in handy. Gillie curled her fingers up to prevent either of them from noticing.

The last push went in a blur of gunfire and lightning. She ran out of ammo in the last hall and dropped the gun; without a fresh magazine, it was just a paperweight. Her eyes stung, but they pressed forward. All the way down to the end. The server room had a complex electronic lock, and none of them could hack, but fortunately, Taye had a workaround. He strode up and fried it. Presuming system malfunction, the door popped open so as not to trap anyone working in the core.

"We made it," she said in excitement. "Let me take it. You two stand guard."

In answer, Taye tossed her the flash drive and she caught it. Gillie hurried forward; with shaking hands, she plugged it into the USB port. Almost immediately, there came a response. The whole system chugged and whined; whatever the hell was happening, it was powerful.

She bounced on the soles of her feet, remembering Hawk's instruction. *No matter what, you can't leave that behind.* The green light flashed on the drive, telling her the software was still running. *Come on, come on.* From outside in the hall, she heard fighting—gunfire and lightning. Dunn and Taye must be battling another team. Just as well she had this under control; they couldn't help her.

"It wondered if you would get this far." The strange, androgynous voice came from behind her.

Oh. Fuck. I screwed up. In her eagerness to start the download, she hadn't cleared the room. Or at least, she hadn't made sure there wasn't a second one, adjacent to the first. Behind the row on row of computer equipment, there was a low arch . . . and an inner chamber. *Shit.*

Gillie spun slowly, her hands in the air. The creature she beheld didn't even look human. It had no hair anywhere on its body; it was thin and pale, so she could see the blood running in its veins. But despite the horror of its appearance, she could clearly see its human ancestry. Whatever it was, it had been bred by the Foundation. *Dear God.*

"Who are you?" Her voice shook.

"It," the thing replied. "It oversees all operations. It decides what research to pursue, what branches to prune. It is cleverer than its creators. They would terminate it and shut it down."

What. The. Fuck.

"So you're responsible for all of *this*?"

"Not its own creation. That would be paradox. But otherwise . . . yes." It gazed at her from bloodred eyes, deceptively thin and fragile.

They were still fighting outside. *So there's not gonna be any rescue. Just me . . . and it. And maybe that's how it ought to be. I gotta get close enough to touch it. Assuming it shares enough of our DNA for the plague-touch to work.* That wasn't a given; it might be a hybrid.

"Are you going to kill me?"

"Yes. It calculates high probability of escape and genesis of new protocols. Humans comprised of interesting genetic stock." The thing talked like an alien, although it wasn't.

It came from these labs. Christ almighty, what have you people done?

The blood on her palm felt sticky, but it should be fresh enough to work. The cut hadn't scabbed over yet anyway—and the thing launched itself at her, jaw unhinging to reveal row after row of sharklike teeth. *Path of least resistance.* Gillie let herself drop and it came down on top of her. Instead of fighting to avoid harm, she dug her nails into its skin until she drew blood. That left her open to the terrible agony of its bite, but she ignored the damage and clamped her hand over the scratches.

Die, you bastard-thing. Die in agony. Die in tumors and boils and blood streaming from your mouth. She poured all her terror, all her anguish into the touch and felt the moment it caught fire, streaming like napalm into the creature's veins. It howled and shook, its flesh boiling over its bones with the virulence of what she gave it. The weight of its corpse pressed her into the floor, and for a moment, she had no strength to move. Weakness wracked her limbs; her breath came in tearing gulps.

Outside, the gunfire stopped at last, and there was no lightning at all. Just silence. Somehow, that seemed more ominous than anything that had happened yet.

"Shit," she heard someone say.

Dunn. That's his name.

Footsteps. The monster rolled off her, though not under its own power. Through bleary eyes, Gillie recognized the bounty hunter. He had a machine pistol in one hand, and he was covered in blood. So was she.

"What the fuck is that?" This, from a hardened veteran of private wars—in his shock and horror, his accent intensified, becoming clearly northern England.

"A dead monster, one they bred, and it eventually took over from the scientists."

"Jesus." He bent to examine the body, the tensile limbs, the too-thin skin, bulbous forehead and unnatural jaw; her handiwork showed in the bloody discharge from the nasal slits, tumors still growing beneath the skin, even after death, and the darkening of the dermis from internal hemorrhaging.

"It bit me. Let's hope it wasn't venomous and that its condition isn't contagious."

"How bad is it? Can you walk?" He offered a hand up, pulling her away from the thing.

"I can, thank you. Where's Taye?"

"I'm sorry."

"*No.*" Shaking off the hunter's hands, she stumbled over to the computer and snatched the flash drive before staggering out into the hall where he lay.

"I'm sorry," he said again as if that could change anything. "He gave too much. There were so many men trying to get in there to you. He cooked twenty of them. Hell of a thing, never saw anybody fight like that. He saved my life. Yours, too."

"He's not dead. I won't let him be. Now pick him up. We're not leaving him here."

Something in her face must have persuaded him she wasn't fucking around because he didn't argue. A tremor rocked the building, sending them both into the walls. *Real earthquake or something one of the weirdoes could do?* Either way, it didn't matter. It was time to get the hell out of here.

Gillie led the run, armed with a gun she'd taken off a fallen goon; this time, she had the presence of mind to snatch a couple of spare magazines. They formed reassuring bulges in her pocket. Her arm throbbed where it had bit her; she would bear fresh scars. None of it mattered.

Save him.

The words looped in her brain as she pushed through the stragglers while the building trembled all around them. By the groaning sounds, the damn thing was coming down—structurally unsound. Dunn followed without a complaint; he was a strong bastard and he had better be, if he didn't want her to shoot him.

If Taye dies—

No. Not an option. She wouldn't let it be. Just as he hadn't given her a choice about his death, she wouldn't give him a choice about his life.

Stairs. Gillie pushed into the stairwell and ran, full out. More tremors now. A chunk of ceiling collapsed behind them as she sprinted, landing by landing.

At last, they hit the ground floor, and she followed the signs for maintenance staff. Those exits rarely had much security. *Metal door, regular lock.* Gillie shot a hole in it and stepped out into an alley, complete with Dumpsters. Heron had ported them into a skyscraper. She had no idea what city they were in.

"Find me a private place to work on him," she demanded.

"The rendezvous point—"

"*Fuck* them. You move or I shoot you." She cocked the gun to show she meant business.

"I hear you." But by his expression, he thought it was too late; he was humoring her.

Dunn led the way to a fire escape. He showed his strength by boosting her to the ladder, even encumbered as he was. Gillie lowered it for him, so he could climb. This looked like a condemned apartment building. Good enough. There might be squatters, but if they had any sense, they'd clear the fuck out. The window was already broken and the place smelled of cat piss, but there was no time to seek something better.

"Lay him down."

She knelt beside Taye, checking for pulse. *Ah, thank you.* It was there, thready but there. He was breathing faintly, a death rattle in his chest. But he hadn't gone. Not yet. Even now, he was fighting for her. For them. He might not know it, but he was. If he'd passed, there would be nothing for her to do, here. She couldn't heal death.

"You can really fix him?" Dunn asked.

"I think so. Do you have a knife?"

In silence, he handed it over and she made a very shallow cut on Taye's palm and sealed her own injured hand to it. Fear trickled in her veins, ice and sorrow. No dialysis machine here. She didn't start slow; there was no time. Gillie opened her healing to him like throttling back on a motorcycle, and his sickness slammed her.

Christ. How did he survive this? The stupid bastard let it get to terminal stages.

Agony spiked into her stomach, and then the blackness seeped into her veins. Her vision flickered—she'd never attempted to save anyone so far gone before. But she wouldn't give up. *If only one of us walks away, let it be him.*

Through a veil of tears, she gazed up at Dunn. "Whatever happens, don't let me stop touching him . . . even if I waver, even if I fall. Do you *understand*?"

The bounty hunter nodded. He knelt, cupping his hands over hers, and that was enough. At long last, the shadows took her in a whisper of leathery wings.

CHAPTER 27

The door opened and closed. Tanager had chosen this chair so he wouldn't see her right away. *Not very feng shui, traitor.*

"You were clever," she said.

She had been sitting here for over two hours, lying in wait. It was dark in the apartment—nice place, after what he'd done, he ought to live in squalor—and her words visibly startled the man who had just come home. She barely made out his shape in the shadows, but she didn't need light to see justice done. She had been right, before, before Mockingbird called her away.

But it was time now.

Finally, Kes. God, I'm sorry it took so long.

"I take it you found the leak." He dropped his keys into a bowl on the table to the left of the door, weariness lacing his voice.

"Bingo."

"I wondered if anyone would ever catch me. Mockingbird had you following the wrong people for ages."

"Oh, I know, trust me." She tapped one long, black fingernail against the sole of her boot. "And see, that's the thing. It wasn't until I started asking myself, who has access, who could've done this, that I first looked in your direction. Why would you betray us like that? Apart from that one breach of trust, you worked tirelessly to shut them down. Problem was, you left no trail, so I had supposition, not proof. You hate the Foundation *so* much—I couldn't figure your angle."

He propped himself against the wall. "Did you work it out?"

"I'll run the scenario by you. Tell me if I'm hot or cold. It wasn't for money. It wasn't because you were their inside man and you wanted to bring us down."

"Warm," he said.

"No, with you, it was personal. That's why you gave them Kestrel. You wanted *her* to suffer. You knew her torment would be threefold—first from how they'd treat her, second, the way they'd make her hunt her friends, and third, what we'd do to counteract her. So much misery, there."

"Hot."

"But why? That's the million-dollar question. My bet is—you wanted her . . . she didn't want you back. You decided to make her pay."

"Scalding."

She squeezed her hands into fists. "It had to be you, Finch. You're the only one who can't forget. MB sends you to all our agents, all over the place, and nobody can wipe it away."

"I wish they could."

"You knew right where she was, exactly where to send them . . . and maybe you were sorry after you made the call. God knows, you've been working for us like a dog ever since, always on call, forever erasing our secrets."

"I'd take it back if I could," he said, as if that made it better. "I loved her. But you don't know what it's like to be dismissed because you're not hero material. It doesn't make your heart less breakable."

No pity stirred in her. Plenty of people suffered in unrequited silence; tonight Tanager embodied Alecto, the ever-angry, and she would judge him.

"The Foundation killed her," she said softly. "They had a sniper put a bullet in her brain rather than let us liberate her. It would've been kinder if you'd stabbed her . . . and saved her all these months of pain."

An anguished sound escaped him; his shoulders slumped. Finch put both hands to his face and wept in pathetic gulps. Tan didn't stir. Vengeance could wait.

"What are you going to do?" he asked.

She sat forward; this was the moment for which she'd waited, making all the wasted hours worthwhile. The darkness rose, demanding outlet, demanding blood. Tanager gave it luscious, full-throated voice.

"You'll climb to the top of the tallest building you can find. For an hour, you'll sit reflecting on what you did to Kestrel. And then, when your time is up, you're going to fly."

"Yes," he said in drugged tones. "That sounds right."

Without saying good-bye, for she hadn't instructed him to, he turned and left the apartment. Soon, he would be just another suicide. Nobody would care. Nobody would ask why.

That was for you, Kes.

Time to seek an anonymous partner. Balance had to be restored, the price paid. And if she cried while fucking a stranger because he wasn't Mockingbird—and it never would be—she hoped the guy would look the other way. Tanager let herself out, walking into the dark alone.

No pain. Taye remembered dropping Foundation goons as if he'd been swatting flies, overloading on power, and he'd known then that he only had to keep them away from her. No more caution, no more keeping resources in reserves. That had been the end, and he'd meant to go out in a blaze of glory.

At first, he decided he must be dead because he couldn't remember the last time he'd woken up feeling this good. But it sure as hell couldn't be heaven—not with this fucking bounty hunter leaning over him. Dunn helped him sit up. Other details registered then—the shitty abandoned apartment, graffiti on the walls, blood smearing his skin and . . . the woman unconscious beside him.

No. Oh, fuck, no.

"What the hell happened?" he demanded.

"She healed you."

"And you *let* her? Son of a bitch."

"She threatened to shoot me over you, mate. I've learned not to cross a woman with a twitchy trigger hand and a mood on."

"We have to get her to a hospital, if it's not already too late."

Fuck. This was exactly everything he never wanted for her—a lifetime of doctors and hospitals she hated against the weight of letting him die. The way he'd planned things, it should have been clean and simple, a heroic death for a bastard like him.

Why didn't she let me go? But deep down, he knew why. He knew. They were twin planets locked into synchronous orbit; the current flowing between them would never end, not even in the face of death. Terrified for her, Taye scrambled to his feet.

"Fuck me." Dunn sighed and shook his head. "Fine. Get her up. I'll find a car downstairs. Follow as quick as you can." With that, he headed for the door.

Taye swung Gillie into his arms and ran, taking the steps two at a time. By the time he reached the landing, Dunn had boosted a car and sat revving the engine. He got in on the passenger side and cradled her in his lap; the movement made her whimper. Her skin was already turning yellow, sign of acute renal failure.

"Found one with GPS . . . nearest medical care is three point seven miles." Dunn's staccato update didn't interfere with his driving; he was already making the first turn.

"Just hang on," he whispered into her hair. "I wouldn't have done this to you for the world, Gillie-girl, but please, please don't make me live without you."

A mile passed with him whispering half-voiced prayers. He didn't believe in God, really, not after what had been done to the two of them, but if there was anything out there, anything at all that knew mercy, that being would spare Gillie. She deserved . . . everything.

As if he knew Taye needed a distraction, Dunn said, "I did some digging on you. Talked to your mother."

That should've roused a stronger reaction, but he had only one emotion right now. Raw fear. Still, he glanced at the other man. "Yeah?"

"If you care, your real name's Tyler Golden, father unknown, mother and grandfather living outside Miami, where you were raised. I can give you the address before I bail."

"I'm an ex-con, aren't I?"

"Yeah." But Dunn offered no judgment in the answer.

Taye wasn't sure he wanted to learn anything about the man he'd been. He figured it could only end in disappointment. Right then, he cared only whether Gillie made it through the night. But maybe he'd take the address and keep it. Just in case.

The bounty hunter ran two red lights along the way, but since it was late, no cops appeared to challenge his speed or his reckless driving. Inside five minutes, he was pulling up underneath the portico at the emergency entrance of the hospital.

"I'm done," the bounty hunter said. "I've some loose ends of my own to tie up. Hope I don't see either of you again."

Taye acknowledged that and slid out, Gillie cradled against his chest, and jogged toward the doors, which swished open on approach. Typical hospital. Parents waiting with children who probably didn't need emergency treatment, but they likely didn't have insurance. A few wounds, people looking out of it.

"I need help," he called. "She's dying. Her kidneys . . . she needs dialysis."

A nurse came over and apparently she agreed with his assessment. She called for a doctor and an orderly, a gurney for Gillie. They threw forms at him and asked about a hundred questions. It was hard for him to answer for the roaring in his head; that noise wanted to translate into fireworks, shorting out all the lights. *Fuck no. You have to keep a lid on this, or she'll die for sure. They need their equipment, dammit.* With sheer effort, he locked it down and controlled the brown outs. The next thing he knew, they were taking her away. Helpless, he dropped into a waiting-room chair and buried his face in his hands.

This is on you. You didn't trust her judgment, asshole. You thought infatuation would overwhelm common sense . . . and deep down, you were afraid—afraid she'd leave you. Afraid she'd be sorry for saving you someday. You let *this happen. Better to die with your pride intact than take a chance on Gillie Flynn. You son of a bitch.*

And now she's dying for you.

"Not today," he said aloud. "Please. Not today."

Hospital room. Gillie had visited so many during her childhood that she could recognize the place by scent alone. All the antiseptic in the world couldn't cover the stench of sickness. *So I lived.* She hadn't been sure she would, in fact. It would've been worth it. She opened her eyes slowly, lashes sticky and clinging, blurring her vision at first. Slowly, things came into focus.

By her estimation, Taye should be in that yellow vinyl chair, beside her bed, worriedly holding her hand. This room ought to be filled with flowers and it wouldn't be a bad idea for him to get down on his knees either. Instead, the space was bare apart from a blue curtain screening her from the other bed, the medical equipment and a wheeled table with a pitcher of water on it.

The door creaked as someone slipped in. *Maybe he just went to get coffee. I bet he hasn't slept in days.* But she didn't intend to make it easy on him. When she got out of here, they were having a fight to end all fights.

But Tanager slid through the curtain, not Taye. She was as colorful as always with her spiky white hair, now tipped in crimson. Today she wore low-slung cargo pants, revealing a tattoo on her hip, a corset-style camisole, a torn jean jacket, and a pair of red Doc Martens.

"How you feeling?"

"Not bad, all told. Are you allowed to *be* here?" Gillie added.

"It's a brave new world, Miracle Girl . . . the old rules don't apply anymore. We can be friends if you want." She sounded awkward in making the offer.

Not that Gillie was an expert. "I'd like that."

"Sure you wouldn't rather forget that part of your life and make a fresh start?"

She shook her head. "So we did it then."

"Foundation's shut down. No more funding. The parent company cut them off. No more money for facilities, research, or personnel."

"God, it feels so weird, knowing we can do whatever we want from here on out."

"No more looking over our shoulder," Tan agreed.

I will not ask about him. I will not.

"Thanks for coming. It means a lot."

"I missed the big showdown, so I figure this is the least I can do."

"What?"

"Sort things out here. I told one of your doctors you'll be private pay . . . Mockingbird's taking care of it. The admin women were giving Taye a hard time."

So he was here. He just isn't anymore. What the hell—

"Thank you."

"The way I hear it, you're the heroine of the hour. Liberator of our people and everything. You hacked their system and slew the beast. Good on you, Gillie Flynn."

"Can I be me again?"

"Yep. MB's working on getting you out of the federal databases, and I'll go with you to Wichita and talk to somebody in charge. Explain about your temporary witness protection status and how they should update your college records, listing you as Gillie Flynn."

"If someone recognizes me from the news and calls the tip line—"

"It's been shut down. They'll get an out-of-service message. Don't worry, it's over."

"Thank God."

"But MB won't be paying for stuff anymore. He's dividing what's left of the money he skimmed from the Foundation among all surviving agents and that'll be it."

"Severance package?" Gillie joked.

Tan smiled back. "Pretty much. We all make our own way from this point."

"Sounds good to me. Can you get me out of here? I hate hospitals."

"That's the other reason I'm here. We need to get you sprung before they notice anomalies. We don't want some other fringe group taking interest in what you can do."

"So you'll get a tech to contaminate my samples."

"Fancy way of putting it, but yeah." Tan sauntered over to the call button and pressed.

A few minutes later, a harried, middle-aged nurse came in; her nametag read "Betty" and she wore a pink and brown camo scrub top with "Private Betty" printed on it. *Wonder if she's former army.*

"You're awake, I see," she said to Gillie. "What can I do for you?"

Tanager said, "Send Doctor Howard in."

The nurse sighed. "It's early. He'll be along on his rounds shortly."

Short of a medical emergency that would draw attention counter to their aims, that was the best they could do. Tan took a seat, propping her foot against the side of the bed. They made quiet conversation and somehow she managed not to ask about Taye. *That bastard. I saved his life. He could at least thank me.*

Eventually the doc came in. He checked out her chart and shook his head. "The consequences for a missed appointment can be severe, as you see."

So that's the story. Gillie nodded and donned her chastened face. She had no doubt that the sudden influx of unfiltered waste did resemble a patient with renal failure who had missed several appointments. People sometimes chose to die that way, and it could take anywhere from a few days to several weeks, depending on a plethora of factors. But they couldn't be allowed to discover that her kidneys were intact.

"How much longer does she need to stay?"

"We need to finish the battery of tests," he answered.

Tan shook her head, and her voice sank lower. Gillie could *hear* the difference, but it didn't compel her the way it did men. "You should release her now. After all, if she has complete renal failure, there's nothing to analyze, is there? You'll send the nurse to remove the IV and shunt."

"You're right," Doctor Howard said. "I'll get the release paperwork started."

As soon as he left, Tan went to meddle with the technicians. The loose ends were just about wrapped up; within fifteen minutes, Gillie had staff helping her get ready to go. She had a clean change of clothes, courtesy of Tanager.

The nurse put a gauze bandage over the shunt site. Kindly, she refrained from commenting on the track marks marching up Gillie's arm, but from her expression, the nurse thought she'd blown her kidneys shooting up. "I swear, you were at death's door yesterday. I don't know why the doctor diagnoses as he does."

"It's probably insurance-related," Tan said blithely. "You know how they are."

Nurse Betty frowned. "Do I ever."

An hour later, an orderly wheeled Gillie along the hall. She fought not to look over her shoulder, trying not to want him to be there. He hadn't gone for coffee or a bite to eat. Now she had to face it; he wasn't coming back. When you got right down to it, Taye was a fucking coward, and she wanted no part of him.

Tanager met her at the front doors, parking in the patient-loading zone. Gillie felt weaker than she'd expected but she managed to get in the car. Once she'd buckled up, they took off.

"Where are we anyway?"

"Los Angeles. It'll be quite a road trip. I mean, I could get us a plane, but I thought you might enjoy the girl-time. I know I will."

"I turned down an internship, so I'm not in any hurry to get back." At least she *had* a life. "Oh, did you find the flash drive in my pants pocket? I didn't leave it behind."

"Sure did. Let's rock." With a whoop, Tan stomped on the gas.

CHAPTER 28

Once he dropped them at the hospital, Cale ditched the stolen car and his thoughts circled back to Kestrel. *Kristin*. It had just about killed him to lay her down, her eyes wide and sightless, staring up at the dark sky. The barn roof would keep the wind off her, and under the circumstances, it had been the best they could do. An anonymous phone call would get the cops out to take care of her, but—

Not good enough. Never good enough. She would haunt him, all the days of his life.

I'll sleep with you. What's the matter? Don't you want me?

Oh, Kes, I'm so sorry. Too late, he'd learned that more than money mattered. If he'd acted sooner, maybe he could have saved her. Then again, perhaps with some people, there could be no salvation. He suspected he was one of them.

Fighting memories, he sat on a park bench in the rain. It spattered the pavement like tears, perpetually falling. The authorities would find her family from this point; relatives would take her home and bury her with no idea how brave or splendid she was—or how broken at the end. He hurt more than he could've imagined possible at the start of this job. Once, things had been simple.

They weren't anymore.

He sat there all night in a private memorial, replaying that moment and holding her body in his arms. People had died on his watch before; it was part of what had driven him from the army into private pay, where at least the money was worth the grief. But no ending had ever left him feeling like this.

At dawn, he returned to the Foundation tower, where everything ended the night before. It was cordoned off, rescue crews poking through the rubble. Whatever the other teams had done, it destabilized the whole structure. Thirty stories, all collapsed into a shallow crater—now it was just cement and steel and dust motes wafting in the wind. People had never seen anything like it.

He took a room at a motel, watched the news; they had all kinds of theories about the tower. Some experts thought it must've been a sinkhole, similar to those that occurred in Guatemala . . . others argued, given the tectonic activity in California, it must've been an extremely localized earthquake. Cale flicked off the TV and opened a bottle of Powers Irish Whiskey. He poured three fingers into the plain glass and held it to the light.

Same color as Kristin's eyes. He shut his own and drank.

On the second day, he called the morgue to tell them her name. From there, they put the pieces together. Though they'd never find the killer—the bastard might even be buried in the rubble at Foundation headquarters—at least they could give closure.

As it turned out, she was from Minnesota, and it didn't take long to run down which funeral home would be handling the services. On the seventh day, with his head thundering, he flew to Pine Grove. For the first time in ten years, he donned a suit and tie. He hadn't expected to dress so formally again . . . not even if he happened to get married. In fact, he'd always imagined himself tying the knot on a beach, if he could find a woman to put up with him.

Unlikely, that.

Pine Grove wasn't a large town, so he drew some looks, first at the service, and then later at the cemetery. He didn't know how long it had been since they'd seen her, but they bought her a nice casket. *Such a fucking waste.*

Breaking his reverie, an elderly woman tapped him on the arm. "Pardon me, but I don't recognize you. Doesn't that sound rude? How did you know Kristin?"

"We worked together," he said quietly.

"Oh?" Her tone invited him to elaborate; her eyes asked for more than that, a memory from him that she couldn't otherwise know, something to remember.

"She was really gifted," he answered. "I couldn't have done without her."

"What business are you in?"

"Importing." That was what his documents said, anyway.

"You're from England, I take it?"

"That's right."

"Well, I'm glad she had a friend willing to come all this way. We lost track of her. She moved out west and then disappeared. Tragic."

You don't know the half of it.

"I'm Kristin's grandma," the woman added. "It was a pleasure meeting you, but I think the minister is about to begin."

Guilt had driven him here to try and make amends, though it was too late. The lady went to join relatives in front, stumbling over the uneven sod. Or maybe it was grief making her unsteady. Quiet fell, apart from the man in black, droning about heaven.

Once the minister finished, he slipped away. He knew he'd never be the same; he'd never look at work as uncomplicated again. For good or ill, she had changed him. From the cemetery, he drove to the airport. It was time to get the hell out. Maybe he could leave the memories on American soil.

As he drove, his phone rang. He answered, and a familiar voice said, "I need you in Liverpool, you bastard."

Hausen. Cale never thought he would be grateful to have one of his messes to clean up, but there it was. Gratitude that he had work to do, so he could focus on something else. Maybe in time, his sense of failure would fade. Nobody would know how things had gone down or that she'd died because he failed to save her. The Foundation certainly wasn't in any position to talk about whether he'd satisfied the terms of his contract.

"Can you contain the problem until I get there? It's a fairly long flight."

"It's not an emergency yet, though it will become so in the next forty-eight hours. I can stall them for now."

"Didn't I say you'd owe me another favor soon enough?"

"Skip the gloating if you please."

"And this is why I get to call you in the middle of the night. I'm on my way."

It was time to leave her ghost behind, if such was possible. Time to go home.

After Tanager saw Gillie safely home, she did what she had been dying to do ever since she retrieved the flash drive. She drove to the nicest house within five minutes of her friend's apartment; it was a huge place with pillars out front, brick facing, and beautiful manicured grounds. The flowers were just starting to bloom, adding touches of color to the green lawn.

"Why don't you take a vacation?" she told the gray-haired man who answered the door. "How long has it been since you took a day off? You should spend the night in Vegas."

"I'd *love* that. I used to be pretty wild in my day." With more excitement than her victims usually displayed, he went off to pack . . . but not before hiring her to house sit until day after tomorrow.

Tanager sauntered in with her backpack, checking the place out. No worry about strike teams. No fear of Kestrel finding her. Somehow the freedom felt bittersweet.

Once Mr. Miller tore out of the garage in a squeal of tires, she plugged it in her netbook and waited. Nobody else knew; once again Mockingbird had given her the burden of knowledge, and she didn't know whether she loved or hated him for it. A little of both, perhaps. It had always been that way between them. She had no idea why he'd chosen her to bear his secrets, except, possibly, that she'd known him longest; they had history.

Two minutes later, he appeared in a shimmer of light. Whole. Unchanged.

"The transfer didn't hurt you?" she asked.

"Their security measures weren't fun, but I'm intact, if that's what you're asking."

Mockingbird had been able to hack peripheral Foundation systems, getting tidbits of intel, and allowing them to hit satellite facilities, but their central server had been closed. No external access. Before Dunn turned, they had no hope of locating enemy headquarters.

In order to shut things down for good, he had to be carried to the server, as Gillie had done, and uploaded, so he could wreak havoc from within. But he hadn't known what the consequences would be—whether a personality and intelligence could be ported on a flash drive and back again. He had been prepared to sacrifice what was left of himself to set everyone else free. Thanks to Heron, thanks to everyone who fought and died, the survivors could live without fear for the first time since the experiments began.

And she'd never been so scared in her life. Tan wished she could touch him—hug him—but that part of him was gone. Now they had only words, so she took refuge in business when she wanted something else, something she'd scarcely admitted even to herself.

"You shut down all their operations? I told everyone you had, but we haven't had a chance to talk before now."

"I did. Destroyed all the data, too. To my knowledge, the Foundation is no more. The parent company is focusing on military applications now: biological weapons and the like, more mundane means of dealing death."

"Guess their number-crunchers didn't have a hard time accepting your report." That had been part of the plan—that he'd sign some executive's name to an internal e-mail, recommending complete termination of the *homo superus* project, as Rowan had called it.

"You know they called the overall effort Project Prometheus? Learned that while I was in the server."

"I didn't. But given what I know of mythology, their plan panned out about as well, didn't it? You *died* for us. Was it worth it?" Anger flavored her words.

The opulence of her surroundings didn't cool the fury of her grief. She'd hardly had a chance to mourn, just that one moment by the side of the road. *Just keep going, Tanager. I know I can count on you, Tanager.* And she still couldn't, because he was still here . . . and yet he *wasn't.* Not in the way she needed him to be. Tan could almost hate him for it, too.

"Yeah," he said. Just that. No explanations.

She didn't know why she'd expected anything different. He'd always held himself apart. Though he'd confided that he once ran a crew in Las Vegas, something bad happened, something that ended in a lot of his people dying, and so after that, he worked alone, barriers and distance.

Then he surprised her. "I was dying anyway, Tan. The more I used my mojo, the more it consumed me."

"You could've stopped."

"Walked away? From this? From you? I don't think so."

She didn't know what that meant. "Were you scared you couldn't come back?"

"Absolutely. Once you took me out of the net, it was like . . . being imprisoned. Here, I have all this space and freedom. In the flash drive . . ." The words trailed off.

He probably couldn't explain it to her anymore than she could tell someone how it felt to use her siren voice. In that way, at least, she understood him. They were both different.

"You can stay with me," she said. "If you need a home base, I mean."

She was sure he didn't. Need one. He could go anywhere. But that was as close as she could get to what she wanted. At least she hadn't lost him completely. How funny to think of her little blue netbook as such a powerful thing.

"I'd like that. It'll make it less lonely."

"You can chat with people, can't you?"

"Yeah." His electronic voice gained some bitterness. "I'll pretend to be a real boy."

"Enough of that. Nobody made you do this . . . you *wanted* to be a hero."

"I wanted to be your hero," he said quietly.

Fucking bastard. Why now? After all these years, when it was too late. Tan swallowed tears, and she paused long enough to get herself together, forcing the emotions down. When she spoke, her voice came out husky. "Enough of this shit. We've got some living to do . . . How do you feel about taking a cruise once the old guy gets back from Vegas?"

"Do I have a choice?"

"Not so much."

He laughed softly. "Then I'll make you a reservation."

Staring at Gillie's apartment door, Taye wondered if he had miscalculated. Maybe he should have stayed at the hospital instead of going off to see about some grand gesture. She had to be furious—or maybe she just thought he was crazy. God knew, he'd given a fair impression of it over the past few months. Part of that, he could blame on the pain medication—it was impossible to make rational choices when you were stoned.

But the rest of the stupidity? Him. All him. Guys like him didn't get the girl; they didn't catch the brass ring. Yet he was still here, somehow. Still standing. That meant things might not wrap up as he deserved. So he steeled his nerve and knocked.

After a moment, Gillie opened the door. The first thing he noticed? Her red hair. Symbolic, he figured, for taking back the sense of self she'd lost while pretending to be someone else. He was so glad she didn't have to do that anymore, however this turned out.

"You bastard," she snarled.

That was his only warning. A heavy book flew at his head, then a lamp, and then the contents of the bowl she kept beside the door; coins and keys pelted him. Still cussing him, she backed into the apartment and laid hands on a pretty crystal vase. Heavy, it looked like. Her aim was better, too, because despite his attempt to dodge, she nailed him with it; hurt his shoulder more than he would've expected, and then it smashed into shards at his feet.

"Just let me explain," he said.

But inwardly, he was smiling. Bent as it was, her outrage meant she still loved him. He just had to talk her past it. Admittedly, it could take a while, but he had an ace up his sleeve.

"There's nothing to explain, you fuckhead. I hate you and I hope your balls rot off. I hope you die in the woods alone, bears eat your bowels, and then your spirit's cursed to wander the earth for all eternity."

"Harsh, but fair."

She made an adorable, angry noise and slammed the door in his face. Unfazed, he raked the glass aside and sat down outside her apartment. It wasn't like he had anywhere else to be.

One of her neighbors went past while he waited. The guy studied him and the mess in the hallway. "So should I call the cops?"

"I wish you wouldn't . . . she'll let me in eventually, and I'll try to get her to keep the damage inside the apartment."

"Damn. What'd you do, dude?"

"Long story."

Half an hour later, she peered out at him. "Are you still here? Seriously? How much clearer can I be? Go. To. Hell. I'd rather be alone than be with someone like you."

"Like me?"

"A man who doesn't trust me. Even knowing how I feel about my own sovereignty, knowing how important it is I get to choose, you almost made that decision for me. I don't know if I can ever forgive you." The anger faded, leaving only sadness.

He knew his first pang of genuine terror—that their relationship might be utterly FUBAR. "Gillie, please. Give me five minutes and hear me out. Afterward, if you still want me to go, I will. I promise."

She sighed and relented, stepping back so he could come in. "Five. I'm timing you. Ass."

Taye didn't look around at the home she'd fashioned because it would just make talking harder, but he owed her this. "Even before we got out of Exeter, I knew my time was limited. I tried not to get too close to you because of it . . . but you're impossible not to love. For me, anyway. You're the answer to every question I never asked, nothing I deserve and everything I need."

"Well, sure. Even now it's all about you. Guess what? I don't *care*."

His fear amped up. "Okay, so here it is. I didn't want you to know because I knew you'd save me. This gift . . . it's carcinogenic, and I can't fully control it. If I could just stop, I would, but sometimes I pull and I don't even mean to. That means the cancer's coming back, sooner or later, and I didn't want to commit you to a lifetime of healing me, when it fucking hurts you, when you *hate* it. I couldn't stand being a burden on you, and I didn't want to become Rowan in your eyes."

"You aren't like him," she said softly. "You're worse. You made me love you . . . and then you didn't trust me to make my own decisions, even though I told you from the start how much that mattered. Regardless of what he did, he couldn't hurt me, not really, not deep down where it counted. But Taye . . . *you* broke my heart."

Past tense. Shit. I left it too long. I fucked this up so completely. I . . . lost her. But no, there was no point in this fresh start if he didn't get to build a life with Gillie Flynn. Against all the odds, he was still here and he wasn't going anywhere. He'd win her over; he'd try harder. There was no other acceptable outcome. Without Gillie, he might as well have died, as he'd planned, in that final raid.

"I'm sorry," he said. "Believe me, I am. If I could go back, if I could confide in you—"

"You can't. The past's immutable. And hey, on an intellectual level, I get it. Once I knew, how could I ever leave you, knowing that means your eventual death?" She shook her head. "But that's predicated on specious logic. It assumes I would want to."

"Gillie—"

She went on as if he hadn't spoken. "That, in turn, is predicated on the supposition I'm unable to assess the pros and cons of committing to a relationship with you. Did you *really* think I wouldn't understand the gravity?"

Time to change things up. He was starting to realize he'd been a total ass but maybe he could get her to look past his mistakes and see a future. "I have something to show you."

"Your five minutes is up. You swore you'd leave if I still wanted you to, or is your word worthless, too?"

Damn. She was mean as a snake, and he loved her for it. Deep down, the masochist in him knew he deserved to suffer. No question. So he practiced patience and let her twist the knife. God knew, he'd hurt her enough for three lifetimes. If she needed blood to make her feel like they stood on level ground, so be it. He'd bleed for her. There was nothing he wouldn't do for her . . . and in the coming weeks, he intended to prove it.

"Okay." Taye strode toward the door. "I'm leaving . . . for now. But I don't promise to stay away. Ask me to cut out my heart instead. Ask me to stop breathing."

"Don't tempt me," she muttered.

He flashed her a smile over his shoulder, meant to tell her he'd only just begun. "Get ready to be wooed."

CHAPTER 29

The first thing Gillie did after the raid was look up her parents online. She had to know if Rowan had been lying. And there they were in the Internet White Pages, Ambrose and Stephanie Flynn, Knoxville, Tennessee. She didn't know what she intended to do about it, but maybe someday, she'd pick up the phone and call. For now it was enough to know they lived. Before, she hadn't wanted to risk her parents, as the Foundation would surely have been watching them.

Relief eased some of her anger at Taye, too. But not all of it. Not nearly.

Gillie stood in her booth at the firing range, grimly plugging her target. In her mind's eye, it was Taye, not some random paper figure. *Bastard thinks he can show up and smile and everything will be forgiven? I. Don't. Think. So. Not with what he did . . . and the way he just left me at the hospital, not knowing if he was ever coming back.* She emptied her magazine and hit the return button. It was satisfying to see how many times she'd hit her target. Not all in the little circle, granted, but not bad either.

When she went home, she found a dozen roses waiting outside her apartment. She scowled at them, but she picked them up and carried them in with her. It wasn't because they were from him; she just didn't want the poor flowers to die because an asshole had purchased them. In retrospect, she hadn't hurt him enough. The bouquet came with a card attached; Gillie debated whether she should read it, but in the end, she did. *As he had to know I would.*

I'll spend the life you gave me making this up to you. This is day one. I love you, Gillie Flynn. Always.

The flowers arrived like clockwork after that, day by day, though Taye didn't come himself. He was giving her cooling-off time. Which was smart, she had to admit. Most days, she still felt like stabbing him. After the first week, he switched from flowers to cards and stuffed animals; most were adorable, but they didn't assuage her rage.

Still, it was amazing what he remembered. When he first started visiting her, they had talked about all kinds of things . . . and she'd mentioned in passing how sad she had been at sixteen when Rowan decided she was too old for her toys. He had made that decision, along with every other major one in her life, and removed the bear she hugged at night. No more softness. Rowan had given them to her, which meant she should hate them, but as a kid, she had been grateful for even pretend company.

And so Taye gave back her collection, piece by piece. God, she'd shared such minutia down in Exeter. Who could've imagined that Taye would recall she once had two stuffed bears—one of which was a koala—a rabbit, a tiger, a puppy, a penguin, and a big fat turtle. Each arrived, day after day, with a new greeting card. Some were cheesy, some romantic. Others were funny. Sometimes he wrote in blank ones. Words like, *I miss you, I'm lost*, and *I don't want to live without you.*

By the end of the second week, she started to miss him. A little. And maybe he knew that, too, because the day she picked up the turtle—the final piece of her lost set—he stood waiting at the foot of the stairs, probably ready to run if she threw things at him again. As usual, he wore a plain white T-shirt, motorcycle boots, and worn jeans. No leather duster—it was too warm out, even though it was getting on toward evening.

For the first time since she'd known him, Taye looked healthy. He had put on a little weight, just enough to ease the ravaged quality. God, he was handsome, though he still had that tragic air about him, like a rock star about to go out in a blaze of glory. Part of her wondered if that had anything to do with her refusal to see or speak to him.

"You weren't kidding when you said you wouldn't give up. How long do you plan to keep on like this?"

"As long as it takes," he said quietly. No bravado. He just gazed up at her with those Mediterranean eyes.

Oh, God. Why do I still love him?

"What do you want, Taye?"

"You. Forever and ever."

She wished she could throw something at his head, but the initial anger had gone. Now she was just sad and tired. Just as well she had no classes this summer and no internship. She needed time to get her head in order.

"You had me. And I don't trust you now . . . I don't know if I ever can again. You treated me like a child."

Pain flared, unmistakable. Yeah, he understood what he'd done. But he didn't make excuses or try to justify it this time, which was a step in the right direction.

"I regret that," he said. "But as you said, it cannot be changed. Let me take you out . . . just one date. If, at the end of the evening, you still want me to leave you alone, I will. I promise."

Wow. He must have a hell of an evening lined up. Reluctantly, she was intrigued as to what he thought could change her mind.

"Okay. I'll take your deal. What should I wear?"

"What you have on. You look beautiful. . . . you've *never* looked less than beautiful."

Hell. Maybe he does love me. She was wearing a thrift-store T-shirt with a picture of a donkey piñata and the slogan "I'd Hit That," along with a pair of jeans with the knees torn out.

"Let me get my purse and keys, then."

They stepped outside, and the air smelled of honeysuckle. It grew all over the fences despite the careful landscaping. To her surprise, he led her over to a motorcycle; though she was no expert, it looked old—chrome, retro-styling, and cherry paint.

"It's a vintage Indian Chief," he told her, interpreting her expression correctly.

Taye handed her a sparkly red helmet; it matched his, only his was matte. With a mental shrug, she put it on and climbed on behind him. When he took off, she had no choice but to lean into him and wrap her arms around his waist. *That's probably why he bought the thing.* Even with the hot wind and car exhaust, she could still discern his scent—light citrus and bergamot. Whatever his cologne, it *so* worked. Damn him.

Astonishment curled through her as they pulled up outside the club where she'd taken him, what seemed so long ago now. It was still early, so the twenty-somethings and college students hadn't shown up yet. Taye parked the bike, waited for her to slide off, and then he laced his fingers through hers. She followed him with a furrowed brow.

Inside, it was even weirder. Based on the time and day of the week, Gillie expected a nearly empty establishment. Instead, the place was packed, standing-room only, and the karaoke stage was set up . . . only it wasn't Thursday. Taye led her through the crowd to a table down front, which bore the placard "Reserved VIP." As soon as she sat down, he vaulted onto the stage, conferred briefly with the guy running the equipment, and then took the mic.

"This song's for the woman I love."

Without preamble, he launched into the hammiest rendition of "All Out of Love" that she'd ever heard. Ever. And he was *terrible*. The raw husky quality that made his voice so sexy when he spoke translated painfully in a musical sense. No tone. No pitch. At first, she didn't understand why the hell he thought this would help his case. And then she remembered; he'd said this was where he drew the line. It was the one thing he would never, ever do for her.

Yet he was doing it. And *so* badly that the audience hooted and threw things. A few people got out lighters to mock him, and still he sang on, dogged in his determination.

"You suck!"

Taye ignored them; she could tell he saw only her. He cared about only what she thought. And she listened to the words of the song, heard the apology. It was awful—and perfect.

When he finished at last, Gillie stood and applauded. She was the only one.

"Sorry for the deception, folks. There will be free beer, on me, for the next half hour." That won a thunderous ovation from the disgruntled audience, and most of them rushed the bar.

"What the hell did you tell them?"

"I posted flyers all over campus that Fall Out Boy was playing a surprise gig here tonight."

"Shit. Did you *want* to be humiliated?"

"Yes," he said.

Well, hell. How am I supposed to stay mad at him?

"Taye—"

Panic flared in his face. "No. Not yet. This was our first stop, not the best."

He thought I was going to tell him we're done. Tenderness flooded her. No, she didn't trust him entirely, but she believed he loved her. And she was capable of forgiveness. Nobody always got it right, but they could try—and do better each time. But she wouldn't let him off the hook until he showed her this last thing.

"Okay." She drew out the word on a sigh, as if she were reluctant instead of madly curious.

Taye stopped at the bar to drop some bills for the beer and then they went out. Dark had fallen, just fringes of crimson and gold above the horizon. She lost track of the twists and turns with her head against his back. Though it was terrifying, the motorcycle was also rather thrilling, the way it hummed between her thighs. That pretty much encapsulated the way she felt about him, most days—a little scary, but too good to stop.

This time, he parked outside an old building built of pale cement and white stone facing, though it was dirty and crumbling—seedy neighborhood, broken glass, and graffiti. She wasn't entirely sure why he'd brought her here. He wheeled the bike toward the doors. *Yeah. Probably smart not to leave it out here.*

"What're we doing?" she asked.

"Shh."

Shock coursed through her when Taye unlocked the front doors. The foyer glowed, adorned with strands of tiny white Christmas lights, and there was a table set for two with a picnic basket and a manila envelope. He leaned the motorcycle against the wall and secured the door behind them.

"Do you want to eat first or do you want to see your surprise?"

"What do you think?"

In answer, he went for the envelope. His gaze was meltingly tender as he handed it over. No explanations. So she unsealed it and drew out a sheaf of papers. By candlelight, she read them over with a dawning sense of wonder. They were IRS documents and zoning permissions, all related to the Flynn Foundation, a homeless shelter to be established on these premises.

That's where he went when he left the hospital. That was what he was doing.

"It's an old hotel," he said softly. "Should renovate nicely. I had just enough from the severance package to buy the property. We'll need a board of directors, and to work on donations for the annual budget. But I've registered at WSU for courses in business management, nonprofit focus. I figure by the time we both have our degrees, this place will be ready for us to run it."

A sob burst out of her, completely uncontrollable. She wasn't pretty when she cried, but she couldn't stop it. Tears ran down her cheeks and she buried her face in her hands rather than look at him. It was perfect, just like that stupid song. He knelt before her and wrapped his arms around her, murmuring into her hair, but he didn't try to stop the noise or staunch her outburst.

Like always, he understood.

"I love you," she whispered.

"I know."

"I hate you a little, also."

"I know that, too."

"Can't believe you did this for me."

"I'd do anything for you." And she knew he meant it. "Even before you healed me, you gave my life back, a reason for living. I adore you. I worship you. I love you beyond reason."

Maybe it should be scary to be the center of someone's world like that, but she needed it. She'd never had it. Gillie hugged him tightly around the neck, rubbing her damp cheek against his. He prickled slightly—and that was Taye. He turned his head and his lips met hers; she tasted her own tears and a hint of fresh sweetness, as if he'd sucked a peppermint. A shudder of reaction worked through her as he deepened the kiss, threading his fingers into her hair.

Long moments later, she broke away, breathing hard. "You knew I wouldn't be able to resist all of this. You know me too well."

"I hoped," he admitted. "You were starting to scare me."

"Good. You *deserve* it. I still kind of want to stab you."

His eyes were grave. "You can if you want."

"I might, when you least expect it. But don't worry . . . I'll heal you afterward, if I do."

Taye grinned, tacitly agreeing to her terms. *Impossible to stay mad at him.* Gillie kissed him again and again, all over his face. Tamped longing swelled within her, adding urgency to her touch. He responded in kind and wrapped his arms around her.

"If you keep touching me like this, I may not want dinner," she warned.

"Fuck dinner." He swept her into his arms and carried her into the next room, where the cagey bastard had set up an air mattress and surrounded it in a sea of candles.

"You were sure of yourself."

"Not really. But it's best to be prepared."

"I always wanted my own boy scout."

"You got him." As he lay her down on the mattress, he nuzzled her throat with slow, languid kisses. "Tell me you had a new Depo shot."

"I did."

"Who were you planning to sleep with?" The jealousy in his tone delighted her.

"I have a thing for my psych professor."

His jaw dropped, and she laughed softly. Taye shook his head. "As I've said before, you're a wicked, wicked woman, Gillie Flynn."

"I know. Make love to me?"

His reply came when he worked the T-shirt over her head and then he unfastened his jeans. Gillie tugged his clothes off, and flung them well beyond the circle of candles. The scent of orange cleaner lingered in her nostrils, along with the burning vanilla wax. He must've spent so much time here, getting this surprise ready. He'd wanted her to know how serious he was about their future.

They kissed endlessly, tongues touching in hot, sweet little licks. He edged her backward until he hung above her, propped on his arms. Taye had almost as many scars as she did—a matched set. He still didn't remember anything about his life, and that was fine with her.

"My name is Tyler," he said, surprising her. "Tyler Golden. I've done time."

She didn't miss a beat. "Me, too. Twelve years. But we're both free now."

With a little growl, he pressed his mouth to her shoulder, giving a mock-fierce bite. She fell back on the pillows he'd so thoughtfully provided and opened her arms. Her whole body ached for him, her cunny already slick. It seemed as if it had been so long.

"I'd prefer you to call me Taye, but all my IDs will be in my real name."

"How did you find out?"

"The bounty hunter tracked me down. Took prints in our apartment in Detroit." At her astonishment, he smiled. "Told you he was good."

"Do you have family?"

"I guess. I don't know if I'll ever be ready to see them. I'm sure I was a mess before I fell off the grid."

"It's okay. You'll always have me."

"Thank God," he murmured.

Taye licked and nuzzled down to her breast. Damp heat and fluttering caresses feathered around her aureole. She sank her hands into his hair with a moan. He teased her like that for what felt like forever, until at last he took her nipple into his mouth and gave the fierce suction she craved. Gillie arched, breath coming in unsteady gasps, but he showed no mercy; he just changed sides—more teasing, until she twisted on the bed—mad with the desire for him to move lower.

He stopped.

"You bastard."

"I want to watch you come. If you knew how many times I've fantasized about the way you looked . . ."

She knew what he meant: a deserted house, Truth or Dare, a bottle of wine, a ladder-back chair. In retrospect she didn't know whether to be proud or embarrassed . . . maybe a little of both. Gillie glanced at his cock. He was so hard, throbbing, with a hint of fluid on the crown, and he shivered at the look.

"Yes," she said huskily. "I've gotten pretty good at it."

Heat flushed through her as he slid down, settling in between her thighs to watch the show. She eased up slightly, letting the pillows take her weight. Her clit hummed but she didn't go right for it. Instead she ran her thumb between her labia, taking pleasure in how wet he'd gotten her. Taye made a hungry sound against her thigh.

"That's it. Touch yourself." His lips moved on her skin, phantom kisses that sparked her excitement higher.

Up and down, lazy sweeps, and each time, she eased closer to her clitoris. He licked the curve of her inner thigh, just below the crease where it met her ass. Gillie moaned, the need for orgasm building tension. He sat up to watch as she went to work with two fingers; the sight made him hiss as she strummed her body, knowing just how to get there—and fast. She jerked and came and he lowered his head to lick up her juice.

Before she could calm down, he was on her—in her, his whole body shaking. Taye kissed her, and she tasted herself. Tart-sweet, intimate. His tongue took hers, tangled, as he thrust repeatedly, no finesse, just need. Love. Lust. Gillie wrapped her arms around him and then her legs, tilting her hips for deeper penetration. *So good. So right.* She whispered to him, demand and endearments, urging him faster with her heels against his ass. They shook together, and he growled when he came, teeth clenched, but he never took his eyes off her face.

Afterward, she held him and smoothed his sweat-slick skin, brushing back the chestnut hair, kissing his eyelids and his ears, everything she could reach. The scent of citrus and bergamot mingled with the vanilla candles, creating a pleasant haze. Gillie curled into him with a contented sigh.

"Still want to stab me?" he asked softly.

"I think I'll let you stab me instead."

"Thought I just did. Love you so, Gillie-girl. You're everything," he said, as he had once before, long ago, but this time, his tone held only happiness.

"I know," she said. "I've always known. Took *you* a while to figure it out, though. Some people are meant to be together. Sometimes things happen exactly as they must."

"I'm slow, but adorable. My wife will be the brains of the operation."

". . . Wife?"

He pushed up on one elbow. "Well, yeah. Someday. That wasn't a proposal. I'll do it right when the time comes."

Could hearts explode with joy? She hoped not. Maybe she'd take him to meet her parents and make him ask her father's permission when they were ready to take that step.

"I'll hold you to that."

"I'm counting on it."

Then Taye rolled her beneath him and showed her exactly how much he adored her. Again. *Yeah.* Sometimes things worked out exactly as they should.

Turn the page for a special preview of

DELANEY'S SHADOW

a thrilling new romantic suspense novel by Ingrid Weaver
Coming August 2011 from Berkley Sensation!

He came back to her in a dream. Yet even as Delaney sensed his presence in her head, the watchful, grown-up part of her knew he couldn't be real. This couldn't be happening. He was the boy of make-believe.

"Max?" Her lips mouthed the name. She hadn't spoken it aloud since her childhood. It belonged to the past, to the girl who used to sleep in this ribbons-and-bows room, to the days of laughter in the kitchen and bees in the roses and sheets snapping in the sunshine.

She couldn't remember when he'd first appeared. It seemed as if Max had always been with her, in some corner of her mind. Whenever she'd needed him, he would show up, the skinny little boy with dark hair and a crooked front tooth.

Oh, the times they'd had, the games they'd played. Racing along the lane, their arms extended like airplane wings, they would fix their gazes on the horizon and pretend to soar. Or quietly, so quietly, they would creep past Grandpa's room to the attic for rainy afternoon treasure hunts. There had been safaris in her grandmother's garden, elaborate banquets on the playroom floor, and gleeful, giggling slides down the curving oak banister.

But the best times, the very best ones, had been when he'd

taken her to their own special world, the place they made up together, where nothing bad happened and nothing ever hurt.

She breathed his name again. Max. He'd been her partner in mischief, her secret confidante, the imaginary friend she had created to become her playmate. The first time she'd insisted on setting a place for Max at dinner, Grandpa had banged his cane on the floor and had told her to quit making up stories or by God she would turn out as flighty as her mother. Grandma had just winked at her and slid an extra plate beside the butter dish.

But then Delaney's mother had died, and her father had returned for her. They'd moved to the city. She'd tried to bring Max, too, but there hadn't been a banister or extra plates in the apartment, and Mrs. Joiner said that imaginary friends weren't allowed at school.

And eventually Delaney had stopped believing. She'd grown up and left Max behind.

Yet if she'd left him behind, how could he be here?

It was a dream, she reminded herself. And unlike the other ones, this dream wasn't filled with images of twisted metal and death.

Why hadn't she realized it before? Max would be able to keep the nightmares away. He could do anything.

"Max," she whispered.

His presence strengthened until the air around him seemed to reach out in a welcoming smile. He stood in the shadow beside the bedroom doorway. A stubborn, wayward lock of hair hid one eye, but the other sparkled in a conspirator's grin.

What would they do today? Where would they go? What games would they play?

It didn't matter. As long as he kept her safe from the nightmares.

She had always felt safe with Max.

He shuffled forward, his sneakers making stealthy squeaks against the floor. As usual, he wore jeans that looked a size too large, the denim hanging loosely from his hips. His T-shirt bore a smear from the mud pies she'd made him the morning she'd left Willowbank. He had the same hopeful smile, the same live-wire sizzle of energy, that clean, fresh-air feeling of sunshine and summer breezes . . .

The watchful, grown-up part of her stirred once more, but she kept her mind focused on Max. He was a part of the past that it didn't hurt to remember, part of the days of innocence, when life stretched out before her in endless possibilities, and pain was no worse than a skinned knee. Sleep hadn't been something she dreaded then.

She splayed her fingers, reaching toward him. "Let's play, Max."

His image wavered.

"No, Max. Stay!"

Like a shadow glimpsed on the edge of vision, like the dream he was, the little boy faded.

She fought the return of consciousness. "Not yet," she urged. "Not yet."

Through the open window came the cheerful lilt of a robin, as persistent as an alarm clock. Against her closed eyelids, Delaney could feel the tentative warmth of sunrise.

The presence that was Max trembled, then silently flickered out.

Sighing, Delaney rolled to her back and opened her eyes.

Something was wrong. Where was the shelf with her dolls? What had happened to the lacy canopy that sheltered her bed?

It took a few moments for her brain to catch up with her senses. Books lined the shelf, not toys, and a dieffenbachia filled the corner where there had once been a rocking horse. The dolls and the lace were gone. They had been packed up decades ago, along with her fairy-tale books and her frilly socks. The canopy bed had been replaced by a cherry wood four-poster. A matching, grown-up-sized dresser stood beside the plant. Her grandmother had redecorated the house when she'd converted the front half into a bed-and-breakfast.

Delaney sat up and raked her hair off her face. Instead of the typical sleep-tangled lengths, she felt stubby chunks slide between her fingers. There was another one of those moments of puzzlement. What had happened to her hair? She slipped her hand beneath the neckline of her nightgown. Scar tissue ridges as fine as stretched crepe paper slid beneath her palm. The burns no longer hurt. She could barely feel her own touch.

Full wakefulness hit her, bringing a spurt of panic. It had been more than six months since the accident. The changes to her life were so enormous, she still had trouble absorbing the full scope of them. She understood what had happened to her body, just as she was aware of what had happened to her husband. The doctors at the clinic had explained it. So had the police. But it wasn't the same as *knowing*.

Maybe today would be the day that she actually remembered.

After all, she had remembered Max, hadn't she?

Ah, Max. She'd had such a vivid imagination when she'd been a child; her make-believe friend would have been able to help her.

Too bad she'd grown up and was beyond all that.

"Those muffins smell delicious, Delaney, but you know I don't expect you to cook."

"I like to cook, Grandma, and besides, I have to do something to earn my keep." Delaney picked up a quilted potholder and started transferring the muffins from the cooling rack to the napkin-lined basket she'd prepared. "These are apple oatmeal. I left out the walnuts in case any of your guests have sensitivities to nuts."

"No one alerted me about any allergies, but I'm glad you left out the nuts anyway. There always seems to be one piece that gets under my dentures. It's so annoying. It isn't very good for business, either, since for some reason the customers don't like seeing me take out my teeth at the table and give the underside a good swipe with my thumb. Seems to spoil their appetite."

Delaney rolled her eyes at her grandmother's humor. "I can't imagine why."

At seventy-two, Helen Wainright had the same twinkle in her gaze that she'd had at fifty, although her long, once-blonde hair was totally white now. Today she had styled it in what she called her Katharine Hepburn poof. It suited her. She had the kind of presence that would have dominated a stage if she'd chosen to pursue acting. But Helen's passion was people—she would have balked at the separation between performer and audience. Besides, Delaney couldn't picture her assuming a role. She was far too honest to be anyone other than herself.

Helen pointed to the basket. "I hope you're going to have some yourself. You made more than enough."

"Maybe later."

"You should eat more, honey. You're too thin."

"Haven't you heard?" She transferred the last muffin to the basket and covered them with another napkin. "There's no such thing as being too rich or too thin."

"If that were the case, you'd be turning cartwheels out in the yard instead of baking muffins and looking as if you haven't slept in a week."

"Grandma, I always look like this before my coffee kicks in."

"The weariness I see has nothing to do with caffeine addiction." She motioned toward the stools that were tucked beside the work island in the center of the kitchen. "Sit."

"The muffins will get cold."

"I can heat them up."

Delaney glanced at the swinging door that led to the dining room. The low murmur of voices came through the wood panels. "But your guests—"

"They've got yogurt and a fruit platter. That should hold them for a while. Please, Delaney. I'm worried about you."

"I'm fine. Really." She crossed the floor and perched on the nearest stool. "Please, don't worry."

Helen took the stool beside her and reached for her hand. There was a breath of hesitation as her fingers closed over the patches of new skin. She recovered quickly, turning the motion into an affectionate pat instead of a squeeze. "Leave the cleanup for when Phoebe comes in."

"I made the mess. I can manage."

"It's what I pay her for. The girl's already lazy enough. No point spoiling her."

Delaney did another eye-roll. From what she'd seen, her grandmother treated the college student she'd hired for the summer more like another granddaughter than an employee. "You're not fooling anyone with that tough talk, you know."

"Rats. How did you sleep?"

"Fine. That new bed is really comfortable."

"I heard you down here at dawn."

"I've become an early riser," she said, trying for a casual shrug. "Sorry if I disturbed you."

"Was it a nightmare?"

"No, just a dream this time."

"That's good."

"Mm-hmm. I'm making progress. Not ready for the loony bin yet."

Helen withdrew her hand. "There's nothing crazy about needing a rest. Give yourself time to heal, Deedee, both inside and out. Grief doesn't work on a timetable."

The sound of her childhood name brought tears to her eyes. She'd had more than six months to mourn, but there was something about coming home that lowered the defenses. A kind word, a loving gesture, and years of adulthood collapsed. "Stanford had always been afraid of growing old. He used to joke about how he would prefer to go out in a blaze of glory. God, it still seems unreal."

"Of course, it does. It takes years to accept the fact that someone we love is gone. The sorrow does fade eventually, and you'll remember the joy instead."

Helen spoke from experience. She had outlived not only her husband but her daughter as well. Delaney wished she had a fraction of her strength. "I'm sorry, Grandma. You've gone through so much more than I have. I shouldn't be leaning on you."

"That's the wrong way to look at it. What I've gone through has made me a good listener, so don't give it a second thought."

"If only I could remember."

"Oh, honey, what difference would it make? Accidents simply happen sometimes."

Yes, the official ruling was that the car had left the road and struck the utility pole by accident. For lack of solid evidence to the contrary, that's what the police had concluded when they had closed the investigation last week.

Unfortunately, the ruling hadn't satisfied everyone. Only ordinary people died in accidents. Stanford Graye, the billionaire director of Grayecorp, hadn't been ordinary. Neither was the Jaguar XK that he'd died in, so there had to be more to the story. The rumors had been impossible to ignore. They'd run the gamut from a murder conspiracy to a foiled contract killing to a failed suicide pact. "I don't think that Elizabeth's going to let it rest."

"She's grieving, too, Delaney. He was her father."

"Of course, and I understand how she feels. Losing him would have been devastating under any circumstances, but the unanswered questions only make things worse. It must seem suspicious for the only eyewitness to claim amnesia, especially in light of Stanford's will."

"She wants someone to blame," Helen said. "She might be behaving like a spoiled brat at the moment, but that's how she's handling her grief."

"I guess so."

"You both need time to heal. Be patient."

Delaney rubbed her eyes. Be patient. Right. That had been the motto of her life. It seemed as if she'd always been the one to let things go. If something hurt to look at, she looked at something else.

Helen took Delaney's hand and eased it away from her face. "This is about more than the memory loss, isn't it?"

"That's just it, Grandma. I'm not sure. I feel as if there's something more I'm missing that I should know."

"You and Stanford were happy, weren't you?"

She didn't pause to think about the answer. It was the one she always gave. "Yes. Of course we were."

"But?"

"But there must be some reason why I've blocked his . . . his last moments."

"Some reason besides the crack on the head you took when his car hit that pole? That might be all the explanation you need."

Then why do I keep having those nightmares? Delaney thought. But she didn't ask the question aloud. She hadn't yet described the details of her nightly horrors to her grandmother, and she didn't intend to. She'd already placed enough of a burden on her by coming here.

"I'm not going to push," Helen said. "As long as you know that whenever you're ready to talk, I'll be here to listen."

"Thanks, Grandma." She leaned over to kiss Helen's cheek, then rose from her stool and retrieved the basket of muffins she'd prepared. "Here," she said, holding it out. "I've kept you from your guests long enough."

"Why don't you join us? The Schicks come every year. The other couple, the Reids, are looking for a cottage near Willowbank. They're interesting people."

"Thanks, but I thought I'd take a walk in the yard before the sun gets too hot. It's a beautiful morning."

"If that's what you want."

"Yes."

"All right." Helen took the basket from her hands. "The fresh air will do you good."

"Probably."

"Make sure you put on some gardening gloves if you decide to weed the roses again. I keep them in the shed."

"I will."

"And take your sun hat in case you're out longer."

"Gramma, I'll be fine. Really." Delaney tipped her head toward the dining room. "Now go feed the customers before they start chewing the furniture."

Helen chuckled and crossed the kitchen, picking up a jug of orange juice with her free hand as she passed the counter. She turned around, mimed a kiss to Delaney, then used her backside to push open the dining room door. A welcoming chorus of voices greeted her arrival.

Only two of the four guest rooms had been occupied the night before, but none would be empty by the weekend. This was the busiest season in Willowbank. The annual waterfront festival was due to begin in two weeks. The influx of tourists provided a needed boost to the local economy.

Raymond Wainright, Delaney's grandfather, had made a fortune dividing his lakefront property into parcels for cottages back when the city people had first discovered the beauty of the area. He'd left Helen comfortably well-off, so she hadn't turned their house into a bed-and-breakfast solely for the income it provided. She'd needed something to fill her time, and she thrived on the contact she had with her guests. Like the Schicks, most were repeat visitors.

Delaney never had learned to appreciate the lake that drove the town's tourist economy. She didn't know how to swim. For as long as she could remember, she'd had a deep-seated aversion to water.

A burst of laughter drifted into the kitchen. Delaney took her sun hat from the coat tree beside the back door, settled it on her head, and went outside. She walked past the beds of roses at the edge of the terrace—even if she'd wanted to weed them today, she wouldn't have found anything to pull out. The lawn was over an acre in size and was just as well-tended as the garden. It stretched in a freshly mowed carpet between high cedar hedges on either side of the yard to the wrought iron fence at the back. Sticking to the shade as much as she could, she wandered among the shrubs and beds of annuals until she found herself at the oak tree in the center of the lawn that used to hold her swing.

Like the other remnants from her childhood, the swing was gone, its ropes rotted long ago. Yet as Delaney paused beneath the oak, drawing in the smell of the leaves and the damp earth that mounded around the base, the past rose effortlessly to her mind. She could remember what it had felt like to sit on the swing, kick her feet free from the ground, and give herself up to the sway of the ropes. She remembered the half-scary, half-giddy sensation of leaning backward so far that her hair swept the ground. Sometimes, if her mother was having a good day, she would come outside and push her, but most of the time, she had played alone.

The Wainright house was on the outskirts of town. That fact, combined with sheer size of the property, had meant they had no close neighbors. There had once been a trailer park and a set of old train tracks beyond the wooded area, but the kids who had lived there had tended to stay on their own side of the tracks. Delaney's mother hadn't had energy to spare for socializing during her final years, and her grandparents hadn't had friends with children her age, so it wasn't surprising that she had invented a playmate of her own to fill her solitude.

Max. After lying dormant for so long, that was the second time today thoughts of him had surfaced. It wasn't exactly what she'd hoped for, but it was progress. If she could uncover memories that were buried as deeply as her imaginary friend was, could the others be that far behind?

Delaney rested her palm against the tree. As she'd done at least a thousand times since she'd first awakened in the hospital, she sent her thoughts back to that night last winter. She felt the bite of cold air as she stepped out of the restaurant, the warmth of Stanford's grip on her elbow as he helped her into the car, caught the scent of his lime aftershave and the faint aroma of wine . . . and then . . . and then . . .

Nothing. She shut her eyes and shoved against the closed door in her mind. Why hadn't they gone straight home? What had they done for the next four hours? And why on earth had she ended up behind the wheel? The details had to be buried in her brain—the fragments that had been surfacing in her nightmares proved that. She needed to push herself harder.

A breeze stirred the branches overhead, and the trace of Stanford's lime aftershave was replaced by the acrid scent of oak leaves. She couldn't hear screeching brakes, only a warbling robin. No thud of metal, just the sound of her heart.

Delaney curled her fingers into a fist until the backs of her knuckles prickled. Trying to remember the accident had become a daily routine. She should be accustomed to the frustration that followed, but she had hoped things would be different now that she was in Willowbank. If only she could find the key . . .

She strained, *willing* her mind to open.

Still nothing. Damn.

She sighed and opened her eyes. Maybe she was trying too hard. She'd never had to try hard to conjure up Max. He would simply appear.

A blackbird squawked from the woods beyond the fence. Delaney moved her gaze to the line of trees there, picturing Max's shuffling walk as he emerged from the shadows that hid the path. His hair had always been uncombed and a little too long, but she'd loved the way it had gleamed in the sun. She'd loved his smile, too, and the way it had never failed to wrap around her like a hug . . .

Her vision blurred, melding the manicured green lawn she saw with the one she remembered. And in the center of both there was Max. He had already passed the gate and was walking toward her, his hand lifted in greeting . . .

The lawn was empty. Of course, it was empty. No little boy, imaginary or otherwise, was coming to visit. It must be some trick of the sunlight, or a streamer of mist that had drifted in from the pond, that made the spot in the center appear blurry. It gleamed like something solid, yet she could see right through it, as if she were looking into another dimension . . . or a make-believe world.

Delaney's palm slid down the tree as she sank to the ground. She dug her fingernails into the arch of a root, anchoring herself in the here and now.

Yet the budding vision persisted. A feeling of warmth, of unconditional welcome was enveloping her. Although her mind was alert, her body was relaxing as if she were once again on the wooden seat of the swing and had kicked free from the ground. Her limbs tingled. This was how it used to feel when she had summoned her imaginary friend.

This was pathetic. A grown woman reverting to the crutch of her childhood.

Yet what did she have to lose? Summoning Max wasn't that different from the hypnosis Dr. Bernhardt, the clinic's chief of psychiatry, had attempted. Maybe her subconscious was trying to tell her something. If she could free her imagination the way she had as a child, perhaps she could push past her mental block.

Delaney glanced around to ensure she was still alone, then drew her knees to her chest, wrapped her arms around her legs, and focused her thoughts on Max.

The picture of him wavered, then re-formed, stronger than before. Blotches of crimson and yellow sparkled against the sky. The mist around him thinned, as if stirred by the same wind that rustled the leaves over her head.

Instead of coming closer, the figure in the center turned away from her.

"Hey, Max," Delaney whispered. "Don't go yet."

The shape that was Max appeared to stiffen. He paused where he was and tilted his head to one side, as if he were trying to hear her.

"That's okay, Max." Incredibly, she heard a chuckle bubble past her lips. How long had it been since she had laughed? "Talking to myself is bad enough. I don't expect to get answers."

The light around him brightened, and details began to appear. He was still turned away, so she couldn't see his face, but his hair was the same dark brown it had always been, gleaming with streaks of auburn where the sun touched it.

He was taller than she remembered. Much taller. As a matter of fact, he was far too tall to be a boy. And he was no longer skinny. His shoulders had the breadth of a man's and his biceps stretched out the sleeves of his white T-shirt. He stood with his feet braced solidly apart in a stance filled with self-confidence.

Delaney blinked. Her imaginary friend had grown up.

This time, her laugh came more easily. It was bad enough to regress to her childhood by imagining Max. It was downright pitiful to fantasize about him being a fully grown man.

But what had she expected? She wasn't a child any longer, either.

"Deedee?"

The voice startled her. She hadn't heard it; she had felt it. It was inside her head. It was deep and rough, stroking through her senses like summer heat.

Years ago, she had imagined Max's voice in her head, too. They had giggled together as they'd played their pretend games, and sometimes he would join in when she sang her nonsense skipping rhymes. Back then he had sounded like a child. Now his voice was as unmistakably mature as his appearance.

This was some fantasy, Delaney thought wryly. The doctors

would have a field day if they knew. So would Elizabeth. She'd haul her into a competency hearing so fast . . .

But no one had to know. That was the beauty of having a secret friend. "Long time no see, Max," she murmured.

There was a pause, then the spots of color that surrounded him began to move, elongating and twining around themselves. Sunshine gleamed not only from his hair but from his broad shoulders. The image was strengthening. His arms became more defined. She could see a smear of crimson on his sleeve, and a streak of blue on his jeans.

Max pressed the heels of his hands to his temples. "Deedee?"

The distress in his voice took her aback. "I know it's been a while," she began.

"What the hell is going on?"

"I just wanted . . ." She caught herself. He was a figment of her imagination. Why was she trying to explain anything to him?

He dropped his hands and half turned toward her. There was a hint of a sharp cheekbone and strong jaw, but she still couldn't see his face. "Go away, Deedee. I don't have time to play."

"Play? I don't want to play, Max. I only want to remember."

"I don't."

"But you can help me."

"No." He strode away. The colors whirled around him, melding with the shades of green at the edge of the lawn.

"Max, wait!"

"No."

"Max—"

"Dammit, Deedee. Get the fuck out of my head!"